POLLOCK'S LAST LOVER

ALSO BY STEPHEN P. KIERNAN

FICTION

The Glass Château

Universe of Two

The Baker's Secret

The Hummingbird

The Curiosity

NONFICTION

Last Rights

Authentic Patriotism

wm
WILLIAM MORROW
An Imprint of HarperCollins*Publishers*

POLLOCK'S LAST LOVER

A Novel of Art and Deception

Stephen P. Kiernan

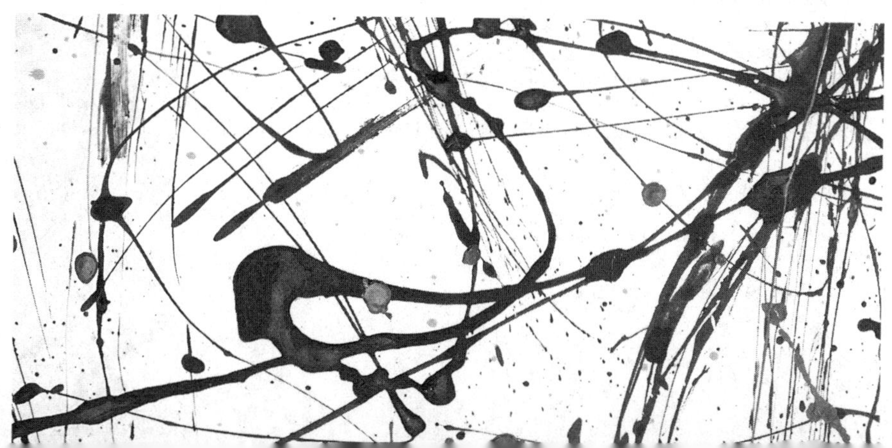

This book is a work of fiction. References to real people, events, establishments, organizations, or locales are intended only to provide a sense of authenticity, and are used fictitiously. All other characters, and all incidents and dialogue, are drawn from the author's imagination and are not to be construed as real.

HarperCollins books may be purchased for educational, business, or sales promotional use. For information, please email the Special Markets Department at SPsales@harpercollins.com.

harpercollins.com

FIRST EDITION

Designed by Elina Cohen
Title art © Nataliya Sdobnikova / Shutterstock

Library of Congress Cataloging-in-Publication Data has been applied for.

ISBN 978-0-06-287847-2

Printed in the United States of America

26 27 28 29 30 LBC 5 4 3 2 1

"The modern painter cannot express this age—the airplane, the atom bomb, the radio—in the old forms of the Renaissance or any other past culture. Each age finds its own technique."

Jackson Pollock, radio interview, 1951

"She actually killed Pollock, she was driving him so nuts."

Andy Warhol, *The Andy Warhol Diaries*, 1989

PROLOGUE

FEBRUARY 2007

From the road, the cemetery looked like any other: gray stones engraved with names and dates, tilting this way and that like so many crooked teeth.

Wyatt drove through the entry, pulling his taxi to one side though there were no other cars. "You have to walk it from here," he said, "if you want the full effect."

As Gwen opened her door, the wind grabbed it, yanking it wide till she hopped out and slammed the door shut. Following gravel tracks into the graveyard, she soon began to see the eccentrics Wyatt had mentioned. A bright shining sphere for a tombstone. A granite bench with a stack of carved stone books at one end. A house-of-cards stack of metal film canisters from a movie projector. A gravestone painted a rainbow of colors, with plastic rainbow spinners on either side, the stone bearing the names of two men.

One grave stood apart—out of sequence, out of scale. It bore neither crucifix nor Star of David. There was no reference to a career or calling, no clever notions like other graves. It looked intentionally bland, but loomed too large to ignore.

A boulder: plain brown, chest-high, and eight feet across. Gwen already knew from her research that it was granite, transported from the dead man's home, and that it weighed forty tons. Fifty years ago, the machine operators had to place it carefully, so as not to crush the casket six feet below. On the boulder's front, a plaque showed a name and dates, its copper tarnished a bright green, but nothing else signified the magnitude of who was interred there.

The wind whipped hair into her eyes, and Gwen pulled it aside to look. The strangest thing of all was the junk piled on the boulder. She'd seen pictures of Jim Morrison's grave in Paris, the flowers and framed photographs fans continually left on the rock star's tomb.

But that was tidy by comparison. The tributes here were a mess, as if someone had axed open a giant piñata: pebbles and seashells, costume jewelry and used-up lipsticks, photographs washed blank by the rain, a pink wig, panties the weather had aged yellow, manila envelopes with scrawled papers protruding, a worn brown shoe. And then, more to the point: paintbrushes, empty tubes of paint, Van Gogh's self-portrait—the one with the ear bandage—on a postcard. And scattered through it all, too many empty airplane vodka bottles to count.

"Blur it all," Gwen told the boulder, "and this might look like one of your early paintings."

She set her green notebook down on the dull winter grass, dug out her phone, and took photos of the visitors' gifts. What would the buried man make of it? A sign of success? Or mere notoriety? No telling, not a word. Gwen thought: *Death might be the most democratic institution of all. Everyone equal, and equally silent.*

"Ask me, that's kinda twisted." Wyatt had idled his taxi up the path, his arm out the window. "Taking pictures of a grave? It's not exactly the view from the Empire State Building, you know."

"I know." Gwen continued circling the giant rock. "But you never—"

One item on the pile caught her breath. A convertible. The little metal kind kids play with, but this one was special. An Oldsmobile, identical to the one he'd been driving that night. Green with a white interior, just like his.

She staggered back two steps. Maybe it was intended as an honor. But someone had included the instrument of his death.

Watching the whole time, Wyatt hopped out of the cab and came over. Gwen turned, handing him the toy car. "Do you know what this is?"

He turned it over. "I have a guess, for sure."

"They caused his death, you know. Fans, I mean." She tucked her wayward hair back again. "Ruth, his lover and biggest fan? He spent months standing at the cliff's edge, no question. But she's the one who told him to jump." Gwen waved at the mess. "And here they're still at it. *Jummpp.*"

Wyatt nodded. "Kinda creepy."

"A great artist went insane. Yet somebody, on a pilgrimage to this place, put a miniature of the man's car on his grave. Do they not understand how he died? What kind of monsters are these people?"

"Freaks and geeks." He handed her the toy car. "Everyone who comes out here, they're either freaks or they're geeks."

She moved back to the boulder. "Then which one am I?"

"I don't see a lotta freak on you. So, I guess you're in the geek category."

They both laughed. "What an honor," Gwen said.

"You should see them in summer." Wyatt chuckled. "All dressed up in fifties clothes. So perfectly bohemian, you know they bought the outfit at a secondhand store the day before." He came to stand beside her. "What sorta zombie saves up empty vodka shooters to bring them here?"

"Now you understand," Gwen said, her voice leveling. She placed one hand on the rock. "Three months ago, a painting by this man sold for an obscene amount of money. Does that make his final painting automatically worth a fortune? Even if, by the time he made it, he was as mad as a rabid dog? And when he wasn't drunk, he was busy screwing some wannabe muse who goaded him into self-destruction?" Her voice rose, her eyes teared up. "There's fifty million dollars at stake, Wyatt. Not to mention my entire career."

"Sounds like a murder mystery. Catch the bad guy before he kills again."

"The killing has already happened." Gwen withdrew her hand. "And not just the guy under this boulder."

Wyatt took off his baseball hat, wiped the brim, tugged it back on. "Maybe we oughta get rolling."

"Does that wannabe deserve the payday of a lifetime? Should she be rewarded for his death? I'm supposed to have answers to all these questions tomorrow morning."

"This place isn't healthy. Let's go."

Gwen bent to pick up her notebook. "I thought coming here would give me clarity. Instead, it's the exact opposite."

"Isn't that always the deal with this guy?" Wyatt took her arm and, with unexpected grace, guided her toward his taxi. "You can look all day long, and you still don't know what in hell he was painting. Except maybe a portrait of his own craziness. He names the thing *Number Twenty* or some other bullshit, and it sells for ten zillion." They reached the car. "Not giving you clarity is his whole damn game."

"Every time you speak, Wyatt, I think you are smarter."

"Yeah, well." He opened her door. "But you still won't go get a coffee with me."

Gwen stepped away, freeing her arm. "I have to get back to the city."

"Of course you do. Whole goddamn world's gotta get back to the city." He waved her in the open door. "All aboard."

As they drove off, Gwen turned in her seat. She took a quick video, then watched it on her phone. One brown boulder of reality, and the cemetery falling away as though distance and time were the same thing, and she was leaving the past behind. Tucking the phone in her coat pocket, she was surprised to find the toy convertible there too. She hadn't intended to keep it, but here it was.

I

JANUARY 1949

Willem works his way through the crowd to a side door, where he sees a short man as fixed in place as a fire hydrant. Willem navigates through smokers, sippers of wine, collectors. Riggins, who owns the gallery, stands beside a desk, wringing his hands. But Willem, a handsome man with a perfect part to his thick hair, persists till he reaches the sturdy man, who that whole time has managed not to blink.

"It's a disaster, Jack," Willem says. "Total disaster."

"Jackson."

"Sure, but you may as well start calling yourself Matisse. Only desperate measures will save the ship from sinking tonight."

Jackson raises his eyebrows, ending whatever reverie he'd been caught in. "What are you talking about?"

Willem leans nearer. "Not one sale," he confides. "Zero. Zilch. Nil."

Jackson shrugs. "It's early."

"Nine forty-five." Willem taps the face of his wristwatch. "The instant the wine runs out, you will witness an exodus worthy of Moses leading his people out of Egypt."

Jackson scans the room. It's a solo show, all the work is his. The paintings on the right-hand wall have abstract shapes in dramatic colors. On the left, wild, vague landscapes in grays and blacks, with the occasional blue as in a vein of ice.

Occupying the entire back wall, there hangs a gigantic work of whirling color and rich texture—which seems to cause aversion instead of attention. Created on fiberboard, because a wood-stretched canvas that big was too expensive, it's a dense layering of green, turquoise, and gray on a rust-brown background, which makes its slashes of calcium white, sports car red, and electric yellow stunning. Yet the nearest people, engrossed in conversation, stand with their backs to the painting.

Jackson snorts like a bull, then bolts out the door and down to Third Avenue.

Willem calls from the top of the stairs. "May I come with you?"

At that Jackson pauses, granting a smile that lasts less than a second. "You have to ask? I'm no fun without you."

"I'm glad." He comes rumbling down. "You know how I hate funerals."

FOUR DRINKS IN, THEY SIT SHOULDER TO SHOULDER AT THE CEDAR TAVern, a dive near Washington Square Park. They're perched well down the bar, so no one will bother them.

"Which does this place smell more like?" Willem asks. "Beer or piss?"

"No difference." Jackson studies his reflection in the mirror behind the bar. Still muscular, still handsome, perhaps a bit loose around the jowls. "Beer is just piss that hasn't grown up."

"Yes. We don't buy beer. We rent it."

"See?" Jackson laughs. "No fun without you."

A commotion by the entrance makes Willem look up. Riggins comes charging through the crowd, elbows out for anyone in his way. "Pollock, you bastard."

"Wrong night for him to collect my debts," Jackson mutters. "We're drinking my last dime."

"You old bastard, you," Riggins says, thumping Jackson on the back, tugging him to and fro.

"What's the matter with you?" Willem says. "Can't you see the man is busy?"

"Very," Jackson says, taking a hard pull of his drink. "Have your secretary call my secretary's secretary."

"Fellows, it's a diamond in a heap of dung." Riggins grips both men by a shoulder. "Our man Pollock had a sale tonight after all."

Jackson draws his head back, attempting to stand, but the place has grown too crowded. "Don't bullshit me. They were afraid even to look at my work."

"Nonetheless. *Number 5, 1948* is now the property of Alfonso Ossorio."

"Who?" Willem asks.

"Ossorio," Jackson growls. "Mister prep school and Harvard, piles of family money—and queer to boot. Small-time painter too."

Willem interrupts the drink he was taking. "He's an artist?"

"A good one," Riggins replies. "With a good eye."

"Sure, if you consider games to be art. Because surrealism is just a game."

"Wait a second," Willem says. "Isn't Harvard the program where you study art but never paint?"

"Ossorio is collecting for his sixty-acre place out on Long Island." Riggins elbows Jackson. "Isn't East Hampton close to your beloved Springs?"

"Too close."

"To inherited wealth." Willem lifts his glass. "And Jackson selling a painting tonight."

"Good old *Number 5*." Scowling, he taps his glass against Willem's. "Though this deal smells like cow dung."

"Doubt it all you want." Riggins grins. "Twenty minutes ago, Alfonso wrote me a check for fifteen hundred. It's in my strongbox till I can deposit it tomorrow."

"I say the deal smells like roses," Willem says.

"Wait a second." Jackson wrestles himself free of both men, working his way upright, pushing outward with both arms. "Give me some goddamn room," he shouts. "Will you people please just—?" And he shoves his arms out again.

They step back, the other drinkers making a retreat until Jackson stands alone. He shakes his head to clear it. When that doesn't work, he presses both temples with his hands. Finally, he taps on Riggins's lapel. "Have you got a cigarette?"

The gallery owner digs out a pack and shakes one free. By the time Jackson fumbles it into his mouth, Riggins is holding out his lighter. Jackson takes two quick draws, then releases a cloud. "No bullshit?"

Riggins shakes his head. "Real thing."

"Well, *ha,*" Jackson barks. He lunges back to the bar, grabbing his beer. "Here's to a good old-fashioned three-day bender."

He chugs the glass dry, then flings it against the wall.

1

NOVEMBER 9, 2006

The Thursday that changed Gwen's life was cloudy and damp, New York City's temperature flirting with the high thirties, but at least the drizzle had stopped. Every few minutes a glimpse of sunlight glinted through breaks in the clouds. The light reflected off the glass buildings of the Upper East Side, as Gwen strode north from the Sixty-Eighth Street subway stop. She crossed the avenues: Second, then First, then onto the far side of York, before turning uptown.

"Any farther east," she grumbled, "this place would fall in the river."

Then she spied her target: the New York office of Sotheby's, the massive international auction company. At two hundred sixty-three years old, this was the singular place to buy Tiffany glass, sell East Asian sculpture, build a collection of rare ancient documents. And, on that day of moody weather, auction one exceptional painting—and she had money riding on it.

When she'd confided her plan to Chillie the afternoon before, to crash a high-security private sale, Gwen predicted the painting would go to a leaper. That's a bidder who waits while others inch the price higher, she explained, and then he—it's always a male—makes a bid high above everyone else.

"It implies that his resources are limitless," she said, "so it is futile to bid against him. The other buyers all fall away in defeat."

She and Chillie worked in adjoining cubicles at Carroll and Bunzel, a Midtown auction house with all the dignity and formality of Sotheby's, but one-tenth the revenues.

"You are completely, thoroughly, embarrassingly wrong." Chillie grinned, shaking his head side to side. "The painting will go to a creeper, guaranteed. Some guy who made his billions one penny at a time. The auctioneer will ask for fifty thousand higher, and this guy will bid two grand more. He's frugal, and he's not giving up."

"The usual wager?" She held out her hand, and he shook it.

"Double, because I don't believe you will even get in the door," he said.

"When I do, I'll send you a valentine."

"You will get arrested. You will be fired."

Gwen laughed. "I'm going to win so many bets, I'll buy the painting myself."

Now that she approached the building, however, Gwen found her steps slowing. Her plan was full of holes. Security was sure to be tight, if only to overcompensate for the company's difficulties in recent years. Some of the senior staff had gone to jail for violating antitrust laws. Somehow, though, scandal only raised the company's profile. It was a sort of compliment, that Sotheby's had grown big enough to merit federal prosecution.

"Not a chance at Carroll and Bunzel," she muttered, shoving a revolving door to usher her in. If nothing else, this morning was going to be educational. She strode under the giant Sotheby's sign and the international flags snapping over the door. The only hard part would be the next three minutes.

Gwen had done her homework: They were using a side gallery on the main floor. That meant she would not have to reckon with the uniformed grouches who provided upper-floor security. As Gwen breezed past, one guard gave the brim of his uniform cap a little tug. She took it as a good sign.

Gwen had been to the main gallery before, when Carroll and Bunzel represented a co-seller. The lot was a dossier of writings by Albert Einstein in his twenties. The papers were not scientifically significant, but his scribbles in the margins shed light on his personality during the productive early years.

The crowd this day was sure to include a corral: Sotheby's employees on the phone with buyers who participate anonymously. Financial heavyweights or international collectors, in either case, they wished to remain a mystery. Not celebrities, though, she mused. Celebrities flaunted their wealth.

Gwen preferred auctions without phones. She wanted to see the bidders, especially their footwear. She had a theory about shoes, how they revealed a person's desire for the auction item and degree of vanity. She and Chillie used to wager based on shoes, but she won so often, he insisted they bet on other things.

How the corral business would change with these new smartphones was anyone's guess. Every bidder could be an ambassador, linked to private money.

With only an approximate idea of where to go, Gwen followed the well-dressed crowd down the wide entry hall. The line led to wooden double doors, where men in gray suits scowled at everyone. She saw the wire that coiled out of the back of their collars, up to a discreet hearing aid–style headphone. One guard brandished a metal detector like a cattle prod. She suspected that they all were armed.

"Good morning, ma'am," said a man to her left, his bow as obsequious as that of the maître d' of New York's finest restaurant. "Bidder or guest, please?"

Gwen gave her biggest smile. "Strictly guest today."

"Yes, very good." He led her to a woman at a table. That was a complexity. She was about Gwen's age, not the susceptible middle-aged male she'd expected.

The woman nodded in greeting. "If you could please show your invitation, or identification for us to match with the invitation list . . ."

"Of course." Gwen reached toward her hip, but when she straightened, her face looked shocked. "I don't have any."

"I'm afraid we require proof of—"

"I know," Gwen told her. "But my purse is gone."

"Excuse me?"

"This is bad for reasons beyond this auction." Gwen turned to the maître d'. "If I've lost that purse, I can't begin to tell you."

"I'm sorry." The young woman held firm. "We're not permitted any exceptions this morning."

"I don't know." She raised a hand to her mouth. "Maybe I left it in the cab?"

"Let her in," said a woman in line behind her. "Be reasonable, people."

Gwen turned to see who was speaking: a stranger, white haired and tall. She wore a black dress, plus several pounds of bling on her wrists, ears, and neck.

"It doesn't appear that she's concealing a machine gun," the woman continued.

"It's not just my ID," Gwen said. "Credit cards, apartment keys, the last of my mother's . . ." She glanced at the stranger, who took her cue perfectly.

"You people could take yourselves a bit less seriously." The woman waved her wrist, jewelry tinkling. "She's not going to run away with a giant painting."

"Is there a phone I might use?" Gwen asked the maître d'. "For a moment?"

He glanced at the line to the table, which was growing like a minor traffic jam. "This way, please."

They entered the side gallery. Chairs sat in tidy rows, with a red ribbon behind the first two rows to separate bidders from audience. On each one there was a pamphlet about the day's lots. At the front stood a pulpit, elevated like the prow of a sailing ship, in front of a velvet curtain. Gwen knew exactly what was behind it.

The audience area was small, a rarity. Generally an audience added drama to the bidding. People cheered or gasped or applauded, like the crowd at a tennis match. They drove prices higher. And later, the crowd worked like a human public relations campaign, telling the auction's story to anyone who would listen. Apparently, publicity was not a priority that day.

Fewer seats, Gwen knew, also meant it would be harder to weasel her way in.

At a quick clip, the man led her around the room's perimeter and through a door in the far wall. On the other side, there was none of the gallery's genteel tone. It was an office, people bustling in the hallway, phones ringing. Someone shouted for Peters, but Peters wasn't answering.

"My apologies," the man said, guiding her into a cubicle.

"I'm the one who owes you an apology," Gwen replied, scanning his work area. The cubicles were not much larger than at Carroll and Bunzel, but the desk chairs looked more ergonomic. The computers had larger monitors too. "Do you have a phone book? I need the number of the city taxi authority."

"This will be faster." He dropped into his chair, tapping the keyboard. "But then I must return to my station."

"Understood." Gwen made an exaggerated nod of her head. "As fast as I can."

He dialed the number, handing her the receiver.

"Hello, I'd like to speak with someone responsible for lost items," Gwen said. When the maître d' glanced anxiously down the hall, she pressed the button to end the call. "Yes, good morning," she continued. "I rode a cab this morning from Central Park West at Eighty-Eighth Street to Thirteen Thirty-Four York Avenue, and I seem to have left my purse in the taxi."

She pretended to listen. "Of course I didn't. Has anyone in human history ever written down the license number of a cab?" Gwen waved a hand by her head as if to say, *What can I do with this imbecile?*

The man was pacing like he needed to pee. "I must go," he whispered.

"I understand," Gwen replied to the phone, nodding. "But I was carrying the last of my mother's—yes? Yes, who am I speaking with?" She nodded. "All right, Henry in customer service. Can I give you my contact information?"

The maître d' bowed in apology and dashed out of the cubicle. Gwen spelled her name and address, taking care not to rush. She gave half of her phone number, checked the corridor, and put the phone down. Taking a deep breath, she studied the man's desk. Two rambunctious toddlers in one photo, then another with both of them in prom tuxedos. A dark-haired woman with a splendid smile, three photos of her.

Gwen took out her flip phone and typed the numbers to send a text message to Chillie: 444, 6, 0, 444, 66. Send.

I'm in.

Putting the phone away, she made herself count, struggling to do it slowly while her blood raced. A little tray on the desk held the helpful man's business cards. She wished there were some way she could send a thank-you note. When the count reached three hundred, she opened the door and found everyone in their seats. A Sotheby's executive stood at the front, thanking them all for coming. Between the audience and the corral, Gwen counted nineteen bidders. She spied an empty chair in the audience's middle row. Mouthing, "Excuse me," she wriggled into the seat.

The executive concluded her remarks to polite applause. Then there was a pause, the air suspenseful, people shifting in their seats. Maybe bidders would get in a lather over something, or egos would collide. Someone might spend a fortune beyond belief, purely for the gratification of winning. Or maybe the object of Gwen's interest, the reason she'd snuck in, would not draw a single bid. Humiliation for the auction house, and for the current owner, an awkward embarrassment in front of an invitation-only audience. In that moment of quiet, anything was possible.

At last Stiles Breuker strode in, through the same side door Gwen had used. The sight of him called the staff to order, and their snap to attention caused the rest of the room to hush. A short man with a blond brush cut, half-Brit, half-Belgian, his age anywhere between forty and seventy, Breuker was renowned for being exceedingly particular. The room must be a certain temperature and humidity. His suit was always gray. For a gavel he used not the customary wooden hammer, but rather a round knot of mahogany from the same tree used to build Benjamin Franklin's favorite desk. And always on the podium's shelf there must be a glass of cool water—no ice, that was absolute, a man busy speaking could easily choke on ice—though no person in the history of Sotheby's had seen him pause long enough to take even a sip. To bidders he was fastidiously fair, and Gwen imagined that, with his sterling reputation, the auctioneer earned a stratospheric salary.

Breuker made his signature flourish, circling the knot of mahogany above his head like a cowboy spinning a lasso, then approached the podium. "Ladies and gentlemen, I bid you good morning." He gave the knot one quick rap on the podium. "Let us commence."

Lot One, a still life sketch by Rothko, nimble and evocative.

Someone wanted it and wasted no time in winning it—his or her haste meaning he or she probably paid too much. Lot Two, a drawing from Willem de Kooning, a cubist nude with spread legs. What was scandalous in the 1950s now barely raised an eyebrow. The pace was steady but brisk, half a dozen interested buyers, all as polite as chipmunks. The rest were saving up, Gwen suspected, for Lot Eleven. This strategy did not make for the best auctions, however, because it restrained bids on the early lots. She observed Breuker working the corners, monitoring the full room with quick, birdlike turns of his neck.

Lot Ten was an incomplete from Motherwell, which drew a prolonged bicker between two people on the phones, nitpicking their way through the mid–four hundred thousands. Then it turned out there was one interested bidder there in person, a handsome Black man in a striking pinstripe suit with a knot pin uplifting his tie. It was a rarity; most non-white people she saw at fine art auctions were from Asia. This man showed expertise, raising his bidding card, using the leaping method, and winning the Motherwell for a clean half million.

Now came the star of the show. The reason Gwen had come.

"Ladies and gentlemen, I give you Lot Eleven."

Breuker paused as the velvet curtain parted. They'd used some kind of clever support system, Gwen realized, because the painting appeared to be floating in the air. When it came to theatricality, she had to give these Sotheby folks credit.

"*Number 5, 1948,* by Jackson Pollock."

It was an explosion, that was Gwen's first thought. A giant detonation. She blinked repeatedly, as if to reset her vision. But the painting remained as it was: huge, as large as a wall; textured in a way no photo in an art book could capture, layer upon layer of paint so that in some places it was several inches thick; passionate, with sweeping swirls of colors and ideas; inexplicable, now that she had looked for a minute, with yellow on top of the white in some places, and under the white in others. As if the thing had been made all at once, the entire image somehow flung whole onto the fiberboard. Which was impossible, because it had been damaged, then repaired twice. So rich with imagery, this was not a painting to see. It was a painting to read.

Did *Number* 5 describe anger? Joy? Chaos? Gwen imagined an orchestra, the musicians all playing whatever melody they wished, yet the cacophony somehow making sense, in a new and captivating key.

Gwen had achieved her goal. She was seeing this painting—privately owned its entire life and about to vanish from public view again—with her own open eyes.

Breuker, giving them all a good gape, droned on with details.

"Ninety-six inches by forty-eight inches, created in nineteen forty-eight and purchased in a Manhattan gallery days later. Provenance is airtight, with only three owners in fifty years—from the original purchase by the late Alfonso Ossorio of East Hampton, Long Island, a collector and artist himself; to the current owner, media executive and philanthropist David Geffen of Los Angeles. Here is a work unique in all the world, Pollock at his highest powers, his full genius on display."

Breuker banged the knot of wood on the podium once. "The floor on Lot Eleven is thirty million dollars, am I bid thirty million?"

A staffer in the corral, phone to her ear, raised a finger.

"Thirty, I have thirty million dollars, thirty million." Breuker pointed at the bidder while scanning over the crowd. "Do I have thirty-five?"

3

JUNE 1949

Willem de Kooning parks his borrowed truck beside the house, immediately noticing that the studio door is open. Someone inside is singing. Or something like singing.

"Knock knock," he calls, poking his head inside.

In the middle of the studio floor sits Jackson, surrounded by newspaper pages. He's unshaven, shirt torn at the shoulder. "Ten after ten," he chants. "Ten after ten."

"Rough riding today, cowboy?" Normally Willem checks for fresh paint on the floor, to spare his shoes, but there's no canvas down that morning. The only work in progress he can see is a bottle of vodka on a side table, about two-thirds of the way gone.

Jackson still hasn't responded. Willem approaches from the side and leans down. "Hello, my friend. How are you?"

Jackson winces as though he's been caught in a bright light. "Ten after ten, that's how I am. Ten after ten."

Willem sits beside him. "What is it, Jack? What about ten after ten?"

"Right here." He thumbs the news sheet in front of him. "Page three of today's *Times*. The Tiffany ad, like always, page three, upper right. Today it's three watches." He turns the page upright. "What do you see?"

Willem studies the advertisement. "Wealth?" he guesses. "Excess?"

"Look at the hands of those watches. All three of them, all set to ten after ten."

He snorts. "That's strange."

Jackson shoves another page. "Cartier ad, lower right on the op-ed page. Look what time it is. Here's Bulova, on an inside sports page. Ten after ten."

"I never noticed that before."

"And you're a goddamn painter. Or so I hear." He tilts the glass in his other hand, but it's empty. "Good Christ, I'm drunk."

"You got an early start." Willem peers around, not seeing the plates and bowls that usually signify the man is at least getting something to eat. "Where's Lee?"

"Lee who?"

Willem winces. "Your loving wife?"

"I know that. I *know.*" Jackson wrestles himself to his feet, shuffles to the side table. "Away. I knew where, but I forgot. Until Tuesday. It's written in the kitchen."

"It's a long way from Saturday morning to Tuesday."

"Yes, my friend. A long damn drunk too." He swings the vodka bottle in the air. "Pretty sure her train gets in at ten after ten."

Willem laughs. "That discovery is certainly stuck in your craw."

"Maybe it means something. A message. Maybe the world will end at ten after ten. Maybe that is the hour of justice and our redemption."

"Maybe it's when we're held accountable for our sins."

Jackson has begun pouring vodka into his glass, but he pauses. "You, Willem? You have sins to be judged for?"

"Well." He looks away for a moment, then back. "You know all too well."

"That wasn't sin. It was joy." Jackson swirls the bottle as though he is mixing a drink. "Also, a long time ago."

"Which does nothing to reduce my wife Elaine's great sorrow." Willem wanders across the large square room. "Change of subject, please. Are you too drunk to register the thing I came here to discuss?"

Jackson scratches his chin on the bottle's spout. "I'm willing to give it a try."

Willem raises a finger. "Don't go away."

He ambles out to the truck, reaches into the bed, and pulls out a painting. It's not heavy, just awkward to carry because of its size. Entering the studio again, he finds Jackson back on the floor, sipping, stirring through the news pages. Only after Willem sets the painting against the wall does Jackson look up.

"What have we here?"

"*Number 5, 1948*, with an unfortunate—"

"Good Christ, what happened?" Jackson crawls closer. "What the hell?"

"Transit damage. The movers were carrying it out of the studio at the end of the show, to deliver it to the buyer, and one of the men stumbled. They were holding the painting face down, because they know absolutely nothing about art and will never be hired by a gallery again. The metal post at the bottom of the stairs scraped off—"

"I can see that." He is not slurring any longer. "I can see that very fucking clearly, Willem."

"—slightly larger than a dinner plate. Riggins spoke with Alfonso, who first demanded a refund. Riggins did his bit, till Alfonso said he would consider a repaired painting. But he will not accept a damaged one."

"Spoken like an artist with the standards of an heir and the talent of a monkey. I've already spent his money."

"Riggins imagined that would be the case." Willem holds his hands together. "Unfortunately, Alfonso has a valid point."

Jackson stands, wavering, then sidles away from the painting. "I liked this one, you know." His throat chokes with emotion. "I really did."

"It's a masterpiece, Jack. Or it was."

"And now I'm supposed to bow to this poser? And fix the damn thing?"

"I believe you mean: Are you supposed to continue to make good money with your art? And to please a buyer likely to acquire more of your works in the future?"

"That trust fund phony? He is my new target collector?"

Willem does not answer, only monitors Jackson as he circles the damage. "They didn't gouge the board deeper than the paint."

"Yes," he says. "There is that."

"There were eleven layers," Jackson says. "Each one had a purpose. A reason. That metal post scraped them all away. And the rest of the thing . . ." He scans it.

"Is the reason to repair it. The painting is damaged but not ruined."

Jackson puts his drink on the floor. "I can fix this."

"I believe you can."

"I have ideas right now. This minute. I could finish before Lee gets home."

Willem brushes off his hands. "Now you're talking."

"Ten after ten," he says. "I'll have it done by then."

"I'll leave you to it." He backs toward the door.

"One favor before you go?" Jackson is still assessing the painting, so close he could be sniffing it.

"Anything for you, my friend."

He holds the glass out. "Ice?"

A WEEK LATER, ON THE SUNNY AFTERNOON OF A BLUEBIRD EARLY-JULY day, Willem returns with the truck. The engine off, he does not hop out right away but sits thinking about what is ahead. Will there be shouting? Violence against the painting? What will be today's version of ten after ten?

Music is coming from inside the house. Jazz—Charlie Parker?—the wailing of a saxophone. He knocks on the screen door, calling hello, and hears Lee from inside.

"Come in, come in."

Willem straightens his back. In the kitchen is a disorder so complete as to look intentional: stacks of plates, food left out on the counter, peelings in a clogged sink. The smell is not strong, but it is unpleasant. And he can hear the drone of flies. If all goes well, later he might help clean the place up.

He continues past the piano. A new work sits on Lee's easel, covered with a gray cloth. In the dining area, Lee sits perched on a sideboard, dressed in overalls stained with many colors of paint, her hair restrained by a red bandanna. At her side is a sketching pad, and a coffee tin of colored pencils. In better light, the scene would make a fair portrait.

Lee is smiling. "Hello, Will. How is my husband's guardian angel?"

"Hardly." They kiss on both cheeks. "You're the one who deserves sainthood. How is everything?"

"Here I am." Lee opens her arms. "Playing goalie on the vodka."

"What do you mean?"

"He has started coming in here earlier in the day. I sit on the cabinet every afternoon, no booze till five o'clock. It's the only way he gets any work done."

"What time do you start?"

"Today?" She smiles wistfully. "Right after lunch."

Willem laughs. "Then how do you work?"

Lee gestures at the tin of pencils.

"But that's not oil on canvas. Not even close."

"I don't mind." Lee fishes through the tin for a pencil. "If I don't look after him, he won't last two weeks."

The screen door slams and Jackson barges into the room. He's holding a glass. Seeing them both, he swerves around and back outside. The door slams again.

"Hello, Jack," Willem calls after him.

"What brings you here?" Lee asks.

"*Number 5*. It's still a problem."

Lee selects a pencil, burnt red by its look, and opens the sketchbook.

"No comment?" Willem asks.

"No one is smarter with money than a rich man."

"Ossorio's concerns are legitimate."

"Yes, and entirely between him and the gallery."

"Normally, yes. But Jackson made a deal: a higher percentage of the take if he shared in the risk."

"He didn't tell me." Lee runs her thumb over the tip of the pencil. "Regardless," she says eventually. "My husband has new works underway, and ideas buzzing in his mind like bees in a hive. He does not need this pretty boy making him work and rework something he finished months ago."

Willem opens his mouth, but checks himself. "I'll do what I can."

Lee brings the pencil to the blank page. "Why is it, whenever something goes wrong, the artist is always the one who has to pay?"

Willem nods. "And pay and pay and pay."

IN THE STUDIO, JACKSON MIXES PAINT, POURING HARDWARE-STORE CANS into larger buckets, leaning into the task with a clean wooden stirrer.

"Hello, Jack."

"I already saw it in the truck. You might as well bring it in."

So, Willem leaves having said only two words, returning with the large fiberboard rectangle. He leans it facing the wall and decides not to speak.

Jackson taps a cigarette out of its pack, takes his time lighting it. "What does the bastard have to say now?"

"Direct quotation?"

"I insist on it."

Willem strolls to the opposite side of the studio. "He said the repair looked cursory. An insulting lack of effort, as though you thought he had no eyes. He said your scorn for him was visible."

Jackson tilts his head to one side. "Maybe so."

"He said the repair area has only three layers, which look pathetically thin compared with the rest of the work. And he suspected that one of the layers was actually the skin of a paint can that had sat open in the air too long."

Jackson laughs. "He actually said that?"

"I'm sorry. I shouldn't have told you."

"The damn fool is right. It's skin from a bucket." He takes a deep draw from his cigarette. "He wants me to repair it again."

Willem goes to the windows, and nods.

Jackson smokes his cigarette. "This is Riggins's problem. I can't keep fixing this painting over and over."

"What do you want me to do?"

He exhales a long plume of smoke. "Take the painting back to Alfonso. Tell him I said he should place it on the ground, cut a tiny hole all the way through, and fuck it."

Willem flinches. He crosses the studio, lifts the painting, turns it around.

"Don't do that," Jackson says. "Don't make me look at it."

"Goodbye for now, my friend." Willem marches out of the studio.

Jackson comes to the studio door, stands picking at the wood for a moment. "Don't do this, Willem. Don't do this to me."

He has already climbed into the truck, and backs it out into the road.

"Don't do this," Jackson yells.

Willem grinds the truck into gear and leaves in a cloud.

AFTER LABOR DAY, OUTER LONG ISLAND GOES QUIET. THE DAYS REMAIN warm, but nights are cool for good sleeping. Summer people have traffic-jammed their way home. Tourists, weekend visitors, and August renters return to the city like the migration of a species of pink-skinned mammals. Behind they leave a stillness. The place feels like a field on the outside of town, grass flattened where a county fair ran for a week and now is gone.

Art Mooney's band plays on the tinny truck transistor, "I'm Looking Over a Four-Leaf Clover," as Jackson drives down-island. He slaps the radio off and concentrates on the route to East Hampton and the property of Alfonso Ossorio. In a place where one-tenth of an acre is considered gold, this place is a full sixty acres. It is called The Creeks.

"If I ever live in a house that has a name," Jackson told Lee that morning, "shoot me. Do it twice, to make sure."

Two minutes along behind the wheel, he pats his pockets and realizes he has forgotten his wallet. Pulling over, he imagines how Lee would react if he went home for it. *Is the money for booze?* she'd ask. He'd lie, then have to buy something else to distract her, and hide the bottle. Bottles.

He could beg Mickey at the store to extend him more credit, but he refuses to. It is mortifying enough that Jackson has to ask Lee for money, except when she inadvertently gives him more cash than he needs for some errand, and he uses the extra to reduce his arrears. A man ought to drink when he wants. A man ought to control his own money. A man ought to—

"Goddamn it to hell." He jams the truck into gear and roars out on the road without looking.

A black sedan honks as it swerves past. The driver shakes a fist in the air.

"I'm thirsty," Jackson yells, as he continues south.

The house is like a picture frame, a two-story brick structure surrounded by vast gardens at a level to rival Versailles. Several servants are weeding and watering as he drives past. The circular driveway, made of small white stones, issues a loud protest under his tires. Jackson measures with his eyes and estimates that the driveway occupies more space than his entire property. As he parks, Jackson considers that he should have come better dressed.

"Too late now," he mutters, climbing down. The sun seems stronger here, though he's driven only ten miles. He licks his dry lips. Forget liquor, he would sell the truck for a glass of water.

The plan was that Lee would call Alfonso once Jackson was on the road, so his arrival won't be a total surprise. Now he stands behind the truck, sniffing his underarms. Would it have killed him to put on a clean shirt?

As he approaches the house, the front door opens. A tall man emerges, dressed entirely in linen. His hair is teased upward and back, as if he were facing a strong wind, his arms wide in greeting. "At last, I meet the great artist in person."

"Alfonso." As they shake hands, Jackson feels short and impoverished. "How are you?"

"Splendid, of course. The rabble departs, and our island becomes heaven again. Would you please join me for a drink?"

"Really?"

"Iced tea or water, that's all on offer today. Do come in."

"Tea is great, but—" Jackson points over his shoulder. "I'm here to make a delivery."

"Lee called with that wonderful news. I've already told John to take care of it, so we might visit a minute. Would that be all right?"

"Sure." Jackson imagines a tall glass of icy cold tea. "Sure thing."

Alfonso leads the way in. The house is cool, as if indifferent to the outdoor temperature. The entryway has a reddish marble floor, with wide white stairs curving upward. The air is perfumed by vases of flowers set on baroque pedestals. The art is classical, Greek and Roman paintings and sculptures, lots of swords, stone butts, and tiny penises. Jackson snickers, then catches up to Alfonso at the screened back door.

"At least put *something* on," he is telling a person outside. "We have company."

Jackson cannot hear the response from outside, but a muscular young man comes to the door with a towel around his waist. "Pardon me, Mr. Jackson," he says, hurrying by.

"Jackson is his *first* name," Alfonso snaps. "I told you that."

The young man bounds up the stone stairs without responding.

"Saint Paul wrote that love is patient." Alfonso smiles. "Wouldn't you agree?"

"Then my wife must really love me. I try her patience around the clock."

He chuckles. "I didn't know you are a wit too. Come, let's sit in the shade."

The patio has half a dozen wrought iron lounges, with flowery padded pillows, arrayed in a half circle to face the elaborate docks. Georgica Pond flashes and sparkles at their feet, stretching south to the Atlantic Ocean.

"This place is really something, sir."

"We love it," Alfonso replies. "But sometimes I yearn for your side of the island. The bay is more serene. In my ideal world, I want my house on your bay."

"I'll put in an order for you, next chance I get."

"*Again* with the wit."

A round woman in a dove-gray uniform arrives with a silver tray, which holds a pitcher of tea and two glasses filled with ice.

"I'll pour, Beatrice, thank you." Alfonso tips the pitcher, and the ice makes a little song as he pours. Jackson can feel his throat's dryness.

"So." Alfonso holds both glasses in his hands. "What have you done with our truculent *Number 5?*"

Jackson ducks his head. "The story is more like what it did to me."

"Really?" Alfonso sips one glass, holds the other close to his chest. "What did it do?"

"Haunted me."

"How romantic. But you should have spared yourself and not kept it from me for so very long. In fact, I was delighted to hear from your wife this morning. I'd begun to grow concerned."

"But I mean *haunted*, sir. Stared at me in my studio day and night for three months. No amount of work, no obsession, would satisfy it. Can't estimate how much time I spent on it. Turns out"—he shifted closer—"within the original concept there was a larger, more difficult idea, more urgent, struggling to be born."

"Jackson." Alfonso waves the second glass of tea. "No 'sir' is needed—or permitted. We are both artists. Men of the brush. We know that all humans are equal before an empty canvas."

A uniformed man approaches with soft steps. "Pardon me, Mr. Ossorio?"

"John, at last. Are we ready?"

The man nods and backs away.

Alfonso raises his eyebrows. "Shall we go see?"

"You're the boss," Jackson replies. But his eyes are on the iced tea. Droplets have condensed on the glass. There's a lemon wedge on the brim.

"I'm so excited." Alfonso takes a hearty gulp from his glass, then sets both of them down on the tray. Rising, he starts back inside.

"Hell with it," Jackson mutters, as he grabs the full glass and chugs it down. Cools his mouth, his tongue, his throat. He even takes an ice cube to suck on.

If Alfonso notices, it does not show. He only holds the screen door wide, then leads Jackson up the main hall and into a side room. Jackson muses that the gallery is larger than the entire first floor of his house.

"My oh my," Alfonso chimes, hands clasped. *Number 5, 1948* hangs on the main wall, under overhead lights as focused as in any professional gallery. Pollock can hardly bear to look at it. The rhythms and cycles of color, the long effort to reveal a concept beyond words, the elusiveness of an idea that can only be expressed in paint. Eleven layers have become fourteen, and in some places, more.

"How nice," Alfonso says, clapping his hands.

"Nice?"

"Don't you think?" He draws close to the painting, slowly moving down its length. "This is good. I'll need to spend time with it."

Jackson can feel his anger rising. "You think this painting is *good?*"

"I do." Alfonso is not looking at him. His attention is fixed on the painting. "Your repairs are quite satisfactory."

"Satisfactory." Jackson's hands close into fists.

"Of course, the delay is another issue. I acquired this painting in winter. Now it's practically fall. But it's here now, that's what matters." Alfonso pats Jackson's shoulder. "Well done."

He cannot get out fast enough, all but fleeing the house. At the pickup Jackson kicks his door, denting it. Then he yanks it open, and storms off trailing a cloud. He is barely out of earshot of the house when he begins shouting at the world, roaring his rage.

LEE IS WAITING OUTSIDE WHEN HE PULLS INTO THEIR DRIVEWAY OFF FIREplace Road. Though she offers a hug, he only paces past her in the dooryard.

"I'm glad that monkey is off your back." Lee stands a few steps back, wary. "One less obsession."

"Yes." He forces a grin. "So, I can get back to new work."

Lee watches him marching. "Now, that is good news."

But he is already at his studio's door. She does not hear the chime of bottles, one in each pocket so they won't touch. She does not smell the vodka on his breath.

By then, Alfonso has slippered back to his gallery, where he decides to place a call. The party on the other end answers quickly.

"Hello, Clement," Alfonso says. "How is America's greatest critic today?"

He listens to the reply, his smile growing. "It worked beautifully, yes. I played it beautifully."

He attends for a moment more, then laughs. "Oh, completely. No attempt to renegotiate, no effort to raise the price. I distracted him by teasing with the iced tea." He switches the phone to his other ear. "It's hanging right here on my wall. I'm looking at it now."

As Alfonso listens once more, Beatrice arrives holding the tea tray. He swaps his empty glass for a full one, dismissing her with a nod. "For the pittance of fifteen hundred dollars, Clement, and the price of patience, the result is indisputable."

He takes a long drink, several swallows, then lowers the glass to his waist. "I have just acquired the greatest work of art of the twentieth century."

4

NOVEMBER 2006

By the time the bids reached sixty million, the auction had found its rhythm. Breuker would suggest a five-million-dollar increase, and no one would bite. He'd propose two-and-a-half million, and the bidding cards would fly up—two, three, even five buyers bidding at that interval, which meant the five-million offer would be surpassed in minutes anyway.

All creepers, Gwen thought. One leaper and that painting would be sold.

Approaching eighty million, she saw something new. Bidders who'd sat out in the lower numbers began to join, as if they'd left the early dickering to the amateurs, and now it was time for big boys to play. She understood why Breuker insisted on a certain room temperature. Between the bidders' passion and the audience's excitement, the place was definitely warming. It was like watching a close basketball game, teams trading the lead so fast it was hard to know who to root for.

There were crowd favorites, though of course the whole corral was on the phone and no one knew the buyers' identities. Still, one girl—Gwen marveled that someone so young had a role in such a significant sale—won her heart. Freckled, red-haired, blushing her whole face and down her neck, she lifted one finger and said, "Eighty-five million dollars."

Breuker leaned forward as if he couldn't hear, but he was missing nothing. Nor was the fellow on the other side of the corral, who maintained a steady blank expression. When Breuker offered a higher bid—eighty-seven million five hundred thousand—the inscrutable man nodded.

And the crowd applauded. Gwen knew this was unusual. The price was nearing record territory, and the bidding had not cooled one degree.

Each new bid brought hooting or clapping, until somehow, as if by surprise, someone had accepted the stratospheric price of ninety-seven million five hundred thousand. Breuker, for the first time in his illustrious career, paused. He reached down to the podium shelf, lifted the glass of water, and took a big enough gulp to reveal him as actually human. Putting away the glass, he lifted his chin.

"One hundred, ladies and gentlemen. Am I bid one hundred million dollars?"

It was madness, and everyone knew it. Gwen felt a strange weightlessness. Yet in the space of three heartbeats, a bidding paddle rose, Breuker prompted the next number, the blank man nodded, and on the auction went.

Gwen noticed that the executive had returned. She lurked by the side door, one hand flat on her chest as if to keep something from escaping. Common practice was that the house received a third of the sale price, with some portion going to the staff who managed the process. The executive stood to make several million dollars. And Lot Eleven still had not sold.

At one hundred seventeen five, a corral bidder jumped to one hundred twenty-five. A leaper at last. Gwen clutched her hands together, realizing they were damp. But someone offered one twenty-six before Breuker had finished recognizing the leaper's bid. No one was scared off. The game continued.

The remaining stretch had an odd atmosphere, like the ship had hit the iceberg but lived up to all the boasts, and did not sink. When the standing bid was one hundred thirty-seven and a half, there were no higher takers.

"Do we have one forty?" Breuker called. "Am I bid one forty?"

He peered over at the blank fellow, who looked away. He caught the eye of the Black man, who shook his head. "One forty, anyone?"

"Yes sir," the freckled girl said into the phone at her ear. Then she raised her whole hand, like a fifth-grader hoping the teacher would call on her. "One hundred forty million."

Breuker went still. It was a kind of compliment, Gwen thought, a one-second genuflection, before he gripped the podium again. "The bid is one hundred and forty million dollars. Do I have one forty-one? Is there a one forty-one in the room?"

No one spoke. No one moved. The people on phones kept their bidding cards down. The executive to the side squeezed both eyes closed.

"Lot Eleven stands at one hundred and forty million dollars, uncontested. Going once, one hundred and forty going twice." Like the pope, he waved an arm above all the people. "Ladies and gentlemen, *Number 5, 1948* is sold."

He rapped the podium with his mahogany knot, as the cheering audience rose to its feet. The executive was clapping too.

Gwen knew perfectly well—probably everyone in the room knew—that this was the largest sum paid for any single artwork, anywhere in the world, ever. Whole office buildings in Manhattan sold for that much money. A part of her wished she knew how much it cost to feed and house a homeless person, and how many of them could live better with the help of one hundred forty million dollars.

The curtain closed over the giant painting, while a movie screen descended from the ceiling. Breuker raised his glass again and drank it dry. After tugging down on the ends of his sleeves, he reclaimed the podium with both hands.

"Ladies and gentlemen, I give you Lot Twelve." A photo appeared on the screen. "Four handwritten letters from Peggy Guggenheim to American art dealers, from her prewar years in France. Item A in this lot, which you now see, includes her plan to smuggle art out of the country in anticipation of a Nazi invasion."

Important records, yet to Gwen they felt trivial. The day's sales should have ceased because of what just happened. Also, Carroll and Bunzel would never mix rare documents with fine art. They drew different audiences.

"We have a seller's floor of fifteen thousand dollars," Breuker declared. "Do I hear seventeen? Is there seventeen thousand in the house?"

The bids were extravagant, as if everyone wanted a souvenir from that historic day. Six more lots sold for far above any reasonable expectation. When they finished, Breuker thanked everyone for coming, and the people responded with a standing ovation. He bowed, then hurried from the stage. As he exited, the executive stopped him at the door to pump his hand up and down.

GWEN SCANNED THE CROWD, HOPING TO FIND HER WHITE-HAIRED ALLY from the check-in desk. She must have left before the final lots, because Gwen reached the revolving doors without spotting her.

One step outside, however, and the woman hurried forward. "Sweet pea, there you are," she said. "I'm so glad it worked out for you."

"Thank you for that experience." Gwen suppressed the impulse to hug her.

"It was nothing." The woman reached out her hand. "Gallagher Shea."

"Ah. Dianne Chillie," Gwen responded, her lie half fumbled. "Nice to meet you."

They set out down the sidewalk, leaving the exiting crowd. Gallagher pulled on a fur stole as they strolled. "So. Are you one of the Pollock lovers?"

"I don't know what that means."

"Some women carry a torch for anguished artists—Van Gogh, Rothko—and none more fervently than today's outlaw. Muscular, magnetic, and mad, born in Wyoming, buried in the Hamptons. I proudly count myself among their number. Given that neither you nor I came here today to place bids, I presumed . . ."

Gwen liked how she left the rest of the sentence unsaid. "I'm not quite a card-carrying member. I came out of curiosity, though I had no idea the price would explode like that. What do you make of it?"

"The world of fine art has been altered completely," Gallagher answered with authority, "and will never turn back. Collecting major works will become a form of investment, as speculative as the stock market. High prices will change the whole market, too, making even common paintings and sculptures more expensive."

"I hadn't thought of that." Gwen was beginning to relax.

"Then what is your analysis?"

"I was distracted about my lost purse."

"Oh yes." Gallagher gave her a long sideways look. "But I won't let you dodge me, Dianne Chillie. Your opinion, please?"

"All right." Gwen was smiling. "Great as it is, we did not just see the finest work of art of all time. So, today's record will fall. Gradually, we will admit that the auction industry's myth about the scarcity of people who can afford to participate turns out to be untrue."

"Yes." Gallagher nodded. "Now we know the price of genius."

"And Sotheby's knows who can afford it."

They reached the corner, and Gallagher put her hand on Gwen's arm. "I should tell you, though, sweet pea, as a friend. You need to raise your game."

"What?" Gwen felt her stomach clench. "What are you talking about?"

"I was behind you, also walking in. So, your taxi story was untrue. You were not carrying a purse either. Women notice other women's handbags, as you know."

Gwen laughed. "You scare me a little. What else?"

"Your name is not Dianne Chillie, or you would have said it more quickly. You should have a consistent fake name ready, so it comes out naturally. Your remarks about the myth of scarcity, and Sotheby knowing who the other bidders are, reveal that you work for another auction house."

"Nice try. But I've told you the truth."

Gallagher laughed. "And I am twelve feet tall." She leaned closer. "I work for a competitor too. See you around."

Gallagher crossed the street without checking the lights. A taxi slowed—miraculously not honking. Gwen waited to see if Gallagher would turn for another glance before disappearing into the maelstrom of workaday Manhattan.

She did not look back.

5

NOVEMBER 1955

Ruth steps off the train from South Jersey with a suitcase in each hand, and the strap of a hatbox over one shoulder. Navigating through the maze and noise of Penn Station up the stairs to Eighth Avenue, the first thing she notices is the bums. Sleeping in the alley, in broad daylight, one of them hugging an empty bottle like it's his teddy bear. She's never seen such a thing, and a tear comes to her eye. With one gloved pinkie, she stops it from marring her makeup.

The second thing she notices is the women's clothes. Here's one in a pencil skirt, hugging her hips. Her walk is feline, but stronger, and Ruth takes a few steps in imitation. There's a woman in capri pants, navy, with a pale-blue shirt, a strand of elegant pearls at her neck. Ruth wants to smell her wrists.

Next come three women in white blouses, elbow to elbow, commanding the sidewalk. Ruth steps aside, impressed. Only as they march past does she notice that all three are wearing bullet brassieres. In the hometown she left that morning, there is only one department store, and the lingerie section sells nothing so assertive.

Ruth stands there, out of traffic, examining the attire she'd put on with pride only a few hours earlier. Saddle shoes, a poodle skirt, it all feels ten years out of fashion. And a long distance from the boldness of these women, their self-assurance.

Is there any way to reach her new apartment without being seen? It's one block west and nine south, and a mild fall day. She reads the fares painted on the door of a checkered cab—25 cents for the first quarter mile, 5 cents per quarter mile after that—and decides this is her first opportunity to economize. Adjusting the hatbox strap like a bandolier, Ruth sets out for her new home.

The walk, she decides, is a perfect metaphor for this moment: striding out of South Jersey and into Manhattan, shedding Ruth the girl to become Ruth the woman. It feels poignant, like a graduation. She is twenty-eight years old.

The brownstone's entry is five stone steps up from the street. She marches right up and presses the bell for apartment 3C. When the buzzer sounds, she knows to open the door quickly. Plodding up the stairs, the suitcases slow her. Two flights up, she sees a door with an A on it, and realizes this is the one with the street views. Apartment B is along the left wall, meaning a view of the alley. Apartment C is in back, and Ruth hopes there's at least a little courtyard to let the light in.

The door of 3C sits slightly ajar, which helps Ruth to relax. How welcoming. She knocks anyway.

"Hello, sweetheart," she hears a call from inside. It must be Lucy. They made the arrangements by mail. "I have an idea," Lucy sings out. "Let's get you out of those clothes as fast as we can."

Ruth blanches. Has the woman seen her poodle skirt already?

"Sound good, baby? Because I'm already—" Lucy comes bounding out of a back room wearing a negligee so thin she looks next to nude. She has strong shoulders, small breasts, and a look of surprise. Ruth drops both suitcases with a thud.

"Oh, honey." Lucy bursts out laughing. "I was expecting someone else. I thought you were coming on the tenth."

"Today is—" Ruth croaks, then tries again. "Today is the tenth. And you must be Lucy."

"In all my glory." Her smile is radiant. "And with apologies. Lucy Steele."

Ruth bows, not quite ready to shake hands. "Hello."

"Let me go get decent, okay?"

"Sure."

"Unless . . ." Lucy hops over, quick as a bunny, to give her a hug. To Ruth it feels like her new roommate is naked, and she has never been embraced by a naked woman before. While she recovers, Lucy trots off into the depths of the apartment.

"How was your train ride?" she calls.

"Fine." Ruth stands awkwardly in the little hallway. "I had a nice walk down. This neighborhood is colorful."

Lucy laughs. "That's a generous description."

There's an authoritative knock at the door. Lucy reappears, still in the see-through clothes. "Pardon me, Ruthie. Just one minute."

Ruth points into the apartment. "Do you want me . . . ?"

"Don't you move an inch, gorgeous." Lucy cracks the door, poking her head into the hallway. "Paul, you beautiful creature."

Ruth can hear them kissing. There's a newspaper on the kitchen table, but when she looks, it's a week old.

"Listen, sexy man. I am horrified to say this, but I made a schedule mistake. I confused the dates, and my new roommate just arrived."

Ruth cannot hear what he says in reply, but the tone is anger.

"It's my fault," Lucy coos. "I promise to make it up to you next time. We'll do something extra special. You dream it up, and my answer is yes."

The man speaks again, this time sounding plaintive.

"Well, I'm disappointed too," Lucy says. "Come here."

Ruth sneaks a look through the door's opening. His blue suit pants are pressed to a sharp crease, his black wing tips buffed to a shine. When his hand slides down Lucy's bottom, cupping it closer, Ruth turns away.

The kitchen is tiny, with a small icebox and a two-burner stove, beside a sink barely larger than a dinner plate. To her right sits the living room: a love seat covered with a blanket, a side table and lamp, a director's chair with a slightly torn seat, and an armless wooden chair, beside which a cello stands stately and dark.

The hallway door shut, Lucy hurries to her room. Before the bedroom door closes, Ruth spies a tiny angled window that looks out on the street. "That's Paul," Lucy explains, "the man who invented eager." In seconds, she returns in a sweater and slacks. "Sorry. I didn't mean for you to see any of that so quickly. But isn't this place cozy and sweet?" She stretches her arms out wide, as if she were referring to a vast estate. "I'm so glad you're going to be my apartment sister."

Ruth is still taking it all in. "Your what?"

"Apartment sister. The girl before you called me that. She also gave me the nickname Loosely, which I liked and didn't like, you know? She eloped with an insurance guy from Sixty-First Street." Lucy lowers her voice. "In the family way." Her volume rises again. "Now she's holed up in suburban Connecticut Shangri-la, baby due any second. I would rather be in jail."

"Are you always this energetic?"

"Not when the tempo is adagio." Lucy laughs. "But, Ruth, you now live in the center of the world. No place moves faster. You'll find yourself on the sidelines sometime and see people at their full intensity, and you'll want to be one of them."

"I'll take your word for it . . ." Ruth replies. "Miss Loosely."

"Ha." Lucy hugs her again. "I knew I would like you. Let's toss your bags and find some chow."

THE BEDROOMS ARE TINY. THE WALL BETWEEN THEM DOES NOT REACH the ceiling.

"If they stop at six feet," Lucy explains, "it still counts as only one room and the landlord's not violating occupancy rules."

The bed takes up nearly all the space in her room, so she hefts her suitcases onto it. But there's a good-size window, and outside stands a leafless tree.

Ruth turns to Lucy. "I think it's going to be all right."

"Of course it is," Lucy sings. "Now, come on. There's a diner I know. Positively infected with men."

Ruth hesitates. "I'm trying not to spend my savings till the jobs start."

"My treat, as penance for flashing my boobs." She snickers, while pulling on a light jacket. "Besides. If we play our cards right, neither of us will spend one shiny penny."

The diner is indeed packed with young men on lunch break, smoking and laughing and wolfing down sandwiches. But the place is not so full that the boys do not make space for Lucy and Ruth on the spinning seats at the counter, crowding alongside to advise Lucy on the menu and ask Ruth a hundred questions. That she has been in the city less than an hour leaves them stupefied with disbelief.

She ducks her head toward Lucy. "I'm a little overwhelmed."

Lucy laughs. "On the sidelines or in the game. Your choice."

THE GALLERY JOB IS BETTER SUITED FOR A CLEANING LADY. RUTH CURLS her upper lip in distaste. The situation is nothing like the man described in his letter. She opens a filing cabinet to find it stuffed with crumpled papers.

"Business records," Trevor says, stroking his mustache downward. "All confused, I admit it."

She finds trash in the coat closet. It gives off a sour smell.

Trevor ducks and bobs. "I've been too busy to keep up with rubbish."

Empty wine bottles in the corners.

"Gives the place some charm, don't you think?"

"It could." Ruth picks up one bottle. "If they didn't have mold inside."

"That's exactly why I hired you, Ruth. My investors, two art-loving brothers from uptown, they love the job we're doing here. But they told me: Everything in order, pronto. Chop-chop."

Ruth, looking for something to wipe her fingers on, pauses to face him. "Can you actually pay my wages?"

"Definitely." His eyes widen. "If you get all of this under control before the brothers visit again, I will pay you time-and-a-half."

"When will that be?"

Trevor shrugs. "When it suits them."

A week ago, Ruth would have rolled up her sleeves and started work. But she has received twenty-four hours of education about New York City, its 1955 glamour and tempo, and she knows the importance of taking charge.

"You misrepresented the position to me, when you knew I was moving here and would have no alternative." Ruth crosses her arms. "This is much more work, and responsibility, than administrative assistant. I think you should pay me . . ." She does math in her head about what is reasonable, an additional dime per hour, then remembers the rates printed on the taxi's door. "Twenty-five cents more per hour. Otherwise, I'll go work at a place that doesn't deceive me."

"Whoa there, Ruth." Trevor waves both hands, as if he were telling oncoming traffic to slow down. "I'm in a pinch here. I didn't mean to take advantage. I'm just overloaded. If you can get this place under control, you'd be my salvation."

Here it is, her first New York negotiation. It feels like jumping from the high dive at the town pool back home. "Isn't salvation worth twenty-five cents an hour?"

Trevor lets his hands fall. "Fine."

LUCY HAS A STABLE, ONE MAN FOR EACH DAY OF THE WEEK. MOST ARE married and visit the apartment when they should be at work. That's Lucy's term: "visit." If she has an audition, and skips it for a guy, she's grouchy the rest of the day.

"I'm a good musician," she explains to Ruth in the booth of a West Side bar. "Dexterity, technique, expression. Teachers, other cellists, they all say so. But I'm an awful auditioner. Sweaty and tense." She sips her wine. "These suitors keep me supplied with lingerie, sometimes they throw in a little cash—not as payment, no, no. Not that kind of girl. Besides, I feel bad for them. They're so under-loved. If you treat him kindly, a married man can be very grateful."

"I need to know something," Ruth says. "One of your secrets."

Lucy's face brightens. "You've got a fella? You work fast."

"No." She waves the idea away. "I want to know where to buy lingerie."

"Oooh. I'll take you, and we can shop together." Lucy raises her glass. "To Ruthie getting sexy."

"And to staying off the sidelines." She clinks their glasses together.

MODELING IS THE REAL REASON RUTH CAME TO THE BIG CITY. AT HOME, she posed for advertisements in the local newspaper: a lilac festival, several jewelry stores (she has long fingers), and one automobile ad that for some reason made people lose their senses. She's wearing tight slacks and straddling the long hood of a bright-red Buick Riviera. Ruth thought the picture made her look sporty. Men saw something else. The dealership took dozens of calls from men wanting her phone number.

"With the right mascara and blush," Ruth's mother said, one hand on her cheek, "you could be a real model."

Her father turned a page in the newspaper. "If you like being ogled for a living."

Ruth wrote to agents, sent photos, left messages—and heard nothing. One agent, when his secretary was out sick, picked up the phone. His name was Craig. She began the pitch she'd perfected, but he interrupted to say if she's not in the city, he will never take her on. "You gotta be available, toots."

Now, after she has been in New York for three weeks, the phone rings. A hand lotion ad, Craig says. Their regular girl got pregnant and her hands are chubby. Ruth thinks that is a terrible thing to say, but she jumps at the chance. She gets lost looking for the company's manufacturing plant in Queens, and arrives late. The shot takes place in an office, papers cleared from the desk. Done in two hours, twenty in cash in her purse.

Soon the phone is ringing once a week. The client is a custom glove maker, Craig explains. Ruth's hands are photographed in the company store before opening time. A client makes scarves and wants one knotted on a woman's neck, with Ruth's hands hovering as if she's just finished tying it. That shoot was in the dressing room area of a department store. A client needs one feminine finger pointing at a listing in the yellow pages. That one, shot in a bank's back office for some reason, takes less than an hour and appears on the sides of buses a week later. Her finger, all over Manhattan. Ruth marvels.

Each time, Craig skims a twenty-five percent fee. If she keeps doing well, he says, he will take her on full-time.

Then he calls about a jeweler who specializes in engagement rings. He wants to lure customers from the excellent but predictable Tiffany.

"Strictly a left-hand gig, toots," Craig says, "but dress up anyway. You never know. He might want necklace shots someday."

By then, Ruth has earned four paychecks from the gallery, and the job becomes part-time because she whipped things into order faster than Trevor expected. To her amazement, she's making enough to pay rent, buy food, and treat herself to something that makes her feel special. A lace-trimmed bullet bra.

"Miss Loosely?" Ruth coos one morning. "How do I look?"

Lucy lifts her gaze from painting her toenails. "Like you're advertising a lot more than diamonds."

"Is it too much?"

"The men won't be watching your hands, I guarantee it."

The shoot is in an actual studio, uptown. The Third Avenue bus turtles through traffic, catching every red light, but Ruth still arrives on time.

The moment she enters the studio, she feels different. Older. Glamorous.

There's a small crowd to greet her, for example. The people know not to shake with a hand model, but they greet her with hearty hellos—Craig; the jeweler, who is a round man with a twinkle in his eye; the photographer, who's so busy with lighting equipment he barely glances to say hello; and the diamond handler.

"I'm Jane, and these are all real." She waves at a display suitcase, the rings held by velvet clasps. She looks Ruth up and down. "I keep a tight inventory. Nobody touches the rings but you and me. Got it?"

"Got it." Ruth smiles. "And thank you."

"Yeah, well." Jane offers a diamond set in platinum. "Let's start with this."

Ruth's eyes go wide. "Look at this rock," she exclaims, sliding it onto her finger. "It's a skating rink."

Craig laughs, but the photographer barks at Jane. "Would you give her the rings in front of the lights, so I can shoot her reaction?" He shakes his head. "Amateur."

Ruth has learned that in New York City, there is no more severe insult.

"*Fine,*" Jane says. "Fine."

"Where do you want me?" Ruth asks the photographer.

He seems to notice her for the first time. "Before we start, I need your John Hancock." He sets a contract on the table. "This says you permit me to take pictures and they can be used commercially. Just a formality."

"The others haven't wanted this."

"Probably amateurs too," the photographer snaps. "Contracts protect you more than me."

Ruth glances at Craig, but he's in conversation with the jeweler. "Sounds sensible," she says, and signs her name.

"Attagirl. Now come along, sweetheart. Careful of floor wires." His hand rests on her lower back, which strikes Ruth as needlessly forward, as he leads her between lighting stands to the backdrop. There's a stool, but when she sits it's wobbly. "Don't trust that thing," he says, shuffling off.

No one notices anything but her hands. Sometimes his camera is inches from her fingers. At first Ruth feels like the rest of her body has no value. The men are all business. And she'd worn something just for them.

Whenever Jane asks for a different shirt—chiffon for a ring, a higher cuff for bracelets—Ruth ducks behind a curtain into a makeshift changing room. The photographer uses that time to change lenses. As he tests his gear, the lights flash, including above the mirror in her changing area, but she gives it no thought. When she emerges, he's waiting.

"Why don't you cut that crap out?" Jane snarls.

"No idea what you're talking about." He turns to Ruth, smiling, and taps the camera. "New roll of film."

Ruth finds the work easy, apart from the stool, which tilts backward every time they want her to pose with it. But that's nothing amid the thrill of wearing diamonds. Emeralds give her a feeling of past generations, sapphires possess grandeur, rubies do nothing for her at all. The photographer turns her hands, angles her arms, pushes her shoulders. She did not expect so much touching. Jane applies light oil to Ruth's knuckles. "To make them gleam," she explains. "We want them gleaming."

The session wraps early. "Clients love that," Craig whispers to her. "We're going to do regular business together, aren't we?"

Ruth wants to leap and scream, but she only smiles. "We are, yes."

"I'll bring contracts next time. Then my take drops to fifteen percent."

The photographer asks if she'd like some fresh headshots. "Since you helped us finish early. On the house."

Ruth turns to Craig. "It's okay," he says. "A.J. here is on the up-and-up."

"Why not?" Ruth laughs while A.J. heads into his office for fresh gear.

Craig leans close. "Nice attire today, by the way. That'll open doors."

Maybe they weren't so professional, after all. As Jane snaps the suitcase closed, she grumbles at Ruth. "Play with fire, you're going to get burned."

"What do you mean?" she replies. "I'm not playing with anything."

"I hope you know what you're doing." Jane handcuffs the suitcase to her wrist, then helps the old man out of the studio, with Craig close behind.

A.J. returns, attaching a new lens. "Okay, now do your thing."

"My thing?"

"We're done selling rings, now we're selling you. Be amazing. Be sexy. Be beautiful." He takes three photos while she digests those commands.

She turns and smiles. "Like this?"

"Gorgeous, baby."

Ruth hesitates. When did she become *baby?*

"Stare at my shoes." A.J. points at the floor. "Now keep your head down, but look up—eyes only." He snaps more photos. "That's good, baby. Really good."

This is more than headshots. It's a portfolio he's shooting, and Ruth is having fun.

Meanwhile, A.J. keeps snapping away. "Shoulders back. Don't slouch."

She frowns. "I never slouch."

"Then don't. And don't make that face. Now, shoulders back."

Ruth obeys, but she can feel her blouse tighten in front. A.J. is moving fast, snapping from above, below, and straight on.

"That's it, baby." He moves to one side of her. "Now bring your elbows back."

Ruth knows that prank from ninth grade: The boys would challenge certain girls that they couldn't touch their elbows behind their back, and the girls would try, and then realize how they had just been displayed. She had been one of the first.

"No thank you."

"Whatever suits." A.J. shrugs, checking his settings. "The camera loves you. These pictures will be amazing." He squints at her. "If elbows are no good, bring your hands by your ribs, with fists like you're spoiling for a fight."

"Like this?" As she complies, her blouse tightens again. She forces a smile.

He drops the camera to his waist. "That shirt is wrecking the effect. Can you open a button?"

Ruth looks around the studio. Everyone has left. Craig vouched for A.J. Jane the jewelry woman knew what was coming, but her warning had been unclear. Ruth realizes the vulnerability of her situation. "I decline."

He scratches his head with a thumb. "The tight front looks trashy, is all."

Her heart is pounding. "An open button is less trashy?"

A.J. steps back. "You're really a rookie, aren't you? I mean, I offer you free headshots, and this is the gratitude I get?"

Ruth cannot help it. She feels dirty. "I think we should try some other poses."

"Fine." He brings the camera to his face, and squats in front of her. "Stretch your neck up, baby. Lift your head like a goose," he says. "Think goose."

When she does, suddenly Ruth feels taller. Regal. Not a goose, but a swan. Her calm returns, her confidence. He's just a guy who photographs women all day, tells them how to pose all day. She eases back into the modeling role.

A.J. shoots her sitting, and standing, and with her body aimed in one direction while her head is turned in another. He tells her to frown, to smile, to laugh. Eventually he brings her over to the wobbly stool.

"Last round. Bend so your forearms are on the stool."

Ruth obeys, but when the shirt hangs off of her, she straightens again.

A.J. wipes the air. "Not to worry, kiddo. I'm shooting profiles." After waving her back into position, he stands to her side and snaps away. "Gorgeous," he says. "Just right." Gradually he drifts away, then begins to circle behind her.

Ruth stands upright. "None of that, please."

"I'm just checking the light." He squints at his camera, adjusting. "You'd better get easier to pose if you want to land big jobs. Awful green to act like a diva."

Ruth adopts the swan pose, and loves the feel of poise and strength. "A new girl has to protect her reputation."

"Sure"—he places a hand between her shoulder blades—"unless it's a reputation of being a pain." And he bends her back over.

"No derriere pictures." Ruth rests her forearms on the stool. "Right?"

A.J. shrugs. "Nothing to shout about from that angle anyway."

She feels a rush of anger. Is she being a diva? Or is he being a pig?

"One round from in front, then we wrap." He points the lens at her face, as she leans toward him, and at the last second the camera tilts ever so slightly lower.

Ruth straightens. "This shirt is too loose."

"What a prima donna. Look." He points at his array of lights. "See how they're all up high? Shining down? That means everything horizontal creates darkness below it." His jaw is tense. "And no camera, no lens, can shoot in the dark." He's shouting now. "So how about you do your job, and let the expert do his?"

Is she being a prima donna? If only there were someone she could ask, someone chaperoning this moment. She grits her teeth and leans over, the stool unsteady under her weight. A.J. lines up with her face, but this time makes it no secret when he aims lower. And some part of her closes, shuts down, while he does what he had intended to do.

Finally, he steps away, winding back the exposed roll. "You'd think I was pulling teeth."

Ruth rises from the stool. "I need to go."

"Sure, get your stuff. Meanwhile, to show I'm a good guy and you're being ridiculous, I'm going to do you a big favor."

Ruth leaves for the changing area to gather her clothes. Big favor? She does not want to know.

Behind the curtain she tries standing tall again. The sense of stature returns. Like it has always been there, but she didn't know. She doesn't need a photographer to tap those resources. Staying for the headshots was a mistake, but no big deal. She took care of herself. The proud feelings are right there, ready when she wants them.

When she emerges, winter coat buttoned for the trek home, A.J. is sitting in his office smoking a cigarette, feet on the desk while he makes a call.

"George, how are you?" He flicks ash in a coffee cup. "Good, thanks, good. Hey, listen. I just shot a new talent, pretty and authentic, a real beaut. You have *got* to have her in your next catalog."

6

JANUARY 2007

In the coffee shop, Gwen bent around the line to see how long it was. The man just ahead of her was unusually tall, and thin like a colt. He wore a slate-gray necktie and pinstripe pants that made his legs look longer. The line stalled, while she measured. Her head was even with his shoulder.

Gwen's new smartphone pinged, and she pulled it out to read Chillie's text.

> **caffeine please god caffeine they're killing me here caffeine fireman save my child**

Her laugh caused the man ahead to turn.

"With all the adverts, that's the first one I've seen in person." He pointed a long, elegant finger at her phone. "I suspect it's rubbish. Do you like it?"

Gwen paused in typing her reply to Chillie. The fellow had bowed a little, and his formality was cute. Also, he had a British accent.

"I love it." Gwen held the phone by her head, like an advertisement. "*Phone* is the wrong name, though. I rarely use it to call. But I text my friends and read the news. I know the weather. I take pictures. There's something new every day."

"I work with antique documents," the man said. "They're all on cloth, papyrus or something comparable. Even stone. The ideas are intended to be eternal."

Gwen laughed. "Rare documents? In the building next door, by any chance?"

"You certainly know this town. Carroll and Bunzel, yes."

"I'm Gwen." She held out her hand. "Fine art."

"Arthur." He shook, firm and quick. "Kind of you to deign to converse with us peasants of the lower floors. How is the oxygen up there on eight?"

She laughed again. "Thin, but not because of altitude. It's the management blowhards sucking up all the air."

"Hey, would you move forward, please?" The man behind them pantomimed pushing, and they inched up to the people waiting ahead.

"I'm sure that will get us our tea much faster," Arthur said.

"Go back where you came from," the man said, "you snotty snob."

Arthur spun to face the man, glowering, suddenly something other than cute. "Careful, puppy dog. Some snotty snobs are taught how to box at an early age."

"Puppy dog?"

"Stop it, guys. You'll get your caffeine soon." Gwen took Arthur's arm, guiding him forward. His muscle felt like a cable, thick and tight. He turned at his own speed.

The silence that followed she took for a truce. After a minute, she leaned close. "Where did you get arms like that?"

"Swimming," he said. "Miles of it, every day for years."

"Remind me never to mess with anyone from rare documents."

Arthur was smiling. "No one is intimidated by a man in a swimsuit."

"You don't wear one of those tiny . . . you know the kind. Do you?"

"Grape smugglers?" His grin widened. "Banana hammocks?"

"Please say you don't. I've been liking you up to now."

He flattened a hand on his chest. "I do possess some self-respect, thank you. I'll be seen in nothing of the kind."

Then it was their turn. He urged her to go first, then insisted that he pay. They strolled to the office and rode the elevator to the third floor, where he stepped off with the same courtly bow, and raised his paper cup. "Cheers."

When the doors next opened, she stepped out on an unfamiliar floor, with two executives waiting to ride down. "Where have I landed?"

"This is eleven."

Gwen backpedaled and pressed eight. The executives boarded the elevator, both wearing skeptical expressions. She smiled. "Too much work on my mind."

On the eighth floor, her giddy mood lasted till she reached her cubicle.

"She arrives," she heard Chillie hiss. "Yesss." With a thud in her chest, she realized she had forgotten. He was rubbing his hands together but stopped when he saw only one cup in her hands. "Um, hello?"

"I screwed up," she said. "I'm sorry."

"You blew off my double espresso?"

"I can explain, but I can't really explain."

"I literally texted when you were in line."

"I know," Gwen conceded. "Then this guy offered to pay for mine, and—"

"You blew me off for a boy?"

"Chillie, I'll run back right now."

"No you won't." He crossed his arms. "The Hawk has been hunting you. She's been down twice already, and it's barely nine a.m."

"Harriette?" Gwen put her coffee down. "Why would she be looking for me?"

"I have no more idea than a tarot reader. And you still owe me for that painting selling to a creeper and not a leaper." Chillie held out his hand, palm up.

"Chillie, that's why she wants me. That Pollock sale. Someone upstairs must have found out I snuck in. I bet that Gallagher woman ratted on me."

"Doubtful." Chillie weighed the idea. "If it were that, they'd let Richards fire you, because he would enjoy it most. One man, single-handedly ruining the reputation of me and every other Black person in this firm." He tapped his palm with the pen in his other hand. "Pay up, girlfriend. Or I'll start adding interest."

"All right." Gwen dug in her bag, found two crumpled dollar bills, and dropped them in his hand.

"Without the courtesy to flatten it for me, despite my utterly decisive victory."

"What does the Hawk want?" She handed Chillie her cup. "You take the rest of this. I think I'm about to be dead."

"It doesn't get you off the hook with me, but thank you." He pointed at her desk. "In case you're not getting fired, take something to write on."

She scanned for the trusty green notebook she brought everywhere, and seized it like she was bringing a friend.

"SHE STROLLS INTO WORK AT LONG LAST," HARRIETTE GROUSED, WITHout lifting her eyes from the computer. "Did we forget to set an alarm this morning?"

"I was early today, as usual." Gwen stood before her desk. "And hello. I heard that you were looking for me."

Harriette peered over her half-glasses. "Early for what? I've been here since a quarter to five."

"Congratulations. Did you want to see me?"

"No." Harriette pouted. "Mr. Pinkney did."

Gwen looked at the closed door to her right. "Mr. Pinkney?"

Harriette stood, rapped on the door, opened it a few inches. "She's here."

"Great," Pinkney bellowed. A native Texan of great energy, he was notoriously loud, regardless of mood. New employees took some time to get used to it. It still rattled Gwen a little. "Bring her the hell on in."

Harriette pushed the door wide and gave Gwen a scowl. Gwen crept forward, till Pinkney could see her from his desk.

"Come in, come in." He waved with both hands. "Not going to bite you."

Harriette closed the door, and he gestured Gwen toward a chair. She sat on its front edge. "How are you, sir?"

"Alive, thank you. Super alive. And why? Because we—you and I—have important business to do today."

"We do?"

"First, context. There are exactly two people in this firm who hate you."

"I can probably guess—"

"That's low for this competitive outfit. Everyone else says you're exceptional."

So, it would be a gentle execution, Gwen thought. *Well, no point in dragging it out.*

"Does this have anything to do with the Jackson Pollock sale at Sotheby's?"

Pinkney's entire demeanor changed. "Who have you been talking to?"

"Talking to? I don't understand."

"Three people in this company know what's going on with Pollock. Harriette, who does not take anyone into her confidence, which is why I trust her. Richards, who would not tell anyone because he dislikes my decision to give the opportunity to you. And me. So how do you know what's going on?"

Gwen shook her head. "I don't. Everything has changed because of that sale, that's all."

She paused. Something was happening; she didn't understand it, but Gwen sensed that she had some sort of leverage. Perhaps sneaking into that auction was not the crime she'd thought. "What *is* going on, sir?"

"Cut to the chase, is it?" Pinkney thwacked a thing on his desk, five chrome balls hanging from a chrome rod, and they clacked against each other in a pattern as he stood and went to the window. While the clacking slowed, he peered down at Midtown—busy, but silent from this height.

"A woman came to my house Sunday afternoon." He tugged his shirtsleeves down. "How she found me, I'll never know. Thank God my wife was in Rome. She came by private car. She was old, maybe eighty, or I would have called the police."

As he spoke, Gwen watched his hands wave and flare and generally expand on his speech. *Basketball coach,* she thought. *Traffic cop.*

"Crazy hair," Pinkney continued, "too much makeup, too much jewelry. She brought something in a huge trash bag. Like they use at construction sites."

"Yes sir." She opened her notebook, ready to write.

"I don't spook easily, but she made me nervous." He chewed on his thumbnail for a second. "She declared that she was Jackson Pollock's lover toward the end of his life. That she was his inspiration. And that he gave her his last painting. She said she watched him finish it three days before he died."

"But Pollock—"

"Exactly." Pinkney raised both arms. "Everyone knows he was too messed up and boozed up to work for, oh, at least the last three years of his life. I said that to her. She just opened that trash bag, and what's inside but a painting. And it's very interesting, Gwen, this painting. Maybe two feet by a little less. But the colors, the layers, the passion? Oh yeah. Bleakness and blood. Very interesting."

He paced behind his desk. "As I'm taking it all in, she says she has kept the painting private all this time. Never been exhibited. But now, realizing the global appetite for his work, she would like the world to see his final effort."

"That's quite generous of—"

"With our firm conducting the auction, and a bidding floor of fifty million." He held his hands wide, then let them fall to his sides.

"Well." Gwen's mouth had gone dry. "That is an opportunity, all right."

"What obstacles do you see?"

She sat up. "Provenance and chain of possession. Confirming the authenticity of the work." She chewed on her pen. "Legal ownership. If the painting was part of Pollock's estate, for example, then it belongs to his widow, Lee Krasner. If not, it could still be a litigation target for a long list of art vultures. Not a simple sale."

"You got it. I asked when she received the painting. Her story was soft as a marshmallow."

"No offense meant, sir, but if she's looking for top dollar, why choose us?"

"None taken. I told her Sotheby's already knows who the runner-up bidders were in November. Call them back, serve the champagne, bang the gavel. Takes an hour. But Ruth, that's her name, she gave us thirty days to move, then it will be Sotheby's. She said we get a shot because all her life she has favored underdogs."

"Do you believe her?"

Pinkney returned to his desk. "I started out here as an auctioneer. Hard to imagine, right? With my bashful personality?" Smiling, he sat. "But I learned to keep a lookout, up there with the microphone, and to know it when I see it."

"Yes sir?"

"The hunger. The ravenous hunger to possess something. She picked us because she figured we'd be hungrier. We'd move fast, before having all the answers. But I could see it. Oh yes." He nodded. "*She's* the one with the hunger. Ruth is not giving that painting to anyone. It's that fifty million she wants."

"And she's starving for it."

"*Yes.*" Pinkney slapped both hands down on his desk. "That's why I want to give this project to you, Gwen."

"To me?"

"I know your biggest deal so far has been in the ten-million range. Blah blah. You see the issues. I've heard you're a workaholic. And this deal is sketchy enough that you will undergo huge professional growth from making it happen." He raised one finger in the air. "*If* it should happen."

"I'm flattered, sir. But wouldn't Richards, or one of the more senior—"

"They'd be drooling over their commission from the first minute. That's no good. We can't afford to be wrong. Our credibility would be shot forever."

"I didn't know we had commissions."

"You typically don't. But with deals this big, you get one percent of sale. If the painting sells for a hundred million, which is possible, you'd take home one million."

Gwen looked down at her notebook, but the page was blank. "I had no idea."

"It's about balance." Pinkney tipped his hand side to side. "This deal is going to eat your life day and night for a month. One month. Not bad, for a million bucks."

"I'll need approval for expenses. I'll need legal to start the estate inquiry. I'll interview this Ruth and measure her story against records of Pollock's painting. Possibly track down witnesses of the work in process, if there are any left."

"That's the spirit." Pinkney shook his fist in the air. "Harriette has a dossier for you on the way out. It's pretty thin. Thirty days, then it's Sotheby's."

"If it's legitimate, let it be us. And if it's junk—"

"Then let the fancy guys sell something that belongs in a garbage bag."

"Yes sir."

He made sweeping motions with his hands. "Keep me posted."

"ARE YOU JUST FIRED?" CHILLIE RESTED HIS CHIN ON THE BARRIER BEtween their cubicles. "Or are you fucking fired?"

"I am very much employed, thank you." Gwen tossed the notebook on her desk. "I've been given an elephant."

"An elephant? So, you got the Pollock assignment?"

"What? Be quiet, will you?" She rushed into his cubicle. "How do you know about that already?"

"I am a gossip, that's how." Chillie snorted. "Or have you not been paying attention for the three years I have been working literally at your side?"

"Tell me how you found out."

Chillie rolled his eyes. "Conflict-of-interest city."

"Tell me or die."

Chillie batted his eyes at her. "I'm not saying it was the Hawk. But I'm not saying it wasn't."

"She tells you secrets? All she gives me is icicles."

"You let her push you around. Push back sometime and see what happens."

Gwen looked at the piles of paper on her desk. "I am going to be six feet underwater for the next thirty days."

"Richard's walking around pissing all over himself."

"Now I know why he has been haunting my desk lately."

"He's angry that he didn't get the job, angrier that it went to a woman, and furious that it went to you."

Gwen tapped the side of her thigh. "I'm not exactly saying he can kiss my ass, but it's close."

Chillie laughed. "But your timing is lousy. I'm having one of my brunches this weekend, and there's an empty spot at the table—"

"On the floor, you mean?"

"Fine, technically. The point is there's room for you. And there'll be a boy."

"Not interested. Especially with this—"

"He's tall. And British cute. And, coincidentally, he works here."

Gwen suppressed a smile. "In rare documents?"

"You've scored Arthur already? You hussy. How was he?"

"I met him at the coffee shop today. That's all."

"Well, love at first sight, I'm sure. He's tall and smart and—"

"Why don't you ask him out, then?"

"Alas, he doesn't play on my team." Chillie made a mock-sad face. "Anyway, one of my usual brunch couples is away, I invited him, and now I'm inviting you."

"You know I hate brunch. It wastes the whole day."

"Leisure is not evil, girlfriend. I'll arrange it so you sit next to him, and laugh and crush and fuck and marry, with me as a bridesmaid, and make babies, babies, babies." He was laughing his way through the litany. "Babies. *Babies.*"

"Will you please shut up?" someone shouted from several cubicles down. "We're trying to work."

He leaned close to Gwen and whispered, "Come for brunch, screw him till supper. You'll be more productive all evening."

"Not listening." Gwen picked up her notebook again. "I'm off to the library."

"There is no sex in the library," Chillie stage-whispered.

"That's not what I'm going for."

THE NEXT TIME GWEN WENT TO PINKNEY'S OFFICE, HARRIETTE SHOWED her the courtesy of looking up from her work. "You again."

"Lovely to see you too," Gwen replied. "I was thinking about you yesterday when I saw a poster for sale."

"Why did you think of me?"

"It was a portrait of Eeyore."

Harriette laughed, one bark. "You've got nerve." She pushed back from her desk and knocked on Pinkney's door. "She's here again."

As they passed in the doorway, Harriette murmured, "Have fun."

"Busy day here," Pinkney said, spinning his chair forward. "Headlines only."

Gwen opened her notebook. "Lee refuses to take my call. Whoever answers her phone says she wants nothing to do with any painting, or Ruth, or us, and to stop calling. Since I've tried at various times of day, I suspect it's Lee herself. Either way, that door is shut like a casket."

"A fitting metaphor," Pinkney said. "Continue."

"The executor of Pollock's estate is dead. The foundation that manages his works says they saw this painting decades ago and dismissed it as not legitimate."

"What do you make of that?"

"Lee handpicked the foundation board. They're not likely to welcome a work from Pollock's lover. Also, the review was only visual. No one did actual forensics."

Pinkney chuckled. "Go on."

"The law firm that handled Pollock's will says their job was completed forty-six years ago. The firm does not have the records on-site. Nor are they inclined to share them. This painting was unknown for twenty years after Pollock's death and therefore would not be in the court record."

Pinkney massaged one fist with his other hand. "All bad news. But I have the feeling you have more to say."

"Two things, actually, and both internal."

He hunkered down at his desk. "Now I'm interested."

"Richards lurks by my desk all day. He does not speak, not even hello. I catch him snooping over my shoulder. When I ask what he wants, he slithers away without a word. He is harassing me. And yes, I used the word *harassing*."

Pinkney put both hands calmly on his desk. "You need to make a choice, Gwen, and you need to do it now. If this painting is what Ruth says it is, you are going to be swimming in shit. Other auction houses will go to Ruth to steal the deal. Art critics will attack you, your credibility, your lack of experience—"

"I don't lack—"

"I'm not saying you need a thick skin. I'm saying you need a hide."

Gwen looked at him blankly. "You're not going to speak with Richards."

"He's beneath your attention. He is also busy managing the auction of a complete suit of armor, helmet to boots, perfectly intact, circa fifteen twenty. I don't want either of you distracted."

"I'm telling you right now that I am distracted by him."

"Have you never learned to do this?" And he gave Gwen the finger.

"I've lived in New York City all my life."

Pinkney laughed. "Nothing I can teach you about that, then. Except to use it."

Gwen put both hands on her hips. "Incredible."

"Show me how tough you are. What's the other internal thing?"

She glared at him, then took a deep breath. "I've been contacted by our forensic staff about this painting. Twice."

"What?" He pounded his desk. "They shouldn't even know this project exists."

"We can guess who told them. Regardless, the 'drooling' you wanted to avoid has already begun. So, I arranged for a third-party forensic expert."

"You're considering taking it out of house?"

"I'm not considering, sir. It's already done."

"There you go." He slapped the desk. "Initiative. Who'd you choose?"

"Matthieu Guerin. You probably don't know him, but he's a perfect match."

"I know of him. I thought his turf was classics. He's a Pollock scholar too?"

"No. But he's scientific, and independent minded."

"Trustworthy and principled?"

"Annoyingly. Resigned from Christie's after twenty-one years because he felt they were exaggerating a Roman sculpture's age."

"Nice. Where is he?"

"Waccabuc, in northernmost Westchester County. He's semi-retired."

"That raises transport issues." Pinkney brushed his hair back with his fingers. "Is Ruth okay with that?"

"She's my next call." Gwen took out her smartphone and waved it. "The minute this meeting ends."

"Wait." Pinkney stood. "You have one of those new gizmos already?"

"I couldn't resist. It makes me so much more efficient."

He hurried around from behind his desk. "Even I don't have one."

The next few minutes had nothing to do with art, but with the CEO's curiosity about a new technology. Gwen demonstrated one feature after another.

"You think people will spend this much," Pinkney asked, "for a phone?"

"Compared with a PalmPilot or BlackBerry? They will stand in line for it."

"Maybe I should buy stock." He wandered back to his chair. "But today's business: You do not feel you can rely on our forensic people to do an objective job."

She tucked her phone away. "Correct. They're too interested."

Pinkney sat again, drumming his fingers. "You're untrusting. I like that."

"I trust you, sir." Gwen grinned, but her jaw was tight. "Oh so much. And you can trust me too."

"Get back to work, young lady. And remind me never to play poker with you."

7

JANUARY 1956

He actually tried the touch-your-elbows trick?" Lucy is laughing hard, incapable of drinking the pink cocktail on the bar before her. "What, is he still in high school?"

"It's not funny." Ruth shakes her head. "It was pure creepy. If he had the guts to straight-up ask me to pose topless, for art photos, I might—might—have done it. This was plain sleazy, and he assumed I was too dumb to realize it."

"You know, the slap was invented to be used on perverts like him."

"Yes. But George called Craig right away and offered me a great deal."

"What in hell?"

"I'll be modeling summer nightwear for B. Altman. Four hours a day in the studio, for a hundred and fifty bucks."

"Hey, for that kind of lettuce, I want A.J. taking my picture." Laughing, Lucy pretends to touch her elbows behind her back.

"I'm serious." Ruth tries a sip of her drink, a crème de menthe concoction, green with a white foamy top. Lucy ordered it for her. It tastes like toothpaste. "I'm worried about this George. I asked Craig to be there. He said George is solid gold, nothing to worry about. But he'd show up anyway."

"Do you trust Craig?"

Ruth shrugs. "He was wrong about A.J. But he stopped calling me toots."

"Progress! Meanwhile, A.J. gets to shoot you again for the catalog?"

"I am not thrilled about that. If he invites me back to his studio to see those headshots, I may take your slapping advice."

"He won't dare. What kind of idiot does he think you are?"

Ruth ducks her head. "A Jersey girl who has only lived here three months?"

"You own these people now." Lucy stirs her drink. "Lock and stock."

"How do you figure?"

"All three of them think they're putting one over on you. They forgot you are a human being, with brains and talent. Plus, you can balance on a wobbly stool."

Ruth laughs for the first time that night, open and easy.

"As your Loosely," Lucy continues, "I predict that you can rule them with a wink. Add a little breathy talk, and they'll all be dancing to your tune."

"But that is not all." Ruth rests a hand on Lucy's forearm. "I showed up late to my gallery job today, and Trevor did not say a word about it. He is too busy complaining. I dive into the bookkeeping, but he is jabbering nonstop. His wife is bigger than the *Hindenburg*, apparently. Is moody, never has sex anymore, and the baby is not due till April. I say, boss, I am trying to work here, what do you need? He says, for me to curate the next show."

"What? For real?"

"I almost fell out of my chair. But he says I have been there long enough. I have seen what people like, what they buy. For this show I pick the artists, and he chooses which paintings." Behind its bottles and mixes, the bar has a mirror up to the ceiling. Ruth looks at herself and raises her glass. "I might be on a roll."

"So, do me a favor, would you?"

Ruth squeezes her arm. "Anything for you, Miss Loosely."

"Don't leave me in the dust."

◆ ◆ ◆

ON THE DAY OF THE SHOOT, IT'S SNOWING: BIG FLAKES LIKE OUT OF CURrier and Ives. Beautiful and inconvenient. Ruth spends half an hour on her hair, but one look out the window and she knows she shouldn't have bothered. Even if she could afford a taxi, none of them are running in that weather. It's a long walk to the Third Avenue bus.

For that crosstown trudge, she opens an umbrella and holds it low against her head. Fortunately, there's no wait at the stop, and the nearly empty bus sails up an abandoned Third Avenue. A few blocks west and she's in the studio, stomping snow from her boots. A.J. is fiddling with equipment, and here comes George.

"I knew she'd make it," A.J. crows. "No excuses for this one."

George is shaking her hand, offering to take her coat, looking her over when he thinks she's not paying attention. *Lucy is right,* she thinks. *Men are so obvious.* Ruth keeps her shoulders back, and smiles, and praises every garment she is asked to wear. Instead of the stage lights flashing, they're on continuously. It keeps the room warm, which is helpful when she's modeling thin sleepwear.

When Craig eventually arrives, Ruth is returning from the dressing area. She's wearing a shapeless cotton thing that looks like a potato sack.

"Waste of talent," A.J. chirps at George. "You mail your catalog to nuns?"

"Button your lip," George snaps. "It's part of our comfort sleep line."

"It's perfect," the makeup woman says, powdering Ruth's forehead. "I have one."

Craig watches, pose after pose, until the flannel sack is done. While Ruth's changing behind the folding screen, he approaches the other side. "I brought those contracts for you to look over."

She is hurrying into powder blue pajamas. "I can't look right now."

"Of course. I'll leave them by your coat. I'm looking forward to doing lots of business with you."

"Oh hey, thanks."

"Is everything okay? You seemed more excited last week."

Ruth pokes her head around the screen. "After you left, the photographer—"

"Enough chatter," A.J. calls, lifting his camera. "We're behind schedule."

Craig's jaw muscles are working. "You want me to deal with him?"

"And wreck my career at the starting line?"

"Let's go, Ruthie," A.J. yells. "Time's a-wasting."

She ducks behind the screen and pulls on the matching robe, plus slippers with a white puff on the toes. The makeup girl comes behind her.

"Let's adjust a bit." She safety pins the nightie tighter in back, below her ribs.

Ruth sees in the mirror how that little adjustment accents her figure without being creepy. "You are good at that."

The girl smiles for the first time all day. If calling someone an amateur is the worst insult, Ruth figures, then praising skill must be the best compliment.

When she steps in front of the lights, Ruth realizes that Craig is bent over, whispering to George, who is nodding.

"What's the problem?" A.J. says. "Is Craig going to wear a nightie too?"

But he takes his time finishing the conversation with George and walks across in front of the lights on his way out.

"I know what to do," Ruth tells herself. She takes the swan pose, the one that makes her feel tall and strong. "I know what to do."

"You say something?" A.J. is hovering.

"Let's get started again." She forces a smile. "I like this outfit."

"Here." He reaches out and, with a firm finger on her chin, tilts her head.

"Hey," George barks. "None of that."

A.J. cranes his neck to look back. "What?"

"You know."

A.J. rests the camera on his hip. "Tell me."

"Do it again and I will fire you like *that*." George snaps his fingers. Rising from his chair, he steps over the lighting wires to stand before Ruth. "I apologize." His voice is paternal. "You have a great figure and a fresh face. You're ideal for our spring-wear catalog. That's three weeks with all-day shooting. You're a good girl, I can tell, and I'll make sure you have a good run of it, okay?"

"Okay," she says, not entirely understanding. The hand-modeling clients had touched her almost constantly. "Very okay."

"Good." George faces A.J. "You and I go back a while, so this is not news. We are B. Altman, young man. Clothes for the whole family, owned by one family."

"I know, I know."

"At B. Altman we do not touch the models. Ever. Ruth here is someone's daughter. For the moment, she is *my* daughter. All posing will be done by verbal cues only. And you will keep your hands on your camera. Understood?"

"Sheesh." A.J. glances at Ruth. "Sorry."

As George returns to his seat, stepping over the wires with care, A.J. leans closer to Ruth: "Not sorry."

"What did I do?"

"You'll get yours." He seethes. "Just you wait and see, bitch."

8

JANUARY 2007

Gwen's day started with breakfast at a diner on Broadway, across from the Flatiron Building, with her college boyfriend. They had parted at graduation not for relationship reasons, but because Neil was headed to Wharton for an MBA, meaning Pennsylvania, and she was going to Stanford for an MA in art history, in California. After the college's ceremony and family brunch, Gwen told her parents she'd be right back. She ran straight to his room, with its bare mattress and empty dresser. Sitting on the desk, she pulled up her black graduation gown, and white skirt beneath, to reveal that she was wearing no underwear. Neil put down his last box, a computer keyboard poking out the top. He locked the door, then dropped his pants to his ankles. While his parents waited down at the car, they coupled like monkeys, her heels hooked around his back while he stood on tiptoe to go deeper, both of them sure they would never meet again.

Two years later, Neil landed a job way downtown, in the Financial District. That same week, Gwen accepted an offer from Doyle Auctioneers, up on Eighty-Seventh Street. They had both been in the city for three months when, rushing to catch subways headed in opposite directions, they crossed paths in Union Square. Within the hour, they were making love at his apartment.

But years went by. There were lovers for him, but not for Gwen because she worked all the time. She called their relationship casual and devastating. When Neil asked her to meet at Tompkins Square Park one afternoon, she went expecting adventure. Instead, he announced that they had to stop playing at sweethearts. Gwen cried and asked him why. Because he had met someone important, he said.

"And because I can get a plumber, a carpenter, and an electrician to my apartment in this crazy city faster than I can get you on a regular dinner date."

"It's my job," Gwen protested.

"It's how you *do* your job," Neil snapped, his frustration revealed.

Gwen sniffled. "What's her name?"

Neil looked up at the sky. "Heidi. It's Heidi, all right?"

"Heidi? You're dumping me for Miss Yodelay-hee-hoo?"

He shook his head. "You dumped me. Two years ago, for Doyle Auctioneers."

Heidi didn't work out, and after that, whenever they ran into each other, they wound up in bed. Until the time she woke to him getting dressed in the small hours.

"We've come to that, have we?"

Neil was startled. "Come to what?"

"Sneaking off in the dark?"

He finished buckling his pants. "What do you want me to say?"

"Wait a minute," she said, rising naked from the bed. "Just one minute."

But by the time she'd returned from the bathroom, he was gone.

Now, six years later, he'd tracked her down and invited her to breakfast.

Why at a diner? she texted.

Increases the odds that we'll keep our clothes on, he replied.

So there she was, taking the 6 train to Twenty-Third Street and walking to the diner. She'd done her preparation online: Neil lived way uptown now. He'd risen in his firm steadily. He was making roughly four times as much as her.

But did he still love the feel of her feet hooked over his butt? Maybe this meeting wasn't another fling, but the start of a more serious connection. Of course, it would have to wait a month, till the Pollock painting was sold, but she was not closed to the idea. Gwen wondered what kind of place he had chosen to meet, till she saw a sign in the diner's window—*Giving people heart disease since 1947*—and she could not help smiling.

Neil was hunched at the counter, reading the *Journal*. In the doorway, she studied him for a minute, his posture no different from when he read in the library in college or crammed for exams on the floor in her dorm room. But then he took up his coffee cup—the old-style kind with a little porcelain loop for the thumb and forefinger—except that he poked his pinkie through the hole instead, turning the cup like he was drinking backhand. It was such a cowboy thing, such an acquired coolness, her stomach turned. And he had chosen to sit at the counter, which meant they wouldn't be facing each other. Gwen paused, considering the idea of leaving, of standing him up and saving herself. Before she moved, though, Neil spotted her.

"There she is," he said. "Lovely as ever."

"Surf's up," she said under her breath, and moved into his shallow hug.

Neil waved at the waiter and pointed at his coffee cup and then Gwen. In seconds, the waiter set a steaming cup in front of her. She added milk and took a sip. "My God, this coffee is awful."

Neil laughed. "Totally cricket piss. But that's part of the charm."

"So, you're a regular here?"

He nodded. "For good luck. I eat at this counter before all of my deal pitches."

Before she could ask more, the waiter arrived to take her order. Then Neil was talking about a recent dinner he'd had with a mutual college friend of theirs, and she didn't get to hear what big deal Neil was about to pitch.

Gradually Gwen realized: He was afraid to tell her. He made insipid small talk for half an hour, while she considered all the other places she would rather be. For this she had delayed starting the day's work? She hadn't had sex in nineteen months, not since that wedding in Vermont. The guy was a soccer coach, older and not very tall, but strong and lean and memorably naughty. Still, she considered nineteen months of unintended chastity a form of failure. Not a chance she was going to ask Neil about his pitch. Let him chat till he ran out of air.

The breakfast's one consolation came with her scrambled eggs: the best hash browns she'd ever tasted. Soft edged, perfectly browned, with a salty pep.

"These are so damn good," she said, offering a forkful to him.

"I'm engaged," Neil blurted. "We've set a date for September."

Gwen's arm went down. "Engaged."

"Gretchen and I are so happy. I wanted to share the news with you personally. And hoped that you would be happy about it too."

Gwen looked at the food on her fork. "Happy?" She jammed the potatoes in her mouth. "I'm fushking ecshtatic."

WITHIN THE HOUR, GWEN STOOD IN LINE FOR COFFEE SHE COULD ACTUally swallow, and there was Arthur again, tall as a telephone pole, on his way out with a fresh cup.

"Hi," she said, with a little low wave. Twenty minutes between men. She couldn't decide if the day felt old, or she did.

"Hullo, love," he said, brightening. "What a welcome surprise."

"How's your day going?"

Arthur pondered sincerely, his face concentrating while he performed whatever calculation would provide an answer. "In over my head, thanks. You?"

Gwen considered for a moment, too, then stepped out of the line. "Why are you in over your head?"

"The usual rubbish. I'm managing the imminent auction of a lovely document. The letter General Eisenhower wrote his wife on the evening before D-Day."

"That's a good lot right there." The growing line of customers crowded them closer to each other.

"Indeed. *I'm well, and love you as much as ever, all the time, day and night.*"

"I hope that's not what you consider 'the usual rubbish'?"

He shifted his weight from one long leg to the other. Gwen realized how far back she had to tilt her head to speak with him.

"Em. This morning, I received a message from a European dealer, complete coincidence, who has an ideal companion document."

"What is it?"

He made his way out of the shop, holding the door for Gwen. "German Field Marshal Rommel also wrote his wife that evening. To alert her that he would be leaving the coast, to be home for her birthday the next day. Of course he had no idea what that day would bring. Yet it reads almost as if he did."

She clapped. "That's auction gold, Arthur. If you bundle them . . ."

"Fool's gold, I'm afraid. The Rommel epistle is presently located in Austria."

"How 'imminent' is the Eisenhower auction?"

"Three days." They ambled up the sidewalk, Arthur sipping his coffee. "No time to confirm the provenance, much less transport the letter here." They reached the company building. "My boss thinks we should take our time and be thorough."

She grabbed his arm to stop him from going in. "Your boss is wrong. Those papers are a complete unit of collection—a pair of marital intimacies from the night before the greatest invasion in human history. They absolutely belong in one lot."

He held that door for her too. "You're rather passionate for a pair of silly letters."

"Not silly," Gwen replied. "Here are both sides' leaders' private words, and the next day, democracy defeated totalitarianism."

They were quiet in the atrium, decorum being essential in their business. Arthur pushed the elevator button, and no one else was waiting, so Gwen continued. "Separately, those letters pull a hundred thousand each. Two hundred if you get the right bidders in the room. But together? Half a million, I guarantee."

He laughed as the elevator doors opened. "You guarantee?"

"I bet on the closing price of lots all the time. I almost never lose."

"Well, but there's no time. How would you make this sale even happen?"

Gwen pressed for the third and eighth floors. "I'd get all the pertinent documents sent to me digitally immediately. It's not even three p.m. in Austria, plenty of time to make it happen within the hour.

Oh, and they should ship the Rommel letter now, by the fastest trustworthy air delivery. If they can't, you should red-eye there tonight, get your hands on it, and fly straight back. If you work the time zones right, you won't even miss a workday."

"Look at your motor running." He grinned.

But Gwen was humming now. "Before you go, send an email alert to everyone invited to the auction, saying the day will offer something extraordinary. Set the publicity team loose too. They'll work the media, which draws an audience and lifts prices. Before your flight, I'd meet with the presentation design team—and security—to build a display so people can read both letters on their way into the auction. Imagine a line of people waiting for their chance to see. And learning that generals, even generals on the Nazi side, love their wives. You'll make the firm hundreds of thousands of dollars."

"This is a lot to do in three days."

Gwen shrugged. "It's only work."

The doors opened at the third floor. Arthur held them open without stepping off. "Grand ideas, Gwen. I wish I had a pen and pad. Just brilliant."

"Wait." She took out her phone and began typing.

"What are you doing?"

"Finding you in the company directory. I'll email you a list in two minutes."

"You like that phone thing?" The elevator door began pinging.

"It's great." She kept working. "Good luck with the sale."

By the time she reached the eighth floor, Gwen had looked up how many UK soldiers died on D-Day—two thousand at Sword Beach and Gold Beach combined—added it to the email to inspire him, and hit send. The doors opened, but she hesitated. She'd forgotten something. Then it came to her, and she pressed the button for the lobby.

Blame it on Arthur again. She'd forgotten to buy a coffee.

AMONG ITS FIVE BOROUGHS NEW YORK CITY PROBABLY HAD SEVERAL million rooms, but Gwen had long known which one was her favorite. When she was in seventh grade, two cool girls from ninth dared her to follow them after school. She did, until they arrived at a building with giant stone lions outside. While she hesitated, the older girls strode up the stone steps and inside. Gwen had to hurry to catch up.

By the time she was inside, the girls had taken the stairway to the right. She ran, catching a glimpse of them entering wooden doors that were propped open. Gwen rushed inside, nearly colliding with them. There her eyes went wide.

The ceiling was high like in a cathedral. There were long wooden tables, with lamps to light each person's work. Bookshelves lined the walls. Giant, church-like windows let in light. Gwen had never seen a more beautiful room.

A barrier stood in front of her, two brass stanchions connected by a waist-high red velvet rope. Tourists took photos from behind the rope: the ceiling, the desks, one another. But the cool girls said, "Excuse me," and marched right past the barrier. One went to the back, found an open seat, and fished a magazine from her backpack. The other plunked herself down midway and took out her homework.

Gwen noticed an older woman holding some sort of tour brochure. "Excuse me," she said. "But where are we?"

"Right here," the woman said, pointing at a map in her brochure.

"Yes, but where?"

"The New York Public Library, dear. And this is the Rose Room."

Forever after, that was where Gwen did her high school homework. And read. And hid from the rain. Anytime she made a new friend, she brought them to the Rose Room. This was the room in which she kissed Jamie Brenner, her first—in a corner, and lips only because they both had braces. Even now, whenever her job required uninterrupted book time, she went here to work. The past two nights she'd stayed up late at home, reading the definitive Pollock biography. Now she needed to understand his art.

Gwen knew she was also procrastinating. She needed to call Ruth and ask for a meeting. But why not see the man's work first?

Gwen set the armload of books down louder than she'd intended.

A man down the table gave a disapproving scowl, then returned to his work.

In no time she had books open and spread all around. She tried to put Pollock's work in some kind of order—not chronologically, but in how wild they were, how passionate, how large. She learned that hundreds of people had declared they owned paintings made by Pollock, only to be disproven. In the 1970s, Ruth had been in that crowd, her painting dismissed as inauthentic. That meant Ruth had not been honest with Pinkney. This was not her first attempt to sell the painting.

Pollock's creations took charge. Gwen stopped reading and simply looked at the pictures. *Autumn Rhythm* portrayed some kind of pagan dance, a frenzy of black and white in dramatic swoops so that somehow the white looked dour and the black looked celebratory.

Convergence 1952 was next to catch her eye. Whirling whites like letters in an unknown alphabet, fire approaching in hot rust flames, while a sweet periwinkle in the background did its best not to be eclipsed by all the energy and jazz.

One after another, they showed something she had never seen before. Were the paintings simply interesting noise, or did they say something coherent? Did Pollock's technique show genius, or madness?

The answers were not simple. The largest book was eighteen inches by twelve. But the paintings it contained were often four feet by eight, if not larger. The few pages with close-ups of details did not make the paintings easier to understand.

Gwen knew already that Pollock, unlike most artists of his time, did not draw the image first. It came directly from his head. Yet somehow the idea always filled the canvas, often with elegance. In fact, her favorite of his paintings, *Mural,* had a recurring series of shapes, and they fit perfectly. But he'd painted it spontaneously, a bucket of paint in one hand, while the other held a stirring stick, or a turkey baster, or his bare hand. *Mural,* she read, was eight feet high and twenty feet long. Gwen doubted that her entire apartment contained one hundred sixty square feet. And he had done it all directly from his head.

"I need to see this in person," Gwen said aloud, earning a snarl from the guy down the table. She turned a few pages and learned that *Mural* hung at the University of Iowa.

Gwen looked up. The light in the Rose Room's high windows was waning. But she knew the Metropolitan Museum of Art was open till nine. She set out for Eighty-Second Street. Enough photographs. It was time to see the real thing.

9

JANUARY 1956

The spring-wear shoot happens in winter so catalogs will be ready for mailing in the first week of March. There are four other women modeling too, of various heights and hair colors, and she can't help comparing herself. One pretty face after another, and one model in particular has cheekbones so sharp she looks stunning. They all have one thing in common, Ruth notices. All of them are chesty. The shortest one is built largest, enough that you'd notice even in ordinary circumstances. Still, the atmosphere is professional. Ruth is pleased to find George praising her work more than the others'. Enough that the short girl gives her some side-eye. Ruth stands tall, as she often does now, and takes it as a compliment.

The shoot involves a complete crew, with lighting designers and makeup artists. One effeminate man paces by the light stands holding a brush and a can of spray. If he steps forward everyone stops what they're doing while he brushes or touches the model's hair, and Ruth can immediately tell the difference. Two women, who look about twenty years old, hand Ruth clothes for the next setup. During her shooting, they fold the previous clothes away.

A.J. is absent, and she feels a weight lifted. This shoot's photographer is slow but always polite. *Lift your left arm, please. Chin higher, please.* Ruth is happy to comply.

She gets breaks, too, while the others have their turns in the lights. On the second day, she brings a copy of *ArtNews* to read, thinking about the show she's curating. George stops on his way past and asks for a look.

"*ArtNews*? Is that so?"

"I work part-time at a gallery."

"To enrich your own painting, I'll wager."

"Actually, I—" Ruth stops, then looks up at him from her chair. "Yes. Exactly."

"Once again, I'm glad Craig sent you our way."

When the shoot wraps, Ruth has the most clothing to return to the dressing crew. The others say their goodbyes and charge out into the wintry city. When she brings her last load, a man is speaking with George, and she stops cold. Though his hair is graying, he is as slender as a teen, maintains an arrogant sneer, and is wearing an impeccable blue suit.

"Here she is now." George waves her over. "Ruth, please meet my friend Ronald Gray. He is an—"

"Actor on Broadway," Ruth interrupts. "As everyone knows. How do you do, sir?" She attempts to shake his hand, spilling garments from her arms. They bend simultaneously to pick up the dropped clothes, and their faces come within inches. He has a quick smile, and eyes such a pale blue, they verge on white.

Rising, Ruth blushes. "This is not the first impression I like to make."

"You could repair it," George says, "and help me out at the same time."

"I would be happy to do both," Ruth answers, her eyes still on Ronald Gray.

"Ronald and I had plans for dinner tonight. But my wife just called, and she's running a fever. Would you do me the favor of dining with Mr. Gray?"

Ruth blinks at George, then at Gray. "Is this a trick or something?"

"A sincere invitation," the actor says. "So that I won't have to dine alone."

She gives him a long look, feeling the electricity between them, enjoying it. "Mr. Gray, I imagine there is a whole battalion of people who would be delighted to have dinner with you. I am happy to take their place."

"Perfect," George says. "And it will require a smaller table than a battalion."

"Please." Gray turns to Ruth, the slightest bow. "Call me Ronald."

"ALL I AM SAYING IS BE CAREFUL," TREVOR SAYS.

"If you would hold up your side," Ruth snaps.

With a heave, together they hoist the heavy clay bas-relief—an image of sunflowers viewed from the side, but arranged in an order that evokes marching soldiers. The wire in back hangs loose as they tilt the artwork toward the wall and the two hooks with reinforced supports. It's a strain, dangling the wire over first one hook, then the other, and when it's done, she gives a great exhalation of relief.

"Next show, we're making him use wood instead of clay." Trevor goes to his desk to pick up the 24-inch level tool.

"That or his work goes on a stand," she replies.

He sets the level on the frame, and it registers half a bubble off plumb. Ruth slides the artwork to the left in increments, fractions of an inch each time, till the bubble floats exactly in the middle.

"Nice work," Trevor says, stepping back. "Now anyone who so much as touches this thing automatically owns it."

Ruth retreats from the wall too. "I love it, though. Very much. Boys going off to war, as sunny and fragile as flowers."

"While we're talking metaphors and being careful." He returns to his desk. "Let's discuss this date you have in a few hours."

She wiggles her fingers over her stomach. "I have an epidemic of butterflies."

"Yeah, but an actor?"

"He is stunning. He is poised. He is—"

"Fifteen years older than you. And it's not just that."

"I do not care about the age difference."

"Me either. But listen." He holds still a moment, thinking. "If you want to play big-league ball—and I think you may be capable of it—you can't be doing it with actors."

"Thank you, I think." She smiles. "But why not?"

"Theater is too uncertain. Actors need to self-worship, or they couldn't withstand the rejections, which even the best of them experience. Besides, if Ronald Gray is not past his prime, he's getting close. You would be an accessory, a bauble to fortify his ego, till the second he gets his next big role. Then he'll toss you like an empty to-go coffee cup."

"I am merely joining the man for dinner. Nothing more."

"If that were true," Trevor replies, "you wouldn't have butterflies. I'm not saying you shouldn't date upward. And I'm not saying you can't date lawyers and doctors, 'cause some of them are bright and decent. Nor finance people. A rare few of them turn their money into philanthropy. But these men are pragmatic. You're practically an artist, Ruth, so you'd get bored. Find yourself an artist."

She blushed a little. "That is kind of you."

"What I *am* saying is not an actor. Look around this room. You did a great job curating this show. These painters are smart, each one. Much more than a pretty face that memorizes lines and knows where to stand when it's time to say them."

Ruth is half amused. "My boss says I should pursue painters only."

"And sculptors. Guys who make things that last, that can be considered over time. All day they're thinking about how we see and remember and memorialize." He picks up the level again. "Find the greatest, wildest, most imaginative painter you can. He will show you worlds you did not even know existed."

"But in general, you approve of . . . let us call it personal advancement?"

Trevor walks over, bringing the level. "You have to be savvy. Don't be their puppet. Make them yours."

"What do you mean?"

"You'll figure it out." He raises the level, bringing it down gently on her left shoulder, lifts it again, and rests it on her right shoulder. "There," he says, "young maid. Now go forth and conquer."

◆ ◆ ◆

RUTH OWNS ONLY A FEW DRESSES, NONE IN THE FASHION OF THE MOment. Ruth lays them out on her bed, standing in underwear while she conducts an assessment, then all but collapses from frustration. "I am sick of counting pennies," she laments. "I am at least five catalog shoots away from affording new togs."

But Lucy is not there to answer. She has a hot date and said she wouldn't be home till late, late, late. Three *late*s typically mean the next morning.

"Caught in the walk of shame," she imagines Lucy chiming from the doorway, high heels dangling from her fingers.

Ruth will pour her a cup of java. "You do not look ashamed to me."

Now the phone jangles, startling Ruth. "Ronald is cancelling," she says. "He found some leggy starlet to take my place."

Her mother once said a girl should never be overeager. She waits till the third ring. "Hello?"

"Ruthie, I'm so glad I caught you."

"Who is this?"

"Brian, Brian Nalen. I'm in your gallery's show next week."

"Of course you are." She sighs with relief. Then pulls on a wrap even though he cannot see her. "Are you excited for the opening?"

"That's why I'm calling. I'm having a nervous breakdown about it. Could you meet me tonight, have a drink, maybe talk me off the ledge?"

Ruth twines the phone cord in her fingers. "This is not your first show."

"My third. But it's different. I'll explain. Do you know the Cedar Tavern?"

"I have heard of it."

She has indeed, with equal parts curiosity, intimidation, and temptation. Located in the dead center of Greenwich Village, the Cedar is notorious for serving Beat poets with half-grown beards, smooth-faced actors bumming drinks from whoever is flush, distracted painters who wear stains of color on their hands and clothes, and—more than any of these groups—herds of look-alike sheep pretending to be artists too. The iron chandeliers are overly bright, Lucy has told her, so that even with clouds of cigarette smoke, the lighting flatters no one. But booze flows through the room like blood in the arteries. Legend has it that the floor is so pickled by alcohol spills, it will last a thousand years.

Ruth has never gone to a tavern by herself. "I am not sure."

"I'm a tornado of anxiety," Brian is saying. "Please."

She checks her watch. Twenty to nine, which leaves enough time for the evening's later plans. To think that five months ago, she went to bed at ten. Tonight, she is dining with a famous actor at that hour. "One drink."

"You're saving my life. See you at the Cedar."

Ruth feels sympathy for Trevor, her boss. All the shows he produces, all the artists he must have to coddle. What it must be like for them, too, to walk through a bustling city with their artistic sensitivity. How do the painters manage? She has still not chosen her dress but decides on her bra first. Confidence time. A night to wear the bullet.

AT NINE-THIRTY THE TAVERN IS QUIET. BEHIND THE BAR, APRONED MEN POLish glasses and wipe the counter. Ruth hesitates in the doorway, getting her bearings. She's wearing a little black dress, under a white linen coat she ironed till it had no wrinkles. Not for the Cedar Tavern, but for after.

Brian sits at the bar halfway back, which quiets one of her concerns. If she arrives first, a woman at the bar by herself invites approaches. She wonders if this is why fashionably tardy was invented.

Brian rises from his stool, gesturing for her to sit beside him, while his other hand waves at the bartender. "Martini for the kitten, Davy, and very dry."

"Is that what I am having?" Ruth's embrace is as light as a rose petal.

"Coffee in the morning, gin at night. It's a balanced diet."

The drink arrives full to the brim, they raise glasses to each other, and she sips. "This place has quite the reputation."

"All exaggerated." Brian offers her a cigarette, and when she waves it away, he puts his pack aside. "There are rowdy nights. But mainly it's artsy types who want something stronger than the double beers at McSorley's."

"I've been told that writers prefer the White Horse, over on Eleventh."

"Rich ones do. The Cedar is more generous with extending credit."

"I heard Dylan Thomas once drank so much whiskey at the White Horse, he passed out in the snow, and that's how he caught the pneumonia that killed him."

"Well, look at you." Brian is smiling. "Miss New York Expert."

"My roommate has made it her personal mission to educate me about this city."

"Greatest one on earth." He raises his glass again. As he drains it, she takes another cautious sip. Already the party around them seems to be picking up. The place is getting smokier, louder.

"So, who are the big names here?" Ruth fiddles with the long toothpick that spears two olives. "What geniuses have you had martinis with?"

"De Kooning is a regular. His paintings are good, but his drawings are super cherry. Accurate like a photograph." He waves a finger at the bartender and points at his empty glass. "Lee Krasner, before she moved out to Long Island. Her paintings might be jive. But you can't look at them without seeing an intelligence at work."

"Who is tops of them all, though? Besides you, I mean." Ruth muses that she seems incapable of not flirting. "The wildest, most brilliant, most—"

"Pollock. No question."

"Pollock? I haven't heard of him."

"And you work for a gallery?" Brian's martini arrives, and he takes a hearty slurp. "Get with it. This is one craaazy hepcat. All but foaming at the mouth."

"Sounds rabid."

"Came from out west," Brian continues, "hired into FDR's Depression project to keep artists from going broke. Painting murals in train stations, like that. Most of them quit being artists in '43, when the project ended. Pollock stuck around, sturdy as a fire hydrant, and somehow won a sweet monthly stipend from Peggy Guggenheim. She paid the down payment for his house with Lee too. And now she gets a slice of everything he sells. The cat's a first-class wheeler."

Brian picks up his cigarettes, looks at Ruth, then puts them aside again. "And his paintings? Ask anyone. Impossible not to have an opinion." He waves at the room. "Either it's garbage, or it's a whole new way of rendering the world." He slurps his drink. "He comes into the city on Mondays to see his analyst and winds up here later. Usually arrives half skunked."

Ruth closes her teeth on one of the olives, sliding it off the toothpick. She notices how closely Brian is paying attention, and does it more slowly. If he's going to drag her down here, he's going to get teased. "Is this Pollock guy the talking kind, holding court till closing time?"

"Nah. He's a brooder." Brian points at a booth in the corner. "His favorite spot. But his paintings are the most wild. King of the jungle."

"Pollock." Ruth sneaks a glance at her watch. "I will do my homework on him. For now, I have to go."

He points at her glass. "You haven't finished your drink."

"I am meeting someone." She slides off the stool. "For work."

"After ten o'clock? You're feeding me a line."

"He is in show business, so his workday is just ending." She stands close, hand on his chest. "See you later."

A peck on the cheek and she's turned to go. He reaches to pull her back for one on the mouth, but Ruth has shucked him and is already gone.

Outside, two men stagger down the sidewalk. One stumbles backward from Ruth, his boots freckled with paint. "Hellooo, girl of my dreams."

She promptly crosses the street to flag a taxi. On her first ride in one, she sat in front. When they reached the destination, the driver explained how it usually goes. This time she flops in back like it's as familiar as her bed. Only then does she realize that Brian did not say one word about his anxiety over the show's opening.

Ronald told her to meet him at Café Nicholson. Ruth has heard the name, because Lucy went there once on a high-roller date.

"Order the chicken in herbs and broth," Lucy advised, her face serious. "And save room for the chocolate soufflé. It's better than sex."

"Impossible," Ruth replied.

Lucy ran a tongue along her upper lip. "Just you wait."

"Mr. Gray is already seated," the maître d' tells Ruth, as he swoops ahead through quiet tables of twos and fours, solemn waiters in tuxedos and white aprons, showy flower arrangements on side pedestals. As they continue toward the farthest corner, as the eyes of everyone seem to follow her, Ruth calculates that the table is perfectly private—after you have paraded the length of the room. When they arrive, Ronald is rising to hold a chair for her.

"Sorry to be late," Ruth says.

"Had you been on time," Ronald replies, "I would have regretted inflicting the weight of punctuality on you."

She takes her seat. "The weight of punctuality?"

He sits as well, adjusts the location of his water glass, shifts his chair. She wonders if he is maintaining his visibility to the room. "If I were not here when you arrived," Ronald asks, "how long would you wait for me?"

"Well . . ." Ruth settles in her seat. "Let me see. You are a formal guy, so you would not be low-class and stand me up cold. You would call, or have someone call for you. Otherwise I guess I would wait an hour."

"An hour?" He smiles, all bright teeth. "You honor me." A waiter appears. Ronald orders a bottle of champagne, then turns to Ruth. "If you approve?"

"Let us celebrate both of us being pretty much on time."

"Let's." The waiter vanishes, and Ronald straightens his silverware. "I would only wait half an hour, though."

"I am insulted," Ruth says, laughing easily.

"You are very beautiful. You are quite young. Half the men in Manhattan would be enchanted to have dinner with you. They might even try to impress you, by choosing to meet in fancy settings." He waves at the room around them. Ruth notices that his hands are perfect: smooth, and manicured. When he gestures, they are birds. "If you stood me up," he continues, "simply did not show at all, and word got around, your social stock would rise. Yes, people know my name. They've seen me tread the boards once or twice. But really, I'm just an overworked clown of the stage, who hates to dine alone."

His voice is like a balloon, rising and falling, only to be tapped upward again. His desire is as evident as A.J.'s was, but with a critical difference: respect. She takes her swan pose—proud, tall, feeling a little thrilled. And makes a decision.

"But why dine alone? What about your wife?"

"She is . . ." Ronald's head hangs, a pause before he speaks. "She is away."

"For how long?"

He looks her straight in the eye. "That's the question, isn't it?"

"Well, Ronald." Ruth rests her hand on his. "That is awfully sad."

He smiles. It is a cool, calculating expression, like a cat holding a mouse with one paw on its tail. Except that the mouse does not mind. He takes her hand in both of his. "I knew you would understand."

IN THE MORNING, LUCY EMERGES FROM HER BEDROOM IN A LONG COTton shirt. "Good morning, beautiful." She reaches back to feel the knots in her hair.

Ruth looks up from reading the paper. "What on earth were you doing last night? For a minute there I thought he was hurting you."

Lucy smirks. "Sorry if we disturbed you."

"Disturbed? I was jealous." Ruth pours a cup of coffee and passes it to Lucy.

"He's a good one, that naughty boy." Lips pursed like she's about to play an oboe, she blows on the coffee to cool it. "May I share details?"

"Miss Loosely. It's not like I'm *dying* to know."

"He used his mouth," Lucy whispers. "And his fingers. At the same time."

"No wonder you were louder than a siren."

She takes one demure sip, pinkie extended. "You could have scraped me off the ceiling."

"You were not the only person who levitated last night. I had an evening with Ronald Gray."

"You did *not*. The actor?"

"The Broadway actor, yes."

Lucy curls her legs under herself. "Tell me absolutely everything."

"We met for dinner, at Nicholson's, thank you very much. I had my first oysters, which I liked, first champagne, which I adored, and first escargots, which no amount of garlic butter could rescue from being disgusting. I ordered the chocolate soufflé, as you suggested, and he fed it to me with his spoon. Then, after, I had my first look at the insides of a suite at the Carlyle."

"*Ruthie.* The Carlyle? You win last night by a hundred miles." Lucy scoots her chair closer. "What's he like?"

"Very wise. He told me things like you said when I was new here." She pulls her thick hair to one side. "He meets all kinds of people, and said he can tell I am special. He said I should never be shy about my obsessions, about men or work or anything, because I am smart and unique enough to get what I want. He said most people do what they are told, and I should not settle for that. But the thing is . . ."

Lucy waits a few seconds. "I can't breathe. Tell me."

Ruth leans forward. "He did not say all of that to get me into bed. I made it clear right away that he could have me. But he waited, because he wanted to get things said first. Ronald is very respectful."

"Listen to you." Lucy laughs. "*Ronald.*"

"That is his name."

"Anyway, you're leaving out the fun part. How was the hanky-panky?"

Ruth pretends to scan the sports page. "Fine."

"You deserve way better than 'fine.'"

"It is always better than 'fine.'" She puts the paper aside. "But let us say there was no mouth and fingers at the same time going on."

"When will you see him again?"

"He has my number, but I am not holding my breath." She laughs, tapping her hand on Lucy's knee. "I did tell him spectacular lies about my acting experience, in case he needs a new starlet. Who knows where life goes? We have forever."

Lucy's face goes dark. "But we don't have forever." She stares into her coffee. "We don't have anywhere near forever."

She watches, waiting, but Lucy remains downcast. "Are you all right?" Ruth asks. "Where did you go?"

"I don't know. Someone must have walked over my grave." Lucy shudders it off. "Anyway. I'm going on a trip."

"Really? This is a morning for big news. Where?"

"Havana." Lucy sips coffee. "To get an abortion."

"Oh my God. You are pregnant?"

"Good heavens, no. It's a terrible prank I do. I was only going to do it once. But the first time worked so well, it's become an annual thing." Lucy unfolds her legs, yawning as she stretches them straight. "Playing in a radio orchestra does not pay well. And there's a point every winter when New York makes me blue. Cold wind through the skyscrapers, slush on the streets, everyone bundled up and closed off. So, I meet with men I've been seeing, and I tell them I need a trip to Havana. They go pale, they start denying. I tell them not to worry, I'll take care of it. Airfare and a hotel for recovery costs seven hundred and fifty, including the procedure."

Lucy reaches over for the newspaper. "That word does the trick. Procedure. They pay immediately. Some give extra. Three fellas are usually enough to get me to Miami and put me up in style. I won't play my trick on last night's naughty boy, though. I'd miss his talents too much. Just pack my light dresses and a bathing suit, and I'm not coming home till the bulbs are blooming in Central Park."

"You are brilliant," Ruth says, "and perfectly awful."

Unruffled, Lucy takes a gulp of coffee. "It's nothing compared to the deceptions these men foist on their wives. And you should see how happy they are to see me go. How relieved. They all disappear forever, too, which is convenient."

"But spring is a long time off. What will I do while you are gone?"

"Not what, Ruthie. *Who*. I suggest round two with Ronald. Maybe the Waldorf next time. Plus, that protective father figure who appreciates a good bosom—George, right? Maybe one for laughs with that photographer? What's his name. A.J.?"

"That weasel?" Ruth sneers. "I would rather catch the measles."

"Listen to you." Lucy leans over and smooches her on the cheek. "I wish you'd become my apartment sister years ago."

"I'm going to miss you so much."

"Sure you will." Lucy sets her empty coffee cup on the table. "Till the first real man shows up."

10

JANUARY 2007

Gwen and Chillie started work at Carroll and Bunzel on the same Monday. On Thursday, they grabbed lunch together at a fast-service sushi stand. He came out to her as the food arrived. Gwen said it didn't make any difference to her.

"My first ally." Chillie rubbed his hands together diabolically. "So begins my plot to take over the company and hire only my people, till the entire staff is gay."

Gwen paused the chopsticks halfway to her mouth. "What happens to me?"

"You're fired, of course. You have till I'm CEO to change your orientation."

Friday after work, they killed a bottle of sugary white wine at an otherwise empty East Side café, and then another. Saturday morning, he called to complain about his headache, and they talked for an hour. From that day forward, they committed to exploring every neighborhood in New York City, and to being each other's guides and guards. To Gwen, freedom from concern about any romantic potential was liberating. Amid Chillie's constant jokes about attractive men, and which of them he desired, they took turns planning weekend adventures.

"I am going to rescue you from boredom," Chillie said.

"I am going to find you a boyfriend," Gwen replied.

Chillie hated the subway. "The crazy people. The hucksters selling stolen candy. The druggies bouncing like pinballs or nodding under an opium shroud."

Gwen gave him a poke. "Those are exactly the reasons why I love it."

Once, a man in their subway car was busking with a mandolin, loud by her ear. She took out a dollar bill, and when he reached, she said, "This is for you to not play till I get off."

Chillie dragged Gwen to Coney Island one sunny summer Saturday. Among the throngs of families and couples on dates, she ate horrible greasy delicious things and rode roller coasters so rickety they could not possibly be safe. When a little boy stepped off the Cyclone roller coaster and vomited on the pavement what seemed like more than the total volume of his body, his father backing away to avoid getting splattered, Chillie laughed so hard she had to hold him up.

In turn, Gwen kidnapped him, despite his protests that nothing was more boring than history, down to the Financial District, destination Ground Zero. In early 2007, five years plus after the mass murder of 9/11, reconstruction was gaining momentum. In some ways, it was like any New York building project: sprawling, loud, the cause of standstill traffic. But the size of the open sky overhead, and the memories still vivid in every New Yorker's mind, gave absence a weight.

Negative space, that was one of the first terms Gwen had learned in the study of art: learning to look at the part of the canvas that was not painted. The classic example was Japanese single-stroke art, in which the painter rendered a black circle in one dramatic swoop of the brush. But the circle was not the important part. It was the shape inside the circle, and outside, that truly mattered.

One day, there would be memorials here, fountains, a museum. For now, Gwen took in the negative space: where the towers had stood, where the fire burned for months, where removing debris took years. Chillie bent forward like a sickened boy.

"Are you okay?" she asked.

He shook his head. "All of my concerns are trivial beyond belief."

Gradually they made other friends, beginning to build social circles. Gwen had flings with Neil, Chillie had a series of romances.

Their Monday gossip was spicier, but shared weekend jaunts became less frequent. As a result, Gwen had never been to Hell's Kitchen, nor set foot in Riverside Park, nor climbed the stairs from the L train at Seventh Avenue to emerge in the West Village.

Now, on another fresh and cloudless Tuesday morning, she was doing exactly that. She'd come in search of a young lover grown old.

ONLINE, GWEN HAD FOUND A TELLTALE PHOTO: JACKSON POLLOCK SITting on a boulder in his backyard in Springs, the town on outer Long Island where he lived with his wife, the painter Lee Krasner. In the picture he's hunched, awkward, squinting in the sunlight. A chesty brunette has thrown an arm over his shoulders and splayed herself across his lap like a cheerleader caught mid-hop: Ruth.

He looks hungover, she exudes enthusiasm. The photo credit went to Lucy Steele, a name unfamiliar to Gwen. The picture was famous because Lucy took it on Jackson and Ruth's last day together. Disaster was a few hours away.

Ruth was attractive enough in the photo. But Gwen found pictures online from her modeling days, and in those she was a beauty. High forehead, lush lower lip, shoulders back like a proud Elizabeth Taylor. A man did not need artistic genius to notice.

After all the skyscrapers uptown and down, Gwen felt the Village was pleasantly human-scaled: trees, small shops and pubs, a bookstore. Quiet, too, given its bohemian past. The streets did not follow upper Manhattan's straight lines, so she relied on the map on her new phone. Finding the right street, Gwen counted building numbers till she reached the one Pinkney provided. She'd persuaded him to call Ruth to arrange the interview. She said his clout would help, but in truth, she was intimidated. If Pinkney noticed, he did not let on. Only waved her out of his office, while telling Harriette to get Ruth on the line.

Gwen stood before a three-story brownstone. An older man sat on the stoop, bent over something, showing the top of his bald head. In one hand he held a block of wood, in the other a short knife. Wood chips littered the sidewalk and his trousers. He was situated in the middle of the stairs, making it impossible to pass.

"Hello?" Gwen said. "Can I sneak by here?"

The man finished the carve he was doing, taking his time to blow away the curl of wood, then looked up. It turned out he was closer to her age. His bright green eyes narrowed in suspicion. "Well, lookie here, Ruth Kligman's latest acolyte."

"She has acolytes?"

He shrugged. "Too profane to be called pilgrims. Too stupid to be called fans."

"I thought it was a requirement for fans to be stupid."

"Can't be a true fan of something you don't comprehend." He scratched his chin with the knife handle. "You're too calm for pilgrimage or fandom. Does she owe you money?"

"We've never met."

"Well, don't believe her about the back rent deadline. No one is going to throw her out."

"I'm sure her rent is none of my business. And between Ruth and me, there's no debt in either direction."

"Oh, there's debt some way. In this life, there's always debt."

"Is that right?" Gwen was tiring of the banter. "What do I owe?"

He considered her more fully, taking his time. To Gwen it felt not like flirtation, but appraisal, which raised her dander. Finally, he swept some shavings away and shifted his backside. "You owe me, for getting out of your way."

"I'll keep that in mind," she said on the way by, "next time I block your path."

The man bent to his block of wood again. "I hope you don't have plans for later. That Ruth can talk."

Gwen pressed the button, heard the door lock buzz her in, and left the carver to his attitude.

"GODDAMN IT TO HELL."

Gwen heard a woman yell it from inside the apartment. The door was open wide. She poked her head in. "Hello?"

"Just a goddamn minute." Seconds later Ruth emerged from the inner rooms—tiny mirror in one hand, lipstick in the other. "If this thing would just behave."

The lipstick had wandered, leaving a bold red mark that strayed beyond her lips—to her chin, her cheek. It made Gwen think of a hyena, lifting its face from a kill. "May I help you?"

Ruth dropped her arms to her sides. "Would you, please? Between my awful eyesight and pathetic tremors . . ."

"Do you have a napkin? Paper towel?"

Ruth revealed the roll of toilet paper tucked under her arm. "Will this do?"

So Gwen found herself standing close, wiping away lipstick where it did not belong. She could have been helping her grandmother. It wasn't just lipstick. The woman was using too much makeup altogether. It caked in the wrinkles around her eyes and made her cheeks look droopy. She also wore too much perfume, flowery and strong.

"There." Gwen raised the mirror for her to see. "All better."

"What a mortification." Ruth withdrew, vanishing inside, accompanied by the hammer of her shoes' hard heels.

Gwen stood in the doorway, wondering what to do next. But her uncertainty was answered in seconds, when Ruth emerged for a second time. Now she wore slippers and moved with a glide.

"Hello, hello, you angel." She wore a big smile. "Hello and welcome." Gwen stood still as the woman held her shoulders and kissed her on both cheeks. "You are a beautiful human being. I love you."

"Well, okay. It's a pleasure to meet—"

"Come, come." Ruth pivoted, wiggling her fingers in the air as she headed into the apartment. "Come in from the cold."

"The cold?" Gwen couldn't help it. She laughed.

"Here." Ruth paused in the hall, pointing at rows of photos. "Me with Franz Kline. Here's Andy Warhol, of course. Rudy Burckhardt's portrait of me, Robert Mapplethorpe—reduced from the giant original. Bert Stern, Irving Penn. Yawn, yawn. Come with me."

Gwen hesitated, hoping that later she'd have a chance to look closer, and followed.

THE LIVING ROOM WAS A MONUMENT TO CLUTTER. EVERY SURFACE WAS busy with seashells or starfish, small wood carvings, a dolphin of blue glass. The corners had cobwebs, and the air smelled dusty, as if the windows had not been opened in years.

As Gwen entered the room, Ruth came and seized her hand. The bones felt like a bag of sticks. "Are you here to help me?" Ruth said. "Or to do me harm?"

"Not harm, definitely. My job is to confirm the authenticity of your painting, so Carroll and Bunzel can represent it for you."

Maintaining the handclasp, Ruth closed her eyes. Gwen wondered if she was thinking, or praying, or battling dementia. Then she fluttered them open. "It is best to begin from a place of trust." She released Gwen's hand and stood square, as if facing a firing squad. "We will learn soon enough whether you are friend or foe."

"Neither," Gwen said evenly. "I am an authentication professional. I have three questions that need answers only you can provide. Once that's done, we will find and gather the people most interested in the item you have for sale. Then we will hold an event designed to generate a market favorable to your interests."

As she spoke, Ruth's eyes had gone dewy.

"But of course," Gwen hurried to add, "I will make the process as easy as I possibly can." She made a little bow. Where had that come from? Arthur?

"Come, then." Ruth extended an arm like a game show model directing attention to a new car—except the car was her living room. "Enter the dwelling of a woman who has been criticized, scorned, and ridiculed, all because she loved and lost."

Art covered the walls, frame against frame with minimal wall space between, the paintings abstract and chaotic. The one exception hung over the fireplace, an elaborately framed enlargement of the very photo Gwen had seen on the Internet: Ruth draped across the lap of a grimacing Pollock.

"That's quite a shot," Gwen said.

"Oh, Jackson." Ruth floated over to it. "Jackson, Jackson, Jackson."

"Excuse me?" Gwen said.

She burst into tears. "I cry now as you did then, my sweet Jackson, at how unfair fame is to genius. I loved you so much. It was beauty and poetry. A love written in the stars. And because it is eternal, I promised to keep that love alive as long as I draw breath. I had no idea I would live fifty years without you." Ruth covered her face with both hands, sobbing.

It sounded, Gwen thought, like the hooting of an owl. She lingered under the room's lintel. The woman seemed unable to pull herself together. It was unlike any client she had ever encountered.

"Fifty years," she cried. "Jackson, Jackson, Jackson."

"Should I come back later—"

"No." Ruth whirled and glared at her. "Love can withstand anything. I need a moment, that is all." She produced a wad of tissues tucked in her sleeve and patted her face. At a wall mirror, she dabbed where her mascara had run.

Gwen continued her scan of the apartment. Persian rugs with worn patches. A vase holding flowers gone dried and droopy. An easel in a corner, its contents covered by a cloth. A side table with tubes of oils in various colors.

"Are you a painter as well?" Gwen asked.

"Once upon a time." Ruth tucked the tissues away, coming nearer than Gwen felt comfortable with. "So young, you are, Miss Gwen. So pretty and unwise."

"Excuse me?"

"Tell me, young lady. Have you ever known a love that would suffer anything, do anything, even burn the whole world to the ground?"

Gwen's agenda was simple, three questions, yet somehow the woman had hijacked it. "Can we talk about the painting?"

"You will never understand it unless you hear the story."

"Actually, I only need to know three things: when he painted it, how it came into your possession, and whether you will—"

"Answer me first." Ruth jangled her bracelets. "Have you known that kind of love? That incandescent intensity that overwhelms your life?"

Gwen looked down at her notebook. "I have known passion and hurt, if that's what you mean."

"No." Ruth wagged her head. "I mean a love to change the world."

"I'm not entirely convinced that *any* two people—"

"Then you will not understand what I have to tell you."

Gwen did not know how to respond.

Ruth spun away like a lover spurned. "You are speaking to a poet." She lowered herself into a stuffed chair. "With a poet's vulnerable heart. The story of Jackson Pollock and Ruth Kligman was written in the stars."

Gwen moved into the room. "If we could focus, please, on the painting—"

"Because I dared to love Jackson," she persisted, "I have been robbed but enriched, abandoned but fed, my name in lights and my reputation in the gutter."

Gwen felt a kind of claustrophobic pressure. She had no time for babysitting. She cleared her throat. "You know, ma'am, I will need to take it for a few days."

That broke Ruth's reverie. "The painting? Whatever for?"

"Forensics. We employ chemists who are experts in brushes, paints, and so on. They have scientific methods of determining the age and circumstances of a painting." She paused to see if Ruth would flinch, but her expression did not change. "In your case this assessment is essential."

Now Ruth was wringing her hands. "Of course you have experts. But must you take my baby away? I don't like being out of its presence."

"My understanding was that you intended for this painting to go away permanently, through an auction."

Ruth looked away. "Much as it pains me."

"If you'd rather not sell, ma'am, please say so now. Relieve yourself of the upset of parting with this asset, and spare Carroll and Bunzel the considerable expense in preparing to sell it." It was a trick Gwen learned from Richards: Never speak of the money a client will make by selling something, but mention the cost to the house of auctioning it. "If you give this painting to the world, it will finally receive the global attention it deserves."

"How will you protect my painting while it is out of my sight?"

"I will personally supervise the packing and accompany the transport vehicle. When we arrive at the chemist's facility—he lives in northern Westchester County—the painting will be in a vault."

"A vault?"

"With controlled temperature and humidity. And steel doors."

Ruth rose from her chair. Folding her hands together at the waist, she lifted her chest like a soprano about to begin an aria. "I want this to happen while I am still alive. I want the world to see this manifestation of our ill-fated love. I want people to know what heights I experienced with the greatest artist of our time. I—"

Gwen interrupted. "May I see it?"

Ruth focused on Gwen, as if waking to her presence. "I suppose so." She hobbled across the room, past the easel in the corner.

"I thought that was it, on there," Gwen said.

"One of mine," Ruth answered. "Me, a lifelong beginner." She reached behind a sideboard, sliding out a rectangle wrapped in blue fabric. "Oh, but this." She carried the painting to an armchair. Her unwrapping was awkward and took a full minute.

"May I help?" Gwen asked, but Ruth waved her away, wrestling with the fabric till it fell away. Blocking it with her body, she turned the painting to face the room, set it on the chair, and stepped aside. "Voilà."

Just as no musical recording compares to a live performance, likewise, the photos Gwen had seen did no justice to the work before her now. The painting was not pretty, but it was not trying to be. A range of colors, a thick texture, fierce brushstrokes showing the painter's passion, all anchored by a mysterious black center. Whoever painted this piece possessed genuine skill and was unafraid to use wildness.

Gwen found herself most affected by the red. It hovered over everything else, like blood thrown on a pane of glass, an inch above the rest of the painting. The effect was not an accident. It was a masterful demonstration of technique.

Ruth stood at her elbow. "You feel its power."

Gwen nodded. "I do."

"You know in your heart it is the real thing."

"My heart is immaterial. I have to prove its authenticity. What's its name?"

"None that Jackson told me. I call it *Red, Black and Silver.*" Ruth tottered over to the photo of her and Pollock. Gwen wondered how many times a day she worshipped at this altar. "Oh, Jackson," Ruth incanted. "Jackson, Jackson, Jackson."

Gwen felt that claustrophobia again. Enough. "When did he paint this?"

"Must you pester me with questions? Isn't seeing enough?"

"How did you come into possession of it?"

"Talking business in front of this painting is like swearing in church."

Gwen scooped up the blue cloth and draped it over the painting. "When did he paint this? How did you come into possession of it?"

Ruth glided to a window, one pointed finger resting on the sill. She paused as an actress might, holding her mark, counting beats till her next line. Gwen wanted to be sympathetic, but she had seen better performances on soap operas.

"We had everything," Ruth told the window. "Love, youth, passion. Until fate intervened without mercy. Jackson was stolen from me, and from the world."

Another three beats before Ruth faced her. Gwen thought: *This is the moment she has lived for. The validation she has desired for five decades. This exact moment.*

Ruth moved a stack of newspapers on the couch. "Would you hear the story?"

"I'm sure it's great, but—"

"You have no idea." She sat.

"It's not my job to listen to stories. My job is to discern if this painting is authentic, and if it legally belongs to you."

Ruth looked at Gwen frankly. "I see you," she said. "I see your ambition. A woman of this era." She picked at the couch. "You cannot understand how and when this painting was made, or why he gave it to me. You need the story."

Gwen lowered herself into an armchair. It was ancient and sagged as if Ruth were pulling her into a trap. "Fine."

"Wonderful." Ruth clapped her hands. Suddenly energized, she bounced up from her seat and crossed to the bar cart. "This calls for a pitcher of martinis."

Gwen swallowed hard. "A pitcher?"

"Of course, Miss Gwen. And, appropriately for a story with an artist as the hero, it starts with color. In this case, the color pink. One night, and the pink dress I wore."

She tilted a bottle of vodka over a glass pitcher and began to pour.

II

MARCH 1956

The life Ruth built in New York over six months collapses in less than twenty-four hours.

First, Lucy leaves for Miami, with a one-way ticket. Their parting hug in the hallway is fierce. Lucy even grabs Ruth's bottom, to pull her close the length of their bodies, before kissing her lips and darting away down the stairs. From the window in Lucy's bedroom, Ruth watches her hail a cab and climb in. The door slams with the finality of a judge's gavel.

All at once, Ruth is standing in silence. It feels vast and lonely. She reaches over to Lucy's cello on its stand and plucks one string. It rings like a melancholy bell.

Time slows. Aside from sometimes noisy renters upstairs, the apartment remains as quiet as a chapel. Ruth slogs home from the gallery and there is no one to complain to about the workload. Trevor's wife is diagnosed with a blood disorder, which puts her to bed under doctor's orders until the delivery. He's cleaning and cooking and only stops by the gallery to confirm that Ruth is there, working away.

Why? Because nearly every artist in the upcoming show submitted a piece larger than the allocated wall space. There's conflict, sending works home, and waiting for replacements that fit, while the opening date approaches without mercy.

Still, the biggest problem is her modeling. The day Lucy leaves, Ruth arrives at the catalog shoot, and one of the dressers accosts her. "What are you doing here?"

Ruth is taking off her winter coat. "I am modeling for the catalog."

The girl gathers up an armful of sweaters, colored in pastels like cotton Easter eggs. "You'd best check with the boss, missy."

"Missy?"

But the girl is gone. Ruth would call her back, and demand an apology, but she realizes she doesn't know the girl's name, and hadn't troubled herself to learn it in the previous weeks. She strides across the set, to find the nice older photographer who always says please. She doesn't know his name either.

"Good morning," Ruth chimes.

"Hello, Ruth." The man bends to unplug an unlit rack of lights, then plugs them back in. The bulbs stubbornly remain off. "Something I can help you with?"

"One of the dressing girls said I should talk to you."

"Oh jeez." He straightens, a hand on his lower back. "I guess George didn't reach your agent in time."

"In time for what?"

"To spare you the trip," he replies. "We finished your part of the catalog."

"I thought we had another full week."

"We do." The photographer shrugs. "But George said you were done."

Ruth scans the room. "Where is he, anyway?"

"His wife has pneumonia. I don't expect him back for days."

"What am I supposed to do?"

The photographer bends again to the light pole. "Unless you know something about electricity, I'd suggest you go home. Sorry, doll, but you've been canned."

Ruth storms away, not sure whether to lose her temper or burst into tears. She's never been fired from anything before.

At a pay phone on the avenue, Ruth dials her agent. When Craig answers, she does not bother with hello. "When were you going to tell me?"

"Wait." He coughs. "Is this Ruth?"

"Yes, Ruth the unemployed."

She can hear Craig's chair creak as he leans back. "What did you do?"

"What do you mean?"

"Your contract was for the whole catalog. But he dropped you with a third of it still to go. George doesn't do that without a reason."

Who are all these men she must answer to? There in the phone booth, Ruth takes her pose of strength. "I have no idea. I was always on time and worked hard."

"Maybe it was not on the job," Craig said. "Did you steal something? Or get caught drunk in public?"

"What kind of a woman do you think I am?"

Craig sighs. "I'm nobody's judge. Do whatever you want. I don't give two sticks, as long as you keep working so I can make a living. I told you at the start that George is a straight arrow. Devout Catholic, church every Sunday. B. Altman hired him because the family who owns the business is also seriously Catholic. Six kids, the whole thing. What George likes about you is innocence. He said that to me. So, you did something, Ruth, or you'd be in front a camera right now."

She slumps against the phone booth's door. Ronald Gray must have blabbed about the night at the Carlyle. There's no other explanation. "What do I do now?"

"Lie low for a week or three. Then I'll make some calls. Whatever you did will be in the past, and we'll get you back to work."

"Easy for you to say. I have rent to pay. And a habit of eating every day."

"That's where George's ethics help. This morning, he messengered me your pay for the whole job. The check is here on my desk."

Ruth rests her head on the metal frame of the booth. "The man is an angel."

"Yes," Craig says. "The only one I know."

PINK, SHE DECIDES. THOUGH THE LIGHTING WHERE SHE'S HEADED ISN'T flattering, Ruth knows what color will stand out. Her plan is to be noticed, and to do it before Lucy returns and talks sense into her. Before another catalog producer can shame her for being young and free. Before another modeling agent can show indifference to her feelings as long as he makes his money.

"No one is on your side," she tells the bathroom mirror, dabbing on makeup. Her pinkie darkens the hollow under her cheekbones, slimming her face. "No one is going to do things for you." Applying mascara, she lectures her reflection. "Every opportunity, you must be bold. It is up to you."

It's Monday. Brian had no reason to lie about someone else's habits: taking the train in on Mondays, then analyst, then drinks. She knows where her quarry likes to sit too. All that's required is courage. And looking like a catch.

Ruth digs through her cosmetics bag, finds the faux gold cylinder she is after, turns its base to spiral out a bold red lipstick. Open-mouthed, she applies it carefully to her lower lip, then mashes both lips together to spread it evenly.

She chuckles. "Look at you."

Ruth pulls the dangling string that turns off the bathroom light. In her room, a pink dress sprawls on the bed. Again, she laughs a little, pulling it on, rotating the hips so it hangs right. "How old are we tonight?" She steps left and right into her pink heels. "Cheat a little, and say twenty-three?" Her reflection grins back from the bedroom window. "All right, twenty-two, if anyone asks. But only for tonight."

She slides into her white linen coat, grabs her little pink handbag, and scurries out the apartment door. Even in heels, she's quick down the stairs. A passing cab slows like a hunting animal, but Ruth waves it on. The walk from Sixteenth Street to Eighth will warm her up, give her lungs a dose of fresh air. She'll need it, before the smoky atmosphere of the Cedar Tavern.

She can hear the place half a block away. Men are crowding the entryway, or perhaps collecting at the door because it's warmer out, the first hint of spring. The gauntlet to get inside could be intimidating. But Ruth puts a bounce in her step. She's doing exactly the right thing.

And then they see her.

"Well, hello, Betty."

"Make way, gentlemen. Make way."

The men are pushing others, clearing a path. Two of them are in a heated argument and haven't noticed. "What I am saying," one of them is shouting, "is if Frank O'Hara wants to play jazz, he should stop writing poems no one understands and take saxophone lessons instead."

Ruth falters. The smell of drink is strong on these men, and she has her first inkling that she might be doing something unsafe.

"Language," the other man replies evenly, his voice not raised at all, "surpasses any musical instrument."

"Hey, guys." A man in a fedora taps the loud one on the shoulder. "How's about making room for the fairy princess?"

"What the hell—" He sees Ruth and stops, mouth hanging open. "This isn't a princess. It's a walking flower."

"Pardon me." Ruth summons her gumption and squeezes through. She's aware of the quiet behind her, but it ends before she's taken two steps inside.

The tavern is louder than before, smokier, rougher. Men crowd the bar, and the tables are full too. If he's not here, she'll leave without having a drink—or permitting anyone to buy her one. A slow scan reveals a few belles, so the crowd is not entirely male. They're all wearing tight shirts and black slacks. And their expressions upon seeing her are exactly the opposite of the men's.

Holding her clutch with both hands, Ruth wends through the crowd. She can see that the last booth is occupied. She is drawing closer when a beer mug comes flying out and smashes against the wall beside the bar.

"Hey, Jack," the bartender yells. "What the hell?"

Using his apron, he wipes the Rorschach of beer off the wall. The barback boy brings a dustpan and broom. People tumble out of the booth, more than she imagined it could hold. One stays behind, hangdog, thin hair on his crown. Ruth stands there until he lifts his face, takes a moment to focus, and opens his arms.

"And then, God sent an angel."

Ruth holds her hand out straight. "You must be Pollock."

"Hah." He shakes her hand. "Jackson."

"Ruth." She slides in across from him. "Why did you throw that mug?"

"Are you the good-behavior police?"

"I am not police of any kind," she answers. "I am curious, though."

His face clouds. "Don't know you well enough."

"Did you do it without knowing why?"

He frowns at her. "Why are you sitting with me?"

"Because you are the one. I ask people, I read and listen. When I say that I want to meet the beating heart of New York City's art scene, the king, the lion, everyone says you."

His grin reappears. "I was almost buying it, till you got to the lion."

"All your friends are artists. In your crowd, talent is normal." Ruth pats her chest. "I am a mere model. And a gallery hand. To me, you are extraordinary."

A bartender appears, setting a new beer before Jackson. "Courtesy of Franz." He turns to Ruth. "What'll you have, miss?"

"White wine spritzer, please."

He takes in her pink dress and walks off muttering. "Why did I bother asking?"

Jackson sits back, one arm over the back of the booth. "Which gallery?"

"Trevor's. I am curating the next show. It opens in nine days."

"I'll come see it."

"Why did you throw that beer?"

"Because Franz said my feelings were impossible."

"Who is Franz, and why did he dare to question you?"

Jackson flinches. It's quick, a wince and then his expression is back to normal. Ruth suppresses her own impulse, almost a reflex, to caress his face.

He takes a moment, assessing her hair, her face, the dress. Whatever made him flinch vanishes, and his confidence returns. Resting forearms on the table, he leans closer. "Imagine you've never seen red. You've been many places over the years, looked at many colors, but never red. You sit down with me, we have some beers, and I start telling you about this great color I saw, vibrant, alive, overpowering all other colors. You say it's nonsense, you've seen all the colors, I'm just drunk."

"But you are not drunk."

"Of course I am. But that doesn't make red not exist. Any more than Franz's ignorance of that particular hue means I made it up."

Ruth's drink arrives, and she thanks the bartender. "But you were not actually arguing about a color."

"No." Jackson leans closer. "We were arguing about everything."

"Help a non-genius to understand."

He raises the mug at her, gulps half of the beer down, wipes his face. "Your wine, for example. There is a factory somewhere, where they grind sand down, heat it up, and I don't know what else. It's hot, they add things, they sweat and run their machines, and they make the glass you are now holding."

Suddenly self-conscious, Ruth puts her drink down.

"Meanwhile, in some completely different place, rustic and remote, farmers grow grapes, laborers pick them, stomp on them. Someone else corks them in a barrel, and later in a bottle. My pal Davy, there behind the bar, he buys the bottle, and the wine comes to you. All of these lives, their dreams, love and loss and terror about the certainty of death. Hell, the person who built this table, glad to be paid for it. Everyone, everywhere. It is coursing through everything in the universe, Ruth, the history, if you allow yourself to feel it. Franz says no, I can't possibly feel all of that, it's just a glass, just wine, and I am full of shit."

"I see," Ruth replies. "You fling the glass against the wall, and we are all offended, because you reveal our disregard for the history of people making the mug and brewing the beer. It is all the color red, and you are a genius."

That fingertip on his lips again. That look of assessment. He sits back as if he has just won a hand of poker. "Do you happen to know what time it is?"

Ruth glances at her watch. "Ten after ten."

"What?" Jackson jolts as though he has been shocked. "Are you positive?"

"I might be running a little fast. Maybe eight after. Why?"

He nods deeply, as if everything before was confusion, but now it all makes sense. "Are you going to get drunk with me tonight?"

"Jackson, Jackson, Jackson." She reaches over, laying her hand on his. It is nothing like Ronald's: hairy, rough, red paint on his thumbnail. She drapes her soft palm over it. "That is why I came."

12

JANUARY 2007

Once the Pollock project began, Gwen developed a routine that felt like hunting: patrolling the streets of Central Park West, looking for her prey. She read that Lee Krasner doted on her dog. In the most recent photo of her in the news, now six years old, she held a Pekingese the size of a loaf of bread. That article also gave broad clues for where Lee lived.

"Stalk her," Chillie said. They'd lingered on the street one afternoon, while he finished a cigarette. "She may not even know you're trying to reach her."

"Let's say by crazy coincidence that I find her out walking Fido. What then?"

"Honey." He exhaled a gray cloud. Most of it missed her, but not all, making her lean away. "You say, hello, we have a painting that belongs to you, can we chat?"

"It's a dumb idea," Gwen said. "And your smoking is disgusting."

"Devon says it's the sexiest thing I do other than sex."

"Devon? I thought you were with Keith. Since when is there a Devon?"

"Since I learned that Devon is another word for devil."

Gwen fanned the air in front of her face. "I am not going to doorstep a widow. I don't care who her dead husband is."

Yet there she was, head pounding from the previous night's martinis with Ruth, starting at Ninety-Second Street and winding south through the brownstones: two blocks away from Central Park, then down one avenue and back toward the park. It was a lovely neighborhood, tidy and quiet. Plenty of people walking dogs, and a few joggers. But no older ladies, or none that she saw.

When Gwen reached the Museum of Natural History, normally the halfway mark, she fought the temptation to sit on the front steps and people-watch till her hangover subsided. Instead, she found a coffee shop, bought herself an extra-large, and indulged in a cab to get downtown.

The carving guy was hogging Ruth's stairs again, but now Gwen saw why. He was bathed in sunlight. A warm place to work outside. He wore a blue beret.

"Good morning," she called. Speaking loudly hurt her brain a little.

"You again?" He puffed on his carving, blowing away a curl of wood. "How much did you kiss the ass of our peculiar poetess?"

Gwen stopped at the bottom step. "You're not very nice, are you?"

"I am but a mere poet," the man said in a falsetto voice, one fist clenched against his chest. *"With a sensitive, vulnerable heart."*

"She's hardly the first creative person to be self-absorbed."

"So there's my answer." He tucked away his knife. "You kissed both cheeks."

"You are something." Gwen shook her head. "You Village people, you masters of affectation. I mean, a beret? Really? Yet you think you do an honest day's work."

He grinned. "Actually, so far today is not half bad."

"Whittling your life away? Sounds grueling."

He turned the block of wood over to reveal a carving that made Gwen catch her breath: the nave of a church, an altar and pulpit, rows of organ pipes, a choir of open mouths and closed eyes. All rendered in a block of wood not ten inches long.

"That's astonishing," Gwen said. "I mean it."

"You want it."

"I'm sure I can't afford it, but of course. It's amazing."

He shook his head. "I could tell you were a wanting person the first second I saw you. This piece will be for sale, once I finish it. But not to the likes of you."

"A wanting person? What does that mean?"

"You should see the appetite on your face. You want this. You can't just look at it, you have to own it. I only sell to people who understand what art is worth."

Gwen laughed. "But that's exactly what I do for a living. I spend all day figuring out what art is worth. It's my job."

The carver shrugged. "Looks to me like it's ruined you."

Gwen put her hands on her hips. "What in the world are you talking about?"

He rose, tucking the carving into the crook of his elbow, and shuffled up the street.

"Why are you such an asshole?" she called to him.

He kept walking, raising his free hand to give her the finger.

THE MOVERS WERE ALREADY THERE, RUTH HOVERING WITH A HANDKERchief to pat the perspiration on her brow. "Why are you building that frame? What is the purpose of that plastic cover? What is the crate made out of?"

The lead mover gave Gwen a pained look, and she drew Ruth aside. "They are professionals," she said. "Experts. They will protect the painting against any possible bump or jiggle, and the cover will shield it from dust."

Ruth blinked at Gwen like a child asking about Santa. "From dust?"

"Now tell me about the man who is always carving on your steps."

"Winthrop? I just love him."

Gwen wheeled to face her. "You love him?"

"Oh yes." Ruth nodded enthusiastically. "He is immensely talented, earns almost nothing from it, and does not care. He was a stone carver, in the quarries of Carrara, Italy. He had a fall, a brain injury. He is gruff, but fascinating. He comes up every Sunday evening, and we have a sherry."

"We're good here," the mover called. "Ready to roll."

"Thank you," Gwen said, still puzzling over Winthrop. "I'll get the signatures." From her shoulder bag she produced a manila folder.

Ruth's hands rose to her mouth. "I'm not ready to sign this painting away."

"Of course not." Gwen spread the papers on Ruth's dining table. "This one is the forensic code of ethics. It says that the person analyzing this work of art will receive the same fee regardless of what he concludes. Your signature"—Gwen handed Ruth a pen as she flipped to the last page—"says that you have read this document."

"That sounds sensible." Ruth scribbled her name on the line.

Gwen studied her a moment.

"Is something wrong, my dear?" Ruth asked.

"You're not feeling those drinks from last night?"

"I am a flower, darling." Ruth smiled. "But I am also made of iron. Two glasses of water before bed, eye mask in place, and I wake up fine. A talent of mine."

"A talent I envy." Gwen spread the other pages on the table. "This explains how scientists will handle the painting—no slicing out a microscopic piece of paint to date the pigments, for example—and states that this research contains no obligations on your part, your ownership remains complete."

Ruth signed without a question.

"Gentlemen?" Gwen called to the movers.

"Ready."

"Now, boys," Ruth sang out. "Don't you hurry on those narrow stairs."

As she spoke, she approached them, swinging her hips like a saucy starlet. Gwen chuckled at how exaggerated the motion was, almost a parody, until she saw that the movers were watching. This woman was nearly eighty, but they looked just the same. "Be good to my baby, will you? Strong men that you are."

"Yes ma'am," the lead mover said. "We'll be careful the whole way."

They hoisted the crate, up and out. As Ruth followed, Gwen tried imitating her walk. It felt silly, a way she had never moved. By the time she'd gathered the papers and reached the street, a mover was padlocking the truck's rear door.

"No company name?" Ruth asked, studying the blank side of the truck. "Don't you want to promote yourselves, like every other business?"

"With our cargo?" the head mover replied. "*Rare expensive item transport company.* I wouldn't want to drive around with that on the side."

The men loaded up. Gwen flagged a cab to the rental office, where a car was waiting. Ruth stood at the curb, wringing her hands. "Be good to my baby."

Gwen climbed into the taxi. "You know I will."

At the end of the block, Gwen turned in her seat. Ruth was bent forward, her shoulders shaking. Beside her, appearing out of nowhere, stood Winthrop, rubbing her back.

MATTHIEU'S WHITE HAIR STOOD STRAIGHT UP, AS IF HE'D POKED HIS FINger in a lamp's socket. He waved madly to Gwen and the movers as they pulled up his driveway. "*Bonjour, bienvenue, bienvenue, tous mes amis.*"

Gwen noticed the woman beside him, young and lithe. They parted with a long kiss, Matthieu ogling her as she walked away. Gwen parked beside a wooden, handmade sign: *The Vault.*

"*Chérie* Gwen." Matthieu was at her car door, air-kissing both sides of her face. "As beautiful as ever."

"You are incorrigible and incorrect."

"What?" He drew back. "You are as lovely as a woman can be, for how little sex you have."

"Ouch." Gwen swatted him. "You're just flaunting your naughty ways. I saw you smooch that youngster."

"Ah, *la belle* Jeanne. With the scent of Marion Cotillard."

"Or a whiff of exploited jailbait."

He laughed. "Jeanne is a painter of astonishing landscapes who needs a place to live and work near the city. She is funny, brilliant, kind. Excellent company."

"I'm happy for you."

"Two problems, though. The young lady is insatiable." He laughed, a hand on his heart. "One of these nights she will kill me."

"Isn't your life goal to die smiling?"

Matthieu's expression darkened. "Second, she will grow restless when spring arrives. Then she will shatter my heart."

"Call me when the time comes. I'll bring champagne."

"You always have the right medicine. And now. *Allons-y.*" He began walking backward to the studio. "Let us see what puzzle you have brought today."

The lab was immaculate, every tool and reference book in its place, the wooden floor old and sloping but as clean as an operating room. The crate sat squat in the middle, looking so plain it could have contained a new toilet. But just beyond it, wall indicators showed a constantly maintained temperature and humidity. Above them a French flag hung from a hook. "So. What overvalued trinket is Carroll and Bunzel peddling to the gullible public today?"

"You know I never tell in advance," Gwen said, sitting on a tall stool. "To avoid leading you in any direction."

"You used the expensive movers, so it's too late." Matthieu took a crowbar and cranked the crate open. "Let the expert evaluate. He is foreign, so he must be right." Winking, he used a scalpel to slice the plastic wrap, which revealed the center of the painting. Immediately, he slowed.

"Well, hello." He went to an inner room and returned wearing white cotton gloves. With care, he lifted the painting out, setting it onto a stainless steel easel. Matthieu stepped back, taking in the whole of it, then leaned close to examine details, reading the painting left to right as though it were a page.

"All right," he said. "This is a fine challenge."

"Tell me what you see." She had her green notebook out, and a pen.

"It pretends to be by a certain artist we might have in mind, before alcohol ruined him. Or madness, you decide. His spontaneity is present, his acute sense of space." Matthieu tapped the gloves' fingertips together. "This item is important. You know what happened at Sotheby's with *Number 5, 1948?* The record price?"

"I was in the auction room."

"Clever." He smiled at her, before returning his attention to the painting. "That sale could not have been cleaner. This one has problems."

"Already? Such as?"

"Evidence of multiple painting sessions, with years between. He may have started this work in nineteen forty-seven and finished it in nineteen fifty-four. That would be out of character. But it is not my foremost concern."

Gwen leaned forward on her stool. "Which is?"

Matthieu breathed in through clenched teeth, as if he were hissing inward. "The artist you and I have in mind? He worked with unstretched canvases lying on his studio floor. This piece is on stretched canvas. And we can see here"—he waved a gloved finger up and down—"how the drips flow. Some of the painting was done upright. He stopped easel work in nineteen forty-seven, after *Full Fathom Five*. For this work to be authentic, therefore, he would have deliberately stepped backward in his technique. What's more—"

Gwen paused in her note taking. "There's more?"

"This canvas is mounted on a wood backing. He never did that. Not one other time in his career."

"So, this is a fake?"

"*Oui, oui*. One of a thousand forgeries. Or . . ." Matthieu rested one gloved hand on the easel, careful not to touch the painting. "Or it is a unique find. Which would make it priceless."

"Do you already know which one?"

He grinned at her. "If I did, *chérie*, I would not be worth my fee."

13

MARCH 1956

By the end of the night, Jackson is a lamb, docile with drink. Ruth has a struggle of it, guiding him up the avenues, hauling him up the stairs, though she enjoys the body contact, the touching by necessity but also growing bold. He sings "Walking My Baby Back Home"—no, he bellows it—regardless of her shushing between laughs. On the landing before the apartment door their kisses are hot and sloppy, their hands everywhere. She leaves him swaying in the kitchen, with promises to be quick. When she returns from removing her makeup in the bathroom, he is unconscious on the bed, face down and shoes on.

Ruth turns off the lamp, surveying his body by streetlight. Thick, sturdy. With those thighs he could pull a plow. His breath is a bellows, deep and slow. She removes his shoes and socks, tilts him to slide his belt out of the loops—an ordinary deed that feels intimate. She reaches underneath, finding him as soft as an airless balloon. She wrestles off his shirt.

"That is all I am doing for you," she tells the body, which does not respond.

Ruth unzips the pink dress, letting it puddle at her feet. She unclasps her bra, tucks it in a drawer, and hangs the dress. Still in panties, she leans over him. "Beautiful man." She kisses his bald spot. "Genius man."

Ruth climbs in. A man sleeping beside her. This man. The idea weighs more than the person. She believes she may never fall asleep. Then does.

In the morning, he is a lion. Ruth is not fully awake when she feels him press against her, his arousal against her thigh. Both of them have the breath of alcohol. He climbs around to mount her.

Her body is not ready. She's so thirsty her throat hurts. But he takes some sour-mouthed saliva and lubricates himself with it. Ruth shifts, hoping her body can accommodate him, guiding him into place, and he thrusts.

It is not a kind coupling. He starts rough, and as her body becomes welcoming, he becomes rougher. She grabs his thigh, tilting her pelvis to take him deeper. Their faces are turned so they will not breathe on each other. He is raw, grunting and severe, until she feels him intensify. She pushes to remove him, but he bears down, approaching the peak of his want. So she must twist with her hips to be free of him, seizing him with both hands before he can complain and, *tug tug tug*, finishing him on her stomach.

"I've made a mess," he pants.

Ruth kisses his shoulder, pulls him belly to belly. "Love glue."

He relaxes on her, his full mass. She marvels at how well her body can bear him. She gives his short hair a deep sniff: Bay Rum aftershave, tobacco, slaked desire. On his part, anyway. If he has any interest in her pleasure, there is no evidence. Here ought to be a pinnacle moment, making love with the great artist himself. For all the tenderness afterward, there is a current of disappointed loneliness.

But something is off, and she realizes he is trembling. It grows into shaking, then sobbing outright. "What's this?" Ruth has never held a weeping man before.

He replies, guttural and dry mouthed, into her neck. She can't hear clearly.

"There, there." Ruth caresses his back. Half submerged in the harbor of her body, he lists away from her face. "My beautiful, tormented genius."

Quaking, he clenches his eyes shut. Ruth responds by humming: "Walking My Baby Back Home." It calms him, the waves pass over, he grows heavier.

"I have you," she says, tilting her hips. "Right here."

They doze a while in each other's arms, until she's aware of him awake again. She whispers, "Were you sad about your wife?"

He shakes his head. "Lee and I have our own rules."

"Then why, my dear?"

He sits up, rubs his face with both hands. "Everything." He rises from the bed, squinting out the window. For the first time she realizes how dirty it is, how grime is muting the courtyard's already lukewarm light. She'll clean that window today, the moment he leaves. He sighs heavily. "Existence. The history of every object. The weight and difficulty of everything."

He starts toward the bathroom, an awkward duckwalk revealing that he had not removed his trousers. They are cinched comically at his ankles. It strikes her as unbearably dear. She kept him company all night, gave him pleasure in the morning, yet in some ways he remains only a boy.

"I love you," she calls after him.

He stops in the doorway, facing down the hall. "Already? Is it necessary?"

She takes in his broad back and round rump. "Yes I do, and for forever."

"All right." He ponders, swallowing, and wags his head. "Then I love you too."

And continues his duckwalk away down the hall.

14

JANUARY 2007

The interoffice email came from another department, labeled URGENT–READ NOW.

Gwen ignored it. She was too busy to care, and the days were ticking by. Surrounded by stacks of legal books about provenance precedents, she had only paused to check her mail out of frustration. Every third sentence in these books, she had to look up the meaning of a Latin legal term.

"Why don't they speak in English?" She threw down her pen. "It's like the adult version of frat boys' secret handshakes."

"Exactly," Chillie answered from his cubicle. "They use Latin that only they understand. Translation is part of what you pay for at ten dollars per second."

He was moving text and spreadsheets from one window to another, deftly and swift, barely paying attention. "It's the same as tech boys and their acronyms for everything. The medical world is worse, I learned that in my awful flu last winter. And in my romantic world—"

"I don't want to know."

"For example, 'playing a man's trombone' means—"

"Stop." Gwen held up both hands. "Ever since you taught me 'tossing his salad,' I am actually antigay."

Chillie laughed. "Resistance is futile. Six more months and you'll be queer."

"Great." She pulled her hair back. "Then there will be two genders I'm not having sex with."

"By choice." Now he was typing at astonishing speed. "Are you going to the party tonight?"

She pulled a book onto her lap, two thousand pages thick in a muted purple cover: *Black's Law Dictionary*. "What party?"

"You didn't see the email? It was labeled urgent." He stopped work, sidling into her cubicle. "Your lover boy hit a home run. Or whatever they call it in cricket."

"What are you talking about?" But she'd found the email and opened it.

"Largest rare document deal in nine years," Chillie crowed. "Attaboy."

There it was: A joint sale of two letters, both written on the eve of D-Day, expected to draw two hundred thousand dollars, instead sold for one million and twenty-five thousand. That price was a signal. People prefer round numbers; if the deal is for an odd sum, it means the auctioneer left nothing on the table.

She read aloud: "The pairing, provenance, and presentation, all accomplished in record time, were the result of exceptional effort by Arthur Hughes."

"Look closely." Chillie tapped his pen on her screen. "You'll find the fingerprints of gorgeous Gwen *all over* this deal. What I want to know is whether you were actually touching him when you gave him the idea."

"You are workplace inappropriate, and I am reporting you to HR." But Gwen was flushed. Arthur had scored a hefty payday—and a department celebration.

"Tell me you're going," Chillie said. "And let's agree to drink too much."

"Hello, ladies." Richards had slunk up to their cubicles. His shirt was stiff with starch. "No one has any work to do today?"

Chillie retreated to his cubicle. Gwen closed the party email. "Interesting question from a person not at his desk."

"I took a break to share some admiration." He touched the gold collar bar under his tie. "For the fine job I hear you're doing with the Pollock painting."

"If it is a Pollock painting," Gwen replied.

"That question could have been answered by people who work here. But in your judicious experience—"

Gwen snapped her head up. "Who told you that?"

He shrugged, holding his shoulders high an extra second as though he were posing for a picture of faked indifference. "People who are upset that their credibility and experience were dismissed by a junior staffer. And a girl."

Gwen felt her temper flare. This was exactly what HR was supposed to police and correct. And what Pinkney was telling her to manage for herself.

"Let me guess," Richards continued. "You hired a girl to do the forensics."

Gwen opened her desk drawer and fished out a pair of scissors. "You know, saying something like that, with a witness, takes a lot of balls."

"Or nothing to fear."

"Either way, I have the solution right here." Gwen sprung from her seat, snapping the scissors open and closed in his face.

Richards made his exit at top speed, Chillie hooting with delight. "Girlfriend," he said, "that's what the twit has been begging for." He laughed louder.

"Will you *please* pipe down?" someone shouted from down the room. "I'm on a call, dammit."

Gwen tossed the scissors back in her drawer. "You talk a big game. But when Richards slithers in, you turn into the great typing scaredy-cat."

Chillie came into Gwen's cubicle again, planting a smooch on her forehead. "There's the woman who can do this project brilliantly."

He'd caught her by surprise. "Thank you," she said, blushing.

"And that is the woman you should bring to Arthur's party."

"If I go."

Chillie pondered a moment, then pointed. "Those scissors are actually mine."

◆ ◆ ◆

IT WAS LOUDER THAN PLACES THE FIRM TYPICALLY USED. HARD WALLS and ceiling, ringing with late '80s disco. *Celebrate good times, come on.* The party started early, when the venue was uncrowded, which made the volume more annoying. Gwen stood in the entry, considering. There were dozens of legal issues with the painting, she hadn't heard from Matthieu, and no cell in her body felt like partying.

Chillie spied her, scurried over, seized her arm. "Come, my love. Fun Gwen awaits." He dragged her through a bustle of coworkers and ordered her a drink.

"Know anyone?" Chillie yowped over the music.

Gwen shook her head. "I never have time to meet other departments."

"With certain exceptions, apparently." He nodded toward a knot of people by the tables, where one man stood a full head above the others. The bartender delivered a glass of something orange with a red floater. "Here's a little gas in your tank."

"Easy." She sniffed the drink. "I skipped lunch today."

"That means you're double thirsty. Chugalug." He clinked his glass against hers and beetled off into the crowd.

Pinkney wasn't there, of course. Richards was working the room, avoiding her too studiously for it to be accidental. If she caught him looking her way, Gwen planned to hold her fingers up like imaginary scissors and chop chop the air.

Meanwhile, she ambled, hovering outside a few conversations, but none seemed easy to join. The drink was delicious and probably dangerous. *Just this one and I'll go,* she decided, viewing the giant semi-erotic airbrush paintings on the walls as if they were actual art.

"Trying to get yourself turned on, girlfriend?" Chillie was back.

"Why is this place so junior prom?"

"Because your crush is here. Otherwise, it'd just be a chance to get drunk on the company." He swapped a new drink for the glass in her hand. "I'm here to help."

"I should go. Those law books, *amicus curiae,* will not read themselves."

"What you should do is go speak to the man like the adult you are. If there's no spark, then squiggle back to your desk and the question is answered. But if there is . . ." He flourished his eyebrows suggestively.

"You are obscene." She swatted him. "But thanks for the drink."

"Ow." Chillie rubbed his arm, feigning the pain. "I'm telling HR."

"We need to change what the letters stand for. *Human Resources* isn't racy."

"Horny racehorses?"

"Habitual regurgitators."

"Howling raconteurs." He winked and backed away.

Horrible romantics, Gwen told herself as she at last caught Arthur's eye. A giraffe among warthogs, he raised his glass. She started toward him, but a managing director arrived first, all handshakes and congratulations. She veered.

A woman was waiting in her path, saying hello over the din by tilting her chin up twice. "Baxter," she said.

"Hi. I'm Gwen."

"I know." She was shouting over the music. "And I don't like it."

Gwen drew back. "You don't like my name?"

"The deal you assembled. Arthur is on my sales team, and I know that you worked the deal to your benefit."

"First of all, you have no evidence of that because there is none. Second, what are you even talking about?"

"Taking a piece of his commission, I imagine that's what you did. Once I figure it out, I am going to hang you with it."

Gwen laughed. "Are you serious?"

"Every other major auction house has seen some scandal. I won't let you do that to Carroll and Bunzel."

Gwen bristled. "Listen, sister. What I did was help a friend with an idea. Period. That you look at collaboration and see corruption says more about—"

"I am not your sister." Baxter spun on her heel and was gone.

Gwen looked around. No one had overheard. "What the hell was that?"

She shook it off and maneuvered around to the far side of the bar.

The bartender finished a drink he was making and leaned toward her. "What'll it be?"

"What's the drink you've been making me?" she asked.

"Tequila sunrise. Like another?"

"Not quite yet."

"I'll check back." He waddled to the other side of the bar, and Gwen spotted Arthur in earnest conversation with Richards. What was that snake up to? Both men were bent forward, heads close as if they were wrestling with some profound question. They reached some conclusion, too, both nodding as if the inquiry had unearthed an important insight. Richards threw an arm over Arthur's shoulders.

Gwen felt a wave of possessiveness. Why was he making pals with her friend? Or crush. Or whatever Arthur was. And why did that anger her? Gwen waved one finger at the bartender.

"Coming right up," he said, filling a glass with ice.

By the time the drink arrived, she'd lost track of Richards and Arthur. Not at the bar, not milling around, not dancing, thank God. She would have abandoned her drink and fled. Sipping it instead, she wandered, ignoring Chillie's antics in her direction, till she found herself back at the airbrush paintings.

"Time to go home." She slugged down the rest of her drink.

"I swear to heaven I did not choose the venue."

The voice came from behind her, but she knew the source and spun toward it. The word *venue*, in his accent, was adorable, and that was something she would never tell him. "Hello, mister celebrated dealmaker."

"Hullo." Arthur made a mock shudder. "But you are the one who ought to take a bow here. All I did was obey the orders in your email."

"I hope they weren't actually orders."

"Actually and entirely, yes. For which I am grateful, nonetheless. Em. Did you know that when we underlings do a major deal, there is a commission?"

"Isn't that a nice surprise?" She tapped her glass against his.

"But look, you're empty." He gestured toward the bar, but Gwen demurred. "Please," he persisted. "It's on the company."

"I need to get back to work."

"I won't hear of it." He offered an arm and escorted her to the bar.

Gwen stayed another hour, mostly at Arthur's side, while Chillie winked from across the room and she ignored him with all her might. She found people to talk to and laugh with. The Asian Art division was full of hilarious people. Gwen suspected they were the smartest people in the firm. They were also clubby. As she approached, for example, they were assessing the mayor of New York City, and the banter was as sharp as a dissection. One woman made a wisecrack that was clearly inappropriate, dissolving their group in guffaws, but she did it in Mandarin. As Gwen stood wondering what she had missed, Arthur reappeared.

"Hello, handsome," she said, tugging on the lapel of his sports coat, then jerking her hand back down. Had anyone seen?

"May I confess something dreadful?" He was swaying a bit.

Gwen really did have to tilt her head back to converse with him. "That's the kind of confession I like best."

"I have been here before. To this place."

"And returned of your own consent? I think less of you now."

"You should." He laughed. It was easy, toothy, and she considered that he might be more drunk than her. "One of the worst blind dates in the history of our species. You know how some of them are so bad, they're funny?"

"All too well."

"This one never reached that blessed altitude. The punch line is a drooling woman poured into a taxi with my twenty-dollar bill in her hand, and my fingers crossed that she will not throw up in the poor driver's back seat. Em. Know what?"

He *was* drunk. He was carrying on. Gwen beamed at him. "Please tell me."

"That night, during the period in which I attempted to hide from her—"

Gwen laughed. "You are horrible."

"I don't deny it. But I learned a secret about this place. I'd like to show you."

"A confession that leads to a secret? Lead on, Sir Hughes."

He took her hand and rushed through the people—many were

dancing now, and regular customers had begun to arrive, adding to the crowd. The music had become more up to date too. The room rang with "Pump It."

"Do you like the Black Eyed Peas?" Gwen yelled over the speakers.

Arthur didn't turn or slow. Could he hear her? Gwen realized she was holding hands with him in front of other coworkers. She loosened her grip. Arthur only held tighter.

Beyond the bathrooms they reached a black metal stairway and dashed up to a little hidden alcove. The walls were carpeted. Lights along the railing flashed down strobe-like on the dancers. Gwen looked for Chillie—he was dancing with a guy not from the firm, but he didn't look interested. In fact, he was scouting the room.

"This is how I want to see the whole world," Gwen said. "With a higher perspective, so everyone's desires and behaviors are in full sight."

"Desires and behaviors are why I brought you here."

She turned from the railing. "What are you talking—"

His kiss interrupted her. For its suddenness, it was astonishingly soft. She was not tilting her head either; he'd bent low for her. It was warm, their faces radiant. Then he paused, drawing back to see how his initiative was received.

Gwen also collected herself to assess. Somehow her hands had gone up to hold his head and pull him closer. He was kissing her again, and now she was kissing him back. Exquisite. Had they invented it?

Meanwhile, their bodies began to get acquainted. He pressed against her, lean and muscular everywhere she touched. She found her legs on either side of his thigh, straddling it as if she intended to climb him. How had that happened?

"Oh," she said in his ear. "Oh my."

Arthur was an expert kisser, deft and quick, then close and tender. He had straightened, but to Gwen just then, tilting her head back felt like surrender. Not defeat, but letting go. His tongue darted across her upper lip, erotic in the best way. She felt like her blood was flowing at twice the normal speed.

The song changed, too loud to ignore. "Hips Don't Lie," its tempo Latin and fast. The crassness of the lyrics was like a tonic, and Gwen stopped kissing. Arthur hovered over her, smiling, but with a puzzled expression.

She was being foolish. Drunk at a work event and making out with a coworker. How did this advance a woman's career? Would it damage her reputation in the firm? How did it prove who made that painting and what it was worth?

"Wait." Gwen stepped back. "One second."

Arthur held her elbows. "You mean you haven't imagined this?"

"Nine thousand times," she said. "But I need to go."

"Oh, don't, Gwen. Please."

"You are lovely." She placed both hands on his chest. "But I am an idiot."

And she bolted—down the secret stairs, through the crowd and out to the street where, unbeknownst to her during the party, it had snowed. There were fresh inches on the trees and sidewalk and buildings, a city gone pretty. She was thirty blocks from home, had no coat, and was wearing flats. Wiping her mouth on her sleeve, Gwen began to run.

15

APRIL 1956

By spring they have a secret routine. On Mondays he takes a train from Springs on outer Long Island, to see his analyst. After, he drinks hard with a painter buddy or two, then finds his way to the Cedar Tavern to hold forth on the power of history in objects, and the inconceivable weight of that past, the sometimes unbearable burden, until closing time or a fistfight, after which he staggers across Washington Square and the West Village to Ruth. She undresses him, makes him drink water, puts him to bed. Intimacy waits till morning, gruffly silent and mercifully brief.

Sometimes he appears at the apartment earlier, before the tavern. He will be starving and wanting sex, and she learns that it is better to feed him first. If he comes to bed hungry, he'll be rough and she'll be sore.

She knows better than to call it lovemaking. This is not champagne with a Broadway actor in a suite at the Carlyle. More like rough crocheting, a hook pulling the yarn of their bodies bit by bit into a complex knot. Some days it is worse. A raw dispensing of his accumulated pain, and Ruth is the receptacle.

One day she has barely returned home from the gallery when she hears her lover's heavy tread. It is a beautiful evening in early spring. Each day the sun sets a little later. She saw daffodils on her walk home, bright and open in the little street gardens of the Village. Now she hears his footsteps climbing the stairs.

Ruth scans the apartment. Not clean, and she would rather have showered, but she opens the door, and he glowers at her from the stairs.

"Bastard is sick, and put a cancellation sign on his office door," he grouses. "He could have called and saved me a damn trip to the damn city."

Ruth pouts. "That is not a very nice thing to say to the woman who waits all week for you."

He stops, still a few steps down. "Sorry."

"It is all right."

"No." He wags his head. "I'm selfish, self-absorbed, and repressed. That's why I come every damn Monday."

"It is all all right." Ruth holds out both arms. "Come, genius lover of mine."

Jackson grouses and grumbles and climbs the last few steps. Once he is inside and she has closed the door, Ruth whispers to him. "I know how you can make it up to me."

"How's that?"

Ruth rests an arm on each of his shoulders. She can't quite attain eye contact, but it's close. "We have never made love when you were sober and fully awake."

Jackson flinches, as he did at the tavern the night they met.

She caresses his face. "It might be nicer for me."

He scans past her, eyes connecting for less than a second. "Fine," he says. "Do you have any bourbon for after?"

Ruth draws his head down between her breasts. She makes him remove her clothes, too, instead of undressing herself. The lure of his buddies will prevail later, but for now he is hers alone. They wrangle and wrestle. Ruth straddles him, guiding him into place. They latch, and for once there is no roughness. Only the crochet. And a long-desired moment when she wails as if she were grieving, her chest and face flushing red, while she surges with pleasure and does not hold back. Eventually Ruth finds herself curled around him, damp with perspiration, catching her breath.

Unlike every other time, he does not cry. So she does not have to rush to comfort him. Simply they lie close and quiet, the sun's last glow spilling in on them. A warbler of some kind perches on the fire escape, trilling for a minute.

"Best part of the day," he says.

"We are living our destiny," Ruth replies. "But will you be all right without your analyst? What can a headshrinker tell an artistic genius, anyway?"

Jackson sighs. "It's more like he helps me to tell myself. Though I do end up hearing his opinions, which are strong. More certain of himself than I will ever be."

She massages his forehead, a thumb working the place between his eyes that is nearly always creased in concentration. "Like what?"

Jackson swallows. "He's kooky, I'm warning you."

"I am dying to hear."

He rolls onto his side, head resting on his fist. "Beer is nutritious."

Ruth laughs and hooks her leg over his. "No wonder you like him."

"Alcohol reduces anxiety caused by obligations and expectations. It reduces inhibition. Alcohol allows the full person to emerge."

"Really?"

"All interpersonal relationships are harmful. They suppress inner freedom."

"He is certain about these things?"

"Ironclad. We should break all close ties. Family, friends, everyone. Liberty from repression and responsibility is the only path to genuine creativity."

"That sounds unorthodox. And maybe unkind."

Jackson nods. "Unorthodox is right. He sleeps with patients and violates other professional boundaries. He approves of us, you and me, because he considers monogamy the worst repressor. A stifler of creativity and passion."

She snickers. "Maybe I like him after all."

"The state took away his license. But he continues to practice, unrepentant."

"A man with radical ideas is bound to be treated like a criminal."

"Yes." Jackson slumps. "We live in the era of Eisenhower. Veterans trained to obey, and men in gray suits whose idea of originality is the color of the band on their hats. But ask yourself: Have you ever known complete freedom?"

"Of course. With you here, just now."

"That was pleasure, not freedom. And I mean complete." He adjusts a pillow under his head. "He asks me every week. It's a huge challenge. Sincerely, Ruth: Have you ever for one second in your life known true and complete freedom?"

She too lies back, her hands as a pillow. "Ever?"

"True and complete freedom."

Ruth searches the ceiling for an answer, a memory, perhaps. But her thinking is interrupted by a clunk against the apartment door. She knows what it is immediately, before she hears the key fumbling in the lock. Lucy is home.

She does not catch them naked. Ruth whips on Jackson's shirt, throwing the sheets over him and shutting the bedroom door behind her.

"Loosely!" Ruth cries as the front door opens.

Lucy bursts in, beaming, but halts after two steps. "What's going on here?" Her grin is as wide as her face. "Am I interrupting something? You saucy girl."

"I am so glad to see you." Ruth hugs her hard, tilting side to side. "Welcome home." She holds Lucy at arm's length. "How tan you are too. Golden woman."

"I know." Lucy giggles. "Look at this." She unbuttons her shirt, tugging the bra aside to show where white skin borders dark. "I wasted so much time down there, sleeping in the sun. It was heaven."

"Delicious," Ruth says. "Did you have legions of suitors?"

"Only one, but he was enough. A fellow from Maryland, he had racehorses. Squired me around town in first class, without mentioning he had a wife until she arrived. That was instantly the end of it, but she suspected me anyway. Purest white-hot hatred I have ever received."

"Oh, let her jump in the sea. I am so happy to see you."

Lucy peers past her. "Do we have company this afternoon, you hussy?"

Ruth takes her straight-backed pose. "I am in love. He is mad for me too."

"Who is he?" Lucy squeals. "Tell me, tell me."

"His name," he says from the bedroom doorway, bare chested in trousers, "is Jackson."

"What the holy hell?" Lucy spins, reaches to pump his hand up and down. Her shirt is still open. "I mean, excuse me. It's an honor to meet you."

"He is a genius." Ruth crowds into the narrow hallway to take his arm. "My lover is the greatest creative mind of this time."

"Nonsense," Jackson says. "He is the thirstiest mouth of this time. I'm going to get us all some drink."

"Please return right away." Ruth kisses his neck.

He tugs his shirtsleeve. "I'll be needing something back from you."

She blushes down to her roots. "Pardon me for a moment."

Before she has closed the bedroom door, Jackson and Lucy have taken each other's measure. They stand in silence. He looks at the bedroom wall, which only rises six feet, and the open air above it.

Finally, he speaks first. "Can I handle that luggage for you?"

"That would be a help."

In two steps he is beside her, his body inches away. They breathe there for a moment. He carries both suitcases into her room. When he turns, she is blocking the doorway, shirt still open. He sets the bags down. "That is interesting."

"What is, mister genius?"

"You. That's quite a tan."

She whispers. "You've no idea."

He whispers too. "I can imagine."

She nods. "I bet you can."

They are silent again, but differently. They have seen something, and it has been declared.

"Hello, everyone." Ruth floats in wearing an outfit all in pink. "Happy spring."

"Indeed," Lucy says, buttoning her shirt. "Happy, happy spring."

Jackson maneuvers to the door, pulling his shirt on. "I'll be going now."

"Darling?" Ruth taps her cheek.

"Right." He kisses where she tapped. But his eyes remain on Lucy, who is surveying everything.

The instant the door closes behind him, she seizes Ruth's hands. "Holy jumping Jackson, honey."

"I know." Ruth laughs. "I can't believe it either."

"Somehow you landed another big fish."

"Comparing Ronald with him is like measuring our brownstone against the Empire State Building," Ruth replies. "This is a great genius with a wounded soul."

Lucy leads her to the kitchen's tiny café table, where they sit knee to knee. "Tell me tell me," she clucks. "I want every dirty detail."

16

JANUARY 2007

Before she reached her desk that Sunday, Gwen knew someone had been digging through her papers. She slowed, as if the person were still there. Her handy green notebook was gone. Her books were not stacked spine on spine, as she always left them to protect their bindings.

Now they were in a mishmash, law and art books mixed. Her notebook wasn't gone but dropped on the chair. The small pottery vase her sister made in high school was on its side, its pens and pencils spilled on the desk and floor.

This snoop made no effort to conceal his visit. She knew immediately who that implicated. "You flaming asshole."

"Who are you talking dirty to this time?" Chillie came bopping in from the elevators. "Do we have a new imaginary friend?"

"Somebody messed with my desk last night. And we know who it was."

"Anyone who wastes precious weekend time on interoffice competition is nuts." Chillie went to his desk, confirming that it was as organized as he'd left it. "If that's not politically incorrect. In which case, I mean 'sanity challenged.'"

"I'm glad to see you working on a Sunday, anyway." Gwen lowered herself into her seat.

"Sorry, sweetcakes." From under his desk Chillie pulled a skateboard, stickers all over the bottom. "I'm just grabbing this. Big boarding date later."

Her shoulders dropped. "I was excited about you ruining my productivity."

"I can do that easily. Just come to brunch at my place, eleven sharp."

Gwen rolled her eyes. "You and your brunches again."

"Your nemesis meal. Why do you hate it so much?"

"I eat too much. Mimosas give me a headache. And it wastes the whole day."

"Tragic echoes of childhood trauma. Try just once. You'll sing with joy."

"Not likely." She dug through the piles of books to find one, and it was still open to the page that had stopped her. "Unless I go dressed like this."

She showed him the picture. A dark-haired woman held her arms down, a bullet bra hooked on her wrists, her breasts fully exposed, with drop cloths behind and a light overhead. The model's face was at ease, her self-possession so complete it seemed she didn't know she was being photographed.

"Maybe not a hit with HR," Chillie said, "but Arthur would approve. Is that our painter's slutty mistress?"

"Chillie." Gwen shook her head. "Neither of those words is okay anymore."

"What do you want? His 'readily available extramarital lapdog'? Besides." He wiggled his fingers at the photo. "You can't flash her softcore at me in the workplace. It's harassment, and I will report you."

"It's art." Gwen showed him the book's cover. "By a photographer named Archibald Jerome. One gallery show in his entire career, but it caused a stir. This book is that show." She flipped through the pages. "Models in stages of undress."

"Archibald Jerome is an unfortunate name."

She laughed. "Clearly his parents didn't like him."

"Does his work say anything fresh about the fashion industry, or the commodification of women's bodies?"

"Not to me." Gwen put the book aside. "In fact, this book looks guilty of commodification itself. The photos are voyeuristic. And the introduction is vague about the models' participation."

"Ick." Chillie shuddered. "Will you discuss this with Miss Soft-Core herself?"

"Can't think of a reason I should."

"The exploitation, of course. Gossip too." Chillie picked up an imaginary phone and began dialing. "Something to discuss with Mister Arthur, too, tra la la."

"You keep bringing him up."

"You both disappeared from the party at the same time."

"And left separately, which I am positive you noticed."

"Guilty." He hugged the skateboard. "But I'm making eggs Benedict. At eleven. Huge fruit salad. Come, eat till you're full."

She turned the page of a law book listlessly. "Maybe I will."

"Yes, and maybe I'll grow horns."

"You already have them, young man. But they only come out at night."

Chillie started to speak, hesitated, then spun one of the skateboard's wheels. "Why do you work so goddamn hard, honey? Give me a reason, I mean it."

"Why?" She pulled her hair back. "Because I want to get out of a lousy apartment. Because I owe too much in school loans. Because I'm good at this work and deserve to rise in the firm. Because women have to work twice as hard, or they'll get paid half as much as men. Even gay men I love like a brother."

He laughed. "I meant a real reason."

"I know I'm ambitious, Chillie. But for me, overwork is a fucking necessity."

They both observed a long silence. The building was quiet, the streets below.

"Babycakes." Chillie rested his chin on the board. "Not denying anything you said. I just wish you could have a life too. Come to brunch, I'll invite Arthur. You can eat till you're full, take him home, do the funky monkey all afternoon. After dinner, you put in a few hours of work, and everybody's happy."

"Sounds like heaven." Gwen rolled snug to her desk. "Maybe next project."

"Go get it, then, girlfriend." Chillie kissed the top of her head. "Love you too."

SHE CAME TO HER SENSES AT STRAWBERRY FIELDS. GWEN HAD WALKED TO Seventy-Second Street, circling through the neighborhood where she thought Lee Krasner lived. But Pollock's widow was not out walking her tiny dog on that gray and gusty day. Gwen had a deep case of the blues as she turned in to Central Park and the monument to John Lennon.

A detailed mosaic made a compass star on the ground, with the word *IMAGINE* in its middle. The last dirty bit of Thursday's snow hid under the metal benches. Two teen boys in preppie clothes and unlaced boots were sharing a joint. Across from them, an old man with a fedora on the ground in front of him took turns blowing on each hand, while his other held a sign: *It is cold and I am blind.*

Ouch. She wanted to tell someone about this man, this moment. But there was no one. No person she could call. Suddenly, Gwen was seized by an impulse, her surrender to the idea both instant and complete. She tossed a buck in the man's hat, ran to catch the bus downtown, and plopped herself in the front row of seats.

For once, Gwen had found a bus with good heat. Perfect for returning to the scene of the crime, the place where Neil announced his engagement. She was in Midtown when her phone rang. "Hello?"

"Henry Huling here. With the Krasner-Pollock Foundation?"

"Oh yes, hello, Henry. You're working on a Sunday?"

"So are you, I'll wager."

"I'm on a break at the moment, but yes. I think of you as being senior enough, you could relax on the weekends."

"It's arithmetic," he said. "To be at the leading edge of anything, you must start every Monday a full day ahead. After a year, you'll be fifty-two days ahead."

The bus was arriving at the Flatiron Building. Gwen hopped off, ducking close to the landmark building to avoid the rain.

"In seven years," Henry continued, "you're a full year ahead. No one will ever catch you."

"I'm not at the leading edge," Gwen confessed. "Just learning a job with all kinds of nuance."

"Then you won't be pleased to hear that we're not going to support the painting."

She stopped short on the sidewalk. "May I ask why?"

"The board has reviewed this particular work before—"

"But the tools today are better. If we could—"

"They are unnecessary, miss. The work is a flagrant fraud."

It was the *miss* that stopped her. The man was defining his territory.

"While I'm delivering bad news, let me add that Ms. Krasner has no interest in being interviewed. Her only comment is 'no comment.'"

Gwen tried to recover. "Does she understand that I'm not media?"

"She is not available to speak to anyone about anything. Not her late husband's alleged relationships, nor forged artworks, nor the pitching staff of the New York Yankees. She will not help your firm, nor that parasite trying to get rich by foisting garbage on a gullible public."

Gwen paused. Clearly Henry was enjoying himself. She gave him an opening to continue. "I understand in the past there were a few counterfeits—"

"A few?" He harrumphed. "Young lady, it was a minor industry. Sloppy imitations, wrong materials, wrong techniques. And none of Pollock's genius."

"Were those the problems with Ruth's painting?"

"In her first attempt at validation, we found no provenance. No record whatsoever of it being made. Our board gave the painting a longer look than most, because of its owner's scandalous claims. The vote was unanimous."

"I heard otherwise." The wind gusted a rinse of chilly rain in her face. Gwen crept around the building's corner. "I heard the fractal analysis people dissented."

"Not people." Henry cleared his throat. "Person. Who later retracted her findings. Which had resulted from an unproven assessment model. Good research on your part, miss, but the board's eyes knew the truth."

"Sounds like solid connoisseur work. Did anyone do forensics?"

"Do you know who the members of that review board were? There wasn't a more qualified body in arts evaluation since . . . well, ever. If they all agree that the painting is false, why incur the expense of forensics?"

"To avoid gnats like me, when the question could have been settled forever. To silence the painting's owner permanently too." Gwen let that land for a moment. "Instead, it looks like you rushed. Like you were determined to reject this painting, right from the start."

"Rushed? I'll have you know that our objectivity—" Henry caught himself.

Gwen waited, not speaking, considering how far past "no comment" he had already gone.

"It is a tragedy to art lovers, scholars, and the world," he continued in a calmer tone, "but Jackson Pollock stopped doing meaningful work years before this opportunist appeared. By that time, lamentably, he was already lost to alcohol and mental illness. If he was unable to paint under the heroic protection and tireless support of Lee Krasner, there is no way he would have been emotionally stable enough to paint for that human trifle."

That phrase—*human trifle*—was like a lawyer resting his case. But Gwen had one more idea. "Will the foundation legally surrender any claim of ownership?"

"What are you angling for now?"

"If the painting someday proves legitimate, your organization won't assert that the Pollock estate owns it. If you're so sure it's fake, there's no objection, right?"

Henry considered, then cleared his throat. "Kudos for your savvy, miss. Plus working on Sundays. I'll keep an eye on your career."

And he hung up.

"Damn." Tucking her phone away, Gwen started toward the diner. The Flatiron Building was under reconstruction again, surrounded by scaffolding so thorough, it looked like a teenager wearing the world's largest braces. She'd been inside once, as an intern, delivering contracts to a man selling a manuscript from the fifteenth century. The slowest elevators in Manhattan, and she loved it.

There was no risk of bumping into Neil now. He was as good as married, living somewhere in Westchester on the road to happily ever after. Did he still handle his coffee cup like a cowboy? *Hook your foot on his leg,* she wanted to advise his wife. *He loves it when a woman does that.*

Now the impulse she'd had at Strawberry Fields felt foolish. Like in college, when she was low, yet played sad music on the stereo. The weather that day was grim, and the wind clammy. Maybe Henry's call broke the sullen spell. Ruth was an opportunist? A human trifle? His insults made her hope Ruth's claims were true.

Gwen pulled her collar up, shuffled down the block to reach the diner, and allowed herself to stop for a good long look. Inside, it was bustling and crowded. Maybe on that sort of day, people did not want to have breakfast at home. They wanted company. A couple stood waiting for a booth. When the woman held up a newspaper article, the man put his arm around her, leaning closer to read it.

"Goddamn it," Gwen said, turning away. But she'd only had a few seconds of escorting her blues southward, when someone called out.

"Gwen! Oh, please be Gwen."

It was Arthur, running from the diner, buttoning his coat on the way.

"What are you doing here?" she said, her tone not friendly.

He drew up. "Enjoying a coincidence. That you should walk by just as I'm thinking of you."

"Aren't you supposed to be at a brunch?"

Arthur narrowed his eyes. "You're well-informed. But I wasn't in the mood."

"Then why are you here? Out of the whole city, why eat at this diner?"

"The usual reasons." He glanced back. "Em. It's good, cheap, and near to where I live."

She narrowed her eyes. "What about the coffee?"

"Oh, that." He rocked in amusement. "Moonlighting as a diner critic, are we?"

"Tell me what you honestly think of the coffee."

"Bloody awful, that's what I think. Nearly bad enough to send me back to tea." He made a mock shudder. "But have you tried their grill-top potatoes? Greasy and salty, yet somehow—"

"The best potatoes on earth," Gwen interrupted. "You'd better not disagree."

Arthur smiled, big toothed and unabashed. "I concur. On the entire planet, none better."

Gwen relaxed her shoulders. It was as though the sun had come out. "Sorry. I'm a grouch today."

"When you peered in the window, it looked like you saw a ghost."

"That's about right. I'm better now."

"Grand. Shall we stroll a bit on this . . . somewhat less than lovely afternoon? A hardy constitutional?"

"Sounds downright healthy."

"Precisely the opposite. Constitutionals bear all sorts of risk."

"Of getting hit by a bus? Or of catching pneumonia?"

"Of having conversations, Gwen. About such things as"—he lowered his voice as if in a horror movie trailer—"*our encounter at the staff party.*"

"You mean the ill-advised grope fest?" she asked.

"I don't think of it that way," Arthur replied, sobering. "Not at all."

Gwen smiled. "Actually, neither do I."

"So." He folded his hands. "Hullo."

"Oh my goodness, Arthur." She rose on tiptoe, gave him a peck on the cheek. "Hello. Now, where are we going?"

"Off to the West Side Highway. There to see the mighty Hudson River, perhaps also casting our eyes upon the far side, and the foreign lands of New Jersey."

"Perfect."

"Then Hi Ho, Silver." He offered his arm, and she took it with both hands.

For half a block they walked in silence, till Gwen broke it. "Do you want to know why I ran away Thursday night?"

"Not yet," Arthur replied. "We've barely moved an inch, and haven't window-shopped at all. Far too soon for serious conversation. Unless you feel it's urgent."

"I think I'm explaining right now anyway. Actions instead of words." She tilted her head against his upper arm. It was as firm as a door. "How are you always in such great shape?"

"Hardly. But I swim. Em. Two miles a day, typically."

She whistled. "That sounds gigantic. When you're in the water all that time, what do you think about?"

"You."

"No, I mean honestly."

"Honestly?" He faced the horizon. "You with no clothes on."

"*Ha.*" It was a bark of laughter. "I guess I asked for that. As Chillie would say, tra la la."

"You know Chilton Eddy? I'm a huge fan."

"You call him Chilton?"

"His work is lightning fast, but he never stops bantering, and never breaks a sweat. Brilliant."

"I'll be sure to tell him." Gwen squeezed his arm. "Do you also know Baxter?"

"Betsy, you mean?"

"She introduced herself to me by her last name, I guess."

"Betsy works in rare documents too. Ancient treaties are her specialty. Real team player, the firm might call it. A huge help with the D-Day letters."

Gwen looked up at him. "I wonder if we're talking about the same woman. At the party she was abrasive."

"Perhaps she was intoxicated?"

"Impossible." Gwen shook her head. "No one at that party was intoxicated."

They both laughed, then happened upon a store that sold antique lamps. They pointed and discussed which ones they could see themselves buying, and which were hideous. Gwen kept one hand tucked into his arm. Sometimes both.

"That one." He pointed at a small Ionic column with ornate porcelain cherubs flying around it. There were more cherubs on the embroidered lampshade too. "We should buy it, bring it to a high place, and fling it down upon the pavement."

She laughed. "Smash it."

"Demolish it."

"Ruin it."

He laughed too. "Annihilate it."

On they played, toward the river and the future.

AT THE HIGHWAY THERE WERE RUNNERS IN TWOS AND THREES, AS IF IMPERvious to the weather, and an expanse of slate-gray waters. Frigid air blew from the north, bearing snowflakes downriver that looked less beautiful than bleak. Gwen and Arthur stayed till she was shivering, at which he rubbed her back vigorously. She tucked in closer, under his arm, aware of its muscular strength, and they circled back toward the Flatiron. They were a few blocks away when it began to sleet, the dreck falling like icy needles.

"Let's duck in here a moment." Arthur pointed at a bodega. "Let me pick something up quickly, and I'll tell you plan B."

"Hurry back." Gwen ducked under the awning, shielded from the sleet.

In two minutes, he returned with some grocery things inside a plastic bag.

Gwen gave him a greeting hug, as if he'd been gone a day or two. "So, what's this plan B you've been talking and talking about?"

"I have been carrying on, haven't I?" He beamed. "Plan B is my apartment."

"Is it near here?"

He pointed across the street. "There. Fourth floor."

"This has all been a setup, hasn't it?" She smacked him on the chest.

"It's true. You've found me out. And I can't tell you how expensive it was to make the rain commence at exactly the right time."

"Some guys really know how to splurge on a date."

"Well." Arthur swayed beside her, a tree in the wind. "Is this a date, then?"

"Close." Gwen pulled on his jacket till he bent enough for her to whisper in his ear. "Very, very close."

He took her hand, and they ran across the street. Flights of stairs in seconds and they'd reached his door. Arthur took out his keys and spun them expertly. "Fair warning: This place has only two temperatures. Arctic and equatorial." He swung the door open, and they charged in.

"Well," Gwen announced, her breath visible, "we're not quite at the equator."

"Soon we will be," he said, adjusting the thermostat, then opening the freezer and tossing in whatever he'd bought, bag and all. Meanwhile, she took in the apartment: larger than hers, with two whole rooms, but messier, the bookshelves loaded with paperbacks to the verge of collapse.

"No looking," Arthur said from behind, covering her eyes, guiding her forward till her knees came up against something soft. She opened her eyes to see the bed, and he was pulling a quilt aside.

"Are we how it gets hot like the equator?" Gwen asked him, stepping onto the bed so that she was temporarily his height, cupping his chin, kissing his mouth.

The radiators began to clank. Arthur lifted her, swept her legs aside, and they collapsed together. He pulled the quilt over them both, and they huddled and hugged till they were no longer freezing. "You smell like summer," she told him.

Arthur winced. "I'm afraid that scent is actually chlorine from the pool where I exercise."

"It *is*." She laughed.

They began to caress, kind touches that lasted until he opened a button of her shirt, just one, and drew back. She nodded her approval, and they hurried to undress each other.

It was not easy, with damp clothes and a heavy quilt. One foot between his knees and she had shoved his open pants down and off. But hers refused to relinquish her ankles, and in the tangle, Gwen lost track of herself. They contorted, the quilt fell away, the radiators rang. By the time she was naked, Arthur had already moved between her legs, and he was busy. Swans and violins, it felt good. But she thought no, she'd be too anxious, it had been too long, could she relax enough to enjoy it? Soon, the question was answered for her, as she clenched and moaned and released. *Well done,* she thought. *Well done, team.*

But he did not stop. Wasn't he getting awfully familiar? And wasn't it fine? The heat was working now, too, steam from the radiators and her throat going dry. Suddenly, there were sunbeams, pouring through the clouds. A high note she sang, as her chest blushed crimson.

But he did not stop. She was sensitive, writhing away. The room had become a rainforest, her mouth as dry as a desert. She wanted to kiss him, to make the experience more mutual.

But he was gentle, and it was so damn good to be given to, after so very long. So sweet to be touched. Besides, the third wave was tall and frothing and suddenly shattered itself on the rocks into a hundred million droplets.

"Hey!" Gwen yelled, twisting, throwing a pillow across the room.

At last, he came up, stretching long beside her. Gwen burrowed backward into him, while Arthur draped an arm, threw a leg over. They nestled like spoons, and his feet were somewhere in the distance below. While she recovered, he kissed her ear, neck, the back of her head. How much a day could change, she thought. What day was it, anyway?

"A-plus," she told him, squirming against him. "A-plus."

"I am feeling rather smug at the moment."

"You have permission." Her voice croaked. She needed water.

"Beg pardon?"

"I know it's first time and all. But after you spoil me like that? I hereby give you permission."

"For what?"

"Whatever you want." She smiled. "Within reason, I mean."

He kissed her shoulder. "Be right back."

As he stood, Gwen rose on an elbow to take in his muscular back and lean legs. Then she lay back, hearing him pull something from the freezer, something else from a drawer. She was dazed, only half present.

As he returned, full frontal, she made no pretense of not looking. Arthur sat on the edge of the bed, taking the top off of a container. "Open wide."

"What is it?"

"Arsenic, laced with strychnine." He waved a spoon. "Trust me."

Gwen did, as he gave her a spoonful of whatever he bought at the bodega. It was breathtaking, cold and sweet. She sat up. "What miracle nectar is that?"

Arthur held up the container. Raspberry sorbet. He scraped another spoonful and fed it to her. Gwen *mmmm*ed till she'd swallowed it all. "You," he said, digging for more, "are a masterpiece."

"What are you doing?" she asked.

"You gave me permission to do whatever I want."

"And?"

"I'm taking care of you. That's what I want to do."

"Good God." She flopped back again. "This was not in my career plan," she told the ceiling. "This is not a good choice for an ambitious person to make."

He shrugged. "Yet here we are, on a miserable Sunday. Eating sorbet naked."

Gwen closed her eyes. "I am so screwed."

"Not yet, you aren't. But in a few minutes, perhaps."

She took the container and dug herself a spoonful, melting it by pressing her tongue against the roof of her mouth. He wanted to take care of her? She did not need anyone's caretaking. But his face looked as enthusiastic as a retriever waiting for her to throw the ball. And the sorbet was exactly what she'd been wanting. And such pleasure was rare. She remembered that man's sign up at Strawberry Fields. *It is cold, and I am blind.*

Gwen spooned out another scoop, a big one.

"In a few minutes, you say?" She fed the sorbet to him, put a hand on his chest, and pushed him onto his back. "How about now?"

17

APRIL 1956

Her agent's prediction turns out to be wrong. He insists the break with George will only affect Ruth for a few weeks, but she still isn't working. There's a smattering of interest when the B. Altman catalog lands in people's mailboxes. But they're necklace and earring jobs, one day and done. Not enough to live on, Ruth confides to Lucy. She spent months banking a little savings, and now she has to spend it. As if she hasn't gotten ahead, as if she isn't a rising star.

The one lucky thing is that Trevor, the gallery manager, reports that his wife had a difficult baby. *Colicky* is the word he uses, which Ruth thought only happened to horses. Fussy all day, wailing all night. At work, Trevor props his head on his hands, smoking cigarette after cigarette, so dulled by exhaustion Ruth has to empty the ashtray for him. One day he heaves a great sigh. "Take the helm, ensign."

He puts his hat on and leaves, taking his pack of smokes with him. Ruth follows his slow shuffle up the street. From one flight up, he looks like a man who is ill. When he turns the corner, she immediately flings the windows open, switches on the ceiling fans, and sets about cleaning the gallery. Brightening it. In a leap of faith in humanity and bedrock belief that no one would steal a work of art, she puts a painting on an easel outside the downstairs entry.

Turns out Ruth is right. People see the painting, climb the stairs, and that first day, two of them buy something. A new routine begins, with a different painting on the sidewalk every day. Turns out the gallery business isn't so bad, if you can tap people's curiosity and generate enough traffic. Soon, new visitors are making a purchase every day. Turns out her trust in people is justified, because each evening when Ruth trots down the stairs at closing, the painting is still there on the easel.

One afternoon, Trevor shows up in a rage. "What do you think you're doing, putting stuff out for free?"

"That is not what—"

"Wait till the artists see." He is shouting. "They'll be furious."

"But the new customers are—"

"You are going to destroy this business, Ruth. Kill it dead."

"Look for a second," she barks, waving an arm. "Just look."

Trevor scans the walls. Half of the space is empty. "All of these paintings were stolen? And you persisted with this stupid advertising gimmick?"

For the first time, Ruth goes behind the desk and sits in his chair. The overhead lights are humming. She folds her hands. "All of these were sold."

"Ruth. I'm tired, but I'm not stupid."

"Neither is Henry Paumgarten. He saw one of his paintings downstairs and came up here spitting fire. Until I showed him that it was the only work of his we have left. All the others are hanging in the homes of happy buyers."

Trevor, hands on hips, turns a slow circle. "Have you told the other painters?"

"Told and paid, boss."

That last word was a bit of exaggeration. But the man did hire her, with no experience, and he has paid her whether business was good or not.

He ambles over to the windows. "Have you kept track of your hours?"

"I have."

"And your overtime? Because the labor law says—"

"Every minute. I need your signature on a check, though. The bank will not let me pay myself."

Trevor leans his head against the window. "Tell you what, Ruthie. I love this goddamn kid, but he's killing me. Agnes has it worse, with the nursing. The doc says he'll outgrow it. I just hope that happens before my wife murders all of us."

Ruth has not moved, not even her hands. "I am sorry to hear that."

He circles the room again, arriving at his desk and gesturing so that she rolls the chair aside. "You're doing great, Ruthie. I'm just beat." He opens a drawer, finds the checkbook, and signs the top check, leaving the rest of it blank. "Figure out what I owe you, and leave me a note breaking it down so I can review it later, okay? Also, add a hundred bucks for keeping this place going."

"A bonus? Mister Trevor, that is so—"

"You earned it." He starts toward the exit. "Just take my advice."

"Yes, boss?"

He pauses at the door. "No kids. They'll kill ya."

INSTEAD, RUTH WANTS TO SEND THAT BABY ROSES. A HUNDRED DOLLARS? With one hundred unexpected dollars, she can afford to wait for the modeling work to recover. She's free to spend evenings with her roommate and Monday nights with her lover. Until one Tuesday morning, after Jackson leaves, when Lucy has something to say.

"Okay." She's sitting at the tiny kitchen table, a knee hugged to her chest. "He's definitely a first-class catch."

"I know," Ruth chimes from her seat on the floor, where she's doing the paper's crossword puzzle. "My genius."

"But how many beers did you have last night?"

Ruth looks up from the puzzle. "I am more of a cocktail girl, you know that."

"How many, would you guess?"

"Maybe one? I probably didn't finish it."

"I had three, hussy that I am." She slurps her coffee, then stares at Gwen meaningfully over the cup.

"Loosely, what are you saying?"

"You see any beers left in the icebox?"

"Should I look?"

"I'll spare you the effort. There aren't any. And he brought a case last night. So, you drank maybe two, and I had three. That means lover boy had nineteen."

"Oh, I know about that," Ruth says. "Alcohol reduces anxiety brought about by obligation and expectations. It allows a person, unrepressed, to emerge and express."

"Excuse me? Drunk means unrepressed? What kind of bullshit is that?"

"Jackson's analyst says so. The man he comes in to see every Monday. In a way, he is part of bringing us together."

"And this analyst is a genius too?"

Ruth nods. "I suppose he is, yes."

"I'd be careful around geniuses, Ruthie. They may not have both feet on the ground."

"Jackson definitely does. And you know what else? We both lost our fathers at a young age. See?"

"See what?"

"Destiny. We were fated to find and love each other."

Lucy looks away, gazing around the room. "Hey, while I was away, did you wash the windows?"

RUTH MAKES CHANGES TO THE GALLERY SCHEDULE, OPENING FOR LATER hours on Saturday, but closing on Sunday and Monday.

"I want time for love," she tells Lucy. "Mondays we sell the least, anyway."

"But Saturday nights," Lucy counters. "Don't you want to be out among people, laughing and drinking and dancing?"

"I only want to do those things with Jackson."

"Does he laugh and dance, Ruthie? Or only drink?"

Ruth smiles. "You have a bad impression. Wait till you know him better."

"He'll need to be way more fun to change my mind. And I want real fun. Like in a circus."

Ruth studies her. "Loosely, did something happen in Florida?"

"Of course not." Lucy's face darkens, though, and in a moment, she is crying. "Oh, Ruthie. I fell in love, like a stupid idiot. With that Maryland horseman."

"But that is lovely."

"His wife didn't think so." Lucy wipes her face on a dish towel. "Once she arrived, everyone shunned me. The last ten nights, I ate dinner alone."

"Oh, honey." Ruth rises to give her a hug. Lucy cries on her shoulder, but as she calms, she pulls the hug tighter. They mash against each other for a minute, not speaking. That's when they notice the noise down in the street.

"What in the world?" Ruth asks, pulling back.

A car horn, blaring and blaring. Lucy, who was still holding on with both hands, lets them fall. "Someone's mighty ticked at the traffic."

Together they go to the window in Lucy's room. Clothes on the floor, bed unmade. Below, Jackson sits in a green convertible with cream-colored seats. It's long and handsome, with smooth contours and a grinning man behind the wheel.

"Come on," he cries, honking again. "Let's go."

"Be right down." Ruth turns to Lucy with bright eyes. "Come for a joyride. It will start the fun."

"You go." Lucy steps aside. "I need to recover from my three beers."

"You sure?"

"Go have your fun, Ruthie. I'll be fine."

"You are the sweetest." Ruth dashes into her room, returning in a red spring coat and a kerchief for her hair. Sunglasses too. Lucy is still at the window.

"You sure?" Ruth says. "Last chance."

Lucy kisses her, a quick brush on the mouth. "You go."

Seconds later, she sees Ruth open the car door and fling herself onto Jackson, who gives her a passionate kiss. Lucy smiles at that. He throws an arm around her shoulder, and they roar away from the curb. Lucy stays at the window, appreciating the quiet street, till two boys come running out with a ball of tape and a stick. Wiping her cheeks, she heads for the bath.

WITHIN DAYS, RUTH BEGINS TO CALL THIS TIME "THE HONEYMOON." THE Cedar Tavern becomes a noisy memory. Jackson has traded two paintings with a woman in exchange for her Oldsmobile and a little cash.

"She got the better deal," he admits, "but I got what I wanted."

He'd banged up his last car, and Lee refused to let him buy another. She manages their money, he explains. "It's better that way. She's more responsible."

"And you have more freedom," Ruth chimes in.

"Exactly." The car trade was an expression of liberty, he continues. His analyst agreed, and Lee can't do anything about it.

Jackson starts coming to the city twice a week. Every minute he isn't in analysis, or rampaging with his artist buddies, he spends with Ruth. Every jaunt starts with him pointing the car north, uptown. Streetlights feel like spotlights, as they pass one by one. Music wafts out of the nightclubs and fills the lobby bars of fancy hotels. The Lenox, the Waldorf. The Plaza, which is insanely overpriced, but has a swanky atmosphere that lives up to the quip of the day: a place to see, be seen, or make a scene. One evening, they witness a couple doing just that, tearing into each other in the lobby in full voice till she slaps him full-handed. It is a louder and harder blow than anyone expects, silencing all conversation. In seconds, men from hotel security usher the woman from the building, while the man goes to the front desk, rubbing his jaw as he settles the bill.

The Oldsmobile has seats as comfy as any couch, an engine full of throaty growls, and a tailwind spiraling in their wake as they cruise the avenues. The city seems to lie at their feet. Instead of circling blocks to park, they always find a place right outside wherever they are going. People wave at the car. Friends call out from the sidewalks. Children pantomime how truck drivers pull the lever to sound their horns, and Ruth reaches over and honks in reply.

"Someone will see us and tell your wife," Ruth says. "But I do not care. I love you with every cell in my body. Every breath, every bone."

Not replying, he smokes his cigarette.

"You don't love me at all," she continues. "You barely like me. You just use me. I am your sex doll. Your plaything."

"Shush." Jackson kisses the top of her head. "You know how I feel."

Ruth wriggles closer, smiling.

"You beautiful sex doll," he says.

She swats him, bright, then curls back in against him, snug.

As spring warms, they drive through neighborhoods from Harlem to Battery Park, from the Meatpacking District to Alphabet City. Manhattan is on display, as if for them alone. The bums congregate on Bowery Street, which makes Ruth self-conscious about riding in such a fancy car. And without even a roof for protection. In that part of town, she asks Jackson to take a different route.

"No one can touch us," he replies. "No one dares."

One evening he parks outside the Carlyle, which makes Ruth's heart skip a beat. But then she laughs. "Please? It will be so fancy and fun."

Ronald the blue-eyed actor is not there. Ruth sits at the little table, musing over her cocktail. Upstairs in that very building, she took the first steps on her path to this moment. What a thrill it would be for her former lover to meet her new love—the former man a one-night stand, the other to last forever.

Then on they go again, weaving through traffic, speeding through yellow lights, creeping through reds if the traffic permits.

"We are not breaking the rules," she tells Jackson. "The rules have gone away."

He is drinking harder now, so she tries ways to keep him coherent. The first idea, one night, is to match him drink for drink.

The fun that night grows wilder, louder, more swirling. And then darker, careening around the city as the hours pass, the streetlights blurring, the bars loud with jazz and later quiet with blues or nothing, as one fellow partier after another crawls off to bed. As the sun comes up, Ruth finds herself with Jackson in Madison Square Park. The first businessmen are marching off to work, with their hats and briefcases, in their gray suits and black shoes.

"Look at the model citizens," Jackson drawls. "One Eisenhower after another."

Ruth is unable to see them. She is busy vomiting over the back of the bench.

"IT'S NOT PRETTY," JACKSON SAYS THE NEXT MONDAY. "I DON'T WANT you sloppy."

"I feel the same way." Ruth bats her eyes. "When you go blotto."

But he keeps drinking hard. So, the second idea is to keep him aroused. Too turned on to get drunk. On stairs she always goes up first, knowing right where he is looking, so she wags. Exaggerating until he laughs and she has him again.

In every restaurant, too, every nightclub, every café corner, she rubs him under the table. It makes him shift and squirm, while she blinks with innocent eyes. In the car, when he throws an arm over her shoulder, she pulls his hand down to her breast. He caresses and cups her all the way down Park Avenue.

One time, his attention wanders, and he sways into a curb. In seconds, a city cop is behind them, flashing the lights on his motorcycle.

"Are we in trouble?" Ruth slides over to her side of the seat.

"Let me do the talking."

"Everything all right here?" The cop shines a flashlight at Jackson. "I saw the way you swerved."

"Sorry, officer." Jackson tips his head toward Ruth. "I was distracted."

The cop trains the beam of his flashlight. Ruth sits with hair askew, dress slid up above her knees. The top button is open, too, revealing the lace of her bra. Switching off the light, he leans on the driver's door. "Looks wild."

"She's very affectionate," Jackson replies.

"Save it till you get home." He tugs his belt. "Don't want anybody run over."

He climbs on his motorcycle and zooms away up the avenue. Jackson has a long exhale.

"Guess what I did after he turned the flashlight off."

He turns. "What?"

Into his hand she stuffs her underwear.

FLIRTATION LIKE THAT HAS CONSEQUENCES, RUTH LEARNS. IN THE MORNing, she is sore. The drink dulls his senses, he starts too fast, he never considers her pleasure. But when she shares details with Lucy, soreness is a boast. And when she climbs into bed that night, his scent in the sheets, she feels almost a pride of ownership.

Increasingly, Ruth and Jackson have the apartment to themselves. Lucy has reconnected with the man who made her howl that night. She's doing just enough musical work to pay the rent. Otherwise, she wants to be available for him.

For Ruth, Lucy's absence means freedom, whether in ardent lovemaking or, on the nights Jackson drinks too much, sparing her roommate his chainsaw snore.

In early morning, she loves following the trail of discarded clothes from the bed to the front door, gathering them. If she hears Lucy on the stairs, she pulls on Jackson's shirt, buttons one button, and waits. Lucy creeps in, but finding Ruth awake, they greet each other with naughty grins.

In May, Lucy says it's love. "I think he might be the one."

"I am so happy for you, Loosely." Ruth hugs her extra-fiercely. "Have you informed him that I will be living with you wherever you go?"

"Oh, sister." They both tear up a little.

The next Monday, Jackson does not show. No call, no message. Ruth paces the small apartment. She has put on a new dress, white with a plunging neckline, a red belt to emphasize her hourglass figure.

"You look like the perfect female confection," Lucy pronounces. "All sugar."

They do the crossword puzzle together, till her beau honks down in the street. Lucy touches her forehead to Ruth's. "Put the dress away for tonight, sister."

"A car accident, do you think? Some illness?"

She squeezes Ruth's arm. "Worrying won't help either of you."

"If he is hurt, no one knows to call me. Our love lives inside a little closed box."

"You can fix that together, after you find out what held him up tonight."

Ruth stares down at the puzzle in her lap. "If your sweetheart proposes, I will be alone in this city."

"Not for one minute," Lucy replies. "I promise."

The suitor honks again, longer.

"Sorry." Lucy picks up her pocketbook. "We have tickets to a show."

Ruth rubs her hand. "Have a wonderful time."

"Love you."

"I love you too," Ruth replies, and they hug before Lucy flies down the stairs.

THE NEXT DAY, IN THE AFTERNOON, JACKSON ENTERS THE GALLERY. IT'S A first. Despite the customers present, she leaps into his arms, kissing all over his face.

"Easy now," he whispers. "Easy."

"I was so worried." But she notices that he did not hug her back. Ruth retreats a step. The customers are staring.

"Let me introduce you," she tells them, "to the great Jackson Pollock."

Wide-eyed, they murmur their hellos. But he glares. "I am not a pet."

"Of course not." She addresses the customers. "I thought you would be interested in the level of artists we serve."

But they are not fooled. Instead of oohing and aahing, or shaking his hand, they say nice to meet you and move for the stairs. Ruth cannot wait for them to go.

"My love, are you all right? I was so worried yesterday."

"I had a problem with the car."

"Are you hurt anywhere?" She runs her eyes up and down his body.

"I was distracted again."

"Without me to distract you? Why, sweetheart—"

"Let me talk a second, okay?"

Ruth calms long enough to take in his expression. It is not his usual Monday brightening. She does not recognize it at all. She retreats to the desk. "Please."

"I am fine, and the car will be fine. It was no big scrape."

She nods. "I am glad."

"It happened during an argument." He swallows. "With Lee."

Jackson never says her name. Ruth feels a weight of dread on her chest.

"She said my 'little spring romance' with you is killing her. She's been hearing about it since the very start. She cannot abide it any longer. She says you and I must part." He glances at her and then away. "You go, Lee said, or she does."

Ruth waits, making sure he's finished. "This is great news," she says. "Now you can make a clean break. We can take the greatest love there ever was and move it upward and outward."

"The thing is."

Ruth observes as he wanders the room, glancing at the walls, dismissing each painting with a cutting glance. He arrives at the windows, where Trevor does his thinking, where Ruth studies the street during slow hours.

"Lee," Jackson continues, "makes my life happen. She manages the money, she helps control my drinking so I can work. She buys the food and cooks it."

"I am an excellent cook. I have never had one chance to cook for you."

His whole forehead is wrinkled with concern. "It's not the cooking."

Ruth's shoulders drop. "My love, what are you saying?"

"Lee is my wife. We have been married eleven years. You know how I feel the weight of history in everything."

"Hold on." She crosses the room to stand near him. "What about freedom? What about rejecting all forms of repression?"

"A lot of words. Good ones, but I don't work in words. I work in images."

"Then how about the image of us flying fifty feet off the ground since the first minute in that Cedar Tavern booth? Can you paint how we are destined to become the greatest love affair of all time?"

He turns, his face contorted. "I can't paint at all. Not anything."

"Oh, Jackson." She caresses his shoulder. "Jackson, Jackson, Jackson."

He leans his head against hers. But turned, her forehead against his temple. This is often a way they rest after lovemaking, which they both recognize.

"What are you imagining?" Ruth whispers. "That we would end? That you would stay out there on Long Island?"

"It feels as far as the moon," he allows. "But it's also away from my drinking buddies. My bad influences."

"We are never going to end, Jackson. You know that. We have a shared fate."

"Maybe I should be dead."

She pulls back, gripping his arms. "Do not say that. Do not ever say that."

"Everybody dies sometime."

"Not you. Never you."

He makes a sour face. "I hate to tell you—"

"It is not your paintings that will make you immortal, either. It is our love. Our destiny will make you immortal."

He lifts his head slowly, as if it is heavy. He scans her face, as if to memorize it.

"There you are." Ruth smiles. "Come to the apartment with me. I will close early, and we will make love all afternoon. We will heal your heart."

Jackson replies by staggering away from her. The gallery suddenly seems to Ruth like a huge room. An entire theater, framed by art and too-bright lights. "Thank you for every second, Ruth," he chokes out. "Thank . . ."

Jackson bolts, thundering down the stairs. The street door slams. Like a judge's gavel, she thinks. The court rules this or that, down comes his wooden hammer, and things will never be as they were.

"But," she tells the room. "But . . ."

Ruth sits in the middle of the floor, the gravity of what is happening gradually reaching her, and begins keening. It grows, till she is heaving with sobs. The room echoes with her grief. Eventually, when the wave of sorrow has passed, and she has floated into deep quiet, two customers poke their heads into the gallery.

"Closed," she croaks. "Closed for the day."

At some point—an hour later? two?—she rises, switches off the overheads, and stumbles down the stairs to retrieve the day's artwork display.

The easel is empty. Someone stole the painting.

18

JANUARY 2007

Their delight went on all night. Arthur's body, his manners, his strength, created a kind of gallantry. When eventually they were starving, he pulled on clothes and went out for Chinese. But he undressed the moment he returned. They ate in bed, feeding each other with chopsticks, kissing between bites, and decided they smelled awful. They showered together, which embarked them on another session. Both of them, damp haired, fell asleep with the lights on.

Gwen had a vague memory of him reaching over to switch off the bedside lamp. He snuggled close, one long arm around her, and again they slept. In the morning, Gwen woke and saw her hair in the bathroom mirror.

"I look like a kidnapping victim." She wet her hair, combing it with her fingers.

"Have you Stockholm syndrome, then? Do you sympathize with the enemy?"

She gave him a long kiss. "If that's what it's called, I want to Stockholm with you again soon."

"Now, please." He began kissing her breasts.

She felt her body respond but squirmed off. "Next time, please. I have to go."

He lifted a pillow away to see the bedside clock. "We're not due at work for hours."

"Maybe you're not." She put on her bra. "I'm already behind schedule."

Arthur sat back. "Are you ditching me?"

Gwen knelt at the foot of the bed, searching. "What are you talking about?"

"What happened last night was not ordinary. Nor was it all libido."

"Where did you toss my underwear?" He pointed at a bookshelf, and she saw where he meant. "I feel that way too. Obviously."

"Make it more obvious," Arthur said. "Be late for work with me."

"One more gander for the fans at home," she said, flashing her behind before pulling up her underwear and jeans. "I can't. Not during this project."

"Okay, then." He fell back on the bed. "All right."

Gwen paused, one boot on. "Are you mad at me?"

"A better word might be besotted."

She donned the second boot and stood. "What does that mean?"

"I'll send you the definition later."

She kissed him softly, lingering, then pulled away. "Till the next time we Stockholm."

FOUR DAYS LATER, HARRIETTE THE HAWK GLANCED UP FROM HER SCREEN, then did a double take. Gwen stood before her, sleeves rolled up, a folio of papers in her arms. "You're up early."

Gwen blew an errant hair from her face. "Is he back from his trip?"

"For all of . . ." Harriette checked her watch. "Nine minutes."

"I've needed to speak to him since Monday. Now would be good."

Harriette hesitated. "I'll ask. But you might sit a minute to cool off. You look like a freight train that lost its brakes."

"I do?" She stomped one foot. "Perfect."

Harriette started to speak, then caught herself and rose from behind the desk. "I'm going to walk slowly. Giving you time to consider what will work for getting what you want. Sometimes it's vinegar. But in Pinkney's office, sugar is often more persuasive."

Gwen lowered her gaze. "Thank you."

Harriette gave her a long look. "All right. Walking slowly now." But she was back in seconds. "He'll see you, but he has a call in five."

"Thank you." Gwen nodded. "I'm going to start easy, at least."

"Hello, hello," Pinkney cried as she entered his office. "I've barely taken my coat off, and here you are."

"You asked me to keep you current, sir."

"Sure did." He slapped his hands on the desk. "What's the news? We all set?"

"A two-part update, sir. Both items are quick."

He fanned his hands at her. "Go, go."

"The foundation has rejected all overtures to approve the painting."

"So, it's ours to sell, if we choose?"

"They also rejected the idea of waiving any future claim of ownership."

Pinkney rapped his knuckles on the desk. "Bunch of weenies."

"The second thing. Richards has been going through my desk. Some of the material is confidential, or under nondisclosure agreements. It's an invasion of my privacy, and a potential lawsuit for the firm if he acts on anything he has read."

"I told you already." Pinkney began stirring through the stack of papers in front of him, opening a folder. "It's time for you to toughen up."

"You did. But with Richards, I'm already tough. It's someone else I need to be tough with."

"I don't follow."

"You. This is your job." She walked up to his desk, putting one finger on it. "It's your responsibility to run a business that obeys the law."

"I ought to fire you right now for insubordination."

"Please do." Gwen straightened. "Except you'll miss the deadline for this painting, so you lose the deal of the year. And you'll be writing a fat settlement check when I sue this place for sexual harassment and wrongful termination."

He sat back, unruffled, hands clasped behind his head. "Is that so?"

"I'll also contact every business reporter in America to tell my side of the story, while the firm's lawyer firmly instructs you not to tell yours. Every decent arts magazine, too, so your cred is shot. I will not stop till I bring this place to its knees, while banking enough of your money that I never have to work again, and I'll do it for sport. Is that tough enough for you?"

Her hands trembling, she hid them behind the folio. Pinkney's face had gone blank. *Don't speak,* Gwen told herself. *Don't say a word.*

He smiled, wide and warm. "Damn," he said. "I had no idea."

Not one word.

"Keep it up like this," he continued, "next year you're a managing director."

"And the year after, I'll have your job?"

"Let's not push it, shall we? The point is, you have a point. Harriette," he called through the open door.

She charged into the room, beaming and bright. Gwen knew instantly that she had eavesdropped. "Sir?"

"Richards in my office before close of business today. Ignore his schedule."

"Yes sir." She gave Gwen eye contact on her way past. A slice of a fraction of a second, but Gwen knew she had a new ally.

"Thank you, sir," Gwen said. "May I get back to work now?"

"I wish you would." He chuckled. "And leave me the hell alone."

GWEN PACKED HER USUAL GEAR—LAPTOP, GREEN NOTEBOOK—THEN considered one more thing. She took Archibald Jerome's book of model photos too. It might backfire. But maybe it would surprise Ruth and trigger some frankness. How does an older woman feel about her naked younger body? Would her answer tell Gwen enough to give the painting a yea or nay?

"What the hell." She tucked the book into her backpack.

There was a wait for the elevator, and when it finally arrived and the doors opened, Arthur was standing inside, alone.

"Oh, hello," Gwen said. "Hi."

"Good morning, Diner Potato-Quality Expert."

They regarded each other, his hand keeping the doors open while she balked.

"I had thought." Arthur cleared his throat. "I might have heard from you. Em. It being four days since Sunday afternoon. And what with my call, voicemail, two emails, and a text defining the word *besotted.*"

"I'm completely tied up with this Pollock project."

"So I gather. And it takes hours to respond to a text."

His expression was not angry, though. Gwen thought he looked more puzzled than anything else. "Guilty as charged."

"I actually deluded myself into thinking I was going to take care of you."

"I don't need taking care of."

"Of course you don't. Though it wouldn't hurt you any."

The elevator started beeping, warning that its doors were about to close. Arthur hesitated, then moved out onto the fine arts floor. He was tall, he was always tall, and Gwen retreated. She had no reply to what he'd said.

"My guess"—he clasped his hands together—"if I may put it into words, since you seem reluctant to do so, em, is that you feel an office romance might interfere with your ambitions. Sunday was nice enough, but an actual relationship would demand time and require a sense of impunity about whether or not the bosses care."

"Look." Gwen shifted her backpack to the other shoulder. "I'm really committed to this project. It's definitely an opportunity to leap to the next level."

He nodded. "Sensible, if disappointing."

"You seem like a great guy . . ."

"I *am* a great guy. Awkwardly tall and formal, but otherwise polite and funny, and generous in bed. Not to mention my excellent taste in sorbet."

"I've really been meaning to—"

"Ah ah ah." He shook his head and wagged a finger at the same tempo. "The interval for expressing sexual thanks elapsed three days ago." Arthur stepped forward. "I remain grateful for the time we had. As for the future—"

The other elevator's doors opened, and Chillie came bopping out with headphones on. "Ho *ho*." He put on the brakes, his grin full of gloating. Carefully he tugged the headphones away, music coming from them thinly till he stopped the iPod. "If it isn't the D-Day letters team. Scheming out the newest conspiracy?"

Arthur bowed in his direction. "Good morning, Chilton."

"Sir Arthur the Twenty-Third." Chillie gave an exaggerated bow. "An honor, as always."

"I'm late," Gwen said, stepping into the elevator.

Chillie turned stiffly. "Have you ever, once in your life, been early?"

"Wait," Arthur said. "Please."

She stopped, her turn to hold the automatic doors back, and for the first time that morning, their eyes met. Gwen's shoulders slumped.

Arthur leaned closer, his head inside the elevator, near enough for a kiss. "My apologies," he said, "for being such a headlong fool."

"No." Gwen looked at him steadily. It took all her strength not to caress his face. "You are a lovely human being."

The warning beeper sounded again. Arthur withdrew, and the doors whisked closed. The corridor was silent.

Arthur straightened, turning to Chillie. "Well, Chilton?"

"Well." Chillie shuffled his feet. "At least you're lovely. Tra la la."

Meanwhile, Gwen gently banged her forehead against the doors all the way down—until the elevator stopped on a lower floor to let in four people from the Asian Arts division. They were laughing and speaking in rapid Mandarin.

AS THEY ENTERED WASHINGTON SQUARE PARK, RUTH TOOK GWEN'S ARM like an old friend. A skateboarder weaved through the walkways.

"I am relieved that Sunday's dreary weather burned off," Ruth said. "I bury myself under blankets on days like that. Did you manage to keep warm?"

Gwen winced. Arthur. "I did. On a bus from the Upper West Side."

"I have not been there in ages. Did you go to the Museum of Natural History?"

"Instead of chatting about my weekend"—Gwen patted her arm—"we need to discuss the painting."

Ruth made a face. "Must we?"

"I've made progress on the legal things. I thought you'd like to know."

"Good of you to do this work, Miss Gwen. Lawyers always overwhelm me. Though I think you could spend more time smelling the roses."

"Excuse me?"

"The pianist back there." Ruth pointed over her shoulder. "He was excellent."

"I didn't notice." Gwen turned. Somehow a man had wheeled a piano into one of the open spaces in the park. A few notes floated vaguely across the air to them.

"You also missed the little girl dancing to his music. One of the more beautiful things I have ever seen. I may remember it for the rest of my life."

They reached the park's center, benches around a fountain. Ruth veered toward the monument, a tall white arch like a doorway into the rest of Manhattan.

"Sorry I missed it," Gwen replied, her tone a bit testy. "But you're expecting a taxi driver to notice roadside flowers while he's busy fighting traffic." She shook her arm free. "My meter is running right now, in fact. You set the deadline—"

"I have my reasons, desperate reasons—"

"Which I respect," Gwen interrupted. "But for something of significant potential value, there's work to be done. I expect a forensic report any minute. We've incurred substantial legal costs. And I still don't know when Pollock made this painting, and how you came into possession of it."

Ruth came to a stop. Investigating her left glove, then her right, she puttered to a bench and sat. Gwen eyed her, not moving. Ruth patted the bench beside her.

Gwen beseeched the sky, then marched over and lowered herself onto the bench.

"Miss Gwen, when you are doing business with someone, what is the most important ingredient?"

She sighed. "That they can afford the thing they want to buy. Or that the thing they want to sell is authentic."

"Both of your definitions touch on what I believe the answer is: Can this person be trusted? You must know without error."

"You've been ripped off repeatedly over the years. I've read that in my research."

"True," Ruth said. "But I knew those people were not on my side and chose to do business with them anyway. Either way, I will not proceed until I know."

"What does this have to do with the painting?"

"I do not know whether you are on my side or not."

Gwen looked across the wintry park, taking that in. "I feel the same way."

"Then the most important thing is not when or how Jackson made my painting. It is how you and I can resolve the unknown about trust."

"If my exertions haven't convinced you . . ." Gwen rubbed her hands up and down her thighs. Her pants were thin for January. "Then what do you suggest?"

"We each share something vulnerable. Something unexpected."

On the far side of the fountain, two men were playing speed chess. Gwen could hear the clack of their pieces landing on the board.

"All right." Gwen opened her backpack and pulled out the book of photographs. "I consider this an unexpected—"

"You are playing with fire, young lady."

"So, you know about this?"

"Know about it?" Ruth scowled. "The filthy creep completely exploited us."

"But he must have had your permission."

"I was livid." Ruth pushed the book away. "We all were. I had already been in the news too much, due to my love affair with Jackson. That snake A.J. deserved execution with a garden hoe."

"Did you take legal action?"

"He had tricked us into signing contracts that made the images his property." Suddenly Ruth cackled. "By then, it was twenty years later. The nineteen seventies. My feminist sisters raised a ruckus. Protests at the opening, all over the news. I spoke at a huge rally right here in this park. The gallery dropped him, the publisher withdrew the book. A victory for solidarity among women."

"It was an accident that I found the book at all." Gwen went to pack it away.

"One second, please." Ruth held out her hands.

"Really?" Gwen said.

Ruth took the book, opening it on her lap at random. "Oh my. Oh my."

She traced a finger down the page she'd opened to. "Sheila. She had perfect lips." Ruth turned the page. "There's Quinn. She married young but lost him in Korea." Another page. "Tori. Well, actually Victoria. Such a beauty, eyes like a doe." Yet another. "Oh, Rosemary, with her sharp jawline. Sons! She had so many. I saw her a few years ago, outside Radio City Music Hall, in a herd of grandchildren. And her jaw? Almost eighty, and still none of this." Ruth poked loose tissue under her chin.

"Meanwhile, on page one hundred and nine." Ruth flipped to her younger self. "This girl. Twenty-eight years old. Three months till she meets the love of her life."

She turned the book so Gwen could see better.

"You are very attractive," Gwen allowed. "It's a flattering image."

"He took it without me knowing. Candid. Authentic. The lighting makes my girls look enormous." Her expression grew wistful. "But look at that smooth skin."

"Do you still feel exploited now?"

"Mixed feelings, actually. A.J. was a creepy little rat." Ruth laughed. "Yet this picture won me attention. I befriended Andy Warhol. Mapplethorpe asked me to pose for him—clothed, which is ironic, given his later work."

"In the Mapplethorpe photo, you're wearing a necklace with a crucifix. Aren't you Jewish?"

Ruth looked up from the book. "Someone has been doing her homework. I believe details like that explain why he photographed me before Blondie or Sigourney Weaver. Even before Susan Sarandon, who was so sensual, naked with a baby in her arms, and a shawl draped to protect her modesty. Do you know the picture I mean?"

"At the firm, photography is a separate department from fine art."

"We all have deficiencies." Ruth tapped the page. "This is good for me to see."

"Why is that?"

"You are too young." Ruth waved a hand up and down at Gwen. "You have no inkling of the future, no grief for a body that will not last. What your current body makes possible for you. What power there is, purely in your physical self."

"If I have any power at all, it comes from sources other than my body."

"So you think," Ruth said. "No need for me to persuade you. Time will do that job, and without mercy."

"Maybe women's power is different today than it was in nineteen fifty-six."

Ruth chuckled. "You should ask someone you trust to photograph you naked. Before gravity discovers you."

Gwen squirmed. "I don't think so."

"One day you will be glad to have those photos." She eased the book closed. "To admire the shape you once had. The skin. The comfort of memory."

Two moms passed pushing strollers. One was staring at her phone.

"I dislike these new devices," Ruth said. "They make people too self-involved."

"I have one," Gwen countered. "It's great for work productivity."

"Not for me." Ruth handed the book over and worked herself to standing. "Never ever. But now I will show you the Cedar Tavern."

She waddled off while Gwen sat stunned. She had assumed the place was long gone. By the time she'd put the book away, Ruth was beneath the arch of the monument. She was in her elevated pose, Gwen thought: straight spine, shoulders back, chin lifted. Ruth had stood that way in her apartment, on the day they met.

"For an age I could not come here," she called back. "The pain was too great."

"The pain of?"

"His departure from me." Ruth waited till Gwen caught up, then continued. "His choice to stay with Lee. His decision to end our love-filled Mondays."

They reached the edge of the park and continued. "Was Lucy any help?"

"She was infatuated with that expert lover, without considering how he learned his skills." Ruth wrung her hands. "I was in a desert. My beloved was gone."

She closed her eyes. Gwen stood beside her, waiting.

"This is the place," Ruth said. "Where we met. Where the Cedar Tavern sold cheap beer and cleaned up broken glasses. Where the greatest minds of an era came to celebrate and argue and fall in love." Eyes still closed, she gestured left. "Right here."

Gwen looked around. There was no pub. "Where?"

"Painters and poets," Ruth continued, "drunkards and novelists. Booths, tables, a long bar. Eventually they kicked Jackson out for life. He had thrown a chair at someone."

"I don't understand," Gwen said. "Where are you talking about?"

At last Ruth opened her eyes. "Here." She waved at the nearest building.

"Where the drugstore is?"

"Yes, and the entry there, where it says 'upstairs apartments.'" Ruth wobbled. "How the mighty are fallen. Once more, memory is a comfort against loss and disregard."

"It's hard to imagine," Gwen said, "all of that creative genius in the same space that now sells aspirin and antacids."

"The banal is always oppressive. I went to the tavern one time during our separation." Ruth faced the drugstore. "Dressed in white, an angel. They fell quiet when I appeared, every last drunken one of them. Talk about power. They knew all about Jackson and me, our destiny thwarted, and it rendered the most talkative people on earth completely mute."

Gwen observed how Ruth did not see the garish store, its posters hawking medicine for colds. Memory was more vivid. "Did you like having that power?"

"I loved it," she replied. "And now I have it again."

19

MAY 1956

Everything about Lucy collapses into love. While Ruth suffers and pouts, a hollow aching in her chest, her roommate buys new clothes, splashes herself with Eau de l'Amour. All for a man who, instead of his actual name, she calls Romeo. On some dates, she does not return till broad day. Romeo has reserved them a hotel room for privacy and abandon. Even after regular dates, Lucy comes humming up the stairs, her lipstick and mascara smeared—to find Ruth in the kitchen, her eyes puffy, the café table littered with tissues.

"Oh, my sweetheart." Lucy swoops down with hugs, kisses on her arms and neck. "My poor bird."

"Do you ever feel dirty, carrying on with a man like this?"

Lucy pulls back. "Are you serious?"

"Do you wonder how he became so skilled at pleasing women? Expertise like his is a warning sign."

Lucy bursts out laughing. She tumbles back against the wall, shaking her head. "Sister, the man is setting me on fire. I am learning that my body is made for pleasure. I don't care who taught him. I'm grateful for what he knows."

"But to stay so many times overnight, when you are not wearing a ring—"

"Now, Ruthie." Lucy puts her fists on her hips. "Romeo loves me, or he would not spoil me this way. Besides, you of all people should sympathize with passion inspired by love."

"Maybe so with Romeo. But you have done plenty of other things—"

"You," Lucy interrupts, "with your married men, are in no place to lecture me. And by the way?" Her voice softens. "I am truly sorry that you lost him."

Ruth digs a fingernail into the table. "Thank you for saying that."

"I know you loved him, and still do." Lucy straightens from the wall. "But that does not make my love for Romeo into a bad thing."

Ruth makes eye contact. "Thank you for tolerating a grouchy roommate."

"I have to get to bed. The sinfonietta is taping a radio show at noon." Lucy takes Ruth's face in both hands. "I love you. So there."

She kisses Ruth's mouth, a waft of booze, and staggers off, pausing in the bedroom doorway to wag her behind. Ruth's laugh rings off the little walls.

EVERY DAY ON HER WAY TO THE GALLERY, RUTH PASSES A CONSTRUCTION site. The men are swarthy and strong, and now that the weather is warmer, they sometimes work with their shirts off. They've dug a shoulder-deep hole in the pavement, to repair something underground. Often when she passes, their bodies are glistening. If she can do it without being caught, she ogles. More often, when she approaches, they take a break to lean on their shovels and whistle. One will utter, "Hubba, hubba," and the rest laugh in agreement. Ruth hurries along, uncertain, but hoping their attention is harmless. It's spring in New York, 1956, and broad daylight. Everyone behaves themselves. One morning, a younger workman yells something vulgar. An older man gives him a swat.

"Sorry," he calls, "our infant here lacks couth."

Ruth spins at the waist and blows him a kiss. With that, the ground rules are established. Ruth says good morning, boys. The men compliment what she's wearing, or needle one of them about it being his birthday and maybe he'll get a birthday smooch. Lucy later teases

Ruth, asking if she has invited any of them up to the gallery, to lock the door and break the rules. Ruth protests; it's Jackson or no one. Still, even Trevor, the gallery manager, knows about "her boys."

"They beg me to introduce them to you," he says. "I explain that if I did it for one of them, all the others would want the same treatment. There aren't enough days in the week for you to date them all."

"I like it just the way it is." In fact, Jackson's departure has given Ruth a kind of numbness. The workmen add color to her days, a little boost. She feels grateful for the gallery job, too, because calls with her modeling agent remain brutally short.

"I don't mind you checking," Craig says, "but you know I'll call you the second I find work for you."

"Do you still represent me? Or did you drop me, like George at B. Altman?"

"You know, toots, I also was counting on that gig to lead to bigger things." His sigh is heavy over the phone. "Remember, I only get paid if you do. The sooner you're back in front of a camera, the better for us both."

Demoted to toots. It stings. Still, Ruth tells Lucy she feels no guilt about the one-night stand with Ronald. She does feel regret, though, that it stalled her career.

Meanwhile, Ruth handles everything about the gallery. She could run the place by herself, and considers approaching the owners to say so. It would mean a huge raise in pay, and in her standing in the art world. But she does not want to wrong the man who gave her a start in New York City.

As Jackson's absence continues, life inflicts constant reminders: the scent of paint in the gallery on warm days, an Oldsmobile convertible passing by, an overheard conversation about the Plaza hotel.

One morning on her way to work, it's drizzling out and the men in the ditch seem not to notice her. She reaches the gallery feeling a little wan.

"Jackson," she says, digging out her keys. "Jackson, Jackson, Jackson."

But the key turns too easily, and in a panic, Ruth realizes the door is unlocked. She dashes up the stairs. How could she have made such a huge mistake?

On the landing, she hesitates. Maybe someone picked the lock. Maybe the gallery is being robbed right now. Does she hear someone inside?

And then a voice: "Ruth? That you?"

Trevor. She rushes in, breathless. "You gave me such a scare."

"You don't have to be afraid." He's sitting at the desk, accounting books open. "Especially with the job you've done here." He taps the page. "Down to the penny."

Ruth gulps, a calming hand on her chest. "Business has been good."

"Too bad about that stolen painting. But I see we covered it." He flips through the pages. "Lucky break that the artist was Brian Nalen. The man doesn't care where a painting goes. As long as he gets the bread."

Ruth surveys the gallery. As usual, morning sun streams in the front windows. But something has changed, and her heart is still beating from the panic on the stairs. She walks to the little closet, hanging her light spring jacket. "So." She sets her purse on the inside shelf. "What brings you in early today?"

"This is my regular time," Trevor replies. "Or it was, and now is again. Today I'm going back to normal."

She emerges from the closet. "The little one is sleeping better?"

"I don't know how couples ever have a second kid. The first one is a warning."

"Same with labor."

"You're right." Trevor turns page after page, not reading. "So right."

Ruth approaches the desk. She keeps her voice flat, so as not to seem antagonistic. "Please tell me why you are being strange."

Trevor jolts, looking up at her. "I am?"

She starts to cross her arms, then decides to let them hang. "You are."

He lowers his head again.

"Are you all right? Your wife? Not the baby, please."

"Two things are happening." He keeps his head down. "They both affect you."

Ruth looks around. "Sometimes this place ought to have two chairs."

Trevor rises, steps around her. "Have a seat."

"This is definitely not going to be good." Ruth perches on the chair's front edge. "Please tell me both things right away."

"First thing." He stands squarely. "The owners love the recent profits lately. They want it to continue, and to grow. More advertising, more frequent openings."

"Great idea." Ruth feels relief, until Trevor starts pacing.

"Second thing." Now he's addressing the floor, his shoes, anything but her. "They see you as a liability."

"A what?"

"You're known now, but not as a seller of fine art. As part of a scandal."

"But I am the reason profits are up. I've been working here alone."

"To them this business is all about reputation."

Ruth stamps her foot. "I refuse to be ashamed of things I have done for the sake of love."

"I respect your feelings," Trevor says. "And I bet you've become pals with some of the city's better artists."

"I have made some friends."

"To me, that leads eventually to showing bigger names here. But today? The owners believe your presence reduces foot traffic. Ordinary people want something pretty, or maybe interesting, to hang above the couch. They don't want scandal." Trevor stops pacing. "There's a reason our customers aren't down in the Village, joining in the decadence. They want to own the paintings that emerge from the chaos, as long as they can stay uptown and not soil themselves by touching the unwashed."

Ruth jumps to her feet. "The *what?*"

"Pretty much exactly how the owners put it."

It is her turn to pace. "I have never met these people, but right now—"

"Believe me," Trevor interrupts. He holds both hands out, as if to keep a dog from jumping on him. "I almost resigned on the spot. But I'm responsible for three people now. The baby changes everything."

Her eyes well up. "Where do I go now? What will I do?"

He returns to the desk for a piece of paper. "You call these people."

He hands it to her. "A summer job, while I find something here in the city for you. I'll be glad to tell people how much you improved this place. I may be tired, but I'm not blind."

"Outside of the city? I am not interested."

"Yes you are." Trevor sits in the chair again. "It's on Long Island."

Ruth goes still. "Tell me more."

"An art school. Mornings for kids, evenings for adults. After work, you can take classes too."

"Where on Long Island?"

"It's called the Sag Harbor Summer Institute. Pretty posh for a day camp, right?"

"Where is Sag Harbor?"

"That's the thing, Ruthie. The whole thing, it's next door to Springs."

Her hands begin to tremble. "It is not."

"Yup." He nods. "One town away from your love."

AFTER HER CALL LANDS THE JOB OFFER, TREVOR GIVES HER THE DAY OFF. Ruth thanks him for a start in New York City she'll never forget. A hug, a kiss on the cheek.

On the way home, she passes her boys. They're sitting listlessly, legs dangling into the hole, or they're standing in it, leaning on their shovels. It's hard labor, and often they slow by midafternoon. But Ruth is floating on air. She stops at their hole and spins in front of them. It rouses the men, murmurs of approval. She keeps spinning till the wind lifts her skirt, and she knows they're getting a gander at her legs. Once more around and they erupt in whistles and applause. She bows, blowing them kisses, and skips away down the sidewalk, dizzy like she's twelve years old.

That night the downstairs door slams, but there is no singing in the stairwell. More like a soldier's trudge up the stairs. It being the season's first warm night, Ruth has left the apartment door open for ventilation. It's late, but she hasn't gone to bed. The idea of moving to Sag Harbor is too exciting. The idea of Jackson. Seeing him, smelling him, touching him.

The footsteps do not sound familiar. Ruth pulls on a robe and hurries to lock the door. Lucy is standing there, pale, looking like she's about to be sick.

"Loosely." Ruth guides her in. "What happened? Are you all right?"

"I am not all right." Her answer sounds mechanical, dull and metallic.

"Did he hurt you?"

Lucy nods her head against Ruth's chest.

"Where?" Ruth looks her over. "I will brain that guy. Where did he hurt you?"

Lucy winces. "Everywhere."

Now things register: a torn dress, no shoes, Lucy's hair a bird's nest. Ruth leads her to the café table. "What happened?"

"I made a mistake." Lucy sits numbly, drops her hands into her lap. "The worst, worst mistake."

"Honey, you are an expert at men. I cannot imagine you did anything so—"

"I proposed to him." She picks at a thread hanging from the tear in her dress. "Nice cocktails, nice dinner, nice hotel room. Sweet, dirty loving, the way he likes. After, calm and cozy, I ask Romeo please to marry me."

"That sounds sweet. Why was it so terrible?"

"Because he's married. I knew that he *had* been, he told me the divorce was final in Nevada three years ago. Not quite. He has a wife and two kids, all waiting on him to come back someday. He sends them half his pay."

"Then why does he get a hotel, when you could be at his place?"

Lucy shrugs. "Maybe he's got a gal there too."

Ruth balls both hands into fists. "He made the mistakes, not you."

"That's what I thought." Lucy surveys her bare feet, dirty from walking the sidewalks home. "I got up, put my clothes on. But you know I am not the silent suffering type. The whole time, I was frying him. Cheater this, liar that. Wouldn't change anything, it felt damn good."

Ruth bobs her head along with the story. "You tell him, honey."

"I did, until Romeo heard enough. He grabs me by the hair, shaking me like a toy in a dog's mouth. That's when he did a number on my side." She starts to cry. "I proposed to the son of a bitch, and look what he did."

Lifting the tear in her dress, she reveals bruises all along her ribs.

"Oh my God. Do you want me to make an ice pack?"

Lucy shakes her head and lets the torn fabric fall. "While he was doing it, he called me the most awful names."

"Hitting you is not terrible enough? The bastard."

"A lot of swearing, till he saw my dress was ruined. That quieted him. He sat down on the bed, and said I was just a fun girl. I would never be someone's true love. Never be a wife. Never a mom. Just a fun girl, till I'm old and flabby. Then I'll be a nothing. Work all my life, and be a total nothing."

"That stinking dog. Invite him for one more romp. I will cut his manhood off."

Lucy raises her face. "I'm not just a fun girl, am I?"

"Not a chance." Ruth takes her hands. "You are clever and beautiful and talented. Plenty of guys will fall over backward to have one minute with you."

"You're a good sister," Lucy whispers, slumping as if defeated. Then she rouses, reaching to see what papers are on the little table. "A map?" She picks it up. "A map of Long Island?"

"A little dreaming," Ruth replies.

Lucy lowers the map. "You never dream without a plan."

"This is not a good time, Loosely. We can discuss it tomorrow."

"It already is tomorrow. It's three hours past tomorrow. What are you up to?"

"I am not 'up to' anything." Ruth tries to tug the map back, but Lucy holds on.

"This is completely the wrong time," Lucy says, "for you to bullshit me in any way. I know you, and how you are always imagining and making a plan."

Ruth releases the map. "You want me to tell you right after your boyfriend beat you up?"

"It is always the right time to tell the truth."

Ruth holds out one hand. "May I please have my map?"

Lucy drops it on the table. Ruth picks it up and begins trying to fold it. "I have been offered a new job."

"Ruthie, that's got to be a relief. Which is it, modeling or a gallery?"

"Neither one." The map is complicated, and she has to start over. "I will be a teacher at the Sag Harbor Summer Institute. Tiny salary, room and board, plus painting lessons. At last, my artistic life can begin."

"Sag Harbor? Isn't that—"

"Close to Springs?" Ruth cannot help beaming. "It is. For June, July, and August, I will be living one town away from my love."

"A guy is trying to be faithful, and you're moving into temptation range?"

"I consider it love-rekindling range."

Lucy's eyes go wide. "Or furious-wife range."

Ruth draws back, regal and unruffled. "You do not understand the power of destiny. How fearless it can make you."

"Fearless or foolish."

Ruth, annoyed by the map, drops it. "I must follow my heart. And fate."

"Sometimes I think I pay closer attention to you than you do." Lucy sits forward in her chair. "A married man broke up with you, to save his marriage, get sober, and work again. The message is clear. I'm sorry, Ruthie, but it's done."

"You are mistaken." She rests her hands in her lap. "I cannot think of one reason why I should not go."

"You can't?" Lucy protests. "Because that's *all* I can think of." She counts down on her fingers. "Eighteen-year age difference. His drinking. His wife. Other directions your life could take, if you let go of this foolishness."

"Foolishness?" Ruth laughs. "Wait one minute."

She hurries off to her room, returning moments later with a copy of *Life* magazine. The August 1949 issue, which she opens and places in Lucy's lap. It's a full spread, pictures of wild paintings, with the artist scowling in the center, and a wide headline: "Jackson Pollock: Is he the greatest living painter in the United States?"

"Where'd you find this?" Lucy asks.

"Trevor got it for me, from a collector."

Lucy closes the magazine carefully. "You really think seven-year-old publicity justifies what you're going to do?"

"Why do you refuse to see?" Ruth snatches the magazine back. "Fate brought us together. And this job came so easily, that's fate giving us a second chance." Ruth sits as straight and proud as a bowsprit. "I will help him continue to make great art. I am his lifeline."

"So, now we part?" Lucy stands from her little chair. "The sisters chapter ends?"

"This is my one and only—"

"I snap my fingers and find another roommate, and she and I go to the Cedar Tavern to laugh at the drunks. Something like that?"

Ruth shakes her head. "That is not what I—"

"Something *exactly* like that?"

Ruth makes no reply, only adjusts the magazine's place on the table just so.

"Go." Lucy shifts the dress to cover her ribs. "Miss Fucking Fate. Go ahead and go."

Hugging herself, she shuffles down the hall, into her bedroom in the dark.

10

JANUARY 2007

The day's first call came early. Gwen had to dig through piles on her desk to find the phone. The caller was speaking before the receiver reached Gwen's ear.

". . . opened my eyes and realized that you are only in this for yourself, and for your company, and I do not feel right about it. Capitalism is fundamentally corrupt. I flinch at the idea of turning a man's genius—"

"Ruth?" Gwen interrupted.

"—into a commodity. It might as well be a pack of gum."

"May I—"

"Yes, an expensive pack of gum. How could I put a price on an utterly unique object, made in an act of brilliance so singular it is sacred. And love—"

"Ruth, if I could—"

"It came from *love*. We had just made love when he made it. We were deeply in love, we were destined to love each other to the end, to the tragic end."

Gwen decided it would be easier to let her finish. She wound the phone wire around her finger and waited.

"I appreciate the time you have invested, but I cannot sell this painting. I want it back from the vault, and back in my living room where it belongs." Ruth began to lose steam. "Where it has always belonged . . ."

Gwen filled the pause: "I'm listening."

"I am allowed to change my mind." Ruth heaved a great sigh. "I had to turn my home halfway upside down to find your business card. It was right here, of course, on the front hall table." She snuffled. "How did I get so old?"

Gwen pictured her, dabbing at her nose with a pink handkerchief. Perhaps there were flowers, embroidered along one edge. "I'm sorry."

"What do you have to be sorry about?" Her tone was accusatory. "What have you done that was wrong?"

"I didn't mean it as an apology." Gwen moved some books, clearing space in case she needed to write anything down. "I meant it as an expression of sympathy."

"Oh, Jackson, Jackson, Jackson."

"Yes," Gwen said, though she had no idea what she was agreeing with. "If you choose not to sell this painting, I completely understand."

"You do?"

"This is the most meaningful object you possess."

"You are not going to try to talk me out of it? Will that get you in hot water?"

"I will get fired." Gwen gazed across the rows of cubicles. It struck her: This was probably true. Maybe she could call that woman from Christie's, the tall one at the Pollock auction, and ask for a job. She glanced to her side. Chillie was eavesdropping shamelessly. He shook both fists in the air.

"The question is," Gwen said, "the real question is . . ." She held still for a moment. Chillie gave her both thumbs up.

"Is what?"

"Do you want the world to know? Do you want the world to learn that at the end of his life, Jackson Pollock had a great love?" Gwen winced but continued. "A woman to whom he gave the greatest gift, his final work? And after fifty years, that woman is willing to share the gift, to suffer the loss of it, in order to inspire all of humanity with the power of love to transcend, to transcend . . ."

Chillie was nodding enthusiastically, but Gwen turned away.

"Well," Gwen continued, her speech slower, "to transcend every damn dull and ordinary thing in this world. And to instruct us that deeper art, and bigger discoveries, all emerge from the primary source, which is love."

There was a long silence on the phone. Gwen felt a little embarrassed.

"Miss Gwen," Ruth replied. "You know just where to hit me."

"Don't we have the same goal? To prove that this painting is Jackson's artistic last will and testament? And that his lover, in an act of stunning generosity, has decided that this rare work should be enjoyed by all humanity?"

"Now you are laying it on too thick."

"Then let's be practical," Gwen said. "We don't have to reach the whole planet. The planet is worked up about, I don't know, the Super Bowl. We want one person who understands. And by beggaring himself, he hopes to enrich the world."

"Amazing. Simply amazing."

"What's that?"

"You changed my mind back. I was up all night, until I made my decision once and for all. Yet you turned me around in about three minutes."

"See? We're on the same side. Any minute now, I hope to receive forensic news. And we can schedule an auction."

Wishful thinking, Gwen knew. Matthieu would take whatever time he needed. She'd learned on earlier cases that if she called before he'd finished, he would throw a tantrum.

"When that happens," Gwen continued, "I will scour the earth to find that one person who appreciates this work of art and the love story behind it."

"Since the awful, terrible night my Jackson left this earth," Ruth replied, "I have never felt more understood." And she hung up.

Gwen let out a long, slow exhale, held the receiver against her forehead for a moment, then lowered it into the cradle.

Chillie gave a slow, steady clap. "Amazing. Academy Award quality."

"That was no act, Chillie."

He consulted a little notepad on his desk. "It will inspire us to transcend? The primary source, which is love? I will scour the earth? By beggaring himself he hopes to enrich the world?" He tossed the pad aside. "Girlfriend, that was a masterpiece."

"Okay, maybe I turned on the violins," Gwen conceded. "But it's also true."

"What is this Ruth hag like, anyway?"

"Not a hag," she replied. "She's sort of camp, you know? The former star of a drag revue, but without the irony."

"You should get her drunk. I bet she'd be hilarious."

"I did, and she was. The first time we met."

"You wild child," Chillie exclaimed. "*Wiiiild chiiiild.*"

"Can you people *please* shut up?" someone yelled from down the row.

Gwen's phone pinged, and she checked the time. "Which reminds me. Coffee fix. You want anything?"

"Since when do you schedule coffee? I thought you drank it round the clock."

"I haven't been sleeping. I'm trying to drink less, and stop earlier."

"I know just the thing to help you sleep." He winked. "Works every time."

She laughed. "Don't you start."

"You don't know what I was going to suggest."

Gwen grabbed a warm coat. "Yes I do."

IN THE ATRIUM DOWNSTAIRS, GWEN HAD ONLY SLIPPED ONE ARM INTO A coat sleeve when someone called her name. She pivoted, and there was Pinkney, accompanied by three men in dark suits, waving his black-gloved hands to make her stop. "There she is. My favorite speed demon."

Gwen slid the coat off. "Hello, sir. What do you mean?"

"I heard how you sped up the guy in documents and he landed a great deal."

Gwen was taken aback. "Who told you that?"

"He did. I stopped by his desk to congratulate him. A pat on the back can go a long way. But he gave all the credit to you."

"I don't know about that."

"Don't deflect me." While one of his assistants pressed the elevator button, Pinkney pulled off a glove one finger at a time. "It's not every day a junior guy breaks a million. I like seeing your influence, your leadership."

"Thank you, sir."

An elevator opened, and Baxter came hurrying out, charging through the suit men. When she saw Gwen she put on her brakes, then noticed Pinkney, and with a grunt of greeting she brushed by. Had Gwen not moved, they would have collided.

"What's that all about?" Pinkney asked.

Gwen watched Baxter spin out the revolving door. "I have no idea."

"I'm sure you do, and if it's none of my business, that's fine." He removed his other glove. "You're aware that our deadline is approaching."

"I think about nothing else."

"Every day that passes since Sotheby's mega-deal, our painting loses heat."

"I am genuinely hustling on this, sir."

"Yet you found time to help a guy in rare documents. I'm not upset about it. But your priorities—"

"Pardon, sir, but sometimes I'm waiting on others. Forensics, for example."

"Oh?" Pinkney pulled up. "What's the situation there?"

"I expect an update later today." Gwen cringed inside. Now she had lied twice about Matthieu. "Meanwhile, I've secured the legal scene. The last guy who might have challenged us, because he challenged ownership of every Pollock painting, died nine years ago. The instant we know the painting is authentic, we can go to auction."

Pinkney grinned. "Most people in the firm don't interrupt me, you know."

"I apologize, sir. I didn't want you to get exercised, when the process is on schedule. Monday is our deadline, and I won't need one extra minute." As she spoke, she felt a hollowness in her stomach. So much work to do, and dwindling time to do it. "You'll have all the information you'll need to make a sound decision."

"We're in a gray area here, but I feel compelled to say one more thing."

"Do I need to take notes?"

"No, just listen. It's fine for you to help a guy, if you have the time. But be smart. You're here to grow professionally. That's why I gave you this damn painting job. Believe me, you want to avoid distractions—professional or otherwise."

He emphasized the last word, and Gwen clenched in her chest. Who knew what gossip Richards or Baxter had told him.

"I assure you, sir," she said, her breath shallow though she tried to sound firm. "I am wise to the *otherwise*."

Pinkney's face lit up. "I knew it. And you know." He leaned closer. "We joked about it a few weeks ago. But I am actually beginning to trust you. Aside from Harriette and my wife, I don't trust anyone."

"Well." Gwen fiddled with a button on her coat. "Thank you, sir."

An elevator pinged, the doors opened, and his men boarded. Pinkney started in that direction but paused. "In fact." He flapped his gloves at her. "In fact, when it comes to this painting, I've decided it should be your call."

"Excuse me, sir?"

"You know the details. You've managed this case at an expert level. Instead of advising me on Monday, you'll be the one to decide if we go to auction."

"I thought you wanted unbiased work on this deal. I'm commissioned."

The elevator started its departure pinging, but Pinkney showed no concern. One of the suits held the door. "That was before I trusted you."

"It's a huge responsibility, sir. To the seller, to the firm, to the art world if the painting is legitimate." Gwen's mouth went dry. "Huge."

Pinkney stepped onto the elevator. "Yes," he called as the doors were closing. "It sure as hell is."

BAXTER BARGED OUT OF THE COFFEE SHOP, BUT AGAIN GWEN DODGED her. The woman charged up the sidewalk, her thick heels clacking like horseshoes in a barn. Gwen wondered what the hostility was about. Either way, she had no time for it. The morning was cold, the shop's windows had fogged, she could not see in. But she wanted coffee.

Of course he was there, taller than everyone, tilting while he waited, this way and that like a bowling pin. He was two ahead of her in line. If Gwen's insides had been jostled by Pinkney, now they were tumbling like a clothes dryer. Yet when Arthur turned around, his face lit up.

"Well, hullo, lovely one." Reaching toward her, he checked himself, and his arm floated down. "What a welcome surprise."

Gwen ducked her head. "Is it welcome, though?"

"Yes." He pointed at the counter. "Buy your poison, and I'll walk you back."

He was sporting a green tie with little blue paisleys. It made his gray vest look sharp. It was all Gwen could do not to grab him. "That would be perfect."

Outside the cold was biting, even with the wind at their backs. "Nice tie."

"Do you like it?" Arthur pressed the fabric flat. "A gift to myself, when the commission showed up in my paycheck."

"Thank you for putting in a good word with Pinkney."

He drew up as if she'd pulled the reins. "That reached you already? We spoke not two hours ago."

"I ran into him. First thing he said was about your deal."

Arthur fiddled with the cup's lid. "Thank you for urging me to do it fast."

Gwen had questions: What was he working on now, how did he feel about her, would he like a kiss? Instead, she said, "You're welcome," and they fell into an awkward silence, marching diligently back to work.

When they reached the revolving doors, Arthur put a hand on her lower back. "I've missed you, Gwen."

It wasn't electricity she felt, not with her heavy coat on. But connection, yes. She looked at his face, the crease of concern between his light eyebrows. "Arthur. I've missed you too."

"It's too cold to stand out here."

Gwen gave the door a shove and went ahead. When they reached the elevators, she pressed 22, the top floor.

"We're off to the Land of Strange Spectacles?" Arthur said, chuckling.

Floor 22 was occupied by an edgy architectural firm. The joke, started by the Asian Arts division, was that everyone who worked there wore odd glasses.

"Higher than that," Gwen replied. The instant the doors closed, she was on him. Kissing his face, neck, his palm as he reached to caress her cheek.

Arthur started to speak, but she smothered him with kisses, pressing him against the wall. As the elevator pinged with each passing floor, he responded more, till they were both grabbing and groping. She had forgotten how strong he was, how firm. She gripped his pants pockets and ground her pelvis against him. He cupped her bottom in both hands. She slid a hand inside his gray vest, which turned out to be lined with satin. He breathed in her ear, and it gave her goose bumps. She held his stomach with her hand like a claw. Familiar and new at the same time, they clung till the door opened, then pulled back from each other.

A man was waiting. He wore black-framed glasses. The lenses were triangles.

"Hello," Gwen chirped, straightening her dress.

"Pressed the wrong floor again," Arthur explained.

The architect assessed them, then boarded, thumbing L. "Not a problem."

"I keep making that mistake." Gwen chuckled, pressing her floor too. "Maybe I need glasses."

Arthur snorted, while the perplexed architect focused his attention on the elevator door.

Making a mistake. The phrase echoed in her head as they descended. Pinkney had explicitly told her to keep everything professional. Yet the feel of his stomach, of her hand inside the vest, was so powerful as she stood beside him. And she had already run hot and cold with him once.

The doors opened. "See you soon?" He was grinning like a jack-o'-lantern

"I don't know." Gwen stepped off. "I have that Pollock painting deadline."

Instantly his face looked wounded, the joy snuffed out. "You don't know?"

And the doors drew closed.

WHEN GWEN RETURNED TO HER DESK, SHE FELT AS OFF-KILTER AS HER dress, which had twisted in the elevator. Before she could visit the restroom to catch her breath and pull the dress right, Chillie finished a call and gave her a slow look. He started to say something but rolled his chair back instead. "Hello."

"How's your day going?" she asked, certain he had noticed, and deciding to pretend nothing was wrong.

"Uneventful." He collected himself. "Before I forget, I wanted to invite you. Sunday, I'm having another brunch."

"Thank you, but that's my last day to work on this project."

"Perfect," he exclaimed. "Celebration time."

She pushed books aside on her desk. "I'll be working till the last second."

"I have an odd number of RSVPs. I need you to even up the fun."

"Did you not hear what I said?"

"Heard it and dismissed it." Chillie shook his head. "You believe that working extra hours on a weekend is going to make you certain about a thing that is clearly not certain. I am offering you a situation that involves breaking bread with Arthur, who I invited, and who said yes."

"Now I'm definitely not coming. Work and pleasure don't mix."

"Don't mix?" Chillie spun his chair. "If work has no pleasure, kill me now."

She wanted to fix her dress, but not in front of him. "Pinkney has all but ordered me—"

"Ignore him, Gwen. You work in separate departments, everyone knows you have a spark—"

"They do?"

He rolled his eyes at her. "You left a company party at virtually the same time."

"That was complete coincidence."

"Darling, you fled in the snow. And he left two minutes later. What else could people think?" Chillie calmed himself. "Gwen. We used to rule this city on weekends. You know that taking a Sunday to enjoy life will not destroy your career. It might even help your thinking."

"Oh, Chillie." She sighed. "I wish."

"Not hard enough."

Gwen's phone rang. She seized the receiver like it was a lifesaver. "Hello?"

"*Bonjour, chérie.*"

"Matthieu." Gwen collapsed into her seat. "Exactly who I hoped it would be."

Chillie rose and ambled away, muttering, "Saved by the goddamn bell."

"*Merci, merci.*" Matthieu laughed. "Life is beautiful. My love is due any minute, though. May we abstain from niceties today, therefore, and talk about the painting directly, please?"

"God yes." Gwen opened her green notebook. "What have you found?"

"*Bouillabaisse.* A soupy mix of plus and minus."

She drew a line down the center of the page. "It's not definitive?"

"It is . . . ambiguous."

"You've had all this time, though."

"Being wrong takes seconds. Being right requires much longer."

"All right." Gwen nodded heavily. "Please explain how it is ambiguous."

"If this painting was made by the artist we have in mind, it is a strange work. Not impossible, but strange."

"What do you mean?"

"The first test is at the connoisseur level. How does it look? This painting has been assessed before, as you probably know, with disputed results. But does it show the quality of craft and control we expect from a formidable artist? Yes. The background resembles granite, its shape is a plausible gesture. The use of white as a kind of reverse shadow, this is very interesting. And the red, *mon Dieu*. Wonderfully impressionistic. Does it portray a human form, its arms embracing the blackness? Or is it a star, spitting fire?"

"What's your conclusion?

"So far? If it is not the painter we think, it is a respectably good forgery."

Gwen started writing on the left side of the line. "Keep going."

Her cell phone pinged. Gwen knew how important this conversation was, but she could not help turning it over.

Call me.

It was Arthur. She felt her pulse rise. **Can't. On a call.**

"The second test is pigments," Matthieu continued. "Are they from the right time? For the artist in mind, the answer is yes. All of the colors were manufactured between nineteen forty-seven and fifty-six."

Gwen continued taking notes. She was the one who would make the decision. The responsibility lay not with Pinkney, but with her. "What else?"

Ping. **You smell magnificent.**

She knew how long that took him to write on his flip phone, where the letter *Y* meant typing the number 9 three times. She started to reply, but Matthieu was forging ahead.

"Yet the pigments complicate matters. All of the colors come straight from the hardware store. No linseed, no blending. This is not like the artist we have in mind, who always mixes or thins colors, to create unique hues of his making. These pigments, you might see on house exteriors, or on the walls of living rooms."

On the right side of the line, Gwen wrote *pigment* and underlined it.

"The third test is materials, which we discussed. Canvas stretched, and on a board. This is not the method of the artist we are thinking of, the master of canvas on the floor."

Gwen kept writing. "That's a big negative, right?"

The phone pinged again. She turned it face down.

"Yes, and so is the fourth test. The artist we have in mind works in giant gestures. *Mural* from nineteen forty-three spans twenty feet. The work you brought here? Sixty-one centimeters by fifty-one. Or, for Americans like your beautiful self, twenty-four inches by twenty."

"Tiny, in other words?"

Matthieu snorted. "A Michelin-starred chef makes a snack."

Ping. She tried to ignore it.

"Why would he paint such a thing? Could it have been a study? A plan for a larger version?"

"*Non*. Unlike nearly every other painter, including expressionists, the artist we suspect made this painting does no advance work. No drawings to guide him, no plans. He paints directly from his mind."

Gwen shifted in her seat. The dress was still pulled wrong. She knew when Chillie returned, he would mention it.

Ping. With an exhale of annoyance, she flipped the phone. Three messages.

When you kissed me, it was too good to believe.

Your bum deserves worship. Or spanking. Both.

When you clawed my stomach, I nearly lifted your dress to your ears.

Gwen snatched up her phone. **When you breathed in my ear I melted. Now leave me alone for this call.**

"Are you there?"

"Yes, sorry." She adjusted her notebook. "Just digesting everything." She sat straighter. "Why would he make a small painting?"

Gwen could hear Matthieu tapping something while he considered his reply. A pencil on the table? She pictured him in his workplace, surrounded by microscopes and books, with the painting on an easel to one side and the French flag flying above it.

"I try to keep noise out of the vault," he said. "Yet I hear things."

"And?"

"Perhaps he made something in order to please a lover."

"Oh." Gwen swallowed hard. "How would that happen?"

"Imagine he wanted to make something quickly. So, he chose an unfinished work he'd kept for some reason. So, it's sized to fit comfortably in an apartment. So, he used ordinary colors, because it was not going to a gallery or collector. Strictly a private gift, never to be seen by the public."

Her phone pinged. She opened her desk drawer and tossed it in. "You can tell all of that?"

"Not without ambiguity. But there are signs that he was being casual. The image is off balance, for example. The artist we're thinking of has an unerring sense of the full canvas. On this work, the red extends to the edge of one side yet stops inches from the edge on the other."

"Isn't asymmetry his style?"

"For a time. By the nineteen fifties he had moved far past that idea. What do you know about the making of this work?"

"Nothing." Gwen scribbled in her notebook, tangled lines like a ball of string. "I've spent many hours interviewing the owner and haven't extracted one word about how and when it was made."

"Evasion always makes me skeptical."

"Me too. And decision day is Monday. How will we sort it out in four days?"

Matthieu chuckled. "Hope for lightning to strike?"

"If that were going to happen, it would have struck fifty years ago."

"I have one other suspicion to share, but it is not about the painting."

"Really?" Gwen drew a box around her notes. "What's that?"

"Who is Lee Pinkney?"

Her hand went still. "Excuse me?"

"Lee Pinkney from your firm called me this morning."

Gwen's spine turned to steel. "There is no such person. The last name is the name of our CEO, and the first name—"

"Is the name of the artist's wife, I know. This false Lee told me that you have a terrible flu. With the deadline approaching, she was calling on your behalf. Do I know for certain whether the painting is by Jackson Pollock?"

"Oh my God." Gwen's hand came to her mouth. "What did you tell her?"

"*Chérie*." Matthieu's voice was musical. "You know I love you. Not one word."

Gwen relaxed one degree. "You are a saint."

"I would never tell anyone. My understanding is with you, my contract is with you. I cannot confirm that I have any painting at all."

"Matthieu, you are my hero."

"Saint, hero, it never stops." They both laughed. "However, my lover Jeanne would be happy to instruct you to the contrary. This false Lee said she was a colleague of yours. But she is not your friend."

"No," Gwen said. "And I know who it is."

"I am not finished with this painting." His voice turned stern. "To sell it in good faith, you need certainty. I will dig deeper and— Oh, hello, *mon amour* Jeanne. *Quoi? Ah oui, je suis désolé*—"

He hung up without saying goodbye. Gwen was already in motion, using the stairway instead of waiting for the elevator, yanking her dress straight on the run.

THE WOMAN WAS PRACTICALLY WAITING FOR HER: SLEEVES ROLLED UP, office chairs barricaded on either side of the desk. She was on the phone but not speaking.

"Hang up," Gwen said.

Baxter's eyebrows rose, but she continued listening.

"Hang up now," Gwen said.

Baxter turned sideways, as if to ignore her. Gwen responded by reaching over and hanging up for her.

Baxter stood, hackles raised. "Who the hell do you think—"

"The most important thing going on in this firm right now is my project. And this morning you tried to steal it. Or sabotage it, I can't tell which."

Baxter sighed. "I'm concerned about the firm's reputation. Your inexperience makes you a hazard."

"You don't even deny it. And you know this painting could be the transaction of the year."

"Spoken like a true Pollock woman."

"What are you talking about?"

"You're a cliché, you and your kind. You love *Starry Night*. Maybe once you teared up over the *Mona Lisa*. You think you're in tune with artists. Pollock comes along, a furnace of creativity, and you identify with his suffering. But his struggle has nothing to do with you."

Gwen made a sour face. "If there is one person I do not identify with, it is Jackson Pollock."

"Oh? Look at how grandiose you've been about this painting—which, should it miraculously turn out to be legit, will still be a minor work. And for that, you are doing direct damage to the women of this organization."

"What are you talking about?"

"Going to an independent for forensics. As if you didn't know that is the only department in this company run by a woman."

"I didn't, actually. But I had three people on that team come to me drooling about that painting. We need much more objective—"

"Don't change to 'we.' You are on your own."

"Seems a little 'we' of you to phone the world-class neutral expert I hired."

"I'm trying to save the company."

"Ridiculous."

"This is a straightforward case, Gwen, and you're making a maze of it. I want to bring it under control, in-house. Where our female-led forensic team determines whether the painting is legitimate. If it is, the auction will be managed by a woman too. Not your arrogant Frenchman, and not Prince Pinkney."

"I remember at the party for Arthur, you accused me of trying to grab his fee, which was total bullshit. Now I realize it was projection." Gwen scoffed. "You want to steal this deal and take the fee. As obvious as the fake name of Lee. Behind your façade of feminism, there's actually greed. You are nothing but an old poacher."

"Well." Baxter's tone changed. "There's the pivotal word." She turned her desk chair and sat. "The whole problem. The word *old*."

"Oh, do tell, aged sage."

Baxter raised a hand, gesturing toward one of the chairs. "Let's pause between rounds for a minute, please, and let me tell you something."

Gwen considered a moment, then yanked a chair around and flumped into it. "This better be good."

Baxter faced Gwen, folding her hands on the desk. "Just before you barged in, I met with two men from accounting. When we were done, they stood, shoving these chairs to the side, totally unaware that they had blocked me in. If my phone hadn't rung, I would have moved the chairs back by now."

"What does furniture have to do with it?"

"They assumed I would do the housekeeping. If they gave it any thought."

"People are inconsiderate. So what?"

"You don't see the privilege in their attitude. And you're the same. You don't know how you got to this moment."

"Sure I do. I was on the phone with my independent forensic—"

"Please." Baxter held up both hands. "Half a minute more."

"If you'll get to the damn point . . ."

"I have worked for years—no, decades—to get where I am. Over that long, painful time, I had to outwit so many stupid men, outwork so many lazy ones, fend off horny cads, ignore sexist comments about everything from my hat to my shoes, and see every opinion dismissed as my gender or my period or the wind messing up my hair. It was hard."

"Said the woman with an office, to the woman with a cubicle."

"You breeze into this place, wag your little behind, and chat up the CEO like you're golf buddies. You don't even notice, much less appreciate, the price that countless women paid to make your career possible. You are clueless." Baxter sat back. "There. I've said my piece."

"You think I breeze around here?" Gwen unfolded her arms. "Lady, I don't wag my ass, I bust it. Hell, I do more work in one day than you do in three. Next time you start thinking about my ass, come on over and kiss it."

"I wish you'd listen."

"And I wish you weren't so competitive and condescending. Women need to stick together. We can't be tearing each other down."

Baxter looked her in the eye. "Ingratitude makes a woman ugly."

Gwen grabbed her chair and set it in place, in front of the desk.

"So." She picked up the other chair. "Does." She slammed it in place too. "Resentment."

WHILE GWEN WAS STORMING BACK TO HER DESK, SHE NOTICED SOMEthing. Maybe it was the weather, since she happened to be catching a sunset over the city at an odd hour. But the quality of light on the west-facing offices was appreciably better than on Baxter's side. It didn't come from the overhead bulbs; it came from the sun.

Had she been taking her position for granted? Weren't her late nights at her desk proof that she wasn't entitled? Wasn't working every Sunday the opposite of privilege?

Her desk's top drawer was open, which made her slow with suspicion. Then she remembered she'd been texting with Arthur. She grabbed her phone and looked.

Where did you go? Hullo?

Sorry, Gwen replied. **I had to take care of something.**

All right. So what was that, the thing you started there in the elevator?

Gwen turned around and sat on her desk. **Being honest.**

Honest about what?

She hesitated. Then typed. **Desire.**

I felt that. But two minutes later, you said you didn't know. Perhaps it was confusion?

Gwen scanned the cubicles. Everyone had gone home. Chillie's desk was tidy, a handkerchief over his keyboard to fend off dust. **Yes, that too.**

I am not a toy.

Gwen considered for a moment. **You are the best toy that ever existed. (wink)**

He did not reply for some time. She imagined him laboring over the letters, as well as what he had to say. He kept her waiting.

> **That compliment is like a bee. A pleasant buzz, but it has the sting of indecision.**

Gwen pulled at the ends of her hair. **It's just that I'm worried about my work. My career.**

There was another pause.

> **People have jobs and personal lives, Gwen. Everyone does. It is normal. We work in different departments, and neither of us is the other one's boss. So what is the problem? You said you were being honest. What do you honestly want?**

She looked at the thread of messages. **With you I could . . .**

Gwen stopped, erasing, trying again. **If only we . . .**

She deleted that too. **You know what I want.**

It was a dodge, she knew, but Gwen sent it anyway. Arthur did not respond. She waited a minute, then turned to face the litter pile her desk had become. On top, an article about determining the age of paint. Under it, an *ArtNews* article about the flood of forgeries after Pollock died. She put her phone aside but checked it every two minutes. Sometimes less. After half an hour, she broke down.

> **Thank you for singing my praises to Pinkney. That was generous of you. Xox.**

Arthur replied at once. **I have a heart, you know. Please don't ride the elevator with me anymore.**

IT TOOK SOME TIME, PRECIOUS TIME, TO PULL HERSELF TOGETHER. GWEN was glad everyone else had gone home. Eventually, she put on her coat again. Off to stalk around Lee Krasner's neighborhood again. Maybe she would find an old lady walking her dog. Maybe they could discuss a working woman's role in a man's world. Maybe they could talk about a painting her deceased husband might have made for someone else, not her.

21

APRIL 1956

The apartment forces Ruth and Lucy to make peace. It's too small for one person to pack her things while another sulks on the other side of a wall that does not reach the ceiling. The conflict seems to be reduced, too, by Ruth's decision to tap her savings and pay July rent though she's leaving in mid-June.

"Maybe you'll come into some cash, and pay for August too," Lucy says. It's early afternoon on a Monday. After walking north on Third Avenue for an hour, they've nearly reached Grand Central Station. Ruth pulls a cart loaded with bags and hatboxes. "That way, you can move right back in when the summer job ends."

Ruth purses her lips. "Loosely, I do not think I will be returning from this trip."

"Whyever not?"

"Jackson and I will be making a life together. The life of art, our destiny."

Lucy raises her eyebrows. "Won't Lee have an opinion about all of that?"

"Only until she sees us together. Then she will recognize what she obstructs. She will step aside."

Lucy makes no answer, only strolls alongside shaking her head. In two hours, the sidewalk will be jostling with commuters, but for now it's not crowded.

Ruth fills the quiet. "Will you be seeing Romeo again?"

Lucy shudders. "I prefer to stay alive. How will you contact Jackson?"

"I plan to wait two weeks, to learn the job. Then I'll simply call him."

They reach a cross street and wait for it to clear. "What if Lee answers?"

"Then I will speak with her, naturally. Love is nothing to be ashamed of."

The lights change, they resume walking. Lucy rubs her forehead.

"I hope this job provides me with lots of time." Ruth bounces on her toes. "To take art lessons. And lie on the beach. And be with Jackson. Have any advice?"

Lucy considers the question. "You're putting all your eggs in this basket. So actually, yes I do."

Ruth laughs. "Fire away."

"No guy likes to be told no. So, if he wants to do something, chances are you'll like it. Or at least can withstand it. And it will be something his wife refuses to do, which means he'll be grateful to you. Say yes."

"You are talking about sex things?"

"I sure am."

"But what if I do not want to?"

"Then know that you are taking a risk. If he starts things, and you're not in the mood? Say yes."

"I do not imagine—"

"He has a dirty idea, and works up his nerve to ask for it? Say yes."

"What if I do not—"

"You've had a fight, and he wants to make up? Say yes yes yes, and he will believe you all three times."

Ruth warbled with laughter. "You are the naughtiest ever."

"Your sister Loosely is advising you sincerely. Say yes, and keep him pleased, because you have little else to offer him."

Ruth stops walking while Lucy continues ahead. "Do you honestly think I have only sex to offer him?"

"'Course not," Lucy says.

But she doesn't elaborate, and they progress up the sidewalk separately till they arrive at Pershing Square. Grand Central's brass-doored entrance is across the street. People pass, all in a hurry. A taxi driver sits on his horn, a long, frustrated blast, as if that will clear the street.

"Ruthie." Lucy takes her hand. "You're smart and creative. Look what you've done with the gallery. You're beautiful, or you could never be a model in this town. I just remember what I overheard, on the Monday afternoons I was around. Many grunts from him, not many cries of joy from you, and not one declaration of love by him. I don't want you to get your heart broken."

"Not possible. Not with the love that Jackson and I share." Ruth opens her arms wide. Lucy plunges in, and their hug is fierce like that between fellow warriors.

"Thank you," Ruth says, "for being my first and best friend in this crazy city."

Lucy pulls back to study Ruth's face, running a thumb along her cheekbone as if she were wiping away a tear. But Ruth's face is dry as she takes up the cart's handle, marches to the doors, and pauses to look back.

Lucy is still there. She waves one hand. "I love you."

Someone charges out the door, a hurrying man with a briefcase, which flusters Ruth out of responding. Isn't that Ruth's modeling agent? Lucy has seen photos, and this man could be his twin. Yet he runs right past Ruth—who, maneuvering her things, does not notice, squeezes through the station's door, and is gone.

Lucy shakes her head. "Boy, are you in for it, kiddo."

THE TRAIN IS UNCROWDED AND SWIFT. WHEN RUTH ARRIVES IN SAG HARbor, a middle-aged couple is waiting. The woman is heavy, solid and sound.

"Esther." She shakes Ruth's hand with the strength of a wrestler. "Welcome."

The man behind her casts an eye on the pile of luggage. "You'd think she was coming for a month's vacation."

"Now, Abraham." Esther rubs his head. With one hand cupped

beside her mouth, she stage-whispers to Ruth. "My husband is a saint."

"How nice for you both." The air is softer here, Ruth thinks, and it tastes of salt. She scans the street, the shops, a honky-tonk inn called the American Hotel. "It looks like a relic from the Old West."

"Abe courted me there, ages ago. The scamp."

"Don't believe a word," Abraham grouses, hoisting Ruth's trunk into the back of his truck. "What have you got in here, a dead body?"

It takes her a moment to understand, but then Ruth gives a quick laugh.

"Oh, my husband." Esther is smiling. "She's on to you already."

"It's easier to find humor when you're not hauling a corpse." He loads the last of her luggage, placing the cart on top.

"Poor fellow hates any task that takes him away from painting."

"Any and every," he mutters. But he opens the passenger door, and after Esther clambers in, he helps Ruth aboard as well.

"Thank you, sir."

As he climbs in on the driver's side, Esther makes an announcement. "Before the boardinghouse, we'll visit the most important thing first."

Ruth perks up. "The beach?"

Abraham snickers behind the wheel, then starts the truck.

"Dear girl." Esther pats Ruth's leg. "The church."

It is Ruth's first time inside a Christian church. She enters nervously but calms quickly. There is no ritual underway, no droning chants or incense. Only a large room full of benches, an altar at the front, and at the back, a wall of clear windows. Sunlight is pouring in.

"Our school is over here." Esther guides her into an annex. The room looks like it could only be an art school: well-lit, tidy, with easels in rows like the windmills of Holland. The walls have cubbies full of paints and cans bristling with brushes. Along the back, potter's wheels sit in a row like honored guests. The place smells of linseed, but with the windows open, the scent is mild.

"It feels clean in here," Ruth says.

"Wait two days," Abraham replies. "The brats will make a chaos of it."

Esther nods in agreement. "Bless every one of their little genius minds."

She leads Ruth down a flight of stairs. A room equal to the classroom above is stacked with old school desks, giant floor fans, lumber and ladders and garbage. "Here," she proclaims, "is our new gallery. Once we whip it into shape."

Ruth flattens a hand on her chest. Turning that junk pit into a gallery will be a full summer's work all by itself.

"Which means me wielding the other kind of paintbrush." Abraham wags his head. "Any damn thing but my actual work."

THE BOARDINGHOUSE IS ON MAIN STREET, BEHIND A LITTLE FENCE. HANDsome and trim, white clapboard and black shutters, with a separate entrance at the rear.

"This door is for you and Shirley," Esther explains. "She's the other assistant."

As Abraham unloads the truck, Esther takes up two suitcases. "Follow me."

Ruth reaches to do the same, but he waves her off. "You'll be toting your share soon enough."

"Shirley is a brand-new graduate of Sarah Lawrence College." Esther charges up the narrow stairs. "A brilliant painter despite her youth."

"She is *so* frightfully young," pipes a voice up on the landing, where Ruth is greeted by a freckled redhead with a searchlight smile. She takes a suitcase from Esther and hurries ahead, speaking over her shoulder. "I'm Shirley, do you like to swim, I get up early to take a dip before breakfast, the water is warm already . . ."

Ruth follows both women into a room under the eaves, with a dresser, a closet, a single bed. On the bedside table sits a lamp featuring a ceramic girl, blond with braids and a light-blue dress, a milk bucket swinging in one hand.

"Isn't this perfect?" Shirley's face is as bright as a Norman Rockwell portrait.

"Make way, make way." Abraham barges in with Ruth's trunk. Setting it at the foot of the bed, he scans the room. "Barely big enough for the luggage and a place to stand. I'll store your unpacked bags after supper."

Shirley takes Ruth's arm. "Is there time for us to go swimming?"

Ruth hesitates. "I am not sure I—"

"A kind offer," Esther interrupts. "We should let our new arrival settle in."

"If you don't mind."

"You betcha," Shirley exclaims. "We can swim later." Lunging, she gives Ruth a quick hug. "Here comes the most fun summer *ever*." She skips from the room.

Abraham grumbles down the stairs. Esther smiles. "Dinner's at six. Welcome."

She pulls the door closed. Ruth flumps down on the bed, which creaks, but the mattress is firm. "Dear Loosely," she whispers. "Everything here is wholesome. I suspect I will teach them a little about decadence."

HER PLAN TO WAIT TWO WEEKS IS DISRUPTED ON THE SECOND DAY. Preparations are complete for the children, who arrive the next day.

"Miss Kligman?" the boardinghouse cook calls up the stairs that afternoon.

Ruth is standing in her little closet, arranging dresses. Almost none are right for the job, which basically requires black slacks and a top that washes easily.

"Miss Kligman, there's a gentleman to see you."

Impossible. She hasn't so much as sent him a postcard. But she bends to the window by the stairs, and there is the green Oldsmobile convertible, idling at the curb. For a moment she staggers, then collects herself. She rushes back to the closet, replaces her orange top with a pink one, gives herself a fresh coat of lipstick.

"Miss Kligman?"

"Be right down," she calls. What else? Her shoes? No, the shoes are fine. A bathing suit? She grabs a bikini from a dresser drawer but is nearly down the stairs before she realizes she only took the top half. She stuffs it away in her bag.

There he is, standing on the lawn by the front door. Hair freshly cut, face freshly shaved, and his eyes are as clear as rain. Ruth leaps into his arms.

Jackson stumbles backward but regains his balance and gives her a good one-armed squeeze. She's kissing his neck and face and mouth, but he turns away.

"Come on," he says. "Let's go somewhere."

"How did you find me?"

Instead of answering, he opens her door. Climbing in, Ruth glances at the house. In the stairs' window there is a shadow, someone crouching. Not until the car moves can Ruth see: Shirley, watching as they go.

The convertible weaves through town, till they reach open road and Jackson presses the gas pedal down hard. "Nine weeks," he says.

"Nine years." Ruth squeezes his arm. "Strong and beautiful as ever."

"I've been eating right." Jackson shakes a cigarette from its pack, puts it in his mouth, but doesn't light it. "Good sleep. Long walks. Daily routines."

"It is all flattering to you."

"Lee has taken to drawing. Anytime I come in the house—to pee, to get some water—she's sitting on the booze cabinet with paper and pencils."

Ruth fluffs her skirt. "I would rather not hear about her."

"Then let's just say I'm drinking much less."

"I saw paint on your nails." Ruth points.

He hides his hand. "I scrubbed hard."

"No apologies, please. It brings me joy to know that you are working again."

"We made a deal." He tucks the cigarette behind his ear like a carpenter's pencil. "If I work till five, she makes me a cocktail for dinner."

Ruth looks away. They're speeding along, the roads arched with leafy elms. The dappled light makes her feel like they're underwater. "More about Lee."

Jackson turns down a sandy lane. "She always helps me. You know that."

"And you know that I am unapologetically jealous of her."

"As she is of you."

So. Ruth has been a topic of conversation. She basks in that news, holding her eyes closed as sun and shadow play with light on her face. After a minute, she opens them again. "Please take me to a beach."

"That's where we are. We have to park here, though, so we don't get stuck."

He steers to the side where the pavement ends. They climb down and follow a sandy path. The sound of the surf grows, and the musky, low-tide scent thrills her. The path opens to reveal a long stretch of white sand, with no one on it. The waves rise as they curl, only to crash and obliterate themselves. Sun glints off everything.

Slipping out of her shoes, Ruth takes a great breath. "Where is everyone?"

"This is Flying Point Beach." Jackson leaves his shoes and rolls up his pants. They stroll above the reach of the waves' spill. "You have to be a member."

"Are you?"

"I would be." He laughs. "If I owned a bank. But no one enforces the rules. At lunch this place is packed like sardines. This late? Mommy's home making supper."

That reminds Ruth, and she checks her watch. If they don't leave in five minutes, she'll be late for dinner at the boardinghouse.

"Besides," Jackson continues, "the club president owns one of my paintings."

Ruth is hungry, but she hooks her arm in his. "We are in heaven."

"It's just a beach. This corner of the world is sick with them."

"It will never be just a beach to me. Forever this will be the location of our rebirth. It is sacred now."

"I don't know about rebirth."

Ruth laughs. "Of course you do."

"I'm doing better. Without that whole life I was leading, I mean. My oddball analyst, my drinking buddies. All traded for a few glimpses of clarity each day. I'm even crying less." He takes the cigarette from behind his ear, digs out a lighter and lights it. "The only bad part is that my work is awful."

"I do not believe that for one second."

"It's true, but it's also all right." They veer around a tangle of dark seaweed. The next wave is bigger, and Ruth runs quick-footed as it chases them uphill. Jackson takes her arms, holding her in place till it pours over their feet. She squeals but does not resist. Once the wave retreats, he releases her. She leans for a kiss, but he has already started strolling again.

"Some days I have clarity." He takes a long inhale from the cigarette. "Some days I see the history within the object. I have brief ideas that images can express. Not the work-all-night power I once had. But not nothing either."

"Sounds like a healthy life for you." Ruth skips ahead. "But you miss me."

He exhales a lungful of smoke. "Oh yes."

"When you cry, it is about us."

"Mostly, yes."

"You see?" She takes his hand and kisses the knuckles. "You have Lee to keep you fed. And me to be your muse and lover, to help you reach your highest genius."

"We know I can't have both of you."

"I am not asking you to leave her. I do not want babies."

"What do you want?"

She faces him. "For us to live outside of society's scruples, without repression or restraint. I do my little art job. You eat your spinach and suffer a bossy wife. I inspire you to your full genius again. After that, things will occur as they are fated."

Jackson stops walking. "No."

"It will be perfect."

"For two weeks my hands shook. Even when I was asleep. It's been hard."

"Because I was not here to love you. Because you were denying your destiny."

"I have been trying—"

"While living with a woman who perches on your liquor cabinet. She is a vulture who treats you like you are four years old."

It is the first time Ruth has raised her voice with Jackson, and he winces.

"I apologize," she says immediately. "My passion got the better of me."

She comes back beside him, but they do not touch, only plod along. Jackson finishes the cigarette, grinds it out on the sand, tucks the nub into a pants pocket.

"Too bad we don't have suits," he says. "The ocean's warm early this year."

Ruth calculates briefly, then pulls the bikini top from her bag. "I have one."

"Do you always carry that? In case of emergency?"

"Fate strikes again." She scans the beach. "But nowhere to change."

"I guess not." He's patting his pockets, but he left his cigarettes in the car.

Ruth hops in front of him. "I should change right here. No one will see . . . except you."

"Please don't." He waves both hands. "I am really trying—"

"So am I, Jackson." She starts to unbutton her blouse.

His lips are pursed, his whole face wrinkled inward like a prune. "I beg you."

"To do what?" Her shirt nearly open, she pulls it out of her skirt's waist to reach the lower buttons. "What do you beg me to do?"

"It's too powerful."

"Why shy away from something strong? Have I become the enemy?"

He looks out to sea, but the ocean has no answers. "The opposite."

She sidles a step closer. "All you have to do is turn around. I will be out of these things, and into my bathing clothes, in half a minute."

"But I want to see."

"Now I think you should not." She tips her head to one side. "Turn, please."

He starts but only goes halfway.

"Jackson." She circles a finger. "Avert."

Instead of rotating further, he stands and crosses his arms. Ruth feels the boldness of it, the challenge. Excitement courses through her veins.

"All right. Be that way." She turns her back to him, pulling the blouse open and off, reaching back to unclasp the bra. She faces him, and he has not moved. The straps slip down to her wrists like elastic handcuffs, and her upper half is nude.

"I'm looking at you," he says.

Ruth assumes her swan pose, shoulders back, head high. "Look all you like."

There is a pause, as when a horse rears back before the starting bell of a race. She lowers her arms, dropping bathing suit, blouse, and bra, all onto the sand.

And he attacks her. They are kissing madly, with the heat of time apart. His hands are everywhere. She rubs his trousers, he is already erect. She undoes his belt, opens the top button, reaches in. He bends her backward as if to lay her down.

"No," Ruth says. "It will ruin the skirt and get sand in my hair."

With a grunt Jackson spins her facing away and pushes Ruth down on all fours. He flips up her skirt, pulls the underwear to her ankles, and thrusts into her. She is ready, there is no roughness, only ease, and ferocity from the first second.

Ruth lifts her head. Sharp grass on one side, the chanting sea on the other. No one else on the beach. She digs the heels of her hands into the sand, to push back at him. He grabs her hips to drive harder.

In minutes they are finished, both of them. He steps away to close his fly. Ruth rises, feeling tall, and taller still, so great is her dignity and pride. She dresses, arranges her clothes, stuffs the bathing suit top back in her bag.

They stroll back toward the car, a pair of upstanding citizens turning for home. Sandpipers rush forward as the waves recede, digging at invisible food in the sand. Her body still feels him, his power and passion. She smells her hand, and it is the scent of him, salt and vanilla root. "You were stronger, just now."

"I feel everything more. It's good and bad."

"Jackson, that makes me feel so—"

He bursts into tears. Ruth stops, observing him in confusion, then pulls him into her arms. "There, there. There, there."

"What have I done?" He sobs.

"Exactly the right thing." She rubs his head, his strong back.

He takes a long time to reply. His nose is running, his breath comes in gasps. "I am so fucking weak."

"No." She squeezes his arm. "It takes enormous courage to be yourself. And for a genius to be himself? His whole huge, brilliant being? That is the difficult thing, and the right thing."

In another minute, his breathing calms. "Do you honestly think so?"

"Jackson Pollock cannot fly with a chain around his ankle. Lee can keep you fed. I will help you fly."

"I hope you're right." Jackson wipes his face. They resume strolling, his arm around her shoulders, her arm around his waist. Gulls cry overhead.

"High tide's coming in," Jackson says.

"How in the world can you tell?"

"Our footprints." He waves an arm down the beach. "They're all washed away."

11

JANUARY 2007

When Gwen returned from the Rose Room, Chillie was banging his head.

"What's wrong?" She flopped her briefcase on the desk.

"Not much. I'm just going insane."

Gwen leaned close. "Over spreadsheets? That should be easy for you."

"So is a maze, if you know the way."

"But you're the expert. What's the problem?"

"Asian Arts has a Ming Dynasty porcelain show coming in London. Those Brits, whose desk hours overlap with mine for about three minutes a day, can't decide what order to rank the lots till they have a full workup of pricing options."

"Why are you doing work for them?"

"Turnover in their office. And persuasion. They have accents that make the dumbest person in their country somehow sound brilliant."

Gwen felt a pang. She missed Arthur's voice.

"Anyway, they need anticipated revenue models, low to high."

Gwen took his mouse and began building stacks of boxes named after the artworks. She still had her coat on. Chillie rolled his chair out of her way.

"You are literally saving me hours," he said. "How did you learn this?"

"Had to." Gwen cut and pasted till there was a file for every option. "There."

He looked at his watch. "I'm waiting hours before I send this. Let them think I was working all that time. If I whine enough, next time they'll ask someone else. Tra la la."

His expression changed, suddenly serious as he glanced over her shoulder.

"What?" Gwen turned but there was no one there. "What did you see?"

"Richards." Chillie tapped his desk. "He had one of those fancy phones, like yours, and he was making a big show of it. Pretending to be on a call."

Gwen shook her head. "What is with that guy?"

"He wishes he was as cool as you."

"Aw, g'wan." Gwen poked his chest.

"It's true true true, cooool girl."

She punched him on the shoulder. "Get outta here, ya big palooka."

They both laughed. Someone down the row of cubicles gave a shout. "Will you two shut up? We're trying to work."

Chillie snickered, then whispered, "Try harder, twerp."

Gwen guffawed, hand over her mouth.

THE PAINTING WAS CALLED *PROPHECY.* GWEN WENT TO SEE IT AFTER ANother fruitless patrol of Lee Krasner's neighborhood. It hung in the Whitney Museum, on the West Side, all the way over in the Meatpacking District. The information card said Lee made it in early 1956, and it was on loan from a private collection. Gwen used to be amazed that people would spend a fortune on artworks, only to lend them to a museum. It was Richards, years ago, who had explained: For some people art was an investment. They put millions down, received a tax break for loaning it to museums for years, then sold it for millions more. The painting would gain value faster in a rarified place like the Whitney.

What struck Gwen was the timing. While Lee was painting *Prophecy*, Ruth was sleeping with her husband on a regular basis. Did she know yet? Did she suspect?

The painting's primary tones were of pinkish flesh, in undefined shapes that implied many things. A face, torn by anguish. A leg, perhaps an arm, and a red shape that could be lips with fresh lipstick or a jagged wound. The background was coal black, making the pink look vulnerable and weak. It was not hard to interpret: Lee's prophecy was pain.

The next painting on the wall revealed the accuracy of Lee's forecast. She made *Three in Two* in the fall of 1956, immediately after the catastrophe. Again, there were pink tones, but now the body parts were severed, with maroon details the color of dried blood. A face turned sideways with grief, a background of blackness.

The card also had a quote from Lee Krasner: "Painting is not separate from life. It is one. It is like asking: Do I want to live? My answer is yes—and I paint."

Gwen sat on a bench. In a way, making art was Lee's form of survival. Painting was her refuge. Maybe work was all she had left.

All at once Gwen felt overwhelmed. Her cheeks were wet.

She had mourned the loss of Neil, though it had been years since they'd been genuine lovers. And Arthur? He was funny and humble and breathtaking in bed, and she had blown it completely. Her suffering was only a fraction of Lee's, and yet: Maybe work was all that Gwen had left too.

She tilted her head back, wiping her face with both hands.

That was when she noticed a humming in her pocket. It took her a moment to realize the cause, and to dig the phone out. The call was from Matthieu. She hurried from the gallery. "Please don't stop," she told the humming. Seeing an exit sign, she rushed into what turned out to be a stairwell. "Hello? Hello?"

"*Mon Dieu,* my dear, beautiful friend. I was afraid I had missed you."

"Me too. How are you? Do you have any news?"

"*Oui.* I found something."

She sat on the top step. "I'm listening."

"It was embedded in the paint."

"Yikes." She stood. "We do not have authorization to—"

"I read the agreement, Gwen. I signed it. And I have not violated it. Nor have I ever in my career broken the research arrangement."

"Well, the way you said it—"

"After all the extra work I just did. I will now receive an apology."

Gwen pressed a hand to her forehead. "Do you have any idea how much stress I am under right now?"

"You fix that with a lover. Not with insulting me."

A lover. Gwen stood blinking. Was every conversation that day going to remind her of Arthur? "Of course I apologize, Matthieu. You are the most trustworthy scientist in the business. You would never violate a contract."

She heard him pound his desk. "There. Now I will tell you about the hair."

"Whose hair?"

"*Exactement.*" He laughed. "Someone's hair on the *back* of the painting. Pollock was bald by the time these pigments were available, so it's not his. The hair I found is five centimeters long, maybe the length of your pinkie. Unambiguously caught in the paint, so the hair source was present at the making."

Gwen felt her heart flutter. "I'm following you. If the hair is Ruth's—"

"*Exactement.* Enjoy the bidding, bang the gavel. But there are two problems."

"I don't have time for two problems." She felt like crying again. "Or even one."

"First, performing DNA analysis quickly is possible, but expensive."

"Expense approvals within the company can take weeks. Please go ahead, and I'll do the apologizing later. Please say the second one is as easy."

"*Mais non.*" Matthieu sighed. "It is the most difficult."

"Do I want to even hear this?"

"To verify the DNA on the painting is only the question. The answer is whether it matches a sample of hair from the owner. From her head."

"Oh no."

"This Ruth woman, she is especially vain?"

Gwen leaned against the wall. "Like a beauty queen."

Matthieu laughed. "So I expected. It would be in character for her to refuse any hairpulling."

"Pulling?"

"*Oui*. We will need ten or a dozen hairs, including *le follicule*."

"The follicle? I have to pull ten hairs from her head?"

"A dozen is better. But yes. Otherwise we cannot prove that she was present at the painting's making."

"You've been thinking this through."

"*Oui*. If you provide a sample by Friday afternoon, I will have a result by Sunday evening."

Gwen took several deep breaths. How could she possibly convince Ruth to give a hair sample? She might as well ask her to skip rope one-handed.

"Are you there?" Matthieu asked.

"I cannot imagine any universe in which she lets me pull her hair out."

"And I," Matthieu replied, "cannot imagine any person other than you who could make it happen."

As they hung up, Gwen was already moving, trotting down the stairs while dialing her phone. "I need to see you," she said the moment Ruth answered. "Now."

23

JULY 1956

Lee finds Jackson in his studio, on the floor with his back against the wall. He's wearing his work boots, splattered with colors, the laces removed so he can step in and out of them without getting paint on his hands. There's no paint in use, however. A blank canvas lies before him, eight feet by twelve. The dollies he uses to hold his paint buckets—they're like the rolling portion of hotel luggage carriers—have a few cans on them, but they're off to the side. Jackson is not hovering over the canvas as he once did, frowning with a concentration so intense it used to frighten her. That's the past, no telling if it will ever return.

Still, he's in a reverie, staring at something in his hands. At first, she thinks it is a letter, which is odd, since she's the one who gets the mail. Amid bills and solicitations, she sets any correspondence for Jackson aside on the piano bench. Now she climbs the few steps from the supply room into the studio itself, the floor creaking.

"Oh," he says, startled. Jackson looks right and left, as if for a place to stash the letter, then relaxes into surrender. "You caught me."

Lee leans over to see the letter. "What fan is kind enough to write—" She sees that it is actually a photograph. Of a naked woman. Whom she knows. "Not you too, Jackson."

"'Not me too' what?"

"Mercedes. She's slept with everyone."

"That's untrue, and you are an awful person to say so."

"All right, fine. She's a beautiful woman who has her pick of lovers. Please don't be her next conquest. Where did you even get this?"

"She gave it to me," he mumbles. "After dinner at Alfonso's the other night. But it's not for romance. If you look at the composition, at the play of light . . ."

"The play of light?" She snorts.

"You're lucky I don't beat you," he snarls. "Bitch."

Lee does not even blink. Instead, she takes the photo and examines it: black and white, an attractive woman lying on a beach at sunset. Half of her body is cropped out. On the rest, seagrass casts a shadow on her skin like zebra stripes. There's a hollow inside her hip, too, its darkness shaped like South America. The photo does, in fact, have a play of light.

"Her husband took this," Jackson says. "A warm image with a cool execution."

"All right, it's interesting." Lee considers the photo. "Frank sexuality, the fertility of her navel. Her body has an unsullied character. Not a mark. Very erotic."

"What do you know about eroticism?" He speaks at the floor. "Ice woman."

"Come to bed sober for once and see what happens."

He points at the photo. "I would never let anyone see you that way. In a painting, perhaps. But a photograph? It makes her a commodity. It lacks respect."

Lee's arms drop to her sides. He looks like a boy. She sits beside him. "We were in jail together, you know."

"Who? What do you mean?"

"Mercedes and I. After the artists' union uprising in nineteen thirty-six."

"Wasn't that Gorky's mischief? I was out of town, I think."

"He and some others." She fans herself with the photo. "Mercedes was sleeping with him. Her list is impressive. Maybe Léger, perhaps De Kooning."

"Willem? Really?"

"Hoffman, too, and he was nearly thirty years her senior. But she got him painting again." She tilts her head back. "Not you, I hope?"

"No." Jackson huffs. "Not yet, anyway."

"Once upon a time, you were unique. Please don't become a cliché."

"Witch," he replies.

"Pig," she says.

"Prude."

Lee gives him a glare. "The organizers were savvy and stayed away. We pawns were arrested, disturbing the peace and so on, and held overnight. As it turned out, Mercedes and I were thrown in the same cell."

"So, *you* slept with her. I'm relieved that you're confessing it at last."

She snorts. "No thank you, Jack. Then she married Matter. I'm told that a number of her former lovers were in the congregation."

Jackson snickers. "We are so vanilla, Lee. We live such ordinary lives."

And they both laugh at that.

She hands the photo back. "What do you like about it? Besides her beauty."

He studies it a moment. "The suggestion of it. The hint of potential pleasure."

"Hint?" Lee says. "She's stark naked. Nothing subtle or nuanced about it. You have a body displayed for men to want to mount, and as it turns out, they do. Later, with a sort of, I don't know, conquering masculine casualness, they attend her wedding. It's quite ugly. I swear, Jackson, humor aside. If I catch you with her—"

"Lee?"

She lowers the photo. "Yes?"

"I'm hungry. Starving. Would you please make eggs with toast and bacon?"

Lee laughs from her belly. "It's either that, or wring your neck."

"No neck wringing today, thanks."

"I could use a bite too." Lee rises, kisses his brow. "I'll bring it out. Try to work."

He hears Lee entering the house, its screen door slapping. In the studio he stares at the large rectangle of canvas on the floor, not a mark on it.

Fifteen minutes later, Lee brings a tray with two plates of food and two iced teas to the studio. He's not there. She carries it around to the front of the house, and there's only her dusty old Model A. The convertible is gone.

"I KNOW A PLACE WE CAN GO."

He is leaning over the car door, waving Ruth closer.

"Impossible." She tilts her head at the playground. Some girls are on the swings, some boys are kicking around a big rubber ball. A few girls sit on the front walk, playing jacks. Shirley squats with them, skirt tucked between her knees. "I have a job."

"A private place." He winks. "Come on."

"I would love to." She cocks her weight onto one hip. "Another beach?"

"I can't remember." He's grinning now. "Only one way to find out."

"Jackson, Jackson, Jackson."

Esther appears at the annex door. She surveys the well-behaved children, beaming until she spies the convertible. Her face darkens. "All right, young artists." She claps her hands. "It's clay time. Sculpture time."

The girls hop off the swings at the highest point, landing almost on all fours. They form a line in front of Esther. The boys have a harder time stopping, till the ball escapes them. Shirley chases after it, fleet-footed, while the boys join the line.

"Miss Ruth," Esther calls, her voice a cheery chime. "Back to work now."

"Ten seconds," Ruth sings in reply.

Esther leads the children inside. Shirley, ball under her arm, runs after them.

Ruth sidles toward the car. "You will have to make your own mischief today."

"But I've been working since before dawn."

"I knew it." She caresses his arm. "I knew this arrangement would help you."

"Come with me. I—" He wrings the steering wheel. "I love you."

Ruth kisses him, and at once he is touching her, his fingers teasing on the side of her breast, so lightly, yet it is like a fire in her blood. She grabs his head and kisses him harder, everywhere on his face, his forehead, his throat.

"Ditch these brats and the wicked witch."

"She is not a—"

"Come with me," he repeats. "Life is short."

Ruth straightens. "That is true. That is indisputably true."

Jackson leans across to open the passenger door. Ruth looks back, hears an echoing sound from inside, the piping of children as they pair off to sculpt together.

"I am awful." Ruth scampers around the car to jump in, to slide over, to snuggle against him. The Oldsmobile roars out and away, like an animal freed from its cage.

THE SUN OF HIGH SUMMER POURS DOWN LIKE IT WILL NEVER END. ONLY half a dozen cars are parked in the sandy lot. At the beach, all the footprints go in the same direction, to the right. Jackson leads Ruth, barefoot, the opposite way.

"They're all going swimming." He points. "We're going to the rocks."

"We should bring a picnic sometime," Ruth says. "A tablecloth, sandwiches."

When they reach a sandy stretch, he unrolls a towel. "Not very big, is it?"

She grabs his belt from behind. "We will have to stay close."

He lies down, and Ruth takes her place beside him. But right away he turns, rolling onto his side to see something. She watches him concentrate, waving his hand over the sharp-edged seagrass. He bends closer.

"What is it?" Ruth asks.

"Goddamn it." He throws a fistful of sand to one side. "You interrupted me."

"Jackson, I am so sorry."

"You broke the thought. You ruined it." He shakes his head, frowning. "It might as well be ten after ten."

"What does that mean? Ten after ten?"

"Another thing you don't understand." He swats at the air. "Why am I with you? Are you trying to kill me?"

"Kill you? No one loves you more on this earth. This whole earth."

"But you interrupt my thoughts with silly questions."

"Let us be calm, my love," Ruth croons. "Lie back a sweet minute."

He reclines, releasing some of the tension. Ruth snuggles nearer. She fiddles absently with a button on his shirt, until he rouses and guides her hand downward.

"Is that so?" She rubs his pants, feeling his response. "Fond memories of our last beach excursion?"

His only reply is to push her head down, as he did with her hand. She lifts it to see that his eyes are squeezed shut. "Oh, my love." She caresses his forehead, rubs in circles on his temples. "Why does that memory make you clench up?"

Again, Jackson does not speak, only shifts on the towel so that her face is lower on him. Ruth realizes then what he wants. She's not entirely reluctant. Lucy's advice rings in her head. If he wants something and his wife won't do it, say yes and you'll keep him.

"Lie back easy now." She mashes her breasts against his hip. "Relax yourself. Maybe you can imagine what you were seeing in the seagrass before I interrupted."

Jackson lets out a long sigh.

"Perfect," she says, while he takes a deep breath, and another. Ruth massages his forehead, his jaw, his chest. She opens his pants, checks up and down the beach, then crouches over him.

Jackson becomes more aroused than in all their Mondays together. He is sober, he has worked successfully that day, maybe these are the ingredients. Just when she is beginning to wonder how long it will take, he cranks his face to one side, a grimace as if in pain, and then he releases.

After, they lie quietly together, limbs like pretzels. Eventually Jackson rolls onto his side again, a hand hovering over the seagrass like a sorcerer casting a spell. This time, Ruth will not speak. She's craving water to rinse her mouth, but does not say a word. His eyes dart from one place of attention to another. Ruth rests her head on his arm.

"It's the pattern." He waves his hand. "Green things going vertically, shadows going horizontally, behind it all, the yellow of the sand. It's like . . . like a . . ."

"Like a loom. Weaving individual yarns into a single fabric."

"Exactly." He seizes her hand. "A loom." Jackson jumps to his feet, like a dog who wants the ball thrown. "I have to go. I need to be in the studio immediately."

WHILE HE'S SPEEDING, TREES CAST SHADOWS THAT RUSH OVER THEIR faces. They do not slow until Mickey's. It's a cedar shack, weathered and gray, with a rusted gas pump and a garage for repairs. Lobster trap buoys ring the front door. Above them hang red and green lights, as if to indicate the building's port and starboard.

What catches Jackson's eye is the Stutz Bearcat, a vintage roadster, fire-engine red and in perfect condition. A boy in oil-stained overalls is pumping gas into it. Jackson careens into the parking area, nearly hitting a frumpy sedan.

"Got any green on you?"

Ruth has been daydreaming on his arm. "Any what, Jackson?"

"I need fuel. But I don't have any cash."

"I rarely . . ." She digs in her pockets and finds a five. "Surprise. Will you bring me a cola? I'm dying of thirst." She licks her lips, to make her meaning plain.

He snatches the bill and trots into the store. Seeing the spring in his step, she thinks: *He is feeling inspired. I am so good for him.*

When Jackson returns, he is guffawing, loud and rollicking, with another man who is also laughing. She remains half turned, as if she's not interested. Tall, slender, wearing a white linen suit, the man has a careful step, and chuckles modestly beside Jackson's roar. Ruth pretends to watch the gas boy.

"Here she is at long last," cries the slender man, removing his sunglasses to eye her up and down. "The mighty muse known as Ruth."

She gives him a cold face. "To whom do I have the pleasure?"

"This is Alfonso," Jackson bellows. He is holding an uncapped bottle inside a paper bag. He takes a full draw from it, wiping his mouth on his sleeve, then throws an arm around the man's shoulders. "Alfonso, my former enemy."

"At your service, mademoiselle." He bows.

"Hello," she says. "But did you say 'enemy'?"

"*Former* enemy," Alfonso says. "We conflicted because I—"

"—he bought a painting of mine," Jackson interjects, and they both laugh.

"We recovered," Alfonso adds. "And now we're gin buddies. If there is a liquor ideal for summer, it would have to be gin. Don't you agree?"

Ruth does not answer. She's watching Jackson swig from the bottle. And he forgot to get her a cola. "I thought you were going to the studio."

He points the bottle at her. "Don't start."

"My dear." Alfonso sidles closer, and Ruth can smell his aftershave. Charcoal and cedar. "He said you were attractive, but oh, what a savory snack."

Ruth glowers. "I am not a snack, Mister Alfonso. I am an art teacher."

"Of course." He dismisses everything with a wave of his hand. "Still. If I were red-blooded instead of pink, I'd want those tits uncovered all day long."

Ruth puts a hand on one hip. "You are asking for a slap."

"Don't worry about him." Jackson sways like a sailor on deck. "Alfonso plays for the other team. No harm intended."

"Please come for dinner," he says. "I behave better with my lover on guard."

"Other team or not, I do not enjoy that sort of compliment."

"But you are splendid, princess. You could spend the whole day topless, and only the clergy would object." The gas-pump boy is standing by, and now he shuffles his weight from foot to foot. Alfonso tucks a bill into the boy's overalls. Then he takes Ruth's hands. "I see why Jack finds you irresistible. But isn't our man beautiful too? If you love that type, I mean. That dark, brooding animalism?"

Ruth feels the warmth of his hands, not sweaty but sincere. Or well-powdered, anyway. "I happen to adore all of those things."

"Well of course you do, princess." His smile returns. "Therefore, here you are, the most logical woman in all of Long Island."

Four women emerge from the store. About Ruth's age, they have cat's-eye sunglasses and dolled-up hair. The tall one declares, "Don't care. I'm going to do it."

Ruth watches her approach, tan and lithe and grinning like a clown, the rest following. If they were males, she would be afraid. Jackson does not see them coming. When the tall one touches his arm, he spins like a startled cat.

"Whoa, there." He stumbles but recovers quickly.

"Sorry," she says, one hand to her face. "So sorry."

"What do you want?" He scowls.

"Didn't mean to startle you. But aren't you that hep artist painter guy?"

Squinting at her, Jackson totters as if he might fall down.

"Yeah." Another of the girls approaches. "With the giant canvases? We're only weekenders, but haven't I seen you before?"

"I live here," Jackson says, somewhat recovered. "Fireplace Road."

The tall girl ignores his reply. Ruth can tell she's doing some math: Here's Ruth, decently dressed, beside well-dressed Alfonso. Jackson wears paint-stained pants and stands apart.

"Come play with us," the tall girl says to him. "Our rental is very near here."

"We have good supplies," calls a girl who stayed back by the sedan. She holds up a grocery bag, its contents clinking.

"You and four dates," adds the tall girl. "All of us big, big fans."

"All right now, girls." Ruth takes Jackson by the elbow. Enough patience, she is thirsty. "You will have to excuse us. He is not feeling well."

"I know why," the tall girl says. "I saw his first slug in the store. Impressive."

"Good day, Alfonso." Ruth corrals Jackson toward the car.

"*Enchanté*, my dear princess. Next week, please, come for dinner."

She helps Jackson into the driver's seat, but when she tries to take the bottle, he jerks roughly away. "Suit yourself," she mutters, going around to her side.

He starts the car, then grinds it into gear and rushes off. Ruth looks back. The girls look like deflated balloons.

A fantasy had filled Ruth's thoughts since the beach: sneaking him into her room for lovemaking, and the fun of having to be quiet. No chance now. The man is frowning, steering with one hand while the other clutches the bottle.

By the time they reach Sag Harbor, he is too drunk for anything. No painting inspired by seagrass and its loom of colors. No affection, either, as Jackson needs all of his attention to keep the car on the right side of the road. She sits against the passenger door, hoping the lack of distraction will improve his driving.

When he reaches the boardinghouse, his tires carve a shallow trench in the lawn, and the car stops with a jolt. She nearly bangs against the dashboard.

"Gone," Ruth mutters, "just like that."

"What's gone?"

She kisses his neck and hops out. "Can you get home safely?"

"Driven Fireplace Road so often, I can sit in back and the car will steer itself."

"Be careful please, sweetheart."

"Faster I go, sooner I'm home." And he roars off, bottle held high like a flag.

Ruth doesn't move till he's gone, then turns to head in. Shirley, on the porch swing, looks up from a book. Ruth stalls, not wanting to interact.

Shirley, however, is all smiles. "Did you have a fun afternoon?"

Ruth nods. How fast everything changed, though, the inspiration she helped him find, and its vanishing the instant he drank. "The tops. How about you?"

"We made hand paintings." Shirley closes the book. "They were so inventive."

"Hand paintings?"

Shirley spreads the fingers of one hand. "First they draw an outline." She runs a finger around her open hand. "The result looks like a turkey. Their job is to decorate it, you know? Feathers, clothing. But they are so clever." She laughs, chirping. "You would've loved it."

Ruth finds herself choking up. Yes, the children's work is rudimentary, like a beginner plunking on a piano. Yet she missed something wholesome, in exchange for a sandy tryst that was wasted when her lover drowned his genius. "I bet I would have."

"Esther expects you to stay after lunch."

"I expected to stay too." Ruth looks up the road. "Something came up."

"Your sweetheart." Shirley nods. "Mister Abraham is annoyed at you."

"I imagine he is. But I'm trying to help a great artist. Anytime I leave—"

"Mister Abraham has to take your place. And can't do his painting, which is why he's here. A break from the needs of college students the rest of the year."

Ruth's shoulders are slumped. "I need to do better." She opens the door to the stairway.

She's still in hearing range when Shirley mutters, "I wish you would."

Ruth feels too defeated to bother responding. She is still thirsty, too.

AT LONG LAST THEY HAVE A NIGHT TOGETHER. IN A SMALL CLUB IN AMAGANSETT, a six-piece band is playing hi-hat jazz. Jackson does not dance, but parks himself beside the punch bowl. Ruth visits him between twirls on the floor, kissing his cheek though everyone can see. And why shouldn't they kiss? What do they have to hide?

Most of her dances are with Alfonso, who is light-footed and quick, attentive until a muscular man half his age appears. Instantly he and Alfonso are in deep conversation. Soon they use the French doors to go out on the patio.

The next time she flounces up to Jackson, he takes her wrist and leads her outside too. It's a hot night in late July, and her skin is shining. Outside, the music softens and echoes. He pins her against one of the trees. A row of oaks, gigantic presences. She feels rough bark through her thin dress, waking all of her senses.

But Jackson stumbles, pedaling backward, arms swinging, till he falls bluntly on his butt. And bursts out laughing.

Ruth laughs, too, pouncing. They are kissing wildly till their teeth touch by accident and they both jerk back. She kneels beside him until the humor wanes.

"Tell me seriously." She lays a hand on his thigh. "Are you all right to drive?"

He's still smiling, cockeyed. "What, are you going to do it instead?"

"If I had a license."

"Come on." He struggles to his feet, but Ruth remains on her knees.

"I am not sure, Jackson."

"Pffff." He waves everything away. "Let's spend the whole night together."

"Honestly? How?"

He scowls. "I have a plan. Unless you want to dance more?"

Ruth climbs into the car. "Tease me if you wish. But all I want on this earth is to be beside you, one precious time, when the sun comes up."

Jackson fumbles the key into the ignition, the big engine roars, and he drives.

14

JANUARY 2007

My advice is to slap her," Chillie announced.

Gwen laughed. "Thank you, but no. She brought us a potentially fifty-million-dollar deal. If she tells me to kiss her ass, I'll ask which cheek first."

They were walking back from getting coffee. The air was frigid, with bitter gusts that seemed to come from every direction.

"From what I've overheard, it sounds like her cheeks are already well kissed. But they need to be spanked."

They reached the revolving doors, and Chillie squeezed in with Gwen so they went through together. As they popped out the other side, he laughed. "Warmer that way, girlfriend."

Gwen shook her head. "There will be no spanking of our client."

"Do *something* differently." Chillie led the way across the atrium. "You've shown the patience of a psychologist, and she has—" He clapped his hands. "I know."

"Why am I automatically skeptical?"

"This woman is an attention addict. You should cut her off. Make it so the only way you will listen is if she is telling you what you want."

"Why are you suddenly all involved in this painting?"

He stopped short. "Do you want the answer of a true friend?"

"Of course."

Chillie met her gaze.

"What?" Gwen said. "You're making me nervous."

"Because," he replied. "This case has brought out all the worst of your work ethic. The obsession, the overtime, the neglect of everything else in life. I want you done with this painting because I love you and it is damaging your heart."

"Jesus, Chillie."

He walked away, Gwen following a few steps behind, head down and deep in thought. Damaging her heart? She vaguely registered the sounds of the elevator doors opening, saw Chillie and other people stepping aboard. She did not notice who until she heard, "Good morning, Chilton."

Gwen froze. Arthur was looking at her, his expression so plaintive, so wounded. She remembered his explicit instruction that she not ride the elevator with him anymore. She stepped out and stood with her coffee cup, agonizing until the doors closed and the elevator whooshed up into the guts of the building.

"YOU'RE NOT GOING TO LIKE THIS," GWEN SAID TWENTY MINUTES LATER. The subway had been warm, but walking to Ruth's apartment was fiercely cold. At least the heat was on. "Not at all."

"For years I had a dog," Ruth replied. "She needed walking in all weather. I miss her, but I do not miss going out when it is this cold. Now." She patted her lap as if inviting a dog to jump into it. "What fresh nuisance have you brought me today?"

"There's no sugarcoating it," Gwen said. "I need a lock of your hair."

Ruth chuckled. "Dear girl, tell me what you really need."

"The forensic analyst found a hair held by the paint for all these years."

Her good humor vanished. "Our contract forbids sampling the painting."

"It was not on the painting. It was caught in paint on the back. It's undergoing DNA analysis right now."

"Please explain."

"If the DNA matches yours, then you were there at the making.

Our questions are resolved. But to find out, to compare, I need some of your hair."

"You mean a cutting? As in snipping off one of my curls?"

"It's more than that." Gwen took a deep breath. "They need the root too."

"You want to pull out my hair." Ruth rose from the armchair, moving to her usual place by the window. But it was fogged, no view of Greenwich Village below. She meandered past the empty easel to the photo of her and Jackson. "Miss Gwen," she said, circling back.

Gwen waited in silence. She knew that persuasion would be impossible.

"I am a creature of some vanity," Ruth said. "I am also seventy-eight years old. Whatever tiny fraction of appeal remains, I cling to it. Do you understand?"

Gwen nodded. "I do."

"There is a day in every woman's life when she becomes invisible. You will see. Pity our egos, that we seek outside confirmation of our worth. But we do. I do."

"I just thought you should know that this avenue is available."

"Kind of you not to bully me into it." Ruth floated to a table where there was a glass of water. She took a slow drink.

"When I awoke in Jackson's arms for the first time, my face was pressed against a polar bear." She chuckled. "He provided no linens or pillows, but we slept on the great thick bear rug on his studio floor. I wondered how many women had been there before me, and then I didn't care. It was my place now."

Ruth paused, and Gwen could see her organizing the story in her mind. Chillie was right. Ruth was taking another dose for her attention addiction, and Gwen was providing it. But she'd known this would happen. On the subway she had set an alarm, for the last minute she could stay and still get back to work on time.

"The studio smelled of paint and turpentine," Ruth continued. "I did not care. I was holding my beloved as he slept. I nuzzled his hair, enjoying his scent."

Ruth sipped her water. "He woke with a start. 'It's already light,' he said. 'We slept too long.' I answered that I loved him. But he was dressing, urging me to hurry. I had left my watch in my shoe. It was Saturday, a day off for the art school. He was pacing. 'Lee,' he cried. 'She'll be up any minute.'"

Ruth gave Gwen a long, steady look. "Too late. We tried sneaking out to his car from the other side of the house. But Lee was standing outside with a cup of coffee. When she saw me, her body seemed to deflate. To cave in."

Ruth rose, walking to the apartment's entry, assessing herself in the mirror. "Lee was not unattractive," she told her reflection. "Small on top, but she wore rider jeans tight, and it worked. She had a severe haircut, though, with stern bangs. I imagine it was practical, to avoid getting hair in the paint, but it made her look cold. I wished to encourage her to grow those bangs out for a softer, less masculine look."

"What?" Gwen sputtered. "You wanted to give her appearance tips?"

"I believed that one day we would be friends. Once she accepted fate." Ruth returned to the room. "She flung her coffee at Jackson, cup and all. They began shouting. I went to sit in the car."

"What were they shouting?"

"How awful I was. A slut, a jezebel, a whore. Jackson argued in a whining tone, he sounded weak. I fixed my hair in the car's mirror and waited. Quite soon, he came around and took the wheel. We had enjoyed lovely times in that powerful convertible. I felt secure."

Ruth sat on the piano bench near Gwen. "Lee had been planning a trip to Paris for months, and would not cancel. She was leaving the next day, for six weeks. When she returned she wanted me, and all evidence of me, scrubbed from their lives forever. Those were her words. Scrubbed like I was a stain, and not his artistic salvation." Ruth put a hand on Gwen's arm. "Do you see?"

"See what?"

"Our destiny, dear. She handed him to me."

Gwen studied Ruth's hand, the rings, wrinkles, and veins. She could feel her reservoir of patience running dry. "That's one interpretation."

"In those days, European travel was an exertion. Train to Manhattan, cab to the wharves, then six days crossing the sea in all weather.

Well. Her train had not yet arrived at Grand Central when Jackson invited me. Fate was swift, and I came to live with him on Fireplace Road."

Gwen's alarm began beeping, and Ruth jumped away. "What in the world is that? Are you carrying some kind of bomb?"

"My phone." She silenced the alarm. "Time's up."

"What do you mean?"

There was a certain thrill—to behave as she'd wanted many times before. Now Gwen would learn if Chillie was right. "I mean that we're finished."

"Miss Gwen, we are decidedly not finished."

"Well, I am." She stood, packing the notebook in her briefcase.

"I do not respond to ultimatums."

"There's no ultimatum here," Gwen said. "You are the one who set the deadline."

"You say that like it was a whim. There is an urgent reason for it."

"Which is what?"

"*This*." Ruth swung both arms wide. "If you must know. My exquisite home since nineteen sixty-six, rent-controlled since nineteen seventy-one. I am behind on rent. So far behind, months and months, I face imminent eviction."

It sounded familiar to Gwen. She was flipping through her notebook to see if she'd written anything down about it, when the memory came to her: Winthrop, the wood-carving jerk who blocked Ruth's stairway. He told Gwen not to believe any claims about back rent, no one was going to throw her out.

"Then why have you stalled our process at every turn? We've committed enormous resources to accommodate you. Do you have any idea how much DNA testing costs? We made a plan. But now? There's no more time or money on our end. This is it."

"What sort of plan?"

Gwen bent over her briefcase. "A national publicity and marketing campaign. A slot in an upcoming auction, which now will go to another painting. It is less valuable, but has impeccable proof of its creation and provenance. Because you never told me what I need to know: when he made the painting, and how you came to possess it."

"What else have I been doing but answering you?"

She straightened. "Walking me down memory lane. All very interesting, but my boss has another case waiting for me. A Roman sculpture."

Ruth crossed her arms. "You are not being very nice."

"I've been nice for a month." Gwen pulled on her coat. Leaving was a gamble, no question. She might be killing the deal. Or perhaps, at last, Ruth would tell the rest of the truth. She extended her hand. "It's been a pleasure."

Ruth turned away. "I do not believe you."

"Suit yourself." Gwen strode off, wondering where the Roman statue lie had come from. She decided to leave the apartment door as she found it the day she met Ruth—wide open. Gwen started down the steps, hoping the scuffle of her boots would echo right back up the stairwell.

15

JULY 1956

When Ruth returns for the last suitcase, Shirley has hopped onto the bed. She's running a thumb down the teeth of Ruth's favorite comb: *brrring brrring.*

"You're leaving?" Shirley chirps.

Ruth falters at her boldness, and the presumption of touching her comb. But she swiftly dismisses it as trivial. Her concern is whether the suitcase will have room for what's left. Beach sandals, her makeup kit. "I must."

"Didn't you promise to work here, though? Why apply for a job if you're not going to do it?" *Brrring brrring.*

"It is complicated." The sandals have sand on their bottoms, so she taps them together over the trash can. A sound like dry rain. "I did not know how much I was needed. You have seen a wild man behind the wheel. But I see the greatest creative mind of our time. His genius is fragile, though. It requires—"

"I know who he is." Shirley runs her thumb down the comb, *brrring.* "I've been worried about you."

"He has so many demons." Ruth stuffs one sandal in the bag, reaches for the other. "He needs a protector."

"What about his wife?"

"She is not up to the job. Right this minute, she has abandoned him to sail for Paris. Besides." Ruth packs the second sandal sole to sole with its partner. "It is my destiny to be Jackson's guard and muse."

"Some say that she's a better painter than him."

"Forgive me, but what do you know about such things?"

Shirley shrugs. *Brrring brrring.* "I've been around in the art world a little. This fall, I'm moving to an apartment in Alphabet City."

"That's tenement land."

"I know. But I won't have much money till my work starts finding collectors."

Ruth holds out her hand for the comb, and Shirley hands it over. "You certainly are confident." Ruth freshens her lipstick, tosses it in the kit, and zips the kit closed. "New York is fiercely competitive."

"Esther and Abraham have made gallery introductions." She crosses her legs at the ankle. "Back home in Ohio, my paintings sold as fast as I could make them."

Shirley blinks at her, all innocence and naivete, giving Ruth a rush of maternal impulses: to warn this girl, to advise her on all sorts of things. But then, on the day she moved in with Lucy, she'd probably looked every bit as green. What a journey it has been. The trip of a lifetime. Let Shirley learn for herself.

Ruth closes the suitcase clasps. "You will do just fine."

"Goodbye, then?"

"Goodbye."

There's no handshake, no sisterly hug. Ruth heaves the suitcase up to hold it with both arms and lugs it down the stairs.

Shirley follows out of the bedroom to stand at the landing. "A good guy helps a girl with her bags."

Ruth pauses, bites back a sharp reply, then decides to give her the last word. Why begrudge Miss Ohio her parting jibe? Why pop her balloon of confidence?

But Shirley's observation echoes when Ruth is outside, sitting on that suitcase, waiting for Jackson. Her other bags are alongside. She's wearing a light-blue pinafore and a cute small hat.

She checks her watch, hoping he arrives before Esther or Abraham happen by. She would rather not face them. And once she is gone, she cannot come back. A drop of sweat snakes down between her shoulder blades, and she stands. The porch is shaded at that hour. She sits on the swing, chewing her thumbnail. She wills herself not to call him.

When her wait reaches half an hour, Ruth goes back inside and asks the house mistress please to use the phone. It takes all of her self-possession to conceal that she is furious. Ruth starts to dial Jackson's number, then stops, and calls a cab instead. He arrives right away, opens the trunk, and when she steps away from her bags, he raises his eyebrows at her, then loads them in.

The taxi smells of cigars. The engine, rumbling roughly, has something wrong with it. The driver takes his sweet time getting in.

"Fireplace Road, please," she tells him from the back seat.

The cabbie launches into a monologue about the weather, heavy dew in the mornings, when Ruth takes a last look back. Shirley is at the window again. Ruth thought her departure would be a moment of triumph. Instead, the noisy car pulls away, and she's hugging herself in her seat.

SURROUNDED BY LUGGAGE, RUTH FACES THE HOUSE FROM THE ROAD. The place is silent. No Miles Davis recording spilling out the windows. No conversation from someone on the phone. The convertible sits in the shade, its white canvas top raised and snapped into place, though it hasn't rained for days.

All is still, like calm water. And her mood begins to shift from anger to worry.

"Jackson?" she calls, sneaking closer. "Sweetheart?"

A blue jay shrieks as it flies over, startling her, and darts into the woods to repeat its cry of alarm.

"Come on, girl," Ruth chides herself. "Broad daylight."

She creeps around the house, is about to turn toward the studio, when she sees something near the edge of the lawn.

There he is. Barefoot. Face down in the grass.

"Jackson?" she whispers. Is he dead? His limbs look flaccid, surrendered to gravity. *Please God, not dead.* She inches closer. *Please.*

When Ruth is ten feet away, he sighs, his back rising and falling. She resists the urge to cry out. Instead, she hitches up her dress and sits cross-legged beside him, angry and relieved, furious and glad. When he rolls onto his side, facing her but still asleep, his skin is flushed with heat from the midday sun. She unpins her little hat and fans it back and forth over his face.

In a few seconds, his eyes blink open.

Ruth smiles. "I am quite relieved that you are not dead."

"Did you think I was?"

"I had already decided which dress to wear to your funeral."

He laughs. Raspy and rough, but she has not heard him laugh in days.

"A little black thing," she continues. "High hemline, plunging neckline."

His laughter grows, a true release, he's on his back roaring to the sky.

Ruth is still livid, but can't help joining in. They take the time, letting out much more than her one joke. Has she laughed like this even once since arriving in Sag Harbor? They do now, till they need to pause for breath, till the joy dwindles.

"Jackson." Ruth presses a hand on his arm. "For a minute I really did think you were gone. It was terrifying. I cannot live without you."

"Still here." Jackson pounds his chest. "Just a rough night." He shifts closer, onto his side, and pushes up her pinafore to rest his head on her bare thigh.

She caresses his scalp. Growling with pleasure, he reaches under the dress, rubbing her underwear, then crooks one finger inside the elastic.

The man has nerve. Standing her up at the boardinghouse. Not apologizing instantly. Not offering to help with her bags, which are still by the road.

Lucy's parting advice comes to mind again. Ruth wants to give him hell. But she says it anyway: "Yes yes yes."

Jackson rises with a growl.

THE COFFEE MAKER IS HUGE, A GIANT PERCOLATOR. "WHERE DID YOU get this beast?"

Jackson is finishing a sandwich. "Bought it from a diner going out of business. Unlike our friends, Lee and I don't take stimulants. Except coffee."

Ruth peers into its reservoir. "You could serve a convention with this thing."

"Not many people visit here, actually."

"I have been imagining that you had no end of guests. Friends, fans, hangers-on. Women in love with your manhood." She rubs her palm on the front of his pants.

"Is that so?" he says.

"It is so, yes." She rubs harder, bold and firm, and in seconds they are half undressed again, grappling on the kitchen floor. When he is on top, the skin of her back squeaks against the linoleum. It makes them laugh together. She bites his shoulder, which sends him off the cliff.

After, while they are cuddling, Ruth utters the one thing she has longed to say in his arms, in his home: "Jackson, I love you."

He hesitates with his answer. Tugs on her ear. "I know," he says. "You can't imagine how much I appreciate it."

Ruth takes that response in, measures it, puts it on an emotional shelf. Rising naked, she starts running water. Jackson rolls on his back, an arm pillowing his head. "What are you doing?"

She lowers the percolator into the sink. "Making coffee."

THE NEXT MORNING, HE WAKES FIRST. SHE CAN TELL FROM HIS NEARNESS, and slow breath, that he is staring at her.

"What are you looking at?"

"Your back," Jackson replies. "Your hair across your skin. It's interesting."

"Mmm. Not sexy? Not beautiful?"

"Interesting is better. Sexy we see and move on in a second. Interesting we stick around to see what might happen."

She remembers the seagrass and its shadow. It inspired him. Another time, they strolled past a dead fish, and he squatted to study the mottled rot of it. There was no sign that he noticed the stink. "You like when one color crosses another."

"Maybe." He trails his fingers on her pale skin, outlining the shape of her hair. "Have you looked at things that intersect? I mean truly investigated them? Two things telling their rich histories at the same time—adjacent, weaving. Complexity is rarely sexy. But it is always interesting."

She backs her rump against him. He chuckles, but she waggles her backside. He kisses her shoulder, and she arches against his arousal like a cat rubbing against its owner's leg.

"I love you, Jackson."

He grips one of her thighs. "Show me."

LATER, WHEN HE'S GONE TO THE STUDIO, SHE SNOOPS. IN THE SPARE BEDroom she finds an easel, a side table littered with tubes of oils, brushes, and rags. There's a canvas, unfinished, and it does not look like anything Jackson would make. The dominant color is pink like exaggerated flesh, with hints of sexual motion. It does not create a feeling of pleasure, though, but of discomfort. Not passion, but violence.

"Let us hope otherwise," she tells the painting.

Ruth wheels away, her yellow summer dress rising. It feels girlish, and reminds her of spinning in front of the construction crew. They applauded. The memory makes her feel grateful and playful.

Downstairs there are seashells, hundreds of them. On the sideboard sits a clamshell nearly as broad as her shoulders, filled with white sand dollars, and miniature trees of pale pink coral. In the next room, one wall is all bookshelves. The books are esoteric: *Byzantine Painting* and *Etruscan Painting*, both by Skira, whoever that is. Thick biographies of Van Gogh and Matisse. *The Meaning of Art* by Herbert Read. *Abstract and Surrealist Art in America* by someone named Sidney Janis.

"Hello, Sidney No-One-Ever-Heard-Of," she says. "And Janis, what an unfortunate last name for a male. I bet they teased you in school."

In a corner she finds a tube amplifier, a turntable, and dozens of LPs. Ruth flips through them. It's jazz, mostly bebop. Monk, Coltrane, Davis. She finds a few orchestral recordings, and the composer is always Stravinsky.

"Time to learn this crazy music," she mutters. "And how to like it."

One album is brand-new, *Ella and Louis*. The cover shows Ella Fitzgerald and Louis Armstrong in ordinary clothes, looking like they've just come from a long day at the office, though actually they've just finished recording. It takes Ruth a minute to figure out how to turn on the amplifier. As the tubes warm up, she slides the LP out of its sleeve and settles it on the record player. She lifts the arm and sets the needle down.

The first song opens with light, friendly piano. Ruth stands and swings her hips, dances over by the dining table, one hand raised, eyes half closed. Ella sings so purely, it's like she's pouring water.

On the second verse, Louis sings, rough and growling. And at the finish, they are in harmony that gives her goose bumps. Their voices are a perfect contrast, hers water and his gravel, and suddenly she is struck by it.

"That is *us*," she tells the living room. "Louis is Jackson, and Ella is me."

Ruth skips to the sink and fills two glasses with water. She dances out to the studio, the living room's music quieter with each step. It's noon on a sunny August day. Though the unfinished painting troubles her, no absent wife is going to interfere with her joy. Ruth taps her fingernails on the window in the studio door and glides inside. Jackson does not look up. He's using a mixing stick in a can of paint, controlling the spill onto a canvas the size of a twin bed, pulling a dolly of other cans with his foot. To Ruth, it looks athletic. She waits. As long as he is working, dancing can wait.

He whistles "Walking My Baby Back Home" absently. It's his favorite song lately, and Ruth likes how it swings. Eventually his gaze rises. "Oh. Hello."

She holds out a glass. "I love you, Jackson."

"Thank you," he says, sidestepping around the canvas. "You read my mind." He raises the glass, drains it in one go, hands it back. "I've been dying."

Ruth weighs the two glasses, empty and full, and takes a sip from hers. Sidles around the studio, hips swinging. "What are you doing today?"

"Not making a painting." He taps the stick against the can. "Searching for one."

"Jackson, Jackson, Jackson." Ruth beams. "Do you not see? This is about me."

"What are you talking about? The world doesn't revolve around you—"

"It is practically a portrait." She waves her hands over the canvas. The base is cream-colored, crossed by brown downward slashes. On top of both layers, strings of green cross in a way that seems haphazard but is mostly perpendicular. "I know exactly what you are painting."

"How can you know, when I don't?" His voice is firmer. "At most, this is a venture. Something that can't be expressed in words or—"

"Jackson, you are wrong." Laughing, Ruth leans over the canvas. "You have painted us, from this morning. This base color"—she points—"that's the skin of my back. Those brown shapes? My hair while I sleep. Green is the color of living things. A sign that you see I am good for you, and our love is good for your art."

Jackson glares like he's scraping her skin with his eyes. "Ten after ten. Ten after ten."

Ruth doesn't know what it means, but she has heard him say it before, under pressure. She may have overstepped. "Why do you put the canvas on the floor?"

He looks down. "So the paint can't run. On an easel, it would."

"Why do you pour it from the cans?"

"I don't. It's not like the philistines who fling colors and hope they land in an interesting way. My work is not about abandon. It's about control." He taps his temple. "A plan in my head. For that, mixing sticks are perfect."

"You could use oil paint. It will not run. Plus, then you could use brushes."

"Wait." He trots down the studio's step. Returning with a brush, he runs it across Ruth's cheekbone, down to her jaw, and lightly under her throat.

She squirms. "It tickles."

"But I don't feel a thing." He tosses the brush aside. "Handle, bristles, it all prevents me from contact, and from understanding. I can't even tell if I'm touching a living thing."

"I think you know that already." As she speaks, Ruth performs a pirouette, her skirt rising as it did in the house.

"Then there's the gravity part," he grunts, tackling her down to the bear rug.

"I loved sleeping on this . . ."

Her speaking ends as he uses his knee to part her legs, pressing his weight onto her. His jaw is clenched, but he whispers, "Gravity pulls like it is the earth's desire."

"Jackson, Jackson, Jackson."

"What the hell does that mean, anyway? Repeating my name that way. I never know what you're trying to say."

She can see the flash of annoyance. "Darling, isn't it obvious?" Ruth touches his face. "It means fuck me."

HE DOES NOT BOTHER TO UNDRESS HER. UP WITH HER SKIRT, UNDERWEAR yanked aside, and although she is not ready, he presses, and thrusts. Ruth cries out.

"You can take it," he growls.

She tilts her hips. Opens wider, letting him in and in and in.

They roll and slide, crossing the studio floor like some clumsy, multi-legged bug, till her knee bangs one of the dollies. The cans clank, but Jackson does not pause. She reaches both hands overhead to the wall, pressing back against him. She kisses his forehead, he gives her breast a love bite and she squeals. It takes him longer. There is no roar in his climax now. The previous day has depleted him, making this session softer, somehow sweeter.

Also, Ruth has a triumph: Before Jackson falls off, he kisses her—and with his old mad intensity. He tolerates her response, too, a bushel of pecks all over.

"Jackson, I love you so."

He collapses on his back. "I believe you've done it. Burned me to the ground."

She kisses his ear. "Thank goodness the condition is temporary."

He regards her with one open eye, then closes it.

She stands, her skirt falling into place, but she slides it to the floor, sheds her underwear, her shirt and bra. "Be right back."

He waves an arm vaguely in her direction, without opening his eyes.

In a minute, Ruth returns with the water glasses refilled. Again, Jackson gives her one eye, then sits up. "You went to the house and back in the nude?"

She sits and sips. "Alfonso advised it. Remember?"

He squints as if she stood in sunlight. "He said topless."

Ruth kisses him. "He also said all day. You know I would do that for you."

He holds still, not responding, not reciprocating. "What if people see you?"

She leans back against the wall. "Then they are lucky."

"Yeah, but."

The room nearly rings with what goes unsaid. *Yeah, but what about Lee? Yeah, but what if she hears about it?*

"You still have not accepted our destiny." Ruth sets both glasses on the floor beside him, collects her clothes, and starts for the door. "Drink your water."

IN THE BATHROOM, THE SHOWER RINGS SHRIEK AS SHE YANKS THE CURtain back. Waiting for the water to warm, she faces the mirror and performs a self-assessment. How many times since age thirteen has she stood before a mirror and found some aspect of herself wanting? Once she grew breasts larger and sooner than other girls, the exam has been daily—and always concludes the same way: not enough of this, too much of that, never all right.

"Careful about them boys," her father had warned. "You oughta suspicion them even more than I do."

A place on her breast hurts from Jackson's bite, though, and she likes it. Feeling his impatience, she is tender between her legs too.

Ruth pulls on a shower cap, turns sideways, and decides that, though she's twenty-eight, she still has a shapely behind. Mostly. She continues her rotation.

There. Green paint, glossy and thick.

Why is that such a thrill? Here is evidence that she cherishes.

Ruth studies the mirror again, in her swan pose—but she hadn't told herself to stand that way. It happened naturally.

She has an idea. Will it anger Jackson, or will he praise her for saying something in paint that cannot be expressed in words? Lining herself up with the white bathroom door, she backs up slowly. It's perfect, a smooth cross-board at a height that matches her bum. Amused, proud, she takes one more step back, her bottom firm against the door, pushing her buttocks, holding fast before stepping away to see her masterpiece. Two dark green ovals with a cleft between. There is no question what the source of the image is.

She claps with joy. "My autograph."

Ruth steps into the rain of hot water, soaping her behind. But the paint is not cooperative. It will take scrubbing. She reaches for a washcloth and finds herself whistling Jackson's favorite: "Walking My Baby Back Home."

26

JANUARY 2007

Ruth strode through the open door, arms crossed like a pharaoh. Down the spiral of stairs, she could see Gwen's hand on the railing, circling lower and lower.

"Wait," Ruth called.

The stairwell echoed, and the hand stopped descending.

Ruth leaned over the railing. "It was sexual."

Gwen poked her head into the open space. "What did you say?"

Ruth scanned the doors of other apartments on her floor. Making a megaphone with her hands, she stage-whispered, "*Sects-you-ull.*"

Gwen vanished, then reappeared. "What are you talking about?"

"How the painting was made. Come back and I will tell you. No nonsense."

Gwen sighed, making sure it was audible upstairs. Trudging, dragging her feet, she privately marveled that Chillie had been right.

"In here, please," Ruth chirped from the living room.

Gwen stopped in the doorway. "I'm listening."

"Please spare me the theatrics. Take off your coat."

"I have a meeting. I'm already late."

"Young lady, that is a lie. Now, sit."

Gwen obeyed, but her sense of humor was gone. Instead, she was simmering.

"So." Ruth folded her hands in her lap. "I want to talk about delicate matters. About giving a man pleasure."

Instantly Gwen's mind leapt to that chilly Sunday afternoon, nearly four weeks past, in Arthur's messy apartment. The joy they gave each other, and how she dared to imagine a future. The memory filled her with longing. And right behind that, the weight of her decision to prevent it from continuing. "I can't imagine any circumstance in which this conversation is appropriate."

"Fine. Be a nun about it. But in my intimacy with Jackson, my satisfaction was not a goal. Or even a factor, you might say. His, however, was paramount. It was essential to his stability. My duty—"

"Have mercy and get to the point."

"Remember that afternoon on the beach I told you about? Jackson was studying the weaving of colors and shadows, he had ideas. But the crucial thing happened immediately after I brought him pleasure: Jackson was inspired. Had I not mistakenly given him money for booze, there would be a painting today. For the whole world to cherish."

"I'm not seeing the connection."

"Some days later." Ruth shifted closer. "I was going to make lunch, and went to ask what he might want. I found him in the backyard, standing there, quite still—looking at the grass, then the sky. Back and forth like that, not speaking, moving only his head. How do I explain it, though? You and I might look at the sky for a minute, and imagine the shapes of clouds. Jackson did not see as you and I see. He did not perceive as we do. He was trying to understand something, the nature of something, what he called its history. After watching him for perhaps twenty minutes, I left for the kitchen. When I returned with a plate, I said, 'Your sandwich is ready.'

"'Goddamn it,' he shouted. 'Can't I get one minute of peace?'

"He was right, of course. An hour invested in studious thought, and I had interrupted. But I knew then, I had learned from the beach, how to help him. While he fought with his rage, I knelt and opened his belt. He said, 'What in hell are you doing?' I put a fingertip under his chin and pushed so he was looking upward. When I lowered his zipper—"

"No more details." Gwen was cringing. "Please God."

"Fine. It was somewhat unpleasant for me as well. But allow me to say that it had the same effect as on the beach. He was inspired. His satisfaction caused him to make a painting that day."

"That day?" Gwen took out her notebook. "Do you remember the date?"

"August fifth? Sixth? Lee had been gone a week or so."

Gwen scribbled notes. "Go ahead."

"Well. He took the sandwich and returned to his studio."

"And that was when he made the painting? Did you see him do it?"

"Look at you," Ruth said. "Rabid with greed."

"This is not greed. This is the end of my patience. And my employer's."

"Miss Gwen, I am counting on your greed. And that of your firm. Carroll and Bunzel desperately wants the commission from a fifty-million-dollar painting. Nearly seventeen million with, I am certain, a considerable gratuity for you."

"If we sell something that later is proven to be a fake," Gwen replied, "we will have sacrificed credibility, which is a certainty that luxury buyers require. It will put us out of business. Money isn't the motivator. Survival is."

"So says the glorified saleswoman. Who does not see the poison of greed."

"Look." Gwen raised both hands, as if in surrender. "Your stories have been interesting. But they are not relevant to the business we are in. Right now is a perfect example. Instead of telling me what I need to know, you're attacking my way of making a living. And telling me about your sex life. Ick."

Ruth burst out laughing. She rocked back and forth, red faced. It took a moment to collect herself, by which time Gwen was seething.

"I know this history is coarse. But, young lady." Ruth wagged a finger. "You are old enough to see the point. My love was nourishing his genius. I was helping, exactly as I had dreamed. Exactly as we were destined."

"Please." Gwen closed her eyes. "Please just tell me about the painting."

"You are about as fun as a dentist's office." Ruth tapped the scissors in her lap. "I went to the entry of his studio, where he kept paint cans, brushes, and tools. His work boots, splattered with colors. Oh, that studio." She stared across the room at the empty easel. "The paint spilled on his floor alone looked like a masterpiece."

All she'd endured over the past month, and perhaps now Gwen would hear what she needed. "When you entered his studio, was he making your painting?"

Ruth huffed with condescension. "He was looking into the trees. Dark green, light green, a blue-sky background. If you stared at what he stared at, you saw how the world looked to him. His paintings were not strange. They were accurate."

Gwen could barely stay in her seat. "When did Jackson start the painting?"

"So greedy." Ruth frowned. "I brought a canvas outside. Tucked a board under it, so the uneven grass would not make the paint run. He began work right away."

"Did he use a dolly outside?"

Ruth shook her head. "It would not have rolled in the grass."

"Then where was the paint? Did he bring colors out one at a time, or all at once? And did he bring brushes, or cans and his mixing sticks?"

"Why are you cross-examining me?"

"If we are going to ask people to spend fifty million dollars, their questions will make me look like a reporter for a high school newspaper."

"Can you not see the beauty of it? That I would lay the canvas down for him. That he would paint from the inspiration I had given him. That he would work while I witnessed. Do you understand the legend we were making?" Her eyes widened. "Tell me the honest truth. Do you understand that this was our destiny?"

Gwen snorted. "You do not want to hear the honest truth."

"In fact, I do." Ruth sat back. "Before I say one more word."

"All right." Gwen spoke with a clenched jaw. "I think this destiny stuff is a hiding place. A bullshit way to avoid admitting culpability."

"Such as?"

"Such as 'it was our destiny,' and not 'we committed adultery.'"

"You have been judging me all this time."

"You seduced a married man," Gwen snapped, "and tried to pawn it off as a decision the gods made. You know which gods? The god of ambition. The god of clinging to a famous person, instead of making your own meaningful life."

Ruth was gasping. "To think that I once thought you were kind."

Now that she had started, Gwen was boiling. "You don't have *any* regrets, do you? No remorse for enabling his alcohol abuse, though it worsened his depression. No apology for blowing off those people with the kids' art school. Not the least pang of conscience for the horror that resulted from all of these things. Aren't you sorry for any of it?"

"Why would I be sorry?"

"Because of your role in causing a terrible tragedy."

"My experience was the most tragic of all," Ruth cried. "Because I survived. I had to live with all of the loss. All the ridicule. No one suffered more than me."

"Not even Lee?" Gwen watched Ruth's face change, as if she'd been forced to drink sour milk.

"Get out." She raised her arm, pointing. "Get out of my house."

Gwen stood. "You understand that this will conclude our business?"

"You terrible auction people. You know the price of everything, and the value of nothing."

"That's Oscar Wilde's line. And he was talking about cynics, not art dealers."

"Jackson painted it right there in front of me, all right? Who else on earth can say that? And what genius emerged from him. Like a river. Like fire."

"Like fire? There's nothing remotely fire-like in this painting."

"You must have no eyes." Ruth rose from her chair, head held high. "It is all there, right on the canvas: *Red, Black and Silver.* The rich red, arched and poised like a ballerina's hand. The black core of deep power. The smooth silver, like moonlight reflected off the ocean."

"Which you want me to sell for top dollar."

"When he had finished," Ruth boomed. But then she caught herself—and in an instant heard what Gwen had said, understood the insult in it, and decided her point was more important than a direct answer. Her voice dropped an octave, and was quieter.

"When he had finished the work, my beloved Jackson said, 'Here is your painting, Ruth, here is your very own Pollock.' That is the story. That is the answer to your pestilent question. He made it in front of me, for me, and gave it to me. And you, Miss Gwen?"

Ruth crossed the room to gaze upon her photo with Jackson once again. "You understand nothing."

17

AUGUST 1956

It is a matter of taking possession, Ruth tells herself that morning. "I have been patient enough," she declares to the house.

That said, she lifts Lee's unfinished painting off the easel in the spare bedroom. She slides it behind winter clothes in the closet. It's awkward, bringing the easel downstairs, till she sets it by the piano, going back for the side table, the paint and the tools. Soon her workspace is all ready, and she confronts a blank canvas.

In honor of her autograph on the bathroom door, which Jackson has not mentioned yet, she chooses a tube of forest green. Ruth squeezes a glob onto a brush as if it were toothpaste, then reaches to the upper right corner. A bold, dark stroke to the middle and curving. Against the pale blank, it is a strong statement. She considers starting every painting this way for the rest of her life.

But she notices a green mark on the shirt she's wearing, which is Jackson's, so she shucks it off. Now she wears only panties. It's August, a cardinal chirps in the lilacs by the door. If ever there were a day to wear next to nothing, this is it.

Ruth globs more green on the brush, making another curve. Inadvertently, the two pair like quotation marks. Is her work already saying something? She picks up another tube, cadmium yellow, and reaches for a fresh brush.

The morning flies. A mess of colors and gestures, while she has no sense of time passing. No wonder Jackson barks when she interrupts. Is she hungry? Or what was it that broke her reverie?

A knock on the screen door. "Anyone home?"

A car must have pulled in. Ruth glances outside, and yes, beside the convertible there is a red-and-white Buick. She doesn't recognize the car, but she knows it's not Esther or Abraham or Shirley, come to fetch her back.

She sets the brush handle on the table, bristles in the air to avoid staining.

"Well, hello there."

Ruth wheels, and the man at the door has let himself in. He is tall, well dressed, and breathtakingly handsome.

"Hello," Ruth manages to say, standing before him all but naked. And yet, after the first fright, she feels a strange confidence. A power. "How are you today?"

He grins like a jack-o'-lantern. "Better now, that's for sure."

Ruth stands upright. "Do you like?"

"My eyes fell out of my head, didn't they?"

She laughs, and he does too. "One moment." Ruth reaches for the shirt—with her bottom pointed in his direction, why not?—and straightens while slipping her arms into the sleeves.

"You didn't need to do that," the man says. "I like Lady Godiva."

She fastens just one button, between her breasts. Otherwise the shirt hangs loose like a windless sail. "It is Jackson's. The shirt, I mean."

The man glances in the direction of the studio. "He's actually working?"

"If you use that word, he will bite you." She loves the word she inadvertently chose, an inside joke with herself. Her breast still bears the shadow of a bruise from his teeth. "Come to the studio. He will be glad for the company."

"Good idea." The man follows Ruth out the screen door. "I imagine my wife would wholeheartedly agree."

Before they reach the studio, Jackson comes outside. Startled, he wipes a sleeve across his face. Ruth knows it's not sweat. Whatever deep sorrow haunts him, he has not yet confided it to her. Jackson backpedals, like a child who has been caught doing something naughty.

But the man hails him, both arms in the air. "Hey, it's Jack the Dripper."

"Willem." Jackson stops retreating, slaps his hands on his paint-stained pants. "Welcome to the place where nothing gets done."

As they shake hands, Ruth notices that Jackson is squinting again. The sun is behind a cloud, and they're all standing in the shade. But his eyes are nearly closed, as if the world has become too bright for him.

". . . and otherwise a middling-to-poor-quality painter, Willem de Kooning, meet the legendary Ruth Kligman," Jackson says, finishing the introduction. If he is troubled by her near nakedness, he hides it well. "Or did you say hello in the house?"

"Oh, we're old friends." Willem is grinning.

Ruth realizes that both men are looking at her. There is that rush of confidence again, a sip of adrenaline. "Shall I make iced tea?"

"Excellent," Willem says. "If I'm not interrupting . . ."

"Are you kidding?" Jackson's laugh sounds bitter. "We could accomplish more by taking a long walk."

"Then let's do that." He puts an arm around Jackson's shoulders, guiding him across the lawn. They're headed toward the trail, which she has been told wends all the way down to the wetlands. Willem has been here before, Ruth realizes. And he showed no surprise to find her there.

"Your lady is quite the firecracker," he says, thinking he is out of hearing. Ruth follows, barefoot in the grass.

"I suppose," Jackson replies.

"You know what happens when you hold a firecracker?"

"Tell me."

"It blows your fingers off."

He laughs, and Jackson nods, but she stops cold. They reach the trail, vanish into the dark of the woods. Ruth undoes the one button, lets the shirt pour off her shoulders, spilling from her back onto the grass. And turns for the house.

◆ ◆ ◆

"HE DIDN'T INVENT IT, YOU KNOW."

Fully clothed now, Ruth looks up from the sink, where she has spent the better part of an hour trying to clean the brushes. There must be some trick, or special liquid, because she scrubs and scrubs, and the water keeps running with a silt of green. It's late afternoon, light leaning under the trees to gild the kitchen.

Willem leans against the door, hands in his pockets. He is suave and gorgeous and reminds her—it surprises Ruth a little—of Ronald Gray, her first conquest in Manhattan: cool but hungry. For an instant Ruth wishes she were wearing only underwear again, to keep things even. "Didn't invent what?"

Willem takes his hands from his pockets to pantomime stirring paint and pouring it. "What everyone credits him with inventing."

"Other artists do it, yes," Ruth replies, "but it is all imitation."

"If you pour me a scotch, I'll tell you the story."

"What is Jackson doing?"

Willem smiles. "Napping on his polar bear rug."

With a smirk, Ruth wipes her hands on a dish towel and drops it on the counter. "Scotch it is."

When she offers him the glass, he takes it in a whole-hand way that traps one of her fingers, and holds. It is subtle, but Ruth unplugs from his grip and returns to the kitchen. "I think you need some ice."

He appears unruffled. "Perhaps so."

She cracks open an ice tray, plunks cubes in his glass. It reestablishes her confidence. Ruth strolls to the living room, knowing he will follow. She takes the club chair, leaving him the wide couch. "You were going to tell me a story?"

Willem lowers himself onto the center cushion. "The legend of Janet Sobel."

"Who is she?"

"Exactly my point. You have no idea."

Ruth shrugs. "I also have no idea how an aircraft flies. But I never worry about one dropping on me."

He laughs. It's open throated, and she knows he is enjoying himself.

"Janet Sobel fled Ukraine during a pogrom at the age of fifteen, arrived in Brooklyn, married a fellow refugee at seventeen, and had five children. But where are my manners?" He raises the glass in her direction. "Thank you, and cheers."

Ruth lifts her hand, holding an imaginary drink. "Cheers."

"Anyway." He takes a sip, nodding approvingly at the flavor. "She begins to paint when she is forty-four. But *paint* is a generous word. Apparently, she disliked brushes. Instead, she used eyedroppers, bare hands, a vacuum cleaner. Eventually, perhaps inevitably, she drips the paint on a canvas."

"On the floor so it cannot run."

"Why, yes." He raises the glass her way again. "Also, it allows the painter to move around the whole work, to approach from every angle. One of Janet Sobel's sons is something of an artist himself. In nineteen forty-five, when Mama makes her first all-drip painting, sonny writes to big players in the art world. Marc Chagall, for example. Sidney Janis."

Ruth can see the book from her chair. "He wrote about abstract art."

"He did indeed." Willem slides back on the couch, looking into his drink. It is Ruth's first inkling that he may be drunk. That he and Jackson got into some mischief besides a trail walk. That Jackson is not napping in his studio, but passed out. "I believe I've underestimated you."

It is Ruth's turn to smile. "You would not be the first."

"Sidney has supported many painters, including me. He brought Janet to the attention of Peggy Guggenheim. At this point I would not be surprised to learn that you and Peggy have shopped at Tiffany together. She loved Janet's work, included her in a group show, then in nineteen forty-six gave her a show all her own."

"When does this story begin to concern Jackson?"

Willem chuckles, having regained himself. "Patience, Lady Godiva. Clement Greenberg, arguably the most powerful art critic in the world, was not going to review Janet's show. Who cares about female artists, much less some grandmother refugee housewife from Brooklyn? Since the show was at Peggy's own gallery, Art of This Century, she made entreaties. Finally Clement capitulated. As a lark, he invited Jack along. It was a great boon to any rising star."

"There he is," Ruth sighs. "My Jackson."

Willem glances at her sideways, waiting to hear the rest of the joke. But there is none. Shaking his head as if to clear it, he sits forward again. "Imagine these two men. Clement, a gruff critic and unapologetic misogynist, grousing at each new painting, calling one 'primitive,' and the next one 'curiously dull,' and so on. Meanwhile, Jackson is silent, wide-eyed, spellbound. He arrives at the painting Janet Sobel called *Milky Way*—it's brilliant, I've seen it. Rich indigo background full of wisps and suggestions, a foreground crackling with passionate circles and spirals. Which is to say, abstract expressionism at its best. There stands Jack in a stupor of wonder, till grouchy Clement tugs his arm and tells him to step lively."

"What I would give to have been there."

"Yes." Willem takes a big gulp from his glass. "The punch line is even better. In a few weeks, Jackson delivers to the world a new painting, and it is a staggering display of creativity. Like a horse, after a lifetime with the reins pulled back, finally given its head. It's called *Full Fathom Five*."

Ruth blanches. "I have never seen that one."

"You would be enriched to do so," Willem advises. "He started with a brush, carefully enough, then skipped gleefully down the path Janet Sobel had cleared. He put nails on the canvas, with paint layered thick enough to hold them. There's a face—not a portrait, it's more primitive, like an indigenous mask. He added coins, thumbtacks, a key. For God's sake, *an actual key in the painting*. It surpassed everything. Atop it all, he applied house paint, using a stirring stick to control how fast the can poured. A tribute in paint and pain, all about the death of his father."

"There is our genius," Ruth purrs.

"That's what Clement said," Willem responds. "He called the painting 'a masterpiece of invention, passion and genius.'"

"But what happened to Janet . . . what was her last name?"

"Sobel? She fell like flotsam from a ship. Critics rushed forward, leaping over each other with praise for Jackson. '*Starry Night* on amphetamines.' 'The muscularity of Ernest Hemingway, the abundance of Thomas Wolfe.' 'In our *allegro* postwar world, it is more than a new way of seeing. It is a new way of feeling.'"

"He must have been breathless, reading such reviews."

"*Life* magazine ran a long article about him, with photos of his work. 'Jackson Pollock: Is he the greatest living painter in the United States?'"

"Did you celebrate all over New York with him?"

"Celebrate?" Willem tilts his head as a dog does, as if not understanding the question. After a moment he straightens, looks her dead-on. "I wanted to kill him."

He drains his scotch, rises, and heads for the door.

Ruth stays in her seat. "Are you saying that Jackson stole the idea?"

"Stole?" Willem puts his glass on the kitchen counter. "More like he exploded it. Exceeded its speed limit, interrogated its potential, and came out the other side with brilliant paintings . . . and an unstable mind."

"Is he really in such terrible condition?"

"No offense, Miss Godiva, and we've just met. But for years now, years, the only thing keeping Jack in one piece has been Lee."

Now Ruth stands. "She was holding him back. Such greatness in Jackson, so much capacity, and always her foot on the brake. His pain is the result of repressing himself, and allowing his wife to oppress him." Her voice quivers with rage. "Now, with the benefit of a love affair granted by the fates, with support and with freedom, Jackson Pollock might go further than any artistic genius ever before."

"True," Willem says, opening the screen door. Evening waits out there, lovely August on Long Island and the crickets singing. "But I just spent the afternoon with him. And he also might go stark raving mad."

28

JANUARY 2007

Gwen laughed. She couldn't help it. Pressed a fist against her forehead, but she was laughing the whole time.

"I can't believe it. The exact moment you're saying I don't understand, you finally tell me something useful. The painting on the lawn story is exactly what I've needed."

Ruth peered down her nose. "I entirely do not care."

"Nonsense. Thirty-three million dollars from the auction will be going to you."

"You insult me."

"By suggesting that you feel the greed you projected onto me?"

"Selling this painting is not about greed. It is about love, and—"

"Destiny, yes, I know. Yawn."

"How dare you? Such disrespect."

Gwen pulled out her notebook once again. "Why didn't you mention the painting in your memoir?"

"I did. Right there in the introduction."

"Sure, in the second edition. Which came out just before the first time you were trying to sell the painting. Not a word about it in the original edition, twenty-five years earlier."

Ruth assessed her with narrowed eyes. "Well, look at the clever girl."

"Buyers will ask. It's best to devise an answer that suits them."

"Devise? One insult after another."

Gwen smiled. "Actually, I think now we understand each other."

"You flatter yourself."

"Perhaps. But if we work together, we might get away with this whole charade. The only remaining issue is how you obtained the painting."

Ruth's shoulders dropped. "Must you always raise a new issue?"

"I asked you this question the day we met. Let's not pretend otherwise. Anyway, there you are. Heartbroken, hospitalized. How did you get the painting?"

Ruth adjusted her clothes. "It does not matter."

"Nonsense. A taxi from the hospital to the house and back?" Gwen paced the room like a prosecutor. "But that would have been a huge exertion. Painful too."

"You are a parasite."

"Also, that would require you to move fast. Lee flew home from Paris the next day. She didn't know the painting existed, though. She wouldn't know it was gone."

"I was suffering. I had lost the love of my life, and my body was battered."

"Or maybe during the funeral, on the fifteenth. Were you up and about by then?"

"No, I was not up and about. My hips have never been right since that day."

"You had a helper, maybe? Lots of people were conflicted about what happened. Clement Greenberg was going to give the eulogy, till Lee refused to let him speak. Others stayed away."

"Clement would not help me. We did not even meet till years later."

"How did you obtain the most important possession of your life? The physical evidence of your grand destiny?" Gwen snorted. "Don't tell me you forgot."

"I was not clearheaded for weeks."

"Weak excuse." Gwen tapped her pen on the notebook. "Too bad Willem isn't still alive."

Ruth picked at her dress. "For many reasons."

"Alfonso, then. Sending a butler during the funeral, tidy as can be."

"I am now remembering that I ordered you to get out."

"What about one of your other friends? Shirley from the kids' school? A nice girl doing a chore for her poor injured coworker?"

"Why haven't you left yet? Must I call the police?"

"Shirley, helping you in the name of love."

Ruth reached to pick up the phone.

"I'm going." Gwen stuffed her notebook away. "But please be aware." She faced Ruth squarely. "This moment isn't any kind of destiny. It is a choice. I'm leaving without a single sentence about the painting's provenance. If I am also without a sample of your hair, I cannot imagine that Carroll and Bunzel will represent the painting."

"I will call your chief executive," Ruth snarled. "We have a good rapport."

"Showing up at his home at night uninvited, yes. It made him so fond of you." Gwen bent over, a hand on each arm of Ruth's chair. "Let's play Cinderella and the glass slipper. If your hair matches the painting, by Tuesday we will have scheduled an auction. Or you can refuse, and by Tuesday you'll have your painting securely returned to you." She straightened. "Your call."

Ruth looked away, wordless.

Gwen hurried out to the entry, then realized she had forgotten her briefcase. She marched back into the living room. "You would think after the fuss I just made—"

She gulped the rest of the sentence. Ruth was standing, one hand on a table for balance, bent at the waist, and, at the sight of Gwen, she bowed her head.

Gwen balked. "Are you sure?"

"Just do it and be done with it."

Gwen approached on tiptoe, but Ruth did not move. She reached for the back of Ruth's head, where removed locks might show less, taking a pinch between her thumb and forefinger. Ruth took a hissing breath through gritted teeth. Gwen tightened her grip, eased slowly away till there was no slack, and pulled.

"Ouch!" Ruth yelled, jumping back. "What the hell?"

Gwen was already poking through the hairs in her hand. "Six with the follicle." She lifted her gaze. "They said I need twelve."

Ruth breathed heavily through her nostrils, a bull about to charge.

She reached up, coiling hair around a finger, glared at Gwen as she tugged, realized it was too gentle, and yanked.

"Goddamn it to hell."

Gwen couldn't help laughing.

"What the holy hell is so funny?"

"That's the first thing I ever heard you say. Through your open apartment door."

"What?" Ruth looked bewildered. "You are making things up now."

"You don't remember? The first time I came here, and your lipstick was a mess?"

"You are driving me mad." Ruth threw the hair at her; it feathered down on the rug.

Gwen knelt, and the dozens of hairs all included follicles. She scooped them up and, along with the six she held, tucked them into a small envelope she'd brought.

By then Ruth had floated over to her preferred window. "I knew Warhol, you know." She was fighting back tears. "We socialized. Irving Penn photographed me. Mapplethorpe too, before he fell in love with giant portraits of penises. Willem and I remained close for years. Whenever I suffer humiliation, I remember that summer in Springs. Alfonso invited me to everything. I lived among the greats."

"I'm sure you did."

Ruth drew the curtain back with one finger. "I wish never to see you again."

"And I wish—" Gwen stopped herself. Why be cruel? This woman, delusional and grandiose as she was, had genuinely suffered. Her memories—and a painting that might be false—were all that she had left.

Gwen folded the envelope into her pocket. "I wish to see you at the auction."

29

AUGUST 1956

Jackson skips dinner, staying in the studio all night. At dawn, he enters the house sailing straight for the coffee maker. Armed with a full hot cup, he ambles toward Ruth but stops abruptly. She stands at the easel, brush in hand, her nudity protected by an apron that bears red and green paint stains. To see what she's making, or to see her intimately, he would have to come in past the piano.

"Good morning, Jackson. I hope you slept well. Is there anything you need?"

"Every object, I have told you, has a deep and profound history," he replies.

"Yes, you certainly have."

"That brush, for example. Is a story about Lee."

Ruth's hand stops mid-stroke.

"In November of nineteen forty-one, she visited my studio on Eighth Street for the first time. After she'd seen my work, she headed to her studio, on Ninth Street. But she was so stirred up, she had to stop and buy a brush on the way." He points. "That brush."

She puts it down with care. "I should have asked before I—"

"It's fine. Someone ought to be painting here. What I'm saying is about *history*." He sips the coffee, wincing at its temperature. "There was a tree. There was a horse's tail. Maybe under that tree the horse ate the sweetest grass of his life. Maybe the horse was bound to the tree and whipped. Or maybe the horse and tree came from different countries, different continents. Do you see?"

"Not entirely." She wrings her hands. "But if you are hungry . . ."

"You can't treat a brush like a fucking toothpick," he shouts. "Every time, *every* time you touch brush to canvas, you bear the tonnage of history. The tree that became the brush's handle, the horse whose hair provided the bristles. Do you understand?"

"I do now, yes." Ruth gives him a wan smile. "Thank you."

He shakes a fist at her. "Do I always have to explain?"

The first fist. Ruth looks at him with every drop of affection she contains. "Not with me, my love. Whether I understand or not, there is no 'have to' with me."

"Finally." He slams his coffee on the counter. The mug geysers, but he is already out the screen door. "Finally."

Ruth, her nose against the screen, watches him stomp across the lawn, kicking and cursing. What did he mean? "Finally" she understands? Or "finally" he has a love with no "have to"?

When Jackson reaches the trail, she wonders if he has liquor hidden in the woods. As he disappears into the trees, Ruth moves to clean the spilled coffee. But she stops where Jackson was standing, because of the smell. It's not alcohol only. Nor smoke, nor sweat, nor the sour breath of morning, though these all contribute.

The scent reminds Ruth of something specific. Driving home with her father on a November day spent in rural Pennsylvania with her grandparents. She was dozing, until he pulled over because there was something in the way. A quiet place at dusk, a remote road. She followed him to where a deer lay across the lane. No sign of injury. But no motion, no rise and fall of the animal's ribs.

"Must be truck hit, to look unhurt," he said. "May's well move it out the way."

Grabbing a front hoof in one hand and a rear hoof in the other, he dragged the deer into the grass. That was when the scent came up, escaped the corpse like a cloud, so that she hurried back to the car, and he was close behind. They rode with the windows open for miles, despite the cold, and the memory of that odor stayed with her. Then it faded, and she forgot, and in April she turned twelve.

Jackson's odor is nowhere near as bad as that deer. But it is pungent, and Ruth can tell it is unhealthy. As if he has a hidden wound, and instead of healing it is festering.

THAT NIGHT JACKSON IS ABSENT, UNFED IN THE STUDIO. IN THE MORNING, the sound of the shower stirs Ruth from her sleep. Maybe when he pulls the towel from its hook, he'll notice her signature on the door. Maybe he'll laugh. She rises, pulls on a summer nightshirt so thin it conceals nothing, and makes the bed as tidy as a bow. As she goes barefoot downstairs to make coffee, the stairs creak with familiarity.

The giant percolator runs like an old engine, wheezing as hot water rises and drips through the grounds. Ruth opens the screen door to sit on the stoop. It's August, dew on the grass, sun through the trees.

"Worse than I imagined," she murmurs. "He needs time. Unwavering love."

A bird bursts out of the lilac bushes, a red male cardinal that zips and rises and lands in the maple. A pair of metal lawn chairs sit beneath. "Oh, to be here in the spring," she tells the bird. "I bet those lilacs make a rich perfume."

The cardinal sings his little song: two upswings like the catcall whistle of those men in the construction project—it feels like ages ago—then five downward chirps like darts, but sweet.

"Jackson, Jackson, Jackson." Ruth picks a dandelion. "May today go better."

With every window in the house open, she hears when the shower turns off. If it storms in the afternoon, she'll run room to room closing them all. For now, she tucks the flower behind one ear and goes inside.

Jackson stands by the piano, startling her a little, so she stops. "Oh. Good morning."

"Coffee, please."

She fetches a mug for him but hangs back a few steps. Can he make it from the piano to the kitchen? Can he take three steps and risk touching her? Apparently his shoes are glued to the floor. "I love you, Jackson," Ruth says.

He extends an arm. "Coffee, please."

She surrenders the three steps. "Is everything all right?"

"Fine, except you."

He saw her marks on the door and didn't like it. That's her first thought. "What mistake have I made? Tell me please."

"Hair in the drain, dammit. I didn't notice at first. Not till the water was up to my ankles, and then my calves. Not sanitary. Not appealing. Your hair is thick as a rope. And it's clogging everything."

"I hate to contradict you, darling. But I had my hair done in the morning of the day I arrived here. I wore a shower cap both times I showered since then. The hair is not mine."

"Who the hell else could it be, then?"

Ruth points at his chest, his arms. "But I will clean it." She leans, rubbing her pelvis against his. "Would you like me to help your mood?"

"Enh," he grunts. But he pushes back, grabs an ass cheek in one hand and presses her. "It's been some days now."

"We should make love constantly. It pleases us both so much."

He's concentrating, she can tell as she flips opens his belt, unzips his pants. Jackson goes completely still. She pulls out the elastic of his underwear, slides her hand down his furry belly. He's as soft as a noodle. She nuzzles him, tries for a kiss, but he shrugs her away. Ruth strokes him, but his body does not respond. She pulls him a little, gentle tugs, and nothing.

"Get off of me," he barks, yanking her hand up and bumping her away.

Ruth did not expect that, and she tumbles, hitting her lower back against the piano before falling to the floor. She lands wrong, yelping, hurting her wrist.

His face is a storm of emotions: guilt, shame, worry, pride, all arriving at anger. "What's the matter with you?" he growls.

"Me?" Ruth is fighting back tears. "My love, the problem is not only me."

"Me? You're blaming me?"

"You do not touch me, or talk to me, or sleep with me, ever since the drinking became severe. And now it has unmanned you. You cannot even help me up."

Standing over her, he makes a fist, clenches it, squeezes.

"Now you are going to hit me," she says, a flat declaration of the inevitable. A tree about to fall on her, impossible to get out of the way. She closes her eyes so she will not see his face when he inflicts the blow.

Instead, she hears a sound like a slab of beef landing on a cutting board. And a second time, quickly. Her eyes flutter open, and there he stands. The skin on his cheekbone is split, his eye socket already starting to swell, as Jackson crumples into himself on the floor, howling, wailing, weeping like the rain.

"Oh, my beloved." She gathers him in her arms. He's sobbing, so much grief, so much buried inside. She tucks his head in close, rocking him back and forth on the floor. "Jackson, Jackson, Jackson."

He clings to her like a life raft. Ruth tries to turn his head so they are brow to brow, but he jerks away to stare ahead. So she rests her forehead on his temple. Every pulse is a comfort.

THEY ARE STILL GRAPEVINED TOGETHER WHEN THERE'S A RAP ON THE door. Willem, returning with a bouquet. Blue and white lupines, their stems torn rather than sheared, which tells Ruth he did not buy them, but gathered them on his way.

"Good morning." He seems unmoved by what he sees. Spotting Ruth's coffee mug, he crosses the kitchen to take a sip. "Looks like the worry I had about you two all night was accurate." He sets the flowers on the counter. "Sorry to see it."

Jackson has burrowed into her, and he makes no move to emerge. Ruth figures that, between the sheer cotton and the way she's sitting, Willem can see pretty much all of her. *So be it,* she thinks, bringing her knees together.

Willem slurps the coffee. "Hey, Jack. How about a smoke?"

He lifts his head. "I could use two right now."

Willem pulls one out, lights it, and holds it toward Jackson. "That's the limit," he says. "I'm not going to smoke it for you."

Jackson unfolds from Ruth and reaches out one hand. Willem slides the cigarette between his fingers.

"Progress." Willem spies a coffee mug on the piano. "I can guess whose this is." He squats with the mug. "Come on, Jack. Mother's milk."

Jackson takes it and sips. Willem ambles into the living room, fooling with things. Music begins. Sarah Vaughan, "East of the Sun, West of the Moon."

He pulls Ruth to her feet, and they are swaying in the kitchen. His hand on her nightshirt feels like he is touching her skin. Jackson squints up at them.

"I brought you flowers," Willem whispers.

"I saw," she replies. "I seem to attract them from married men."

"Touché." He twirls her once and releases. "Now Jack." He reaches out both hands. "I don't want to dance with you. Let's take another walk. After we get an ice bag for your eye."

"Thanks, Willem." Jackson puts the mug down and clambers to his feet. "Man's got to stand on his own two."

"It's true."

Jackson studies Ruth's face. She can't tell why. What she knows for certain is that he did not hit her. The rage was all within himself.

"Come on." Willem takes Jackson by the elbow. "Let's do the ice later."

They shuffle out the screen door. Ruth lingers near, eavesdropping again.

"So, what did she hit you with?" Willem throws an arm over Jackson's shoulder. "Rolling pin? Frying pan?"

"No no," Jackson protests. "It's not like that at all."

She sees them pilot toward the trail. The last time, Willem returned too familiar, and Jackson spent the rest of the day sleeping off his drink. "Not that way," she yells. "Go somewhere else."

Willem looks back, but she's inside the screen. Still, he veers, steering down Fireplace Road. It's safe, at least for the mile until the dirt becomes pavement.

Ruth steps back from the door. There's nothing broken, no blood to clean up. The next song begins, "Nice Work If You Can Get It," Miles Davis on his mournful horn. Ruth puts the flowers in a vase and holds it under the faucet. But she stands there a long while, staring out the window, before she remembers to run the water.

◆ ◆ ◆

LATER HE LETS HIMSELF IN AGAIN. RUTH IS PAINTING IN UNDERWEAR AGAIN.

"Hello, Lady Godiva."

"Pardon me," she says, trotting upstairs to pull on a sundress.

"No need to do that for me," Willem calls. "Chagall paints stark naked."

When she returns, with sun through the windows behind her, her shadow stretches ahead on the kitchen floor. That means Willem can see her body's outline in the dress. *Let him look,* Ruth thinks. She knows what her destiny is. "Where is my Jackson?"

"Asleep on his rug."

"Again?"

"Sober this time. Whatever you two are doing all night, it's burying him."

"We two?" Ruth adjusts her dress. "He has not come to bed in a long time."

"Oh." Willem's confidence is so vast, this flicker of self-doubt stands out. "Some of the time, he's trying to paint. He wants to make you proud."

Ruth flattens a hand on her chest. "Did he actually say that?"

"He implied it." Willem nods toward the door. "It's cooler outside."

"Of course." She grabs her glass of ice water, considers getting him one, too, then doesn't. They stroll out to the metal chairs under the maple tree. The skies are clear, a steady wind from the Atlantic stirring the leaves. It feels cleansing.

Ruth sits. "This morning, I thought we were in for a storm."

"The humidity broke." Taking the other chair, Willem reaches for her glass. She hesitates, then hands it over. He helps himself to a long drink. "He had relations with my wife, you know."

"From what I gather," Ruth replies evenly, "all of you had relations with everyone's wives. The lucky ones had Miss Mercedes too."

He laughs, long and loud. "Once again, I've underestimated you. But there's one thing you don't know, and I want to set it right."

She gazes down the lawn toward the wetlands. "All right."

"I did Jackson a bad deed yesterday. In my sermon about Janet Sobel."

"The woman who got no credit for what she invented?"

"Not none. But it's like the Wright brothers' first flight. They went a few hundred yards, and now people fly across oceans. Janet Sobel spilled paint, but Jackson took it to new countries. New continents."

"Tell me something I do not know."

"I can tell you what his gift is, if you like. His particular talent."

She adjusts her dress again. It's too loose in front. "I have my own ideas."

"Sure. But let's say you were making a sign to sell an icebox. On the top line you write *for sale*. Below, you write *refriger,* and you've run out of room."

"Unless I measure first, you mean."

"Exactly." Willem rattles the ice in the glass. "When I am painting, I always measure. By the time I put paint on canvas, I've drawn the damn thing a dozen times, trying to get it right first."

"Sounds sensible."

"Unless you're Jackson Pollock. He doesn't sketch beforehand, doesn't measure, doesn't plan. It all happens in that chaotic skull of his. Yet it comes out perfectly. He knows precisely how big to make the letters, somehow, so *refrigerator* fills the space perfectly, with no room left over."

"That sounds too simple. A parlor trick, rather than genius."

Willem raises his eyebrows. "It is difficult enough to navigate a small canvas, and a small idea. You start with one concept, and you paint it. But then you have all the rest of the space, to fill with something fascinating or beautiful or at least original. It can be terrifying, and that's on a painting the length of your arm. Jackson uses giant canvases, and without any plan, yet he has brilliant ideas for every inch and corner." He rattles the ice again. "It is like waking up in the middle of the ocean, thousands of miles from land, and knowing exactly where you are."

Ruth beams with pride. "No wonder he exceeds all of us."

"The story of the Peggy Guggenheim commission." He tilts the glass, shaking ice into his mouth. "Sorry. Walking him calm made me thirsty. It took a few miles."

"Two fresh glasses in just a moment."

"You're nicer to me than I deserve."

Ruth smooths her dress. "I have no idea what you deserve."

"I think you do," he says, chuckling.

"Peggy Guggenheim, you were saying."

"She was already supporting him, you know. Buying every work he made. The rumor is that she paid for this house. Once she gave him a solo show in her gallery, and it bombed. Sixteen paintings, only one sold. But Peggy had an idea that suited her vanity and would pique the appetite of the critics. She commissioned a work for her apartment in New York."

"I have heard about that painting. Legendary."

"Do you know why it is twenty-two feet long?"

"I assumed so that it would be the largest work of abstract expressionism ever?"

He shakes his head. "That's exactly how wide his studio is. He couldn't go bigger."

Ruth laughs. "Is that true?"

"The problem was that he procrastinated. She ordered the painting in July. He promptly bought the canvas and brought it here. Day after day, Jackson spent hours in a turned-around chair, resting his forearms on its back, staring at the void. Twenty-two feet of possibility. Like moving a mountain with a spoon."

"But we know how it all turns out," Ruth interrupts.

"Wait, though. As Peggy waited, summer passed without paint touching canvas. Then fall. The work was due in November, but the date came and went. Early in December, Peggy issued a deadline. She was having a party for a friend in January. Jack promised he'd get to work. Christmas Eve, friends came for dinner, peeked in the studio. The canvas was blank. Peggy announced that if the painting did not arrive in time for the party, her support of Jackson would end forever."

"Exactly the wrong thing to say," Ruth says, caught up in the story despite her desire to remain indifferent to Willem.

"The worst, yes. A week before the party, Lee snoops, and the canvas is without a mark. He hasn't even started. He sends her to her parents' house, but she returns the day before the painting is due. Not one brushstroke, not one drop."

A grasshopper leaps onto Ruth's calf. She startles, then calms, feeling its tiny legs cling with surprising strength. "I dislike this story. Continue."

"Just after sundown, he begins to work. First, he made eight . . . oh, what to call them? Let's say eight sections of activity, left to right. And three zones from bottom to top. A total of twenty-four regions, defined by wild black paint, yet as neatly spaced as the word *refrigerator*. They don't limit him either. It's more like they each give him a stage to stand on. He puts fresh ideas in each section, dancing and fighting and struggling, all of it in motion. You know when you hear a great song, and you can't help tapping your foot? The visual version of that."

"I need to see this one in person."

Willem nods emphatically. "It displays genius as though it were an everyday possession. Miss Godiva, my composition skills are every bit his equal. Franz Kline is just as stylish, especially in using negative space. Lee's work is wild, and sometimes wilder."

"I am acquainted with her painting."

"But understanding how to merge space and expression? To join form and content? Jackson is better than everyone. Do you hear me? *Everyone*. As they say in the Village, dis cat gots all de chops."

Ruth laughs a little. "What happened to the big painting?"

"The unthinkable. It took him fifteen hours to paint, eight or so to dry. He rolls the canvas, brings it to Peggy's apartment to mount. But her wall's not twenty-two feet long after all. It's twenty-one feet, four inches. Jack has a tantrum, screaming and stomping. Servants go running, calling everywhere, trying to track Peggy down. Jack finds her liquor cabinet and hits it hard. When she arrives . . ."

A plane flies overhead, buzzing low and loud. It swoops in from the ocean, swings inland down the island, with Manhattan far in the distance like it's almost forgotten. There's no point talking till the plane has passed. And then it's gone.

Willem clears his throat. "Peggy's getting dressed for the party, people are arriving, and Jackson is belligerent drunk. One of the servants tells her the canvas is too long. 'Then cut off whatever you must, but I want it hanging in fifteen minutes.' And she scurries off to welcome her guests."

"I never heard this part before."

"They cut eight inches off one end and throw it away. They marred a Pollock masterpiece beyond all repair. Can you imagine? Some bartender with scissors, hurrying for the boss? While the artist is too blasted to object? Peggy invites everyone into the room, like an unveiling. They gasp and clap, the cameras flash, she takes a bow. Jackson is stunned. He asks the caterers what happened to his painting. When they explain, he walks straight through the crowd, into the living room, and pisses in the fireplace."

"No!" Ruth bursts out laughing. "Genius and madman in the same person."

"Now I know you love him for real," Willem answers. He's laughing too. "Our beautiful Jack, our gifted Jack, our insane Jack."

AS THE SUN SINKS LOW, THEY STROLL TO THE RED BUICK. RUTH KEEPS A safe distance. When they've nearly reached the car, she stops. "It was nice to see you again."

Willem tilts his head forward. "The pleasure is all mine."

Ruth takes her swan stance, her strength and foundation. "Not all."

He smiles. "Joust all you like. It thrills me more than I wish to admit. But we both know. You simply must get this situation under control."

"You think I somehow do not want to?"

"You are upsetting him. It's evident."

"Upsetting? I worship the man. I do everything he asks. You cannot imagine. Everything."

"Look." Willem stuffs his hands in his pockets. "I'm just saying, let's not create ourselves a Van Gogh situation, all right? His face is already battered."

"I insist that he phone his analyst every day."

"That quack?" Willem scoffs. "He thinks drinking is good, and more drinking is better. He calls common sense 'repression.' The idiot even condones adultery. Approves it, as if—" He catches himself. "Begging your pardon."

"I am here for love, not praise."

"Get both. Give both. Just keep him calm." They reach his car, he opens his door. Ruth remains on the opposite side. There will be, she has decided, no embrace.

"Keep him steady, Ruth, please." He climbs in, starts the car, leans over to speak across the passenger seat. "Keep him alive."

No parting words from her, no touch of any kind. Only watching the cloud of dust he makes, as it trails him up the road until he reaches pavement.

RUTH WISHES THEY HAD A DOG. SOMETHING ALIVE IN ADDITION TO HER, to help Jackson find balance. And keep her company. She misses the kids at the art school. Self-pitying Abraham. Esther, who teaches art but is not an artist. Ruth's mood feels like an odd form of loneliness: angry.

Glancing back, she notices that they left the water glass by the chairs. She should pick it up. Instead, she ambles to the studio, crickets singing her on the way. At the door she takes deep breaths, lowers her shoulders, knocks. When there is no reply, she opens the door. The air is dusty, late sunlight streaming into the room.

Jackson sits against the far wall, smoking. He does not greet her. His eyes are squinted nearly all the way closed. She sees a blank canvas on the floor.

"Did you invent it?"

Exhaling smoke, he raises his chin at her.

"Drip painting, I mean." Ruth stays on the step, outside his workspace. "Did you invent it? Or did you steal it?"

He draws on his cigarette, the tip glowing. "You know how I feel about the history of everything. I did not even invent my own existence."

"I know, but—"

"I didn't invent paint, or canvas, or expression. Not art, not criticism, not sex, not God, not the dollies I move the paint with." He boots one within kicking range. "I didn't invent the studio or the brush or the dipping stick. I didn't invent collectors or galleries or money."

"And yet, I feel that in some ways I invented you."

He exhales out his nostrils, a squinting dragon. "I existed for eighteen years before you were born."

"In body, yes." She wants to adjust her dress, it's too low in front, but decides against it. Perhaps he will unsquint his eyes, and desire her. "A man can be remade many times. I started a new life when we met. Maybe you did too."

He continues smoking. "It's not dripping. I am painting. I have as much control as any ass at an easel with a brush." He waves a mixing stick. "It's a technique, that's all. A method."

"I love you, Jackson."

"Sshhh." He stands, lifts a can, uses the stick to guide paint onto the canvas. It's bluish gray like slate, like a winter sky. After several swings of his arm, Jackson reaches back with one foot, without looking, and pulls the dolly along.

"When I'm uncertain about something," he says, "I do its opposite. Anything to avoid predictability."

Ruth stands agog. This is the most he has spoken in days.

"Instead of using black to create depth and shadows, I'll use white. The inverse of a shadow, which makes the initial object, despite its limitless history, original. This is how to articulate an idea that can only be expressed in a painting."

"You have said that before," she says. "What does it mean?"

"You cannot paint a story any more than a story can show a painting. Here is my version of shadows." He dips a mixing stick into a different can, moves his arm beside the gray curves, and the pigment that dribbles off the stick is a chalky white. "Even inverted, there are shadows and light."

Ruth is wishing she had a tape measure, to see if the studio really is twenty-two feet long. On the far side, she notices a painting with a hole in the middle. A creamy base the tone of her skin, marks across in the brown of her hair.

"Jackson." She rushes over. "What happened? Did something fall on it?"

"That?" He's still spreading a white shadow, cigarette smoke haloing his face. "I kicked it."

"But you made it the first morning I was here. The idea came from us in bed."

"Perfect example of what I was saying. You can't paint sentiment. You can only paint light, and seeing the history of a thing. Truly seeing."

"But as a symbol, Jackson. Of our history."

"A souvenir." His eyes are squinted again. "As art, not interesting."

"It was *us*, Jackson."

Dropping his cigarette on the floor, he grinds it under his boot. "It was shit."

Ruth gulps for breath. There are things she is bursting to say. About disappointment, about being taken for granted. But it will only send him spiraling. Another night he'd drink himself stupid and behave cruelly the whole next day.

Ruth whirls as if to run, but only staggers out of the studio.

30

JANUARY 2007

Gwen had a runny nose when she stepped onto the elevator. Her mind was whirling with urgent tasks. How would she deliver that hair sample to Matthieu? What if it matched, and the painting was legitimate? She'd been skeptical for so long. Still bundled against the winter chill, she juggled her briefcase, a cup of coffee, and the napkin she was dabbing her nose with. The doors began to close automatically.

At the last second an arm speared between them, a long-fingered hand. Startled, Gwen jumped back as though expecting a blow. The doors pulled open, and in stepped Arthur. He wore an antique pilot's hat with the ear flaps down, so cute Gwen's heart all but melted.

He pressed a floor button, then turned to her. "Tell me one thing you like about me."

She blinked at him. "What?"

"Anything you wish. Big or small, important or trivial. Please."

Flustered, pulled completely out of her train of thought, Gwen spoke from an impulse, and where she was looking. "You have a perfect ass."

Arthur burst out laughing. "One desires to be remembered uniquely. And I did set the parameters rather widely."

"I'm sorry." She laughed too. "It's just the first thing—"

"Intelligence, sense of humor, compassion for the downtrodden." He wagged his head. "But no."

She glanced down, as if her coffee contained some information she needed. "My life has been insane, Arthur. But every so often." She sighed, looking him in the face. "No. Every two minutes. Every two minutes something reminds me of you."

"Gwen." He tugged on her sleeve. "Lovely Gwen."

"When I saw you the other day, I immediately remembered your text that you didn't want me riding the elevator with you."

"Rubbish on my part." He took off his odd hat. "I spoke in a fit of pique. And disappointment."

"So I stood there feeling like an idiot."

Arthur laughed again. "That is what Chilton said for the entire ascent."

"That I am an idiot?"

"That we both are, when we obviously belong together. He only repeated himself a dozen times, though." The elevator stopped, the doors opening to the top floor, home to the quirky architecture firm.

"Are we here to buy designer glasses?"

"To show you a secret place." He lifted away her coffee cup and reached out his other hand. Gwen looked at it, then took hold.

That floor was something of a maze. The architects were so busy designing useful spaces for their clients, their own environment was byzantine.

"What is this secret place? And how did you find it?" Gwen gripped his hand as they weaved through narrow hallways.

"Overhearing Asian Arts people. One elevator ride, they were joking about going one floor higher. Took me a bit to realize some of them get stoned up here."

"No wonder they're always cracking up."

"The rooftop regulars gave themselves a name: 'The Bunzel Dynasty.'" They arrived at a metal door: *Emergency Evacuation Only, Alarm Is Armed.*

"Here we are," Arthur said, setting her coffee cup on the floor.

"Be careful—" Gwen began, but he pushed, and the door opened without a sound.

First, they felt a blast of bitter cold, the same wind that had scoured Gwen on her way to and from Ruth's apartment. He led around the corner of a bulwark, which blocked the wind. Ten more steps and they reached some sort of vent. It issued a steady flow of comfortably warm air.

Instantly Gwen felt her shoulders relax. "This is great."

"Sorry I don't have a big ganja spleef for you, mon, but I don't partake."

"Something about you saying the word *spleef* is adorable."

They both chuckled, and then it arrived: the awkward moment, when they were alone and had privacy, yet everything was uncertain. Neither knew how to fill the void. Arthur solved the problem by moving closer, bending from his height.

"What are we doing?" Gwen tilted her head upward, her hand on his chest.

And they kissed. This time it was not the hurry of the office party, not the passion of his freezing apartment. It was gentler, familiar, patient. Sweeter by far.

After a while, Arthur drew slightly back. "Better than I remembered."

"Yes," Gwen replied. "And better than I've been dreaming."

"I know you are driven in your work. But I believe . . ."

Gwen's mind wandered. The envelope was still in her pocket. Matthieu did not even know it was coming. What would she do if the results weren't ready till Tuesday?

". . . and must decide whether there is room for another person in your life. That is, em, room for me." Arthur finished what he had to say, lips pursed, eyes wide.

Gwen felt awful for half listening. Her brain felt full. She pulled him closer, arching her body upward. "I wish I could . . . I just wish."

"What is it?"

"Be taller. Corny, I know, but I want my heart against your heart."

Arthur bent, wrapping his arms around her, then straightened, and lifted her off the ground. "Like this?"

His arms were cables, solid and strong, and for a moment she felt weightless. Was that his heart or hers, thrumming between them? "I think I have an answer for you. An answer you might like."

He pressed his eyes closed, then opened them again, innocent as a lamb. "Tell me the whole truth."

"Well, the whole truth is that I am incredibly preoccupied right this second. You caught me by surprise, hopping on the elevator like that. But the larger—"

He lowered her to the roof again. "The painting."

"We had a major breakthrough about twenty minutes ago. I need to notify one person, just one quick text, and then you'll have my undivided—"

"Of course." Arthur retreated a step. "I surprised you when it was convenient for me. I'd been scheming for weeks. No telling what I'd be interrupting."

"Thank you for understanding. This will take less than one minute."

"Please." He nodded, giving her room, putting his hat back on. "Sorry to interfere."

"You're not interfering," Gwen said. She dug out her phone, searching for her text thread with Matthieu. "This will be very quick."

But there were multiple texts—from Harriette the Hawk, from Chillie, from the legal department. She barely glanced at them, only the first few words, before she tapped out her message for Matthieu.

I can't believe it. We have a hair sample. Dozens, with follicles. Only problem is

The vent behind them made a metallic groan, and more hot air poured out. Gwen held up one finger. "Almost done."

Best way to get it to you? And if I deliver it tonight, will that be enough time for results by Monday morning? And Matthieu! If we get a match? Does that overrule your other concerns?

"There." Gwen raised her eyes from the phone.

She was alone. She looked around the vent, searched behind the bulwark. New York City lay spread all around below—steam rising from the orange pavement spouts—and above, January sky in all directions.

No one else up there. Arthur gone.

31

AUGUST 1956

She wakes during the night because Jackson, beside her, is shivering. Ruth pulls the sheets and light summer blanket over him, slides her body close against his, wraps him in her arms. He is fully clothed, she is naked.

"Are you all right?"

"The booze is making me sick." He coughs. "Or maybe I'm already sick. The booze is making it worse."

She waits a long time, but he does not add anything. "Maybe," she whispers, "maybe tomorrow you could take a day off from it. And see how you feel."

"Horrific dreams tonight." He backs against her. "Monsters."

"Who? Who are the monsters, darling?"

"Everyone. The critics, Clement, Peggy, Willem. That girl teaching at the art school. All innocence, but inside she is judging everyone and finding us inferior. Everyone is a monster." He coughs again. "Except you."

"I certainly hope so." She kisses his shirt on the shoulder. His body has calmed, the shivering is fading, a thunderstorm floating into the distance.

"Even Alfonso," he says. "Trying to run me over with his car."

"Alfonso is your friend."

Jackson shakes his head. "Not in my dream."

Ruth considers for a moment, then sits up. "I'll be right back."

Moonlight shows the way, and displays the shape of her body. Ruth returns holding the poker from the fireplace. She climbs back into bed with it.

"There. Now you have an army to protect you."

She snuggles against him again, the poker close on her other side. "Let anyone dare try to hurt you," she tells him. "Anyone."

They lie together, eyes open in the dark.

IN THE MORNING, RUTH HEARS MUSIC FROM DOWNSTAIRS. THAT PIANIST, what is his name? His melodies are pretty, and he's always doing something strange with the rhythm. She feels uplifted. Jackson is awake, and playing music.

She hops up, making the poker clang on the floor. His clothes are on the floor too. She'll clean up later, make the bed later. Dressing fast, she all but skips down the stairs, which creak like the voice of an old friend.

"Just in time," Jackson says. He's at the stove, the first time she's ever seen it, wearing a too-small apron, scrambling eggs, adding what she suspects is too much salt.

Ruth slides her arms around his waist, kisses the side of his neck. "Did you get some decent rest?"

He nods. "I needed it. I feel great."

"Great?" she says. "*Wonderful.* Who is this pianist?"

"Brubeck. He does to music what we all should be doing to everything. Grab some plates?"

Ruth floats to the cabinet, takes down plates, sets the table.

"Sit," Jackson says, frying pan in hand. "Go go go." He comes to the table, portioning out eggs for them both.

Ruth applauds. "My hero."

"It's just breakfast." He tosses the pan clanging in the sink, brings coffee for them both. He sits and dives in, shoveling the food.

Ruth is content to watch and sip.

"What? I'm starving." He points with his fork. "You too, while it's hot."

She squeezes her eyes closed, defeating the tears, and opens them to see him pause for a slug of coffee, then another forkful.

"How about we go to a beach today? It won't be summer forever."

"A beach? An actual beach?" Ruth picks up her fork. "I love you, Jackson."

"Mm." He continues chewing. "You too."

It's enough. More than enough. It is a victory. Now she does weep. And tastes the eggs, which are almost ruined by salt, and eats every bite.

JACKSON INSISTS THAT SHE NOT PACK A BAG, SAYING THERE'S FOOD AT the beach and he wants it to be simple. "Let's be spontaneous and get out of here."

She puts on a bathing suit and light cover, pops on her sunglasses, and dons her hat with the largest brim. Ruth starts to put on her wristwatch, then changes her mind and leaves it. Downstairs, Jackson is wearing shorts and sandals. Seeing her, he slides on his sunglasses too.

"The perfect beach bum," she chirps as they march outside.

"One day's rest from that damn place." He nods toward the studio. "Time for some peace of mind."

"What do you think about, in all those studio hours?"

"How I used to paint." He starts unsnapping the convertible's top. "How I used to be Jackson Pollock."

"But." She stands in front of the car. "But you still are."

He pauses. "Not even close."

"Who taught me that everything has a huge history? And why would that not include you?" She opens the door on the passenger side. "My job is to help you turn your history into new and greater art. All you need is faith in the power of my love."

"You think that will get me painting again?"

"With all my heart."

Jackson snorts. But he continues taking the top down, while Ruth climbs aboard and preens in the mirror. They don't speak during the drive south on Fireplace Road, except to praise the cool morning air. When they reach pavement, Jackson accelerates. Wind nearly snatches her hat, but she clamps it down. He puts an arm around her shoulders.

"I feel like we're back in New York, when you first bought this beautiful car."

He nods and drives faster.

It's a straight route, one left turn and the world opens. Even from the parking lot she can tell the beach is long and wide. There's a classic pavilion, a cedar-shingled bathhouse nearly a hundred yards long, with whitewashed porches along its length. Through the high arch of its entry, Ruth can hear the surf pounding. Kettledrums and pouring rain.

"Oh, heaven." She's sitting up, alert as a bird. "I already love it here."

He concentrates on parking. White lines on the blacktop show where each car should go. "Thought you might."

They stroll through the entry, as casual as movie stars. At once, the span of the beach opens before them. Ruth grabs his arm. "Jackson, Jackson, Jackson."

He pays for an umbrella, two beach lounges, and two large glasses of iced tea. They stake out a place, and a muscular beach attendant brings everything they've rented.

"Two of everything," Ruth says.

Jackson tips him, she can see that it's generous. Then he arranges her chair, which is more like a canvas sling, setting it in reclining position.

"Oh, Jackson." Ruth's eyes are bright and fixed on him. "Metamorphosis."

"What's that?" He's unfolding his lounge, which is rusty and resistant.

"Is that the right word? When something changes completely?"

"I didn't change." He pulls off his shirt. "Just got some sleep."

She runs a hand down his chest. "If you say so."

The wind steals her hat, but he hops after it, then uses one of his sandals to keep it in place. They lie back, eyes closed, listening to children squeal as they run in and out of the water, or murmur as they build sandcastles. A couple nearby discusses whether Eisenhower should be reelected. The man does most of the talking. The tinny snack bar radio plays "Heartbreak Hotel" by a popular new singer named Elvis Presley. Gulls, hovering in the hopes of stealing a French fry, repeat their shrill cry.

Ruth had not slept well, though, and in minutes she is dozing. When she wakes, she has no idea what time it is. Her tea has tipped into the sand, and when she reaches for Jackson, he is not there.

"She surfaces at last." He's standing a few feet away. "I've been watching these surfers."

Ruth shades her brow. Out beyond the swimmers, three young men as fit as gymnasts are riding the waves. They're quick footed, and never fall. When their ride is done, they slide down into the wave. "Like ballet on water," she says.

"Ruth." Jackson is jumpy, she can tell. "Do you want lunch?"

She shrugs. "Sure. A little something, because I had a big breakfast, thank you. Definitely something to drink."

"The food at this snack bar is awful."

"Truly?"

"It will make you sick." He grabs his sandals, tucks her hat under his chair. "I'll zip to town and get us decent sandwiches. Be back in a wink."

Ruth sits forward. "Take off your sunglasses."

He does, but his eyes are so squinted she cannot see them. She takes off her glasses anyway, trying to make eye contact. "Where exactly are you going?"

"Mickey's. What's the problem?" His face looks boyish. "I was going to get you a roast beef sandwich, with tomatoes and a little horseradish."

Ruth relaxes. "That sounds delicious."

Jackson points over his shoulder. "Enjoy the radio. I'll be back in five songs."

Reclining again, she puts her shades back on. "As long as they skip 'Heartbreak Hotel.' I have heard that one enough this summer."

Jackson leans over and kisses her. It's a surprise, and she reaches up to hold his head. They kiss for half a minute, her body stirring. "Five songs?"

"Six, tops." He jogs away across the sand, into the shadow of the pavilion.

◆ ◆ ◆

AT TEN SONGS SHE STOPS COUNTING. SHE WATCHES THE SURFERS UNTIL they are repeating themselves. Now the couple is arguing about atomic bomb testing at the Bikini Atoll. The woman is speaking, she's far more informed, and Ruth can hardly bear overhearing it. A toddler on the other side is fussing.

"I know," she murmurs. "I would like some lunch too."

When she hears "Heartbreak Hotel" begin on that radio, Ruth jumps out of her chair, jams the hat on her head, and storms away down the beach.

She does not feel one wrinkle of worry. He did not have an accident. No, what he did was lie. She could all but taste that sandwich. Five songs. What nonsense.

Her stride is furious, chewing the distance till she is far down the beach. Ruth turns, and the pavilion looks small and distant. The price of this walk will probably be sunburned shoulders. And a Sahara of thirst.

Nonetheless she takes her time returning. She strolls along the edge of the ocean, water cooling her feet. Occasionally, a stronger wave dissipates with foam ankle high. It's refreshing, calming. She decides to take a swim.

Ruth wades into the sea and immediately feels the water pulling at her. It's more than a wave retreating. There's an undertow, invisible and sinister. She's been warned about such things, but never experienced one. The next wave is strong enough to knock her back a little, and the retreating water nearly tips her over.

Frightened, Ruth runs for dry sand. She realizes that the swimmers are all clustered up by the pavilion. The locals know.

It's later than she thought too. Families are packing up, children fussing. Ruth proceeds slowly, giving him time. When she reaches the chairs, Jackson will be there.

But he isn't. She sits again, not sure what to do. She has no money. She could ask the people inside to use their phone, but who would she call? Shirley? Willem?

Ruth observes the surfers, who show signs of tiring. They fall sometimes, their rides are shorter. The waves are weakening anyway, as the sun sinks. Someone's father walks down from the pavilion to call the surfers in. Only when they come trotting up, boards under their arms, does Ruth realize that they are boys. High school age, no wonder they were so nimble.

She stays till the beach is empty but for her. The muscular man who carried their umbrella appears, apologizing for having to collect everything before closing.

"Not to worry," Ruth tells him. "Thank you."

At the pavilion, she hoses sand off her feet, slips on her beach shoes, and escorts her hat out to the parking area. There are still a few cars parked here and there. The wind has died, the sun is low, there is nowhere for Ruth to sit.

She settles for the pavilion's stoop. There are pebbles underfoot. She sifts them hand to hand, tossing them one by one down the pavement. The lights go off behind her, and the beach attendant comes out.

"Ma'am, is everything all right?"

"Thank you," she says. "My ride should be along any minute."

He tugs on his Dodgers cap. "Are you sure, ma'am? I hate to leave you here."

"I am not in any danger, am I?"

"No ma'am. Only there's not a lot of traffic here at night. And I had to close up, so you can't really call anyone."

"Thank you for your concern," she says. "My husband unexpectedly had to work late. He will be here in no time."

A car pulls down the beach road, tooting the horn.

"See?" Ruth says. "There he is now."

He gives the tip of his cap a tug. "Good evening, ma'am."

"I appreciate your concern."

The man's truck is parked in the far corner. He strolls to it, unhurried, and drives off. Meanwhile, the arriving car stops beside one of the remaining two. A man gets out, thanks the driver for the lift, then both cars drive off. Ruth is alone.

"Well," she tells herself, "it is definitely too far to walk."

An hour or more passes, she estimates by her stomach's growl. She can picture exactly where on the dresser she left her watch. But would knowing the time make a difference?

"No," she says aloud. "Only one thing would help right now."

NOT UNTIL AFTER DARK DOES A CAR ARRIVE, SWERVING DOWN THE HILL TO pan its headlights across the parking lot. Then the lights home in on her, the car accelerating till it stops, parked askew from the tidy white lines.

He leaves the engine running, sets the brake, and hops out. Ruth holds both hands up and out. "Do not speak," she commands. "Do not say anything."

"But—"

"Not one word." She wags her forefinger. "Not one."

Taking her swan pose, and feeling it down to her toes, she strides past him. He smells of peppermint, as clear a sign as if he stank of whiskey. Ruth stops in front of the passenger door, not lifting a hand till he opens it for her.

They pull out of the lot, and up the hill to Fireplace Road. Instead of going right, toward home, he turns left.

"Where are we going?"

"Alfonso's. For dinner."

"I am wearing a bathing suit."

"And I'm still in shorts. I asked, and he said it was fine."

"Where did you see him?"

"Mickey's, like I said."

"Like you said? *Like you said?* You also said you were bringing me a roast beef sandwich. Instead, you marooned me and spent the day drinking with him."

"That's not what—"

"Spare me your bullshit."

He drives in silence.

"If I were not starving, and dying of thirst, I would insist on heading home. How far is his place?"

"Two more minutes."

"It had better be acceptable that I'm in a bathing suit."

With a finger, Jackson draws an X on his chest. "I promise."

◆ ◆ ◆

"HELLO, PRINCESS," ALFONSO SAYS AT THE DOOR, KISSING HER ON BOTH cheeks.

"Your home is incredible," Ruth says, taking in the stone entry, the manicured gardens, the torchlights. "Beautiful and grand."

He assesses her attire with a glance so swift and decisive she cannot feel insulted, only impressed. "Lovely Ruth, come away with me a moment, please."

Jackson looks off while Alfonso leads her in. They pass through hallways, sitting rooms, arriving at a side room, and its closet, where various dresses hang. "Help yourself to whatever fits. We'll be on the patio in back of the house."

"I am mortified," she says. "He promised me that beach attire would be fine."

"Princess." He gives off that same peppermint scent. "You know better than to believe a man who's been drinking."

Ruth gives him a level look. "Currently that category of men includes you."

"Ha." His face lights up. "Touché."

RUTH CHOOSES A BROWN DRESS THAT IS INTENTIONALLY DRAB. A RED belt, or perhaps gold, might make it work. Instead, the fabric hangs like drapery. A perfect way to shame Jackson. Her skin feels brittle from too much sun, but her anger feels like the burn is all inside. She wanders through the maze of the house until she finds a bathroom.

Ruth runs the water, bends her face under the clean chrome faucet, and drinks. It's like salvation, cool and soft. With every gulp her mouth softens, her throat cools. When she straightens, wiping her mouth, she looks in the mirror.

"Dear God." Her face is parched and pink, with white ovals where her sunglasses were all day. Her hair looks comical. Teased by wind, doused with salt, it has twice the normal volume. She starts the water again, thinking to repair it, but changes her mind. "Wet it now," she murmurs, "and you will have the drowned-rat look."

She marches back to the hallway and follows the sound of laughter.

From the patio door, she sees Jackson sitting across from Alfonso. It's not until Ruth steps out on the porch that she discovers there are other guests. A gorgeous man, mid-twenties in age, seated beside Alfonso. On the host's other side, Willem, looking resolutely away. On his right a much younger woman, attractive, muscular like an athlete, and their age difference rivals the one between herself and Jackson. Ruth recognizes her from pictures. Willem's wife, Elaine. Everyone greets Ruth, but they're stiff with trying to conceal their intoxication.

A waiter bends near for her drink order, and she asks for three waters. The others request gin and tonics. When the round arrives, they all take demure sips. Except Ruth, who chugs her first glass empty without shame.

The cocktail hour is prolonged. A grandfather clock inside rings eight, then nine o'clock, while the pulsing crickets and slow dusk of August quiet the world. A sea vessel—a red light and green light and otherwise invisible in the dark—blows its mournful horn. The conversation consists primarily of gossip about this painter and that gallery, this collector and that critic, Jackson contributing a growl from time to time. Ruth only opens her mouth to drink water or devour salted nuts from a silver bowl on the table. She tries to imagine Jackson with Elaine, and decides it was too long ago to care. She weighs whether to get drunk too. But she hasn't eaten and doesn't want misery tomorrow.

The only person speaking less than her is the young man beside Alfonso. He's a specimen, his body statuesque, his face smooth like he shaved only moments before she arrived. As a servant delivers a fresh round, and the clock is ringing ten, the boy stands.

"I will die of starvation," he says. "I'm going to see if there's anything for dinner besides cashews."

"Stay fortified." Alfonso watches the boy enter the house. "And slender."

Jackson says something so garbled she cannot tell what it is. About the young man, she guesses, because Willem laughs but Alfonso frowns.

"You are less fun when you are this drunk, you know. I make no secret of my life. It takes no intellect to ridicule the beautiful."

Jackson responds by grabbing Alfonso's drink and chugging it down, gnashing the ice with his teeth.

At that point, any decorum vanishes. Elaine is shouting now, and Ruth realizes that the woman is every bit as drunk as the men.

"A baby," she tells Ruth, her words loud and slurred. "Can you believe it?"

"Pardon me." Ruth blinks. "What are you talking about?"

Elaine looks like she's just put on boxing gloves and is ready to go a few rounds. "You don't know because you are stupid."

"Now now," Alfonso chides.

"A mistress, right?" Elaine bites the air in Ruth's direction. "I know you know what that word means."

Ruth, instantly glad that she is sober, does not reply. She only wishes her hair was not huge from the salt water that afternoon.

"Willem's mistress has delivered a baby," Elaine announces, in acid tones. "A daughter, whom that whore Gillian Breck intends to give Willem's last name. Johanna de Kooning, isn't that sweet?"

Everyone is silent, and Ruth feels the woman's pain, but Elaine continues. "She'll go by Lisa, poor bird. Today a child, tomorrow a walking embodiment of my shabby husband's repeated infidelity."

"Gillian?" Jackson's eyes clear and he turns to Willem. "Isn't she the illustrator you met at the Cedar Tavern?"

"Really?" Ruth chimes in. "That's where Jackson and I—"

"Yes," Elaine barks. "Where immoral expressionist sharks go for new meat."

"As if you have been a saint," Willem says, his dander up at last. "Shall we make a list? Rosenburg, Hess, Egan—"

"This is getting ugly," Alfonso says, though Ruth thinks he does not look particularly dismayed. More like he is enjoying it, like this is the party he wanted.

"—not to mention my friend Jack, here."

Elaine is on her feet. "Every one of those men has helped your career."

"So generous of you." Willem sneers. "To open your legs for my sake."

Suddenly everyone is shouting at once. It's like a storm. Bending to conceal herself, Ruth rises and slinks beyond the torchlights. Then she ambles farther on the grass. Distance quiets the noise, and she feels herself relaxing. Reaching the bay, she finds a long wooden dock. At its tip, however, she finds that her woes came along too. She is famished. Hurt from being abandoned at the beach. She wishes the moon were shining on the water, but it is barely a glow in the east. Maybe she can find something to eat. Maybe the gorgeous boy is smartest of them all.

When Ruth returns to the patio, everyone is gone but Willem. Turning at the sound of her step, he rises from his chair. "It's Lady Godiva."

"Hello, Willem." She smirks. "Jackson did not tell me that dinner came with a show. And here I am, wearing a borrowed potato sack."

"Potatoes never looked better."

"Where did everyone go? To the castle boxing ring?"

"I don't care if they dove into the sea." He turns in the light, handsome and unruffled. "I am insane with desire for you."

"Really?" She smiles at him. "How would you rate it?"

"What do you mean?"

"Your desire. On a scale from your wife Elaine to your mistress Gillian, where does your insane desire for me rank?"

He peers past her into the dark. "I don't know what to say."

"That is actually a perfect reply." Ruth kisses his cheek—brisk with a citrus aftershave—and heads into the house, where she will shed the foolish dress like a bad habit and look for Jackson.

In her clammy bathing suit and wrap, she finds him at the bar. "Take me home now."

"One minute." He drops ice cubes into a glass.

Ruth swats the glass away. It shatters on the marble floor, ice and shards in all directions. "Take me home *now.*"

He obeys in silence, as sullen as a teenager. When he backs the convertible from its parking spot he goes too far, and some yew bush branches poke in at them.

"Are you all right to drive?" she asks.

"Who else will do it?" he snarls.

Ruth rests a hand on his arm. "Kindness, please. I've had a hard day."

"I'll give you kindness." Jackson guns the motor. They go fishtailing out of the white gravel driveway and onto the road.

Ruth has no idea how fast the convertible can go, and at first, she is astonished, even impressed. But when they swerve to avoid an oncoming farm truck, and nearly go off the shoulder, her perspective changes.

"Darling." She braces herself on the dash. "Would you please slow down?"

He looks at her for less than a second and continues speeding.

"Please. You are scaring me."

He stomps on the gas pedal. The engine roars, responding with a power that feels like enthusiasm, pushing her back in the seat. *Like an undertow,* she thinks.

"Please, Jackson. Please slow down."

He careens up the road, crossing lanes, swerving, one time jerking the wheel as if to avoid hitting an object in the road—when there was nothing.

"Please," she cries. "I am begging you."

On he speeds, taking a corner that throws her against the passenger door. When they reach the curve on Fireplace Road, where the pavement turns to dirt, the convertible spins one hundred eighty degrees, nearly flipping over. It comes to a stop, swaying on its struts, facing the direction it had come from, without hitting anything.

Jackson idles there, looking around. Ruth, weeping, clutches the passenger door's armrest. She keeps her head down, but her body is trembling.

Jackson needs three back-and-forths to point the car the right way again.

"Lucky no one was coming," he says, cowed. No reply but her sniffling.

For the remaining mile, he drives at a low idle. When he parks at the house, Ruth flees the car and runs inside. He kills the engine and lights a cigarette.

She comes out with bread and apples. The screen door slaps shut.

"Ruth," he says, reaching an arm toward her.

For a second time that day, she strides past him.

"Ruth. Come on." He stands in the car, then yells. "Where are you going?"

She charges up Fireplace Road, vanishing in the midnight dark.

THE FIRST TWO SLICES OF BREAD DO THEIR JOB, FILLING HER BELLY. THE third is too bland, and she's become thirsty again. That first bite of apple? The flavor, the wetness, it feels nearly sacred. She holds the fruit in her mouth before chewing or swallowing, making herself take pleasure.

"Quite the day," she tells the crickets, the nightbirds, the silent trees. On she strides past dark houses, a few barns, an unoccupied bungalow. Her skin hurts, her heart aches, and she is *still* wearing a bathing suit. At last, the moon rises, blue light filtering through the trees. By the time Ruth tosses the apple core into the grass, she can feel herself recovering.

Until she senses that someone is following her.

It is a strange sound, not familiar, not Jackson's tread, and gaining ground. Her heart is in her throat again. What a day, what a night. Who would be out at this hour, but someone as desperate as her? He's coming too fast to outrun, and where could she go, anyway?

It's not one person. It's two. Ruth hides behind a tree, overhanging the road so thickly no moonlight can enter. An oak, with acorns littered beneath. Hearing the pair's tread, she presses herself back against the bark. And there is the hulk, its deep breathing, coming closer, closer, right up to her.

A horse. Ruth exhales with relief, resting against the barrel of his ribs. Patting his sides, his sleek hide, she can tell he is well cared for.

"Look who got out of his stall tonight," she says. "You beautiful boy."

The horse sneezes, clears his throat.

"Wait." Ruth reaches into her cover-up's pocket. "I have something for you."

She holds the remaining apple in her palm. The pony clasps it in his huge teeth, and there is a sound Ruth remembers from girlhood. Her father took her to a horse farm, where she fed the animals carrots.

The sound of a large mouth chomping down something sweet, it gives her warm memories.

"Apple is your name." She takes his bridle. "Now where do you belong?"

After turning in the direction they both came from, Ruth lets go. Sure enough, Apple leads, large head bobbing. She repeats his name, she pets him, and on they go. After ten minutes, Apple veers left. Ruth follows him into a dooryard and past, to a corral in back with the gate open.

"The case is solved." As the horse moves gently into the corral, she pulls the gate closed and fixes the latch.

"Thank you, Apple." She rubs his chin. "You led me homeward too."

At the house there's a light on over the sink, like a bit of warm welcome. Until she sees a stack of unwashed dishes. How many days ago was breakfast?

She turns the faucet, intending to clean up, then changes her mind, shutting off the water and the light. There's another on the stairs, coming from the bathroom with the door propped open. A towel hangs on the hook inside, but she thinks it's impossible that Jackson has not seen her autograph by now.

She switches off that light, entering the bedroom in the dark. Jackson is not snoring as he usually does on drinking nights. Shedding her clothes, she climbs into bed with her back to him. How can she help this man, when genius is so close to madness? Had he almost killed them? Can she explain how badly he treated her, without sending him into a spiral? How will she cool her roaring furnace of rage?

Jackson stirs, rolls over, snuggles close. She stiffens. He reaches around, caresses her shoulder, cups one of her breasts.

"You have got to be kidding me," she says.

At once he retreats to his side of the bed.

32

JANUARY 2007

When Gwen reached her cubicle, Chillie was sitting in her place, feet up, reading a magazine. "Is this your desk now?"

"Girlfriend." Chillie put his feet down. "I thought you were never coming back."

"For a while I thought so too."

"Good results?"

Gwen was still digesting what happened on the roof. Not ready to discuss Arthur's disappearance yet, she handed him the envelope. "Check this out."

Chillie peered in. "This is your natural color?"

Gwen shucked off her coat. "It's from Ruth."

He tossed the envelope onto her desk. "And this is interesting why?"

"Because we found a hair on the back of the canvas. If the DNA matches—"

"Boring." Chillie stood. "I have something much more important to discuss."

"I promise, that sample of hair is very—"

"Boring."

"All right." Gwen crossed her arms. "Tell me your momentous news."

He rolled the magazine into a tube, which he spoke through like a megaphone. "I am hosting another brunch this weekend. And you are attending. Tra la la."

Gwen froze, boggled. "Have you been smoking something for the last month?"

"This is an opportunity for you to try being human again."

She counted down her fingers. "First, you already told me. Second, you know Monday is decision day on my Pollock painting." And third, she could not even say. Something about her heart hurting, and it being her own fault.

"So now it's *your* Pollock painting?"

"If this deal happens and my bonus is a million dollars, I promise I will buy you exactly one drink. A small one, with bottom-shelf booze."

Chillie laughed. "We're starting late this week, because all the spectacular people I've invited are decadent on Saturday nights and want to sleep late—exactly the crowd you should associate with. Including Devon, who you have been too obsessed with 'your' painting to notice has been calling me hourly and sending me texts that get me so hot and bothered at my desk I've had to come sit at yours—"

"Excuse me, but ick."

"You can arrive at two, and still have way more fun than sitting at home biting your fingernails over how some hussy got her mitts on a forgery of weirdness."

"You know, that's part of the problem."

"Having brunch too early?" he crowed. "If you'd only said—"

"The painting, Chillie. God, is your skull made of rock?"

"Will you two please pipe down?" someone shouted from down the row of cubicles. "We're trying to work."

Chillie gave the finger in the shouter's general direction. "What about it?"

"I hate it." Gwen leaned closer. "I've seen nearly all of this guy's work now, in person or in books. The only painting I dislike is the one I'm preparing for sale."

"Irony is dripping all over this project. Like maple syrup on the blueberry pancakes I'll be serving with thick-slice bacon on Sunday afternoon."

"It's impossible for me to be there, and you know it."

"Every one of my guests is ambitious, hoping to rise and make a difference. Yet they all have lives. Lovers, hobbies, insane marathons they want to run."

"May I interrupt?"

It was Harriette the Hawk, and Gwen all but hugged her. "Please do. And can you somehow get this productivity sponge out of my workspace?"

Huffing, Chillie went to his own desk, where he immediately began typing.

"Are you busy?" Harriette asked.

"Insanely," Gwen said. "Why?"

"The boss wants his phone lesson now."

"What? Did he forget my deadline?"

"I reminded him. But he has two other recent phone buyers coming to his office. So, by *now* he means *now*."

Gwen closed her eyes. She needed to follow up with Matthieu. She needed to get the envelope to the vault. She opened her eyes. "I'll be right there."

"Thank you. He has a meeting just wrapping up."

Gwen checked her phone, to see if Matthieu had responded to her text. And, hurrying for Arthur's sake, she had forgotten to hit send.

"Aaahhhh." She pushed the button, then leaned into Chillie's cubicle.

"Busy, busy," he said. "Busy bee, too busy to talk now. Bzzz bzzz."

"I need you to save my life."

"Not listening." He typed away. Gwen looked on his screen, and it was gibberish.

"All right, then." She pulled her hair back. "On Sunday I'm going out to Pollock's place. To see his home, his studio. If I catch the crack-of-dawn train, maybe I could be back—"

"For my party!"

"Shut *up*," someone yelled down the row.

"It was the bacon that persuaded me."

Chillie clapped his hands. "How do you want me to save your life?"

Gwen held up her phone. "Call me in nineteen minutes. If I don't answer, keep calling. Every two minutes till I answer. You'll save me from a stress stroke."

"Look." Chillie put his hands on his thighs. "I know you're not really going to come on Sunday. But I'm worried about you. You look semi-electrocuted."

"What a compliment."

"You don't need to cover every angle. You just need to find decisive evidence. The rest will become trivial."

"But I have tons of decisive evidence—for and against."

He shook his head. "Then it's not decisive. Anyway, after this deal is done, as someone who loves you? We need to have a serious talk about your priorities."

"Chillie." Gwen looked down at her hands. "I really appreciate—"

"Go." He waved her off. "I'll call in nineteen."

On the way to Pinkney's office, Gwen wrote a follow-up to Matthieu. But when she reached the waiting area, she saw that her typing was full of errors. If only the phone could take dictation. Every day she had ideas for what else it should do.

"Well, hello there."

Gwen lifted her eyes from the phone. A tall woman with white hair stood with one hand on her hip. Gwen struggled to remember.

"It's Gallagher Shea, sweet pea. From the Pollock-fest at Sotheby's."

"Oh my God." Gwen laughed, and they had a quick clench of a hug. "I've been meaning forever to thank you for getting me into that auction."

"I should thank you." Gallagher laughed. "Coming to your aid meant no one asked to see my credentials. Innocent spy from Christie's that I am."

"You are so calculating, I love it. What brings you here?"

"Managing director opening." She shrugged. "He won't offer me the job, nor would I accept it. But why waste an opportunity to size each other up? I heard about the whale you've landed."

Gwen wilted. "Not even harpooned at this point. Legal, forensics, the whole tangle. And Monday's our deadline."

Harriette was at her elbow. "The boss will see you now."

"Invite me to the auction, would you?" Gallagher said. "It was all over your face at Sotheby's."

"What was?"

"Sweet pea. You're a proper Pollock woman now." She patted Gwen's hand and set off toward the elevators. "Welcome to the club."

"I hope not," Gwen called after her.

"Toodles." Gallagher wiggled her fingers in the air.

Harriette spoke louder. "Mr. Pinkney will see you *now.*"

Gwen hesitated. "Can you get me a courier? For a delivery outside the city?"

"You know we don't cover that sort of thing."

"Then I need a car. Can you rent one for me, please? Right after this meeting."

Harriette gave her a stern look. "You need to get a hold of yourself."

"What I need is not to have unscheduled bullshit come up when I am up to my neck with doing my actual job."

"For the moment, this bullshit *is* your job." Harriette pushed the door open. "Found her, sir," she sang. "Here you go."

When Gwen entered, she found that the boss was not alone. Richards sat in one chair, so absorbed in his phone he did not look up. Across from him sat Baxter, looking as smug as a cat holding a mouse by the tail.

Pinkney was tapping his phone and scowling at it, and tapping again, until finally he tossed it on his desk. "Goddamn thing."

"I can't stand it," Richards said.

"Hello?" Gwen said. "Did you need me for something? Because if not—"

"Yes yes," Pinkney answered. "We want instruction."

Richards spoke without lifting his gaze from the screen. "My PalmPilot came with a whole book of how-to."

"Same with my BlackBerry," Pinkney added. "Meanwhile, we've all seen you wielding your thing like a computerized sword."

Gwen scowled. "Now?"

Pinkney opened his arms. "We're all here."

"Whose idea was this?"

"I forget," Baxter said, not bothering to conceal her grin.

Gwen faced Pinkney, hands on her hips. "You know I have a deadline—"

"Then let's get going," he interrupted. "Besides, by now your gut knows if it's legitimate or not. Down deep, you already know."

"I don't understand this thing," Richards said. "You have to figure everything out."

"I second the motion," Baxter replied. "It didn't even come with a manual."

Gwen felt like she was about to burst into flames. "That's the whole point. To make it instinctive, so you don't need manuals or instruction."

When she stopped speaking, all three of them were staring at their phones. "Right?" she said. No one answered.

Gwen could feel heat rising on the back of her neck. She was working as hard as possible for this company, and for what? To teach them a thing they could learn by themselves, if they used their brains instead of their position.

"People? People?" She snapped her fingers. "All eyes here." As they raised their heads, she pointed at her face. "You look at your phone when I say so."

"Bossy," Baxter grumbled.

Gwen spun toward her. "It's hard to learn while you're grunting like a pig."

Pinkney laughed. Baxter glowered at him, but he shrugged. "It was funny."

Soon her phone would ring, and by then she needed them to have learned enough for now. The pressure felt immense. She had to get the hair to Matthieu.

"All right, buckle up," Gwen said. "Now lift up your phones and follow along with me." She pointed. "This is the home button."

33

AUGUST 1956

Somehow, in the morning, Ruth's rage has vanished. Wafted away in her breaths. Evaporated. In its place, there is a plan.

She hears Jackson downstairs and does not get up. After a while he calls from the bottom of the stairs, "I made coffee."

She pulls the sheets up to her chin. Later, she hears the screen door slam. Ruth hurries to the window in the spare room. Yes, he is going to the studio. Downstairs she makes two phone calls. Then she showers, dresses, and packs a bag. She puts it in the convertible's back seat and knocks on the studio door.

"Come on in," Jackson calls.

Ruth enters briskly, but her step slows when she sees him. He is standing in the corner, sheepish like a scolded boy. His hands are empty, and he is barefoot.

"I need a ride," she informs him.

"Where to?"

"The train. It departs in twenty-five minutes, but I would like to go now so I will not worry about making it."

His face droops like a sad clown. "You're leaving me?"

"I am going to the city for the weekend. My analyst is there. Also, my sister Lucy is desperate about some guy again."

"Your analyst came home in the middle of August?"

"Yes. And he made time for me tomorrow."

Jackson considers. "You are leaving me."

"No. We are knit together, Jackson. You are the genius, and I am your muse. Can we go now, please?"

"Did you have coffee this morning?"

"They sell it in the dining car, but thank you."

By the time he finds shoes and climbs into the convertible, he is weeping openly.

"Jackson, I need you to collect yourself. I need you to be a safe driver, to go at a reasonable speed, and to make sure I catch the train."

"What time does it leave?"

"Ten-forty."

He untucks his shirt, using the tails to wipe his face. "Ten-forty. Much better than ten after ten."

That again. Ruth gives him a perplexed look, but he starts the engine, and she locks her face forward.

The station parking lot is nearly empty, yet Jackson parks in the far corner. They get out of the car, and he hoists her bag for her.

"Thank you." Ruth holds out her hand. He hesitates, then passes it over.

The bell begins ringing, and a conductor calls for boarding to begin. People say their goodbyes and get in line. A car arrives briskly, and a young man hurries out. "Scott," a voice from inside yells. "Your suitcase."

Scott runs back and is about to dash for the train when an elderly man raises his hand. "You're all right, son," he says. "Boarding began just this minute."

While Scott and the others board, Jackson and Ruth remain by the car.

"I promise."

Ruth has been concentrating on the boarding, wondering when she ought to get in line. When she will step away from Jackson. "Excuse me?"

"Not to drive that fast again. Not to scare you." He drags his shoe in the gravel. "I promise."

"You are the most brilliant man on earth." She kisses him, he rests his hand on the small of her back.

"Please don't leave me, Ruth."

"Jackson, Jackson, Jackson." She caresses his face. "You are part of me. I can no more leave you than I can leave my leg."

"But . . ." His throat chokes up. "But."

"I am with you forever. I am your true wife of the heart and of fate."

"Last call," the conductor yells. "All aboard."

Ruth takes her bag and trots up to the train. When she reaches the car's steps, she blows him a kiss, and boards. Jackson stays. He cannot tell which window is hers, or if she's even sitting on this side, but he waves in case.

The train leaves with a long blast of its horns, an uncertain harmony that makes Jackson cover his ears. He continues to hold his hands up for several minutes, until the elderly man who told Scott not to worry shuffles over.

"Are you all right, sir?"

Jackson lowers his arms, squinting at the man. "Do I know you?"

THE DOWNSTAIRS DOOR IS OPEN. RUTH CLIMBS, HER HARD BREATHING revealing what kind of shape she is in. In the narrow hall, she rests for a moment, then knocks.

"I gave at the office," Lucy sings from inside, as she opens the door. "Oh, hooray!"

"Hello, my sister—"

Lucy leaps, seizing her in a fierce hug, swinging side to side. When she starts to release, Ruth pulls her back. "Not yet." And they hug half a minute more.

Lucy scurries back into the apartment. "I need to make some phone calls."

"They cannot wait?"

"Not if I'm going to clear my calendar for you." She picks up the receiver and waves Ruth forward. "Come in, come in. Make yourself at home. This is your home." Lucy begins dialing, fumbles, lowers the phone. "I am so jazzed that you are here."

Ruth kisses her hand. "Me too."

While Lucy takes care of obligations, Ruth pokes into her old room. Unoccupied, the bed not wearing so much as a pillowcase. But the fan she left is still in the window. She flops on the mattress, its creaks familiar like the stairs in Jackson's house.

"There." Lucy sails in through the bedroom door. "All set. And you are welcome to move back in this afternoon."

"How can you afford to leave this room open?"

"Remember old woman-bruising Romeo?"

"How could I forget?"

"Three weeks after you left, he showed up with a dozen roses. On our stairs, wearing a black suit on a damn humid night. He apologized over and over. He promised to treat me better, to give me the respect I deserve. He also gave me a check for two thousand dollars, I suppose to prove that he meant business."

"What did you do?"

"Deposited the check, of course. First thing the next morning, and it cleared. Also threw the roses in the trash, thank you. I told him I would think about it. But would you believe it? I haven't been able to find five free seconds to do that part."

Her snickers turn to laughter, and Ruth lies on the bed laughing too. When did she last laugh? She can't remember.

"Either I attack you right there," Lucy chimes, "or you get up to splash your face, or whatever you need. But do it quick, because we're going out on the town."

When they step outside a few minutes later, Lucy is wearing a blue beret, cocked at a sharp angle. She takes Ruth's arm and sets off south, into the Village.

"Besides depositing checks," Ruth says, "what else have you been doing?"

"I bought a hat."

"So I see. A sexy one, by the way."

"Thank you." Lucy takes a little bow. "I had this crazy idea. Instead of acting like a virgin in public and a hooker in private, I could drop both phony acts and be myself. Still naughty as a goat, but I'd better like the heck out of the guy first."

"The one and only Loosely."

"I want to tell you something about that nickname. But here we are."

They are standing outside the Cedar Tavern, and Ruth feels her chest clench.

"Returning to the scene of the crime," Lucy jokes, but when Ruth doesn't laugh, she pulls her face-to-face. "This is okay, right? Coming here?"

"Sure," Ruth says halfheartedly. "We'll see how long I want to stay."

"Roger." Lucy takes her arm again and breezes them in the door.

It's late afternoon, hours too early for the crowd that might recognize her. They slide into a booth, Lucy removing her hat and shaking her hair free. The bartender waves, which they read to mean he'll be over soon.

"You." Ruth is smiling. "Are as beautiful as ever."

Lucy grins. "Kiss me, you fool."

They both laugh, but Lucy's face swiftly turns serious. "You know, my old Romeo, he wasn't completely wrong."

Ruth grabs her wrist. "Yes, he was. There is no excuse for a man to hit a woman."

"I don't mean that. He can go straight to hell for that. But when he called me nothing but a 'fun girl'? It was humbling, because he was partly right. That whole trip to Havana thing? Very deceptive and dishonest. *No bueno.*"

Ruth fiddles with the saltshaker. "I suppose not."

"I had a good run," Lucy continues. "But I'm done with that game. Now I'm asking around about instructors, to see if I can take my cello skills up a notch. Maybe find a seat in a small orchestra—or a quartet, I'd love to play in a quartet."

"That is why you are so beautiful. You are doing good things for your life."

"Annnnd." Lucy smiles. "And I took up my old hobby of photography. I was actually the first girl ever in my high school to be editor of the yearbook. It turns out musicians love having their picture taken, and they all need headshots. Even though they have no money, they will pay nicely for a good promotion portfolio."

"Well, look at you." Ruth is beaming.

"You were my role model, Ruthie. Nobody handed you anything. You saw it and you went for it. The day you left I took a long bath, and saw those bruises turning yellow on my ribs, and I knew what I needed."

"A shotgun?"

Lucy doesn't laugh. "Self-reliance. And a bit of ambition."

"Oh, Loosely, I love you."

"I love you too, and that name is the last thing. Then we talk about you."

"I prefer the topic of your life, actually."

"It's time for Loosely to go away. I was actually named after my grandmother, who was tough and smart and hilarious. Her name was Lucille."

"Lucille." Ruth takes her hand. "Have you tried it with many people?"

Lucy ducks her head. "You are the absolute first."

"Lucille. I love it." She squeezes her hand. "Lucille it is."

The bartender arrives, wiping his hands on a towel. "Apologies, ladies. How may I wet your whistle?"

"Martini for me," Lucy says, giving Ruth a wink. "I'm making changes, but I haven't lost my mind."

"Same here, please, with extra olives."

"Coming right up," he says, backing away.

"So," Lucy sings. "Life on the island with your genius artist. I want to hear everything. How's the school? Are the kids a hoot? How many beaches have you been swimming at? How is your great love affair?" She whispered, "How is all of that sex?"

"Oh, Lucille." Ruth looks at her, sharp and proud, and bursts into tears.

34

FEBRUARY 2007

She boarded a train so early, the city was still dark. It left Penn Station in minutes, and most of the seats were empty. Passengers got off in Bay Shore, in Islip. By the time the train reached East Hampton, she was the only rider left.

There was one taxi. The driver, head down, wore a Yankees cap. The angle of his lean against the car made her think he was dozing standing up. But the station door scraped as it closed, and he woke.

"Hello, miss." Rousing, he shook himself. "Where can I take you this fine day?"

It was drizzling and gusty, and definitely not fine. From the top of the stairs Gwen could see his eyes were bloodshot. "Are you sober?"

"Yes ma'am. Working two jobs means a guy may not look his best."

"I'll need you for about two hours."

"With pleasure." He opened the car's rear door. "Thousand bucks."

Gwen laughed but said nothing. Only stood still while a damp wind pulled at her coat.

"Okay, okay," he said. "Eight hundred. 'Cause I like you."

She descended the steps. "I'm glad my laugh was worth two hundred dollars. But I'm not one of your millionaire summer women."

He looked her up and down. "Don't believe you one inch."

"Before you stands an ordinary human, crushed by Manhattan rents. I'll pay you fifty an hour, while we drive to three locations. Or"—she waved at the empty station—"you can drive all the other customers."

"Fifty an hour?" He made a face. "You're paying for gas too."

She liked him, his shamelessness. "What's your name?"

"Wyatt, at your service."

"Wyatt at my service, I'm not paying for gas. But if you do a good job, I promise your biggest tip of the day."

He crossed his arms.

"Don't get pouty," Gwen said. "You know it's a fair deal."

"So, where you gotta go?"

She held up three fingers. "A house, the site of a car accident, and a grave."

"Shoulda guessed." Wyatt took off his cap, then tugged it back on. "Girl like you comes out here in February, it's gotta be another freak for the crazy guy."

"I object to your language, sir."

"What? 'Freak'?"

"No." She stepped past him, sliding into the car. "Girl."

"HERE WE ARE." WYATT PULLED IN THE DRIVEWAY. "THE MADMAN'S CASTLE."

Gwen peered out the window. The house was underwhelming, a shingle-sided two-story cape with a shed addition. It sat on a flat lot, bereft of gardens. Beyond the winter lawn lay a brown stretch of meadowland, and a glimpse of blue water. No sign of genius or passion. It could have been the home of a local accountant.

"You expected fancy, right?" Wyatt snorted. "When a guy's that famous, you figure big bucks."

"I did think it would be impressive in some way."

"So. Next stop?"

"Not quite." Gwen opened her door. "I need to see if I can find any answers."

"Hell, I got answers like dogs got fleas." He threw an arm over the passenger seat. "What's your question? Fire away."

"Maybe later."

Gwen climbed out, and a gust slammed the car door behind her. Ahead, a slender wooden post held a warped sign: *Closed for the season.*

"You'd think they could have planted one bush to adorn the place."

She peered through the front door's windows. An open kitchen, a four-burner stove. A toaster so antiquated, it was cute. Spices on a rack. Squinting, she could not read the labels, but recognized a red bottle of Tabasco sauce. Everything seemed frozen in time: the rusty oven fan, the hooks that held fraying oven mitts.

The striking thing was seashells. A giant white one, filled with conchs, sat on a side table. More kinds of shells on the shelves. Blanched pieces of brain coral. Though it had never come up in her research, this household walked the beaches.

Or perhaps Lee had collected it all, in the years before she returned to New York City. In her long widowhood.

Gwen crept around the house, peering in. There was a handsome round dining table with twelve chairs. Shelves of books, a record player, a rudimentary amplifier with its tubes visible. A couch and facing armchairs.

"Not much, is it?" Wyatt called. Gwen glanced his way. He appeared to be warm, though he was only wearing a sweatshirt.

The Cedar Tavern had become a drugstore. By comparison, this was not bad. She snooped in the bay window. More shells, a piano coated with dust.

"Not much, no. But I bet the water view is great from upstairs."

"In summer there's tours, crowded every day. Weird people. Go figure."

"Maybe they're like me, Wyatt." Gwen had reached the front again. "Maybe they're hoping to find some evidence of how such original, wild, perplexing art was made here. Something to explain why it ended so badly."

"Yeah. But it's just a house. No secret sauce."

She stepped back, peering at the upper windows. "I wish I could get upstairs."

"From what I hear, you'd see walls papered with labels from different liquors. That, and portraits of women's backsides."

Gwen laughed. "In fact, there's one in particular that I'm interested in."

"Kind of liquor?"

Smiling, she shook her head. "Ass."

Wyatt stood, watching her stroll across the lawn toward the studio. He took off his baseball hat, scratched his head, then set it back on again.

35

AUGUST 1956

She can barely describe the call as a conversation. At least he answers the phone, though apparently "hello" is too much work.

"Jackson?" Ruth asks. "Are you there?"

He grunts. So, he is in one of his moods. Well, Ruth gave him reason for it.

"I miss you," she says. "I am coming home today. I am bringing my friend Lucille." She reaches over the kitchen table to rub Lucy's hand. "For the weekend. Our train arrives at twelve-thirty. Will you please pick us up? We can go somewhere fun for lunch."

"Twelve-thirty."

He hangs up. Ruth, stunned, listens to the dial tone. But in two seconds she is nodding. "That sounds lovely." Pause, while she mock-listens. "Oh, you naughty." Pause. "I love you too."

As she sets the receiver down, Lucy eyes her. "You sure this is a good idea?"

"It is perfect. We need to get some sand between the city girl's toes."

JACKSON IS LATE. APPROACHING WITH THE WIDE GAIT OF A SAILOR, HIS squint is so severe, Ruth marvels that he can see at all.

"We need to find your sunglasses," she says, kissing his cheek.

"All right." He remains hunched over.

"Sweetheart, you must have slept in your studio again." Ruth puts one hand on his chest and the other on his back, and he straightens slightly. He gives off a strong smell—alcohol, only muskier and more sour. "Here is my lovely friend, Lucille."

"We've met," Lucy says, a bit stiff in her back. "Nice to see you again."

He nods at her. "Hello."

"Jackson." Ruth nods at her bag on the station's steps. "Would you please manhandle that for me?"

He hoists it up and heads for the convertible. Ruth notices Lucy's bag and sweeps it up herself. "So light," she tells her friend. "It feels like you packed air."

Jackson climbs up behind the wheel. Ruth goes to the other side. "I apologize," she whispers to Lucy. "Sometimes he has moods."

"Believe me, I've seen worse." But Lucy marvels. To think that she had found Jackson attractive. Now his eyes are barely open, and he needs to bathe. She regrets every flirt with him. The loyalty of her friend is far more valuable.

Ruth opens the passenger door, tilts the seat forward. "Your chariot awaits."

Lucy scrambles into the back. "These are some snazzy wheels."

Jackson is silent. Ruth tumbles in back too. "On our way to the prom."

Lucy laughs. "Robbie Santos is cute, but he's awful handsy, you know?"

"You say that like it is a bad thing."

And they're both laughing, as Jackson stomps on the gas. The convertible's big engine throws them back in their seats.

AT THE HOUSE, HE CHARGES INSIDE WITH THEIR BAGS WHILE RUTH AND Lucy climb out of the car. In seconds he is back, tromping off to the studio.

"All righty." Ruth claps her hands. "How about I make us all some lunch?"

There isn't much food, she discovers, but enough to make chicken salad that she scoops onto lettuce on three plates.

Lucy is using an old wire swatter to kill kitchen flies. "This is fun."

Ruth chuckles. "You are lethal with that thing." In the shed she finds a wooden box, which she overturns under the maple, adding plates, glasses, a pitcher of iced tea. After knocking, Ruth enters the studio.

Jackson is sitting on the step, weeping into his hands. When he looks up, mouth open with anguish, Ruth imagines a fledgling bird, beak wide for Mama and whatever she brings.

"Oh dear." Ruth gathers him close. "Did you worry about me returning?"

Sniffling, he nods.

"Jackson, Jackson, Jackson." As before, on the morning he punched himself, she presses her forehead to the side of his head. Feeling the pulse of his temple, she hopes it comforts him as much as it does her. "I told you. I am your wife forever."

He nods again, hanging his head so the tears darken her skirt.

"Darling, when did you last eat?"

He shrugs.

"Have lunch with us. Come enjoy my friend. Food will make you feel better."

He stands, following hangdog. Ruth spots his sunglasses on a shelf. "Here. These will help too."

He slides them on. Lucy has wandered down the lawn, but she returns with an easy sway.

"It looks like the ocean is relaxing you," Ruth calls.

"Just to breathe salt air," Lucy answers. "It's heavenly."

"Come and sit, dear Lucille."

Ruth hands them their plates, Jackson accepting his with a grunt. She pours tea from the pitcher into tall glasses, ice tinkling as it falls.

"So, Jackson." Lucy settles on her chair. "Have you had a good summer of work? Or does my sister distract you too often?"

"Well." Jackson sits. "I'd have to say . . ." He raises a hand to wipe his face, which spills tea on his plate. "Damn it." He jumps up, dumping the tea and salad onto his pants. "Aaaarrgh!"

He flings the plate away and whips the glass into the side of the convertible, where it shatters and leaves a dent.

"Say anything," he snarls at Ruth, who is still standing, holding the tea pitcher. "Say one fucking thing."

Ruth lowers her gaze. He kicks the ground and stomps off toward the road.

After a moment, Lucy collects Jackson's plate and sets it on his chair. She takes Ruth by the shoulders and makes her sit.

"He is not always like this."

Lucy puts a finger on Ruth's lips. "You need to listen to me for a moment."

"I know what is happening. I can help him."

"Tomorrow I will be on a train back to New York. You are coming with me."

Ruth's hands wrestle one another, twisting her fingers. "Do you think I am in denial here? Do you think I am unaware that his illness is beyond my ability?"

Lucy kneels before her chair. "I suppose not."

"Am I supposed to abandon him? Take the train, and leave him to the wolves?"

"I don't see any wolves."

"There are ten thousand wolves. All of them in his head."

"When you put it that way . . ."

"I love him. And he loves me, in his fashion. We are in this mess together."

Lucy pulls a clump of grass. "There will be a price."

"Lucille, I am paying it already." She waves toward the shed, where Jackson is standing, staring at the sky. "So is he."

Lucy considers him in the bright seaside light. "Let me take your picture."

"What?"

"I brought a camera. You two do have a unique love. I want to capture it."

Ruth ponders the idea. "We should have lunch first. Give him time to cool off. Then we can see if he is willing."

"Well." Lucy goes to the little table and raises her iced tea. "Cheers."

◆ ◆ ◆

AN HOUR LATER, JACKSON IS STILL CONTEMPLATING THE CLOUDS. LEANing against the shed, he has extended both arms like braces, as if he might fall.

"What do you think?" Lucy wields the flyswatter again, smiting passing bugs.

"I have a way to restore his good humor," Ruth answers. "And to inspire him, but I am not in the mood. Definitely not. Perhaps you could chat him up a little?"

"Why the hell not?" Lucy starts across the lawn. "He doesn't bite, right?"

Ruth puts one hand on her breast and remembers. But Lucy and Jackson strike up a conversation. No tantrum, no tears. She points the flyswatter at the chairs, but he shakes his head. She waves it at the convertible, but again he declines. She gestures somewhere else, Ruth can't tell where, and he ambles in that direction. Lucy runs inside, returns with a camera, and Jackson is sitting on the big rock in the backyard.

He supports himself, one hand on the rock, while Lucy begins taking pictures. She circles to see where the light is best, the shadows most defining. Jackson follows her instructions to turn his shoulders, lift his chin.

"Ruthie," Lucy calls at last. "Come join us."

Ruth skips over, enthusiastic. "This is the first photograph ever of the two of us together."

But then she sees Jackson's face up close. A wooden mask, pretending to be happy. His eyes are squinted down so hard, she cannot see his pupils.

"Climb on him," Lucy commands. "Be his lover."

His shirt is disheveled, pants a mess, and she's bare legged. But here is proof, she thinks. Evidence, should the world ever doubt.

So Ruth does as she's told. She throws a leg across his lap, and starts to slide off. He grabs her knee with both hands, she clutches his arm, they find a balance.

"There you are," Lucy says, camera to her eye. "Love knows no age."

Ruth is beaming. Though his back is hunched and his brow furrowed, Jackson also manages a narrow smile. That is the instant Lucy snaps the shutter.

"I got it," she crows. "Can't be sure till it's developed. But I got it."

"Got what?" Ruth asks.

Lucy laughs. "You two should sit on this rock more often."

Ruth feels herself slipping again, and stands. "Thank you, Lucille."

Jackson puts a hand frankly on one cheek of her backside. "Why don't I drive you ladies to the beach?"

"Really?" Lucy snaps her camera into its case. "I'd love that."

Ruth considers. "Can you fend for yourself? And collect us later?"

"I will." He starts toward the car. "Gather your stuff."

THEY AGREE UPON SIX, AND WHEN THE GREEN-AND-WHITE CONVERTIBLE pulls into the lot that evening, the large clock in the pavilion reads two minutes till.

"There." Ruth exhales, lets her shoulders drop. "Right on time."

"And now you're free of the weight that burdened you all afternoon."

"I apologize, Lucille. You know I worry."

"Not without reason," Lucy jokes, but their laughter is choked off when the car bumps a wooden post at the end of the lot.

He's not crying when they get to the convertible. He even changed his shirt. And he is standing behind the steering wheel, arms raised.

"G'afternoon, lady and lady," he cries. "Hail to thee both."

"Jackson, Jackson, Jackson." Ruth and Lucy climb in back again. "Thank you."

"I come bearing good news."

"Oh?" says Lucy, fastening her wrap.

He slides down into his seat. "Alfonso invited us to dinner again."

"Who is Alfonso?"

"A collector of Jackson's work."

"Made of money," Jackson adds. "And good booze."

Backing away from the post, he swings the car around and drives them out to Fireplace Road. Again he turns left, down island.

"Sweetheart." Ruth rests a hand on his shoulder. "Once again I am wearing beach clothing."

"S'fine." Jackson waves her off. "Very informal t'night. Some band playing."

"My bathing suit is damp," Lucy says. "I'd prefer to wear dry clothes."

He shakes his head. "We'd miss the band."

THE DRIVEWAY IS PACKED. MEN WITH LITTLE RED FLAGS GUIDE DRIVERS on where to park. Ruth and Lucy see the problem right away. The people getting out of their cars are in formal evening wear: ladies in long dresses and twinkling jewelry, men wearing tuxedos and stern expressions.

"Jackson," Ruth calls once they've parked, but he has charged ahead.

Lucy takes her arm. "We are the wrong monkeys for this circus."

"Let me fetch him, and we will go home."

By the time Ruth reaches the front door, Jackson has found Alfonso—who is wearing a dark-green velvet dinner jacket and a yellow bow tie. They are arguing.

"This is a special event to celebrate the peak of summer." Alfonso rests a hand on Jackson's shoulder. "Which calls for special—"

"Hands off, pooftah." Jackson shakes him away.

"Pooftah?" Alfonso laughs out loud, then squares off with him. "I love you, Jackson Pollock. And I wish with all my heart that you would get well. But tonight? Time for you to go home."

Jackson peers past him. "Who's this snooty band you're showing off with, anyway?"

Ruth stands near, listening, as a well-dressed couple squeezes by. Only after they've passed does she recognize them: Esther and Abraham from the art school. They continue without a glance her way—not out of scorn, but because in this setting, in the wrong clothes, in the company of a drunkard, she is invisible.

"Jackson. It's not a band." Alfonso makes eye contact with Ruth. "It's the New York Philharmonic."

"Are you serious?" Lucy asks. "At your house?"

"Jackson," Ruth snaps. "Look at me."

He turns, eyes on fire. "What?"

"You will drive us home now. We will put on proper clothes and return to enjoy Alfonso's incredible generosity." She takes Jackson's arm. "Come. Come along."

He shakes her off and marches away kicking the air.

Alfonso approaches Ruth. "I'm so sorry. Will he be safe behind the wheel?"

"You have no reason to apologize," Ruth replies. "I do. And he has promised me he will drive slowly."

"Once again the most rational woman in all of Long Island." Alfonso takes her hand and kisses it. "Princess, we will delay the performance until you return."

"You are so generous to me." She kisses his hand in return, which makes them both laugh. "Are you sure you play for the other team?"

Just then the gorgeous young man appears, delivering a glass of champagne to Alfonso, then melding back into the crowd. He smiles. "Absolutely certain."

IT'S A BEAUTIFUL NIGHT, RUTH THINKS, TO DRIVE FAST. SWEET AUGUST air, the empty roads, their sea-salt hair whipped by wind in every direction. They're both in back again.

She leans over to Lucy. "Remind me to wear a hat for the trip back."

"Aren't you frightened? He's going so fast."

"This road is nearly all straightaways. And we are close to home now."

Lucy lays a hand on Jackson's shoulder. "Would you mind slowing down? I'm feeling carsick."

He twists free and continues at the same speed without a word.

Lucy touches Ruth. "Will you talk to him?"

Ruth leans over the seat back. "Jackson?"

His mouth is open, as if he's biting the wind. "What?"

"You're going to kill us," Lucy yells.

"Never." Ruth shakes her head. "Jackson is the best driver that ever lived." She rubs his back. "A brilliant genius knows what speed to go."

Lucy's eyes bulge. "You people are insane," she yells.

"Jackson," Ruth shouts over the air noise. "What is in your gigantic mind right now? Is it an idea that cannot be expressed in words?"

He cackles, his eyes wild. "It's ten after ten, you wretches. Ten after ten."

Lucy looks at Ruth, terror plain on her face. She screams herself breathless, then gulps air to fill her lungs again. The sound she makes next is so loud, so curdling, it wounds Lucy's vocal cords as Ruth covers her ear on that side.

"Remember how you said you would not frighten me again?" Ruth drapes a hand on Jackson's shoulder. "You promised."

"After ten after ten after ten," he bellows, and stomps the pedal to the floor. The wind roars like a lion.

36

FEBRUARY 2007

Wouldn't have killed them to plant something."

Wyatt gestured at the ground. "When they bought the place, the barn was here." He walked a shape in the rough grass. "All these years, and you can still tell where the slab was."

"I wonder why they moved the barn."

Wyatt pointed toward blue water in the distance. "Blocked the view."

They reached the studio, a simple square with a shed on one side, its cedar shingles weatherworn to a handsome gray. Gwen scanned the property from there. "It's more private over here too."

Again she had to satisfy herself with peeking. From the door's windows she saw rows of shelves, coffee cans bristling with brushes. Tubes of paint, which must have been Lee's. Also Jackson's buckets, with stirring paddles stacked to one side. A pair of boots with the laces removed, paint drops all over them.

She stepped back. "Too tidy."

Wyatt snorted. "Like they're gonna leave it a pigsty?"

"There is a process," Gwen explained, "of turning an artist into a commodity. Even the wildest ones. There's no mess, no torn canvas, no mayhem."

"Maybe so. But this place needs signs." By the high windows,

Wyatt set up a stepladder he'd found somewhere. "Info stuff since there's no tours here in winter."

"You mean like 'Here lived Jackson and Lee, they painted x and y.'"

"Yeah. For off-season weirdos like you."

Gwen gave him a look, but he was smiling.

"Or a kid in a booth bored to death. Charging admission, selling postcards."

"Yes, with a cruel case of acne." She bent to the windows, snapping pictures with her phone.

"You bought one of those gadgets? Ask me, it's a waste of money."

Gwen shrugged. "It's in case I forget anything, which I will. And I don't have to hit the number seven four times to text the letter *S*." She climbed a few steps on the ladder. "This is where it all happened." She rose on tiptoe and peered in.

The studio was immaculate. No cluttered dollies, no rags, no ashtray full of butts. Any evidence of actual work had been sacrificed to myth. One man's torment was good for little more than a higher number when the auctioneer banged his gavel, *sold*.

Except for the floor. And what she saw there nearly knocked her off the stepladder.

She couldn't tell what kind of wood it was. Something dark brown. But there were spills, thousands of them, all over: black, white, red, yellow, blue, green. Blotches and drips and one bare footprint. The mess was accidental of course, creativity's excess, evidence of imperfect humanity. But to Gwen, that stained floor was as beautiful as any painting. It choked her up. Here, a man had tried.

All that time wanting to redeem himself, to regain the early years' house-on-fire genius that somehow had abandoned him. For the first time, she understood Jackson's later years, the weeping and fury and drink. No wonder his works were chaotic. *He was trying.*

Gwen felt a weight of sorrow in her chest. An affection for Pollock's suffering heart and damaged mind. She stepped down to the winter lawn. "Let's go."

"Cool with me." Wyatt put the ladder back and hustled to meet her at the car. "Funny thing?"

"What is?"

"I picture this guy, right?" He sniffed. "I don't know. Genius or crazy or both. Anyway, he's stomping around this place drunk as a monkey, foaming at the mouth and screwing who knows who. But then he goes into that . . ." He jerked a thumb at the studio. "Garage, really. Goes nuts in there with buckets of paint, canvas on the floor for chrissakes. Makes a total mess. And it sells for ten million bucks." Wyatt adjusted his Yankees cap. "Pardon me, but it's all one big what-the-fuck."

"All true," Gwen said. "Except try one hundred and forty million."

He stopped cold. "Bullshit."

"Last November. I was there when it happened."

"So, you're a summertime princess after all?"

She shook her head. "I work for a company that sells art. Someone says they have a painting made by your drunken monkey. My job is to find out if it's fake."

"You can tell a painting is fake by seeing the guy's house?"

"I couldn't predict whether coming here would help or not." Gwen gave the place one last look. "Okay, tiger. Let's visit the scene of the crime."

"Tiger, huh?" He opened her door and winked. "You have no idea."

THE DRIVE FOLLOWED FIREPLACE ROAD. SEEING THE ROAD SIGN GAVE Gwen a chill.

"Hey," Wyatt said from the front. "When we're done, you want to grab a coffee or something?"

"I don't have time. Thank you, though."

"I know a nice place. Real warm. Raw bar opens at ten a.m."

She fiddled with her green notebook. "How long have you been divorced?"

He wrung the steering wheel with both hands. "You know, there is such a thing as being too smart for your own good."

"How long, though?"

He scowled in the rearview mirror. "About a year, all right? She gets the girls on Sundays, for church, so I work an extra shift. Wyatt's life of joy and adventure."

They rode in silence, and much sooner than Gwen expected, he pulled over. As she climbed out of the car, trying to get her bearings, Wyatt pointed at the road. "See that place where the blacktop changes?"

"I sure do."

"Town line. Different surfaces, paved by different companies, in different years. So that night, the surface changed on him, right before they barreled up." He waved at a mild curve ahead. "Right there."

"That doesn't look very dangerous."

"At high speed, it doesn't take much."

Gwen scanned the scrubby brush, the bare trees, winter's bleak attire. "What a shame, you know?" She kicked the gravel. "What a waste."

"My kid brother, Tony, he was a motorcycle racer."

"Yes, and?"

"Started with motocross, because you don't need a license. Fourteen years old, a hundred pounds, tops, racing on three-fifty bikes weighing more than four hundred pounds. And he's good at it, the real thing. Win here, win there, trophies on the shelf, you know? Sixteenth birthday, he gets out on his first hard track. Asphalt. Flips on third lap, damn near tears his head off."

"Was he badly hurt?"

Wyatt tightened his jaw. "Dead before he stopped bouncing."

"Oh, I'm so sorry."

"A century ago. Point is." Wyatt raised his chin at the curve. "Point is, some people are slow cooking, like you and me. Some are made to burn fast."

Gwen gave him a long look. "You're smarter than I first thought."

"Yeah? You want to get that coffee?"

"You know we have one more stop."

"Whoopee." He circled a celebratory finger in the air. "The cemetery."

37

AUGUST 11, 1956

On Fireplace Road, pavement turns to gravel at the town line. On the south side lies moneyed East Hampton, with a few modest homes, but enough mansions to generate property taxes that provide for a better school, a handsome town library, and smooth roads. To the north is Springs, second home to a few of the wealthy, but mostly farms and homes, plus small properties within the reach of people like Jackson Pollock and Lee Krasner. In their time, Springs has no library, the school is tiny, and the town's method of slowing cars on loose gravel is to build a curve where the pavement—and traction—ends.

No one knows what speed the green convertible is going at seven p.m. on August 11, 1956, as it reaches the road change. When Jackson sees the curve and slams on his brakes, the tires grip the soft gravel, leaving a track whose depth later leads detectives to conclude that he was going eighty miles per hour.

Despite his braking, the car skids off the road's right-hand shoulder, tugging the wheels hard toward a stand of trees. Jackson jerks the steering wheel to the left, correcting, overcorrecting.

The vehicle charges across the road, still at high speed. It soars off the left shoulder, briefly airborne before diving into the dirt like a whale sounding for the deep. Detectives later measure, and calculate, and conclude that the convertible went from eighty to zero in the space of about fifteen feet.

The sudden stop catapults Jackson over the windshield. His body is still fourteen feet off the ground when his head strikes an oak tree seventy feet away. The impact is not enough to stop his body's momentum. He glances off the oak, flying another twenty-five feet before flattening the underbrush, face down.

Lucy has been clutching the front seats with all her strength, so her body flips upward, legs high in the air as the rear of the car rises, then slaps down upon her much as a flyswatter crushes a fly.

Ruth spirals sideways out of her seat, over the hood before the car finishes its cartwheel, tossing her in the dirt, where she spins like a bowling pin till she comes to rest against a clump of wild honeysuckle. In a minute she is breathing, and standing, though she does not remember regaining her feet. Her dress has lost its top two buttons, which means whoever comes to rescue them will be ogling her, and she gathers the fabric in one fist. But she has forgotten something urgent, what can it be?

Her body feels wrong. Twisted, as though her hips and spine are not aligned. It doesn't hurt, or not terribly, anyway, as she spits dirt from her mouth, blinks it from her eyes, probes with a pinkie to dig it from an ear. A few steps and her hips hurt sharply, which causes her to remember.

"Jackson?" she calls into the darkness. "Darling?"

It also registers with her that the car is upside down, hard against the ground. "Lucy." Ruth takes more steps. Pain shoots up her leg, and she falls against the car. Perhaps Lucy tucked herself down in the seats, and is unhurt. "Lucy?"

Later at the inquest, people who live two miles away will attest that they heard a woman screaming. But now there is no sound from under the car. Only the clicking and ticking as the engine cools. Then all is silent.

Ruth swats the tire, which is now at chest height, and her hand stings. "You only got to be Lucille for one day."

Her hips hurt now. Ruth tries to twist them right, and the pain is blinding. But when her head clears, she sees in amazement: One of the headlamps is still on, casting a cone of yellow on the road. It looks like theatrical lighting, an effect for the small stage the crash site has become. People will see that light. Help will follow it.

"Jackson?"

She limps forward, lowering herself gingerly to the ground, and turns to rest her forehead against the side of the headlight. The bulb gives off heat, thin but she can feel it. Everything else is broken. From that moment on, Ruth vows to herself, she will accept whatever comfort she can find.

38

FEBRUARY 2007

Under the high dome of the main hall in Grand Central, Gwen stood by the four-sided clock, wanting to be kissed. Was the idea from a book? Some cheesy movie? She vaguely remembered a couple's passionate embrace right where she was standing. She longed to be kissed there, by Arthur. She felt hollow with want. And what—having seen the heartbreak of Pollock's grave—what should she do now?

Answer her phone, ringing in her coat pocket.

"*Chérie* Gwen! You sent me the hair so late."

"I know, Matthieu." She started walking. It was Sunday, and she had a routine to maintain. "You have no idea how hard it was to convince that woman—"

"No time for chitchat. I begged a favor, and I have results."

"You are a miracle." Gwen stopped. "Is the hair hers?"

"Ha," he scoffed. "It is not even human."

"What do you mean?"

"Did the artist we have in mind own a dog?"

She was looking for the crosstown shuttle. "Not that I know of."

"My technician says the hair came from a furred mammal. Bobcat, coyote, wolf, and so on."

Gwen felt a tug in her gut. "How about bear?"

Matthieu laughed. "Did our artist have a pet bear?"

"Never mind." Again her power in the decision, unsought, unwanted, was growing. There was a bear. Jackson and Ruth made love on it. Should she tell? Or keep it to herself?

"My technician did not rule out bear, mademoiselle. It may be possible."

Gwen tried to calm herself. "Definitely not Ruth's hair, anyway."

"Correct, alas. Meanwhile, Jeanne and I are flying to Paris Tuesday, so I've arranged for your movers to take the painting. You will alert the client?"

"Of course." She heard the shuttle rattling into the station. "You're a prince."

"Also correct. *À bientôt.*"

Entering the subway, Gwen ran out of habit, caught the crosstown train to Times Square, then rode the 3 train north to Lincoln Center. When she reached street level, the same raw wind that had chilled her in Springs was whistling through the West Side. She flipped up her collar and buttoned her coat tight.

Gwen had canvassed those streets so many times, she knew by the trash bags piled on the sidewalk on Tuesday nights that Wednesday was collection day. Yet in all those rounds of the neighborhood, she hadn't seen one aged lady walking her little dog. A dark-haired guy jogging with his chubby beagle, yes. A blonde propelled by her enthusiastic black Lab. A hired walker wrangling a knot of leashes for six dogs at once. But no one resembling Lee. Why would today be any different?

Gwen aimed for the park, planning to work north. It was tolerable, except when she faced west. The wind was biting. "This is a total waste of time."

Yet she continued up Central Park West, deciding to go as far north as Seventy-Second Street. Then she would concede. There was no more information to be gathered. She would take the southbound bus home, the same one that caused her to run into Arthur—also early on a Sunday afternoon.

Gwen felt nostalgic as she reached Strawberry Fields again. It was still cold. She was still blind. Still desolate with yearning, and she turned to go home. Across the street, in front of the Dakota where

John Lennon had been shot, a gaunt woman was walking her minuscule dog. Its little legs kept busy, trotting while the woman leaned into the bitter wind.

Gwen ran. There was no need, except to quell her disbelief. At the sound of approaching boots, the woman turned her frail frame. She was much older than in the pictures, but Gwen had no doubt. Here was Lee Krasner, in the flesh.

"Sorry to bother you," she said, pulling up beside her. "I'm—"

"I know who you are."

"I've been trying to reach you. The foundation blocked me. I left messages—"

"Nineteen." The little dog tugged on its leash, pulling Lee forward. "Nineteen messages in twenty-six days."

"I'm sorry."

"So far, two apologies in half a minute," Lee observed.

"Well, my reasons were important. Why won't you speak with me?"

She sniffled. "All you offer is a new mess. The old mess is large enough."

"But you might be—"

"I am honoring my deceased husband. It's a form of fidelity."

Gwen needed a moment to take that in. Lee was still plenty sharp. She had interrupted more times than Gwen had apologized.

"Besides." Lee jutted her jaw forward. "You ask the wrong questions. You think this is about a painting. But it could as easily be a paintbrush. The object does not matter. The question does."

"Which is?"

"Wait." She dug a quavering hand into her pocket, which caused the tiny dog to dart back, yipping, leaping off its hind legs. He reached surprisingly high. Lee gave the dog a treat, and he darted away, all pride, tossing his head side to side.

"Did you know," Lee said, "she sued me for her medical bills from the crash?"

"Actually, I—"

"Did you know she took up with Willem? For four years. He and Elaine stayed married, but they were never right again. Separate dwellings, separate rage."

"I had heard—"

"Did you know there were others, in a nearly continuous line? Carlos Sansegundo? Franz Kline? Jasper Johns, though I'm told he did not favor women. Some sort of entanglement with Andy Warhol, who protested that it only went as far as kissing. Meanwhile, Willem unveils a painting titled *Ruth's Zowie*."

"*Zowie*? No, I hadn't—"

"Did you know." Lee gave a feeble cough, then turned her head and spat. "That Ruth bought a house in Springs? No one could miss her, the painted pony. Wearing some absurd hat, boobs spilling out of her bathing suit. And telling everyone she was a poet? It was dreck. Sugary as cotton candy, and as profound as a thirteen-year-old's fantasies. One poem had Pollock on a white horse." Lee laughed, but she was gritting her teeth. "Can you imagine?"

Gwen's gloved fingers had begun to ache. "I did read her memoir."

"Then you have suffered." Lee grimaced like a gargoyle. "Alfonso would host readings. Real poets—O'Hara, Ferlinghetti—with Ruth as the opening act. He meant to provide her an opportunity, but it was cruel. People laughed openly."

Gwen waited for more, but Lee seemed to have lost steam. "You said I am asking the wrong questions."

"The Hamptons intelligentsia could not decide. Mock Ruth, or celebrate her ironically? That's how they treat everyone. Till she became part of the furniture."

"I imagine that made her struggle for attention even more."

"At that time . . ." Lee glared, annoyed by the comment. "I, too, asked the wrong questions. She was eighteen years younger than Jackson, after all. Then one summer it was different. No more showgirl body, no more lush hair. She looked like us." Lee wiped her nose. "That is when I realized she was pathetic. A parasite, yes, but to be pitied."

"You feel pity toward Ruth?"

Lee coughed. "She will always be the sycophantic strumpet who hoped to save my Jackson by living with him, and instead in twelve days he was dead. But yes, eventually."

They reached the corner. Lee produced another treat, and the dog leapt as avidly as before. Then she struck out across Columbus Avenue, bent into the wind like a sailboat's prow. Gwen held close by her side.

"For as long as there has been marriage," Lee continued, "women have stolen husbands, and men have gladly let themselves be stolen. If I remained enraged and heartbroken by that alone, I would be a cliché. That was not her crime."

"Did Ruth commit a crime?"

Lee sniffed. "You are being sarcastic, I hope. She committed countless crimes. The one that matters is that she caused the death of the greatest creative mind of the twentieth century. She killed the art that did not occur because of her. The hearts and minds not enlarged by seeing those works."

"I had not thought of that." Gwen's feet hurt from the cold.

"That is why I am speaking with you. She called it love and destiny. In fact, it was only enabling. She fancied herself a muse. In fact, she was a siren, singing her song of seduction, luring the depressed alcoholic directly onto the rocks."

"Which brings us back to the original questions," Gwen said. "Who made the painting, and who owns it. If we go to auction—"

"Damn it." Lee stamped her boot. "You're not listening."

They had reached Amsterdam Avenue, and Gwen waited again. But Lee didn't cross. She poked a crooked finger at Gwen.

"Approve that painting, and you give the woman enormous wealth she did nothing to earn. But that's a fraction of the value. Last year, a single Pollock painting sold for one hundred and forty million dollars. If she deprived him of twenty years of work—he was only forty-four when he died—then she robbed him of billions. Worse, she stole from the world the pleasures of those paintings. The incomparable experiences of them."

"Let's agree on all of that," Gwen said, her legs shivering. "We still have a painting, maybe by Jackson Pollock, in the possession of a person who maybe owns it, and who wants to sell it. What do we do?"

"Dismiss any debate about whether it is authentic, or legally hers. The right question is whether she should benefit from a tragedy that she caused." Lee seized Gwen's arm with both bony hands, yanking her close. "What reward should she receive? What does she deserve?"

"I don't know what to say. I just—"

"I'll say it, then." Lee's face compressed into a sneer. "She does not deserve the oxygen she breathes. And if she falls, let the vultures have their day."

She jerked away, gnashing her teeth at the wind, charging across the avenue. Halfway there she dug out a treat, and the little dog leapt with all his might.

GWEN CAUGHT THE 3 TRAIN DOWNTOWN. SHOULD SHE GO TO THE OFFICE? Would Pinkney want her decision written, or delivered in a presentation? She had no idea.

As she drove the green convertible up and down her thigh, a man staggered into her subway car from the one ahead. A drunk, she thought, noting the bent tortoiseshell glasses barely hanging on the tip of his nose. But as he straightened she saw that, no, he had been preventing a box of chocolate bars from spilling. Gwen turned away, but he had seen her, and now he was making his way up the car. She tucked the toy car into her coat pocket.

"Good, delicious chocolate," the man was saying. "Only one dollar."

Gwen took out her phone, pretending to read a message that demanded her attention.

"Good, good chocolate." He drew closer. "Just one buck."

She tried to make herself small, but here he was, directly in front of her, swaying with the subway's motion.

"Darlin', I can tell right off you could use some sweetness in your life. What's a dollar to a pretty girl like you?"

"No thank you," she said, and it felt like capitulation.

"You don't eat candy? You won't help a man on hard times?"

"No thank you." Her voice was firm.

He leaned back, assessing her over his glasses' thick lenses. "You are a closed box."

"Excuse me?"

"Everything you do." He gripped an overhead handle. "Friends, job, love. Closed box, shut tight."

Gwen held up her phone, as if it would shield her. "Please leave me alone."

"I won't hurt you." The man pushed his glasses up into proper position, his eyes suddenly changed. "All I offer you is life. Sweet, sweet life."

The train stopped, the doors opened, and though she had no idea what street it was, she ran past him, up the stairs and out to the street. Closed box? Closed box?

She surfaced at Fourteenth Street and Seventh Avenue, the West Village in a Sunday afternoon quiet, and Gwen calmed quickly. But the cold was there, too, as windy as it had been uptown. Gwen was surprised to find that she was still holding her phone. She considered for a moment, then called Pinkney at home.

He answered with a chuckle. "I wondered if I would hear from you today."

"I went out to Springs," she answered.

"Fun. See anything meaningful?"

"I can say with complete certainty that Jackson Pollock is dead."

Pinkney laughed. "You are way more entertaining than the basketball I'm watching right now. Kobe Bryant is single handedly slaughtering I don't even know which team"

"For some reason I thought you'd be working."

"Currently surrounded by finance spreadsheets. You're working, too, and you have a decision for me."

She took a deep breath. "I do."

Gwen could hear him shifting, getting comfortable. She backed into the entry of a bridal shop, out of the wind, surrounded by mannequins in white dresses.

"Go," he said.

Closed box, she thought. *Don't be a closed box.*

"The paint hues match the era," she began. "Some technique does, too, though it's mostly brushstrokes he'd abandoned years before. The work is way too small, and the canvas is attached to wood, which he never did before or after. Provenance is basically zero. Lee says it's all a greedy woman's lie."

"You conversed with her?"

"That would be a kind description. She's still as angry as a blister. Anyway . . ." Gwen took a deep breath. She would not choose. She would inform him and let him decide. "At this point you might want to rule the painting out, but there are things that tip the scale in the other direction."

"Such as?"

"There was a hair on the back of the painting. A DNA matching test was—"

"DNA? What the hell?"

"Ruth says they had sex on his bear rug. And the hair on the painting was some kind of mammal. So, it's possible—"

"No no no," he interrupted. "No pun intended, but you're splitting hairs. That's not what we do with our buyers. It's like selling someone a mansion, huge and gorgeous, but there's a chance the volcano in the backyard might erupt. You don't start working the odds of it blowing up. You go look at another house."

"But the DNA test—"

"We can't auction something we have doubts about." He sighed heavily. "Tell me. Can we in good conscience and solid certainty call this painting 'by Jackson Pollock'?"

Gwen waited as an ambulance went by, its siren jangling her thinking. "At best," she said eventually, "we could call it 'attributed to Jackson Pollock.'"

"Well, damn. When did you know all that? About the brushstrokes and all?"

Gwen looked at the mannequin brides. "Three weeks ago."

"You should have decided then. And saved yourself a pile of work."

She stammered. "I don't . . . I mean, I suppose . . ."

"Don't worry, it was your first big case. Too bad, though. This one could have been a plum."

Gwen expected to feel relief. Instead, there was tension—in her back, arms, stomach. "What if Ruth goes elsewhere?"

"Our hands are clean." He chuckled. "In fact, I hope she goes right to Sotheby's. They'll still be drunk on last year's auction, I bet they leap."

"I wish there'd been a different outcome."

"Me too. But it says something about your integrity that you didn't approve this painting right out of the gate. A million dollars will bias most people."

"Thank you, sir."

"You're definitely not one of those Pollock women, are you?"

"I hope not." Gwen stood taller. "I hope there aren't any more of them."

"I can see why you'd feel that way. I'll handle the notification."

"I did all the work with her, sir. I ought to bear the bad news."

"I want to. She jerked you around. Besides." He coughed. "A funny thing happened this morning. A woman called to withdraw from our managing director search. She was a finalist, too. But she said you would be a better fit."

Gwen felt a strange lightness. Around her, the wind tumbled a brown paper bag down the dirty sidewalk. Yet she felt euphoria.

"How about that?" he continued. "A woman supporting a woman."

"How about that?" she echoed.

"Got me thinking. How about you and me meet first thing Monday?"

"Tuesday, sir." It was a groundbreaking reply, and terrifying.

"Excuse me?"

Gwen steeled herself. "Today is Sunday. I worked all day yesterday, and six hours so far today, and the Pollock details aren't tidied up yet. Return of the painting, and so on."

"Well, then chalk up another funny thing for the day. I've never had somebody balk at a potential promotion."

"I'm not balking, sir. I've worked seven weeks' worth of hours in the past four. One recovery day is a small ask."

"You should be on Kobe's team. " He laughed. "I'll tell Harriette to fit you in Tuesday."

Gwen ended the call, then switched off her phone altogether. Tucking it away, she looked around herself. There was a whole city, chilly and bustling, a woman pushing a stroller, another going for a run, a guy trying to get his lighter to work so he could have a smoke, two teen girls sharing a gigantic coffee. She had the same liberty now, she had earned and bargained for it—and now that her day had slowed, she did not know what to do with it. Celebrate, or cry?

She ambled east, and with each avenue she felt lighter, and more curious about the fact that there was no place she had to be. She could go wherever she wanted. And as she wandered into Union Square, she knew where that was.

She was almost jogging by the time she reached the building on Thirteenth Street, just west of Third Avenue. Chillie's apartment was on the third floor and would be crowded with people celebrating a day of not working, better known as brunch.

She thumbed the 3N entry button, like she had many times before. Normally she heard a buzzer in return, which meant Chillie had unlocked the street door. But there was no answering buzz. She tried again, and still no response.

"Must be on the fritz." That also was nothing new. She pulled out her phone to call him, turning to lean against the door, and there at the corner stood Arthur. When they made eye contact, he started to walk away.

"No," she called. "Wait."

He stopped, hands in his pockets, and looked up at the sky.

"I'm glad to see you," she said, trotting over. "I have missed—"

"I am astonished." He continued gazing upward. "You actually put aside your device to speak with me."

Gwen held up her phone so he could see it was turned off. "I owe you an apology."

"You owe me three apologies."

"Only three?" She put the phone away. "That seems a little low."

Arms crossed, Arthur stared down the avenue. "Feel free to start anytime."

"I'm sorry I was hot and cold with you, and torn between work and you. It was not respectful."

"Go on."

"I'm sorry I ran from the disco, when we were in the middle of showing how we actually felt, and it was amazing."

His face became less stern. "To your credit, a truly awful song was playing."

Gwen reached to touch him but stopped herself. "I'm sorry that I used my phone for work stuff when you took me to the freezing roof. I wasted a great romantic opportunity to kiss you while the hot air poured out around us."

He scuffed his shoe on the sidewalk. "Of the hundreds of thousands of women I've brought up there, you are the only one who missed the magic of it."

She took hold of his coat's lapel. At last, he looked at her directly. The electricity was still there for her, the chemistry. "You're a great guy to be making jokes, Arthur. But I needed to learn some things, and that unintentionally coincided with you. I'm sorry for that."

"What did you learn, Gwen?"

The way he said her name so warmly, she nearly folded against him. But she pulled herself upright. The man was so damn tall.

"I learned that for all his madness, Pollock was trying, and that's true for everyone. From the floor in his studio, I learned that a mess has its own beauty. Also true for everyone, I think. And from a random sage on the subway, I learned that I should not be a closed box."

"A closed box? Em. I think I know what he meant." Arthur tucked a bit of hair behind Gwen's ear. "What does all of that mean in terms of me?"

"I want a second chance."

"Eleventh chance?"

"Okay, eleventh, but starting now."

"You'll understand if I trust your deeds more than your words."

"Okay, yes. So, first deed. I ask you, please, to take tomorrow off and spend the entire day with me."

"I have nine hundred commitments tomorrow."

"Which is why you are free to say no. But I want you to know that I am prioritizing you, effective immediately."

He leaned back, one eye squinting. "What have you done with our Gwen?"

She raised her arms, then flapped them down against her sides. "You're looking at her."

He studied her with narrowed eyes. "Hullo, you."

"Hello, Arthur. I have missed you. But here I am." Her throat tightened. "Also, I have a gift for you." From a coat pocket, Gwen produced the green convertible. "There's a whole story about this little car, it's very sad, and I would love to tell you. Then you can either keep it, or throw it in the Hudson."

"Thank you. So far, I lean toward keeping it, but . . ." He weighed the toy car. "It does feel quite throwable."

"Maybe the future starts with us being public, together, in front of other people." Gwen hooked a thumb over her shoulder. "Such as brunch?"

"I've attended many brunches with Chilton and his friends, hoping you would be there." He raised his shoulders and dropped them. "Today would feel like a performance. Perhaps some future Sunday?"

"Absolutely. But can we grab a bite somewhere? I've been on the run since before dawn, and I'm starving."

"I know a diner not far away, Twelfth and First. But I must warn you." He had a stern expression. "The hash browns are consistently mediocre."

"This is the kind of candor that makes for stable relationships," Gwen said, her face also serious. "But much, much more importantly, how is the coffee?"

"Good," he answered. "Quite good."

"Great?"

"Excellent."

She stepped closer. "Brilliant? As you would put it?"

"Bloody smashing." He extended his arm ahead and they set off, lighter with every step. Halfway across Third Avenue the pavement material changed, smooth into rough, and they did not even notice.

"Nutritious for the soul?" she asked.

"Nectar of Shangri-la."

Laughing, Gwen bumped against him. "Sex?"

His eyebrows rose, and he whispered, "Sex with you."

"Oh Arthur." She leaned against him. "Heaven?"

"Yes." He put his arm over Gwen's shoulder and pulled her close. "Heaven."

AUTHOR'S NOTE & ACKNOWLEDGMENTS

In the winter of 2014, I started writing a novel about Jackson Pollock, but I couldn't make it work. Another idea was pulling at me, and I could not resist. The result was *The Baker's Secret*.

In 2021, I wrote *The Glass Château* under the influence of Marc Chagall's stained-glass windows and learned how much art can add to a story. I toyed with trying Pollock again. Of course, his art is not friendly like Chagall's. It's abstract, wild, and often hard to understand. Still, the strange beauty of his paintings captivated me.

The research process provided two compelling new ideas. First, I learned things that called into question the myth of Pollock as a Hemingway of the canvas. Second, I found that the stories of women in his life were often more interesting than his.

To bring the story from history to fiction, I sometimes digressed from the record. So here is some clarifying information:

Sotheby's did indeed sell a Pollock painting in November 2006, for a record $140 million. But it was a private deal, not an open auction.

Pollock was indeed married to Lee Krasner, whom some consider a superior artist, and they lived in Springs, New York. In the months before his death, he had an affair with Ruth Kligman, a model and aspiring artist eighteen years his junior. He actually did trade two paintings for a green convertible, which he drove to New York City weekly to see his analyst.

That therapist, Ralph Klein, was one of an unorthodox group of analysts who later helped to found the controversial Sullivan Institute for Research in Psychoanalysis. According to the definitive biography (*Jackson Pollock: An American Saga*, by Steven Naifeh and Gregory White Smith), Klein counseled people to break free from repression and hostility, in order to lead lives of freedom and creativity. After reportedly dismissing Pollock's drinking problem, Klein encouraged him to act more often on his sexual impulses. Pollock spent the subsequent weeks propositioning women, some he knew and some total strangers, without success. That was when he met Ruth.

In reality, she attempted to sell *Red, Black and Silver* many times. Sources disagree, but it appears that at least once she represented the painting as her own work. There also were times that other people represented *they* owned the painting, to prevent the Pollock-Krasner Foundation from denying its authenticity purely because Ruth had possessed it. When she wrote *Love Affair,* a memoir of her months with Pollock, it made no mention of his last work. Years later, she published a second edition—adding a prologue about the making of *Red, Black and Silver*—before trying to sell the painting again.

Ruth's memoir also details her affair with a famous Broadway producer, who gave her all sorts of ambitious advice. The actor Ronald Gray is a fictional person only.

The novel's settings are genuine: the Cedar Tavern, Fireplace Road, the beaches, roads, and towns of Long Island. On any given day, even seventy years after Pollock's death, you can find all sorts of talismans on and around his grave.

Ruth did take a job with a summer art school in 1956, but the version here is entirely fictional. Alfonso Ossorio owned a palatial property in East Hampton and did indeed commission the New York Philharmonic to perform at his home. The Clement whom Alfonso called after hanging Pollock's repaired painting was Clement Greenberg, arguably the most powerful American art critic from the 1940s–1960s. Although the Whitney Museum has shown the work of Lee Krasner for decades, I'm not aware of any time in which *Prophesy* and *Three in Two* were displayed simultaneously, and adjacently.

During the research, my sister Casey sent me *Brushed Aside: The Untold Story of Women in Art* by Noah Charney. That is where I learned the story of Janet Sobel. She made her drip painting *Milky Way* in 1945, two years before Pollock began using that technique. Clement Greenberg called her work "primitive" coming from a "housewife," though later he softened, characterizing her as "a forerunner to abstract expressionism."

Janet Sobel died in 1968. Today, *Milky Way* belongs to the Museum of Modern Art in New York City.

Several characters are based on a combination of people—Lucy, for example. Ruth did have a cellist roommate who told lovers she was pregnant in order to fund her winter trips south. But a different friend was riding in the convertible on the night of the crash.

Pollock really did pee in Peggy Guggenheim's fireplace.

The authenticity of *Red, Black and Silver* remains controversial. In 2013, a retired New York Police Department forensic detective declared that he had found a polar bear hair on the painting—a clear link to Pollock's studio. However, a member of the disbanded Pollock-Krasner Foundation responded that the painting still did not look like a genuine Pollock. Even granting that the painting was made in his studio, the bear hair did not prove who had held the brush.

By that time, it did not matter to Ruth Kligman. She died in 2010.

Which leads to the greatest liberty I took: Pollock's widow, Lee Krasner, died in 1984. But in this novel, she is very much alive in February, 2007. On the subject of *Red, Black and Silver*—and Ruth—I wanted to give her the last word.

Research is central to my books, even when I bend what I've learned. So I want to thank the people who helped me along the way.

Lori Scotnicki, an antique and art appraiser who worked at Skinner Inc. in Boston (now Bonhams Skinner), gave me a tutorial about the inner workings of major auction houses. Painting conservator Suki Fredericks, who introduced me to the issues of art forensics, was an important early support. So was Richard Kerschner, an expert in the transportation of valuable artworks and the issues of provenance.

I learned more about the fine art auction industry from Michael Hughes, who was with Christie's New York office when we met, and who now heads the Chinese department at the global auctioneer Bonhams. His assistant at the time, Helen Dennis, was also helpful; after working with collectors and galleries, she is now primarily an artist.

You may recall the scene in which Trevor and Ruth are hanging a bas-relief of sunflowers as soldiers. That idea came from *The Nature of Memory*, an actual (and amazing) work of art by sculptor and installation artist Nancy Winship Milliken. It debuted in 2023 at Saint-Gaudens National Historical Park in Cornish, New Hampshire.

I visited the Pollock-Krasner house on Fireplace Road several times and spent enough semi-obsessed hours in the studio to become enamored of the paint spills on the floor. The Stony Brook Foundation, an affiliate of Stony Brook University, now manages the property, which is a National Historic Landmark.

Among the people I met there, thanks go to James Walker, Theresa Davis, and David Salter (who shared his Pollock ghost stories). Fellow visitor Mike Price—a retired ship captain from Minnesota who wants to be an art history teacher—specified for me exactly where Pollock went off the road.

Along the way I had steady and wise support from my agent, Ellen Levine, a trusted ally who never fails to think of ways to make my books shorter. The novelist Dawn Tripp read a very early draft and gave me a good talking-to. That's what friends are for, and in fact, she helped the book change direction in crucial ways. The novelist Justin Cronin calmly pointed out several gaping holes in the plot, while the novelist Wendy Walker had expert suggestions as well.

I am grateful to the New York Public Library for providing an unparalleled workspace—the gorgeous and studious Rose Room. Gwen goes there often in this book, just as I often write there when I am in the city. Thanks, too, to the Charlotte Library, small but mighty, for once again saving me via interlibrary loan.

Handing a manuscript to an editor is an act of faith. This is my sixth book to benefit from the guidance of Jennifer Brehl, editor and friend, over a span of fifteen years. She has helped me from first sentence (in *The Baker's Secret*) to last (in this book). She has also marshaled the resources of William Morrow for marketing and publicity (especially my dear friend Tavia Kowalchuk), and the art department—in particular, Mumtaz Mustafa—for eye-catching covers as well as gorgeous page designs *inside* the covers (the stained-glass title page in *The Glass Château* was perfection). Thanks to them, one and all.

One other person merits mention here, because he encouraged me to give Pollock a second try. A brilliant novelist and playwright, he has helped my career with guidance and inspiration countless times over the years. More importantly, he has repeatedly been an essential friend in hard times. For these reasons and others, I am proud to dedicate this book to Chris Bohjalian.